TAMARA DUDA

DAUGHTER

English translation by Daisy Gibbons

mosaicPRESS

Library and Archives Canada Cataloguing in Publication

Title: Daughter / Tamara Duda ; English translation by Daisy Gibbons.

Other titles: Dotsia. English

Names: Duda, Tamara, author. | Gibbons, Daisy, translator.

Description: Translation of: Dochka.

Identifiers: Canadiana (print) 20220223548 | Canadiana (ebook) 20220223580 | ISBN 9781771616720 (softcover) | ISBN 9781771616737 (PDF) | ISBN 9781771616744 (EPUB) | ISBN 9781771616751 (Kindle)

Classification: LCC PG3950.18.O75 D6813 2022 | DDC 891.7/914—dc23

Published by Mosaic Press, Oakville, Ontario, Canada, 2022.

MOSAIC PRESS, Publishers
www.Mosaic-Press.com
Copyright © Tamara Duda 2022

MOSAIC PRESS
1252 Speers Road, Units 1 & 2, Oakville, Ontario, L6L 5N9
(905)825-2130 • info@mosaic-press.com • www.mosaic-press.com

A NOTE ON READING THIS BOOK

The events and stories presented in *Daughter* are not fictional. They have been drawn from the personal experiences of the author and those of acquaintances she made while working as a volunteer and intelligence agent for the Ukrainian army. Each character in the novel is based on someone the author personally knew — from the enigmatic Komar to Elf, Donetsk's adopted 'daughter'. Some are still alive and well; others have passed on. Elf's grandmother is the only character without a real prototype: the courageous Baba Olya is an homage to the figure of the Ukrainian grandmother-protectress.

A testimonial by the real 'Elf' has been provided at the back of the book, alongside a handful of other testimonials written by the author's acquaintances who were involved in the Ukrainian war effort. Their style and prose differ to the novel's, as they are honest accounts by people recalling their lived experience, and they provide an insight into the lives of people who continue to live in Europe's only warzone.

Daughter is a testament to the Russian invasion of Ukraine and a eulogy to the people the war has taken. For this reason, the author felt a translation into English was necessary, in part to raise awareness among an Anglophone readership. You are advised to bear the above commentary in mind as you read on.

ДОНЕЦЬК
DONETSK
ЗНАМ'ЯНКА
розважальний
Шахтаре

INTRO

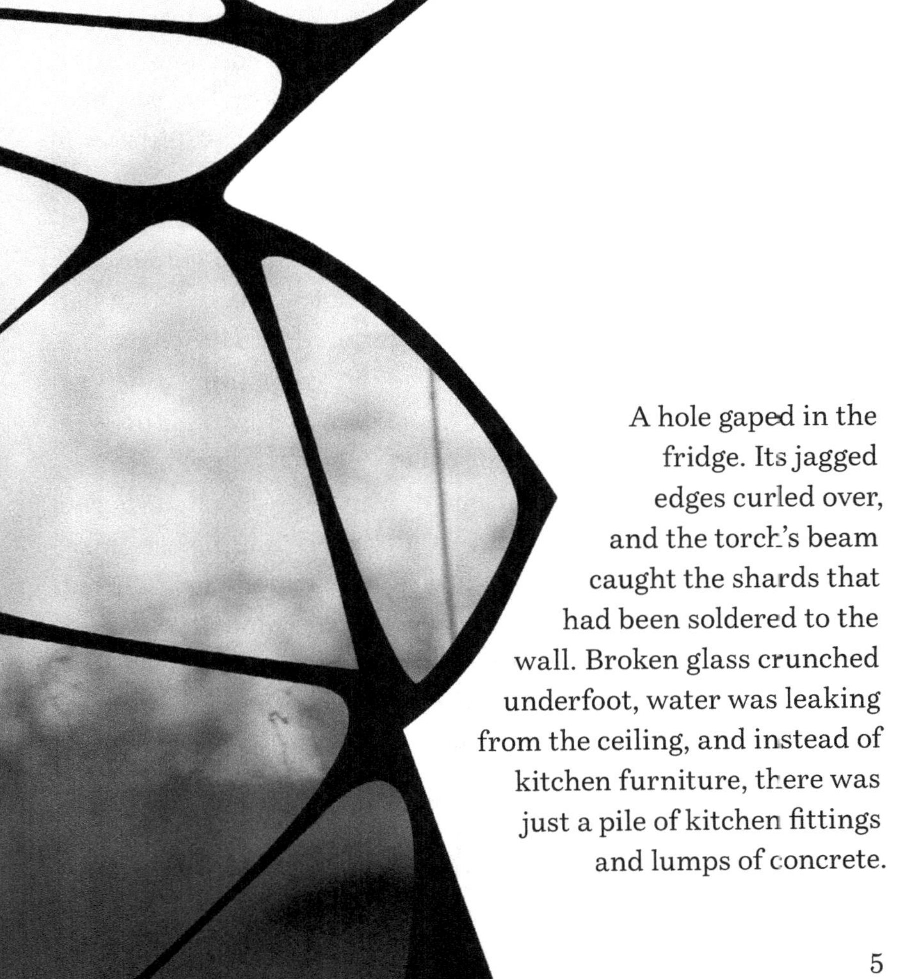

A hole gaped in the fridge. Its jagged edges curled over, and the torch's beam caught the shards that had been soldered to the wall. Broken glass crunched underfoot, water was leaking from the ceiling, and instead of kitchen furniture, there was just a pile of kitchen fittings and lumps of concrete.

It appeared that I now had nowhere to live — nice one, Captain Obvious! — and nothing to eat, since our backup supply of food had been destroyed, along with the fridge.

This episode can effectively be thought of as the starting point of this story, just like any other of the series of events that had preceded it, which have become intertwined in a perfect chain of cause and effect, where not a single link in the chain can be erased or bypassed. But for me, as for all of us, what matters is not the beginning, but the end. And the end is that I am alive.

I could have buried this within me, to tell the truth; if it were not for the thought that maybe somewhere in Antwerp (lovely name, I adore the way it rolls off the tongue) or maybe in Madrid, or, we could even say, in Kyiv or Vinnytsia, lives a certain thirty-year old woman like me. Perhaps she also is without a family or children. Like me, she stays late at work, making her stained-glass pieces; maybe she paints, bakes bread, or does tests with her students. Perhaps she's not doing anything at all, and is living off some royalties (another great word). Today, she has downloaded a chocolate cake recipe from the internet and stands over the batter, mixing the cocoa with butter, not suspecting that her established, cosy world has already shattered into little pieces.

It is like radiation. You cannot see it; you cannot smell or taste it; it floats, transparent in the air; and you would do well to either drink iodine, or run away before it is too late.

I would ask my unknown friend in Antwerp — 'Listen, do you have somewhere to run to? Have a look, and then have a think where your money and documents are; check your bag is packed, with as many valuable things as you can carry. Among your most precious valuables, make sure you have two tins of food, a first aid kit with some doses of morphine, a torch with extra batteries, a good knife, and a change of underwear. Write down the contacts of any people you could stay with, and draw a map of any roads or directions that you are going to take.'

If you suddenly decide that you want to stay, whatever the

reason, but primarily because of your own naivety — say, you cannot stand to leave your workshop; you feel sorry for your dog, or your neighbour; after all, there might be a hundred reasons why you would want to stay — you are going to have to change. In order to survive, that person you know as *you* will have to die. Behold! Your house has burnt down. Look! Your car has gone up in flames, as has your collection of porcelain bells and your library of books. That is not all though, you understand? Perhaps it is a part of your body that is now gone. Think what it might be like to live without arms, legs, or with your ear cut off. Accept that you will face rape, or any other abuse, and disassociate yourself.

Prepare yourself, and be vigilant. In order to survive, you would eat earth. And one day, you yourself will feed the earth.

LEAD CRYSTAL

WHITE UPON WHITE

My memories only start from the age of nine. Everything that happened before is a *terra incognita*, a blank slate, upon which feature no memories, nor images. Lost somewhere in the midst of this white reverie is my mother. My mother had to exist, right? Yet, in our house, no one talked about her. My questioning fell upon the deaf ears of my father, who only once let slip that she was called Maria, and that she died young. Whether this was true or not, there was now no way of making sure. I clearly took after my mother, since my father was short, stocky, with a pronounced belly, and premature baldness. I did not so much as grow as put on length in all directions. Everything about me was too long: my feet, my toes (I would court my toes as a child, and it seemed almost as though I had an extra one), elbows, ears, hair.

My face was graced by an aristocratic, pointed beak, taking the attention away from my overly thin, bloodless lips. Picasso would have found my physique inspiring, but this was little consolation for a girl who was the last in the class to need a bra; even then it was an A cup.

To add to this picture, I lived through reading; I would swallow books on the go, on school breaks, at night under the covers, and under my desktop in class. I devoured the written word like a locust; I did not care what it was I read. I would linger over a scrunched-up newspaper used for seedlings; I would become engrossed in junk mail leaflets. I would diligently study volumes of Russian classics with the same level of interest as the new light romance paperbacks.

To top it all off, I loved physics. For hours, after making my room as dark as possible, plugging every crack against the light in order to make my own *camera obscura*. I would endlessly experiment with lenses. I then became interested in electricity. Other girls dreamed of future husbands, flashy cars, and holiday resorts, whereas I fancied myself as something of an electrician. I was fascinated by the laconic beauty of the diagrams; I attentively and mechanically made drawings of the circuits; some of them were actually paradoxically absurd, but I had no one around who would appreciate this particularly keen sense of humour.

In any case, who would I even show it off to? As is probably now obvious, I was not the most popular girl in old Dobrovytsia. I do not think that anyone in my town knew what my real name is. I was known as 'Elf', by my teachers and neighbours. It was a silly childish nickname, which must have come from somewhere — but I cannot be sure where; I doubt my father came up with it, since he referred to me as 'Hey, come 'ere' — and it stuck, like chewing gum in my hair. I would like to think that behind my back they called me something else, but let's be realistic here: behind my back, no one even mentioned me at all.

We have a saying: when the horse offers the farrier its hoof, the frog also holds out a leg. You could use that to describe me: how could I compare myself to our amber mining princes here in Polesia? I could not compete with the high and mighty with their chic sense of style, which was like mother's milk for them, something that comes from having money. It was laughable to compare us. I never burnt through cash like the rest of them, (I had never even lit a cigarette, let alone burn anything else). I never even crashed a car, not even some cruddy rustbucket. I never left a trail of suitors in my wake, because for seventeen years no one even wanted to be a suitor of mine.

Thinking upon my future, I once came to the disappointing conclusion that this was just not the place for me. The town which built upon and lived on the trade and production of amber simply had no place for a girl as built like a beanpole. If only there would have been some dowry, or some land for my hand, anything! Plus, we were poor and rugged, like church mice; how else anyway, when old *Misko*, my father that is, would only ever be sober once a year, on Good Friday, which would result in him enduring the most infernal suffering?

Imagine my surprise then, when returning home with my school graduation certificate in my hand (I did not go to the graduation ceremony itself — and how would I have paid for it, anyway?), I found my father standing there rather sad and quiet, and, ahem, upright.

"So, my daughter, come 'ere, we need to talk."

What was going on? Were we being evicted?

It turned out that the answer was yes and no. In the midst of yet another alcohol-induced torpor my father had had a revelation. He saw an angel appear unto him amongst a radiance of snow-white robes: a heavenly voice pronounced him a deadbeat good-for-nothing; a heavenly hand walloped him across the cheek; and a heavenly foot gave him an almighty kick below the belt. Mykhailo Pavlovych saw clearly now: life cannot go on like this, and that was when the paranormal activity began.

Within a week my father had sold our flat, obtained a Polish visa, and ordered a bus ticket to Przemyśl. His was now the fate of an economic migrant to Poland or even Germany, and therefore, 'daughter', he needed help packing his bags.

"What about me though, Dad?"

"What about you?"

"Where am I supposed to live?"

"In Donetsk, with your grandmother."

That was how, at the age of seventeen, I found out that I have a grandmother. I already knew about Donetsk from the newspapers.

* * *

If you've never gone by train in Ukraine, then *Donbas* trains are not the best way to get acquainted with this mode of transport. I, however, had no choice, and two days later was standing on the platform, clutching a bag of clothes to my chest, a suitcase full of books, and a cage with two Angora rabbits. A neighbour had brought the rabbits over at the last minute.

The rabbit is a rather timorous beastie — it wasn't like I had a wild stallion on my hands. I arranged the cage on a luggage rack behind some mattresses, and swiftly forgot about them. Besides, there was much for me to think about.

From the few words my father had shared on the matter, I understood that his mother (and so my grandmother, or *baba*) was called Olha Ivanivna, and that they had not seen each other in a good ten years. I learned that one day he left with his documents in his pocket, and vowed never to return unless it was utterly necessary. The utter necessity — me, in this case — led to a formal familial reconciliation, and after a few short discussions, it was agreed that I would be taken in on a temporary basis.

I was going to live in Donetsk's Kyiv district, on Blahovishchenska street. I shared the full details of my story with my fellow travellers, a pair of pensioners and a shaven-headed, middle-aged man in a leather jacket. At this, the old folks looked at me and asked for the address again.

"Have something to eat, child,"[1] sighed the old woman, and gave me a tomato and half a chicken.

The man in the leather jacket was silent, and then out of the blue decidedly to tell us about the time he killed a Vietnamese man at the bazaar when he was a young man.

I tried my best to soak up the sense of romance in the journey, something I had read so much about. I listened to the clattering of the wheels against the track, which other authors would pronounce either comforting, or sinister, whereas I found myself questioning the reliability of the train's design. The carriage creaked too loudly, the shelves sloped too steeply, an empty beer bottle rolled about on the floor, and the damp sheets stank of sweat and mould.

In the morning, we were awoken by a crunching sound. One of the rabbits was sitting on the table and was munching on the chicken skeleton. The empty cage sat there, a hole in it gaping open, and there were no traces of the second rabbit.

That was the state that Baba Olya first saw me in: dirty, dishevelled, with grazes on my hands and bruises on my knees. The conductor and I had scoured every inch of the carriage, probing every shelf, suitcase, and toilet — every nook and cranny. We shook out the upholstery and made every passenger get up off his seat. The bloody animal had vanished. I'm almost inclined to think it had been flushed down the toilet.

"Oh well, it happens," sighed Olha Ivanivna. "Your father should have known that animals don't really last long here. Except mice, of course. Let's go home."

---

1   Throughout the text, italics are used in direct speech and quotations to denote when a character is speaking Russian or a predominantly Russian mix of Russian and Ukrainian. All other dialogue and quotations were originally written in Ukrainian.

And that is how we began our lives together.

My new home was an old Khrushchev-era apartment block that smelled of urine, cats, and meatballs. My room overlooked the local college, and every morning I would watch the students as they had a cigarette before class. My grandmother's room looked out onto the privately owned, one-story houses below (although this concept of 'private' was somewhat conditional). I remember how striking I found it, that Donetsk was full of these one-story houses, that for such an industrial city it had such a small-town feeling to it. It took me a long time to get used to the high fences, the small slate roofs, to the tangles of weeds outside of every house, and to the general sense of neglect. Everything that could be stolen was tied up to something. All the houses had been patched up here and there, standing on rotten wooden pillars, and peppered with soot.

The soot was everywhere. The flowers on the trees quickly withered and disintegrated. The first snowfall would stay a glistening white for about an hour, maybe two. Your new shoes would be ruined the first time you went out in them. Every outing would turn into an ordeal, a battle against the dust, mud, and the dry wind. Instead of walking to places, I developed the habit of scurrying from wall to wall; not raising my head, not looking anyone in the eyes, not attracting attention.

In my first week there, I got a job as a cashier at a supermarket. After a few weeks I was promoted to manager, and a year later I became a senior salesperson. We hardly lived in the lap of luxury, but my grandmother's pension, along with my wages, was enough for food, to pay the bills, and to put some money away for a rainy day.

Our life was alright enough. It could have been worse; the days went by, and we managed. Looking back, I am grateful for this pause of several years that fate dealt me, allowing me as it did to grow up, gather my strength, and get used to the reality of life on the Donbas.

The reality of life here caught up with us at three in the morning on the 18th November 2007. I remember the evening well. My grandmother and I had settled in for the evening, with her watching her soap opera, and me behind a book, huddled close to the only working radiator. It was the middle of the night, when the quiet outside our windows was disturbed by the sound of sirens. The whining of the sirens was so loud that the walls shook. We jumped out of bed and ran outside. In the glare of the streetlights, I could see the white, waxen face of my grandmother, her hands shaking.

"My dear girl, there's been an accident."

There was indeed an accident. There had been an explosion at the Zasyadko mine, a kilometre underground. There were more than four hundred workmen on their shift at the time; three hundred had made it to the surface. One hundred miners remained in the slaughterhouse, and for two weeks we waited with everyone as the rescue operation went on. On the 3rd of December, after a series of repeated explosions, the decision was made to flood the shaft.

For two weeks, the sound of keening hung over our neighbourhood. For two weeks they held funerals. For two weeks, my grandmother and I prepared *kolyvo* and baked funeral buns. Three people had died from our block of flats alone, and two were still missing. We spent the whole time with others. Together, we went down in a crowd and set upon the mine in search of information. Together, we went around the funeral directors, ordering coffins and wreaths, and together we attended the cemetery. Other people's children stayed in our block; we all ate at a big table in the yard; when someone had got hold of rumours or news, we went through all the stages of grief, shifting from hope to despair and back again.

I had long felt like a stranger in this city; it still frightened and alarmed me. However, something then changed. The house which you grieve in will never be completely foreign to you.

That accident, that terrible sound of nightly sirens, was when the fates of the Donbas and my own began to intertwine. It was from that very moment that I count down the events that prompted me to make a decision. That winter planted the seed of the person whom I have become: an insurgent, a spy, and a saboteur.

* * *

My days with my grandmother, Olha Ivanivna, passed quietly. We measured the passing of time with trips to the bazaar, with the stuffed cabbage leaves we made for Sunday lunch; we shopped seasonally, never planning further than that. We had an unspoken rule that I would not ask about the secrets of the past, and she would not press me about future plans.

Perhaps our neighbours talked about us behind our backs, but no one said anything to our faces. Well, except for Stepanida Viktorivna from No.28, but that was no surprise. There are people who represent the 'spirit of the age', its guiding reason, its brains. Old Stepa, on the other hand, was our block's liver. Through her passed all its toxins, all its hives of gossip, scandal, and hatred, which the snakes in the grass and the old Komsomol leaders on their pensions like to feed on.

Sometimes in life, people praise you or give you compliments, but you feel instead as though you've been spat on. I never heard that woman ever start a sentence without saying 'eh': *'Eh, what a lovely daughter you have, she's just like my granddaughter. Eh, how old is she, a year old? Still not walking, poor love? Eh, what a shame.' 'Eh, your new haircut really suits you. Well done, at your age it needs cutting a bit shorter.' 'Eh, I saw your husband at a café with some woman. Eh, I'm so sorry, men are all the same...'*

However, when it came to my grandma, she chose the wrong woman to mess with.

"Eh, these young people! They all want for nothing, want for

no one! I see yours stays at home all the time. They're all like that, they don't want any children, no husbands, am I right!"

My grandma carefully put her bags down, took her glasses off, and wiped them clean.

"So, tell me, Stepanida, so what's this about then? You're the village witch here — else what the hell are these people muttering on at me for? Where's the justice in that?"

Meanwhile, a certain Vitalik started coming by my work. He started popping in twice a day to pick up some bread, or some beer, or something. The women quickly cottoned on to what was going on, which I found embarrassing. When he finally invited me out after my shift, I was too awkward to refuse. And when he took me home. And when he took me to a hotel.

If I was able to call this a love affair, I would have told this story in more detail, with beautiful turns of phrase and all that. But in truth, there are no beautiful turns of phrase for what happened here. When it was all over, I just could not understand why this act causes us so much strife. So many works of literature, so many tragedies, all because of this — some bodily movement?

"How are you doing, are you ok?"

"Super, thanks. I'm going to the bathroom, alright?"

Returning from the bathroom, the man was already asleep, having pulled out the blanket from under him. It seemed a shame to wake him, so I lay a towel over myself and fell asleep. After all, a towel is enough for someone of my stature.

In the morning, Vitalik awoke first, patting me on the back protectively, like I was pet, and grimaced — after all, a woman weighing forty-two kilograms needs to be touched carefully, there are not that many places to pat her comfortably — and told me that we were going to have dinner at his mother's place later.

I did not want any mothers involved, but here we were again; I felt too uncomfortable to refuse, especially since he promised to pick me up right from my shop. Indeed, there he was, at exactly seven o'clock, standing there solemnly with a magnificent bouquet in his hands.

"What beautiful roses... Thank you! You know, I've never been given flowers before."

"Yes, only, um, you understand... The flowers are for my mum, since we're going to hers to visit after all."

"Oh, sorry, my mistake."

'Mum' met us in the hallway, handing me a pair of silly pink slippers with white spots to put on and invited us into the kitchen. It was clear she had found out all she needed to know about me on that trip down the hallway, because by the time we had sat down at the table it was all over. With every piece of cake that he forked into his mouth, his mother's lips would become thinner and thinner, Vitalik would grow paler and paler, and the pauses in conversation reached a theatrical level of tension.

"Eh, the way you speak is so interesting, in Ukrainian. *Are you from the West?"*

"Actually no, I'm from Donetsk. I grew up in the Rivne region as a child."

"Just as I thought. Eh, careful, he bites! [this was as I approached the parrot in its cage]. *How do you say 'parrot' in Hutsul? A 'cock-a-doodle-doo' or something, right? Tell me, do you have cows in your village? What do you do with them, do you milk them?"*

"Ah, no, not really. That is, people do milk them, but we didn't have any cows."

"Your parents don't live with you, I guess? Eat, eat, have some chocolates, Tosenka bought them. Haven't you eaten today, Vitalik? You were so late; I've been waiting since seven. I'm always so worried when he's held up, after all, he's on a strict diet. I'll tell you about it later, he cannot eat any reheated food, only freshly-prepared food, we make our breakfast, lunch, and dinner in small portions, I'll show you the pans."

It is important you understand me correctly: I fled. After

another one of those pauses in conversation, I got up from the table, excused myself, and asked where the bathroom was. After I had reached the toilet, very quietly I tiptoed to the door. I flew out of the flat as if they were at my tail, not waiting for the lift, jumping four steps at a time. I only realised when I had run two bus-stops away that I was splashing about in the puddles in those same pink slippers that she had given me.

I stood in the middle of the road, looking at my feet, laughing. I was laughing so hard that I was hiccupping, snot bubbling out my nose, till tears were coming out my eyes. I laughed like I had never laughed in my whole life, like I was unhinged, almost soaring into the clouds with this feeling of incredible, inhuman relief. Let's assume that I had just had sex and had a relationship, shall we? However brief, if only for three days, who cares? I would not die an old maid; I would have something to say for myself, should someone ever ask me. The mother; I am going to blame everything on his mother. 'We were ideal for one another, but his mother was against it, and I — *ha-ha-ha* — I thought against it — *oh, I can't, I can't* — and I made the decision — *ha-ha...*'

There was another thing that I understood at that bus stop: I shall never, ever go back to that supermarket. I swear, I am willing to sleep under a bridge, I will go by foot, I will sell my kidney, only I will never, ever be a senior, nor a junior cashier, I will never stack another shelf and I will never wear that uniform again.

Have I already mentioned that my family coat of arms (if I had one) would have the motto 'Never say never'?

* * *

Looking back, the thing I found most surprising was that my grandmother was not surprised. Everything that happened afterwards, she accepted as a given. There were no arguments; she did not ask me any questions; I got no unsolicited advice. She listened silently to the news that I was now out of a job. She nodded along as I summarised my brief love affair. Nothing changed at home, only we would make stuffed cabbage rolls on Tuesdays, instead of on Sundays.

I was restless, however. I could not sit in one place, I had to get out. I could not sleep; I could not eat. I was experiencing a previously unknown feeling: I was overflowing, flooded with energy. My hair stood on end, my ears were full of noise, and my fingertips burned. I paced the tattered rug in my room, running from wall to window and back.

Eventually, the moment came when I realised that I could not stand it anymore. I could not look out onto this street any longer, at these wet fences; I was being suffocated by the dust; I did not have the strength to breathe, my chest felt tight. The grey boxes outside the window, the grey passers-by, everything was grey, like an old stage scene dusted with powder.

I went out with all my money and went to the only art supplies shop in the area. Surprising myself, I bought a dozen brushes and filled a whole basket with acrylic paints. White, silver, blue and pink — that was all there was. I then went to the chemist and bought a bottle of white spirit.

Getting home, I tore off my jacket and threw off my shoes without stopping. I would not and could not waste a second, like a drug addict on their way to get their fix. Never in my life had I had such a feeling of obsession, although right now I didn't have the time nor the desire to analyse the root of it.

I wiped the window down with the spirit, getting it on my hands and on my trousers. I did not have a palette, but what difference did it make? I squeezed the paint onto a plate, with no remorse, a whole half a tube straightaway, and began to paint the windowpane. I knew exactly what I wanted to do, without having a clue how to do it. Those moments were ones of pure exhilaration, of unbridled inspiration. I worked standing up, although after a while I made some sort of scaffolding out of two chairs.

I drew winter. I painted the cold weather, which I remembered from my childhood; I painted our Polesian sun over the river Jordan. The window dazzled with thousands of snowflakes, the patterns overlapping each other in a complex web of invisible lines. My paints started to run out; I added salt, talcum powder, and flour; I broke and crushed up lightbulbs; helped myself to a needle and a feather, breathed on the window, and my breath froze on the glass. Hour after hour passed, and step by step the street outside disappeared. The room glowed with flashes of white, pink, and red that blinded the eyes.

"This was supposed to happen, clearly."

"Baba?"

Baba Olya was standing behind me, and tears were running down her cheeks.

"How long have you been standing there? And what was supposed to happen?"

"The apple doesn't fall far from the tree... Your mother loved embroidery, my girl. She would pick up a needle and that was it, she was turned off to the world. You could shout, say something to her, practically hold a fire under her nose and she wouldn't turn her head. And the things she would come up with! I'd never seen anything like them, neither before nor after. You'd look at it, and it'd be one picture; blink, and it'd be something else altogether..."

I held my breath, afraid to move. I was positive that my grandmother had never known my mother, she never mentioned her, after all. Yet now it looked as though she knew her, and knew her well at that?

"Baba, you're going to have to tell me about her. I want to know who she is, and how she died. I have the right to know."

"Yes, of course. I can only tell you what you can understand... because no one understood her. We called her Stunde, this Maria, after those old puritan evangelicals we used to have here, the Stundes; like them, she was not of this world. My Misko, your father that is, he wasn't right for her. But nobody was right for her, if you thought of it like that. I couldn't say — no one could say, really — why she liked my son, they were like that old tale of the swan and the pike… She was always quiet, always lost in her own thoughts. You would say something to her, and she would reply, but she would always look at you from afar, like she was looking at you down a telescope. And she looked so surprised every time, as if it was the first time she'd ever seen you."

People in the village would bet on how long they'd last together; no one gave it more than a month. But as luck would have it, seven years passed. You were already big enough by then, you ought to remember. Your father was a security guard then, he'd work one night in three. One night he went on his shift, and then he came back, and your mother wasn't there. He didn't hurry off to find her at first; he thought that she must have gone out somewhere. It was odd how she'd left her daughter at home and hadn't taken any bags or money, but, you know, maybe she didn't need them. When it got closer to evening, however, they began looking for her, and then they called the police.

The police came with a dog, and the dog caught the scent without a problem, and immediately chased it from the house into the field. The field started right outside the house, and a little path led across it. They ran along the path up to the crossroads, and stopped. It was a maize field, on both sides, and at the place where the roads parted, right in the middle, there were traces of a fire. Someone had started a fire, which was so huge, it had burnt a hole half a metre into the ground. No one knew why there was a fire there, only that had been one.

The scent was cut off around the fire. The dog also pulled back, tail between its legs. They combed through the ashes — what did they want to find there? — but in vain. There were just ashes, nothing else. And no one has seen your mother since. A year later, we were given a document saying that she had gone missing, and that was it. Your father was dragged into the police station about eight times, but he had been at work all night, and the cameras there showed that he didn't move from his post. Me, the neighbours, we were all interrogated, but it led to nothing.

After that, life in the village wasn't for us anymore. People are like that — they like to talk; they can't keep their mouths shut. They would hiss at us behind our backs, then right at us, and in the end our house was set on fire. Luckily, your father hadn't gone to sleep yet, and we rushed out the house just as we were, taking you with us, grabbing our documents. We lost everything: all of our possessions, our furniture. The log house burst aflame, as doused with petrol, and burned down in seconds.

After that we parted ways. You and your father went to Dubrovytsia; they gave Misko work there, and I came here, to my sister's. After that, well, you know your father, when he gets in his own head. He wouldn't write, he wouldn't phone, he just disappeared, and it was only now he got in contact, asking if he could bring you here.

My grandmother fell silent, and I didn't speak.

"My girl, it's better not to stir up anything now. What happened, happened. But you know what — your mother also sewed, white upon white. Whole canvasses, people would come from Kyiv and Lviv to get their hands on them. They were alive, these works, just like this window here."

BLUE GLASS

A ONE-IN-A-MILLION OFFER

My life completely changed
after that. The shop assistant was gone;
in her place now stands a young, ambitious artist,
whose formidable talent has enraptured curators and art
connoisseurs from around the world. I am now in charge of
several serious projects, including the Dior catwalk
at Paris Fashion Week, as well as opening
my solo exhibition in Tokyo.
Or not.

We commanded considerable popularity amongst our neighbours, of course. Valentyna Stepanivna, Oksana, and her sister-in-law came to have a look at our 'winter window'; even Petro, being our 'kumpel', as the Germans say, came, stood, had a cigarette, and then asked for a bite to eat. This, however, did not solve our money problems.

We had a little bit of money set aside to tide us over for a month or two. Therefore, the next logical step was selling something I had made.

At first, I took to decorating wedding china and tea sets. I would draw lush flowers, little butterflies, animals, and children's faces, all very nice and sweet and pedestrian. I then had a phase of drawing angels, so we had angels nestling on various plates, beer mugs, shelves, and key hangers. Cheery-looking dolls took up all the free space in our already tiny flat. I had to go into our savings pot to buy a book on Italian frescoes for inspiration.

After about a year I received my first order for a stained-glass window. It took me a long time to bear parting with the thick, uneven slabs of church glass, with their blemishes and air bubbles. The mosaic came together by itself, almost by its own accord: it was so clear which fragment fit together with the next, and which ones, on the other hand, could not, and needed a buffer between them. I did not think about either the customer's taste nor how feasible the design would be. I did not care where this window would be placed; I understood that a special interior would have to be designed around this piece, but this piece was worth it.

The client arrived in person, accompanied by four bodyguards. The guards waited silently in the corridor, and our client came into our one-bed flat just as silently, glanced in the kitchen, and then stopped in front of the finished artwork. She stood there for a while, the pause dragging on, the only noise being the creak of the parquet floor under the feet of her escort.

"Turn on the light. Yes, good. Hold it up against the window."
She turned to me. "I want to buy another eight of these from you.
Under the condition that you won't make something like this for
anyone else here in Donetsk for two, maybe three years."

We settled on this arrangement. Besides, the amount of money I got for it meant I could spend the next two, maybe three
years doing nothing at all.

After getting to grips with my craft, I came up with an idea.
It came to me in a dream, floating in front of my eyes as clear as
day. I saw a magnificent, shimmering ball, which illuminated
everything around it with its glittering presence. It would em-
body the very essence of joy and purity. It would have to be
a diamond-like candelabra, with a complex system of edges and
angles that would cast a three-dimensional, structured shadow. Should I make it out of crystal glass? Murano glass? I spent
hours designing it, and finally came to the disappointing realisation that I would not be able to manage it by myself. Someone would have to do a fine solder according to my designs, so
fine that it could almost be a job for a jeweller. I needed to find
a locksmith-cum-jeweller.

I do not know what it's like anywhere else, but here, all roads
lead to Granny Masha. Known by some as Marchykha, by others
as Mariia Pavlivna, she knew everything about everyone, like
an old *mafioso*, with Putylivka district's most useful contacts,
acquaintances and connections at her disposal. In a fortunate
turn of events, she was also my grandmother's sister-in-law, and
as such, the field meetings of the local Inquisition would take
place over lunch in our kitchen. It was Marchykha's light hand
that would fill our house with Avon powders and creams from
Oriflame. As of late, the local Pentecostal community had become the new source of inspiration for our dear relative. At our
place they now sang, quoted the Scriptures, and led discussions
on salvation. I found these women wearisome, but it was moder-
ated by the fact they would not enter my workshop, and I learnt

how to sneak into the kitchen, light as a shadow, without making a sound.

"Auntie Masha, you couldn't suggest any good metalworkers, could you? I need someone to weld together a particularly delicate design, but neatly and cheaply."

"Well, you'd better go to our Roman. Rom's got a golden touch: he could shoe a flea! He was remarkable, but he had an unlucky turn of fate, you see. He worked as a foreman for us, then studied to become an engineer, but then something happened and he became paralysed. He had a drinking problem for a while, but then he came to and opened a workshop. He now spends his days doing repairs. Go down there, have a chat with him. Oh, and take him this magazine, I forgot to give it to him."

The next day, with a copy of *The Good News* in my hands, I was walking through the industrial area of the city. Somewhere amongst these hangars and garages was the place I needed, but I just could not work out where it was. Just before I left the house, I had decided to change out of my battered, comfortable trainers into a pair of more presentable, but heavy, boots and now I was suffering indescribably, as my shoes were rubbing the back of my ankle.

Ah, here it was. The workshop occupied several garages and some outbuildings, and gave off a general appearance of an abandoned scrapyard. Inside, a man was sitting in a wheelchair between two tables, intently sawing at some wood.

"Hello! I've been sent by Mariia Pavlivna. Look, she asked me to bring this and…"

He threw down his glasses with one hand, the piece of wood with the other, and his face, contorted with rage, came right at me.

"Oh, go stuff it up your arse! You tell that old cow, if she sends me another one of you bible-bashers, she'll be picking up the pieces!"

He kept shouting, getting more and more pent up, but by

then I stopped listening. From my brief but instructive interaction with the local drug addicts I had taken away one thing: run away at the first opportunity. Do not explain yourself, do not engage in conversation, just run away. I was out of the garage like a bullet and slammed the heavy metal doors behind me in one motion. There was a simple bolt on the door on the outside, and I drew it shut in a flash.

There was a second's pause in the workshop, and then the door shuddered, like a battering ram had hit it. I counted to three, then something made of glass flew at the metal and shattered. Suddenly, grey smoke appeared underneath, and the owner, inhaling the smoke, stopped swearing and began to cough.

I scurried away to a safe distance, forgetting all about the blisters on my feet, and stopped. But what if he choked to death? He was still a person, even if he was a crackhead.

I had to go back.

The garage was full of smoke, but I could not see the fire. There — a fire had started next to the table with the gas canisters. The old headcase had thrown a rug on it and was whacking the flames with a jacket. But the cluttered narrow passage was too narrow for the wheelchair to turn around in, and those gas canisters standing over there were going to blow all this junk up till kingdom come.

"Get out of here, now!", I kept saying to myself, at the same time running to the rescue. I rolled the gas canister away, grabbed another jacket, and also started attacking the source of the blaze.

"There's a fire extinguisher on the wall, grab it!", he wheezed next to me, and I even felt surprise at how deftly he was reacting to the situation, rather than hallucinating pink unicorns or whatever druggies were supposed to see.

Although it was too difficult to reach from a wheelchair from where it was fixed to the wall, the fire extinguisher was in working order. With a whoosh, it spewed a stream of foam which momentarily covered the whole floor and all the chairs and tables. Within ten seconds, the fire had been put out.

We looked at each other, and my druggie friend spat, coughed, and held out his hand.

"Roman. So, what was it you wanted?"

"If I'm honest, I want a hexoctahedron, forty centimetres in diameter."

"What? Are you high?"

* * *

"…I'm asking you one more time. Just change your outfit, is it really that hard? Think about it, no-one here gets that sort of style, those ancient trainers of yours. Go on!"

"Alright, let's end this, once and for all — well, or until next time, I know you'll never give it a rest — I have to be comfortable, I shouldn't have to be distracted."

"I don't get it — why can't you be comfortable in a dress? I have one, it's your size, just try it on, that's all. Just try it on."

Ah yes, that old chestnut… If it were anyone else, I doubt I would have tolerated it, but our dear Maryna was special. She was our style icon, the very bastion of chic and glamour with her carefully sculpted figure, heels, cleavage, nails; her aesthetically-coiffed ponytail which emphasised her perfect cheekbones and slender nose; her husky voice with its perfectly-projected changes of pitch. Maryna was a diamond, all dazzling jewellery with a no-less dazzling smile.

She was a genius negotiator, our secret weapon. She did not have a single lost contract in her portfolio — her belt hung heavy from the scalps she had claimed. This woman was always the centre of attention. Whenever she entered a room, everyone present would hold their breath for a second, and after this pause the tone of the conversation would change.

In essence, Maryna was the showcase of our company, our business card, and our mascot. Only a narrow circle of the elect would have guessed that the company also had brains, a stomach, and legs.

Maryna appeared at our workshop a year and a half after we started work. I had already moved into Rom's hangar and we more or less shared the responsibilities: I thought up and drew new designs; bought glass, enamel, and resin; took photographs of our works for catalogues; wrote up a small advert and performed a whole load of other small tasks. Roman soldered and welded the structures, laid out the glass in patterns according to their design, assembled, carved, guarded, and transported the pieces in his Opel customised for disabled people. Then two lads came to us to do any odd jobs we needed and for cutting glass. Then there was Don, our faithful hacker who ran our site and used photoshop; Borysovych, our general factotum and security guard; and Larysa Petrivna, our part-time accountant who would come to prepare our quarterly tax reports.

At some point, we happened upon the problem of a name. Between us, we just called it 'The Company', but that wasn't really enough for the general public.

"You understand," said Roman, reading a general course on 'Donbassology', "the name has to be something substantial, something beautiful. Something rich. It should have the word 'golden' in it. And something else exotic, beginning with 're', or 'ra'..."

"Ridicule? Rapunzel? Rheumatism?"

"Come on you, I'm being serious here. It should be something romantic, but also positive."

That's how, after lengthy discussion, we came up with the (English) name — don't laugh! — of 'Golden Rose'.

That period merged into one amorphous blob of fatigue. Sometimes I would switch off right at my table and would find myself on an old couch, having no idea who carried me there and when. My weight dropped below the critical forty kilos, and it began to affect me so much that I had to factor in the direction the wind was blowing on my way to and from work, otherwise I would be carried off. I passed out while working at my glass windows a couple of times, at which point Roman started watching how much I was eating and made the boys turn up at work with snacks.

I still remember the unbelievable clarity of vision of that time. It was as though the veil of perception that masked the world's beauty had fallen away. I was suffocating from pure delight, from the all-encompassing and infinite beauty that saturated everything around me, that flowed through the air, that penetrated my arms, my eyes, my chest. I absorbed the perfect harmony of the sweeping apple trees and oak leaves. I could spend hours looking at my own hand against a lamp, studying the perfect weave of blood vessels and capillaries. I took a coal-black glass base and decorated it with heavy crystal droplets, so that the light, reflecting off every second face, would refract off the third and return to its source, scattering into pure, spectral components and coming together again in a prism. It was here, in this perfect purity of light, this impeccable clarity of form, where I found magic.

We got along with barely any problems, and we worked quickly, like we were possessed. I would see the finished product in my mind's eye and then try and convey the idea to our technicians. The lads would try to meet me halfway; I would barely say a word and they would get it, and the pieces would come alive in their hands. We went through several options and settled on making little lampshades, which would be the easiest products to sell on. We would produce each one in a small series of no more than five pieces, each having a detailed certificate identifying its composition, weight, and serial number. Sometimes, if I was in the mood, I would take on making children's nightlights, vases, even making a dreamcatcher out of differently-toned pieces of glass.

After about a year we bought our first glass-blowing oven and industrial gas furnace. For Roman, this meant a significant reduction in our spending on raw materials; for me, it signified new horizons in terms of three-dimensional modelling.

Maryna came to us on the recommendation of one of our regular customers and ordered an exclusive chandelier for her bedroom, to which I, quite reasonably, replied that we do not make any 'non-exclusive' products. My first impulse was to decline this commission. Seeing the men's reaction, however, I realised that it was too late. I think Roman even bargained with me on behalf of the client, knocking off the price for our 'dear guest'.

I made her a chandelier, and I did it myself, not trusting anyone with any of the soldering. For three weeks, I wouldn't leave my oven's side, literally embroidering a glass web. What I came up with in the end was a huge dandelion, fluffy and weightless in appearance, which looked as though you could just give it a puff and it would take flight. The little glass 'parachutes' clung to each other chaotically, in no order — but turn on the light in a dark room, and this chaos would revert to order. At first glance, the careless lines of the chandelier would give off a geometrically uneven shadow. If properly hung up, however, readable words and symbols would show up on the wall, most of them obscene.

At its first showing, we kept playing with the light switch, unable to stop. The customer ran from the chandelier to the wall, covering the shadows with her hands, the whole company bustling after her.

"How? How did you do that?"

"Listen," Maryna said to me, when we were all laughing and chuckling at the scene, "I know you don't like me. Don't deny it! Women have never liked me, they've hated me my whole life, that's the price you pay for men adoring you. So, even though you don't like me, I'm asking you to take me on in your team. I want to work with you. I want to sell these things; I want to hold them in my hands. Believe me, you won't regret it."

And I did not regret it.

* * *

Of course, our day of reckoning came. It had to happen sooner or later, and we were lucky that it happened later. Our small company grew into a likely target for extortion by the Donetsk mafia about a year before the attack even happened. I spent the whole year waiting in a state of nervous apprehension. We had no support, no protection in the local administration or any local circles of influence, and this meant we were left in peace while no one still knew about us. We could fudge the books and hide a team of more than ten people for a month or two, at a maximum, but soon we would be in trouble.

I started memorising people's faces on public transport, making sure that I was not running into the same people twice. I wrote down the car number plates in the yard; I made friends with our neighbours. We would not keep cash at home or at work, we would not discuss anything important on the phone, we would not meet up with strangers, and we would tell each other where and when we would be at any point. We had a notification system for each member of the team, putting chips in our phones, so that we could find their location even when the device was turned off.

Not everyone was a fan of this; some even openly sabotaged it, but we were lucky. We were very lucky: we didn't have just one paranoid person lurking in our company, but two. I wouldn't have been able to convince them on my own, but our *sensei*, the security guru Borysovych, was on my side, and anyone would be a fool to oppose Borysovych.

Our old man had had such a rich past that even he got confused as to which one of his many stories was an anecdote he'd heard, and which was genuine. Moreover, Borysovych was the source of several legends that he had generously launched into the world. He seemed to have gone to prison at least twice, and his arms and shoulders had gone dark in patches where tattoos had faded and healed over. He was well over sixty, and he was remarkably resilient, flexible, and strong for his age. He could shoot from any barrel and could beat our boys at the shooting range even when blindfolded. In fact, we started to go to the range using his armoury, and the lads managed to get their weapons permits. Borysovych was Roman's contribution to the corporation's assets, alongside the garage, the tools, and his old Opel. There was something that happened in their pasts that had intertwined the fates of these two lone rangers and had led to Borysovych acting as Roman's devoted carer, and later, all of ours too.

It was at the request of our head security guard that we did not advertise our presence here in Donetsk. The shop was closed to the public, strangers were not allowed in, and we installed good doors and bars on the window from the very beginning. There had been a couple of incidents of petty crime, but the authority of our boys and their connections had been enough to repel any attacks. We had a couple of attempted robberies, but the security alarm went off and the group of security guys had rushed in.

We did not leave a mark on the city's public space. We did not put up any advertisements, nor did we hang up any billboards. We didn't have a shop window, we did not rub up against the tax or city administration, nor did we have any contact with the press.

Customers found us via our site and via recommendations, which we had been getting more and more of recently, even getting a backlog of potential customers. Unbeknownst to us, we had become fashionable, and more and more, our clients snapped up our products without even haggling over the price. I began to decline work if I did not like the customer — something that would have been absolutely unthinkable a year ago. Nevertheless, the more eccentric our behaviour was, the more desirable and scarce our chandeliers and stained glass would become, and accordingly, the higher the price.

Floundering under the weight of all our orders, we were forced to admit that it was time to make a qualitative change to our company. That, or we remain a small gang, and we continue working as an artisan studio, or we make a fundamental decision and go to the next level. We hire people, expand our floor, rent more equipment, and put lines of models into production.

"Borysovych, how much time do you think we've got before we become a target?"

"Until September, no longer. And that's not for certain. So save up as much as you can, and as Auntie Sonya said, *arbeiten* — get to work!"

Business went on as usual. Roman and Maryna were involved in the hiring process; I did not interfere, in fact, I took on everyone and taught everyone who was willing. We paid them well and on time, even organising hot lunches in the workshop. I put a few job vacancies on the internet, but the lads laughed at this. "You'll learn. We have our own internet here in Donetsk. Borysovych said that there'll always be people when you need them."

People did come: some disappeared after their first shift; others still stood enraptured next to the crucibles, and we guessed who would be part of our team by the excitement in their eyes, by the light drumming of their fingers, by their absent-minded expression, a mix of impudence and awe. We were approached by leavers from the local state residential school, whom the state had expelled into the world with no safety blanket to catch their fall; we were approached by former miners and teachers; we even had a taxi driver — although his career behind the wheel of a taxi was a short one. We put a team of seamstresses on the mosaics, since laying out coloured glass had something in common with beadwork.

The autumn of that year turned out to be a fruitful harvest. It was like nature, living by her own laws, suddenly exploded and went into overdrive. It all started with the honey. There was honey everywhere, honey markets sprung up, one after the other, like a relay. Honey was sold on the streets, at people's doors, overwhelmed beekeepers clogged the phonelines of wholesalers, who would take honey for twelve *hryvnia* a kilo. Then came the vegetables: heaps of cabbages and peppers, piles of potatoes, beetroot, carrots, and onions. The women on the street corners were standing on heaps of conserved vegetables and fruit, trying to turn over these unexpectedly generous gifts of nature. My grandmother was rushed off her feet trying to preserve everything, the jars taking up every free inch of the flat, and I would spend the night at the shop in order to avoid the all-pervasive smell of *lecho* ratatouille. The last stage was the mushrooms. It seemed they didn't only propagate in the mines. There were so many above ground that people were not picking them one by one, but mowing them down with scythes, and I even had to take a day at home to sort through buckets of *openki* mushrooms.

The same thing happened in businesses. Everyone was raking it in and parting with their cash, like it was their last day on earth, buildings were going up in four shifts — contractors were torn between choosing dozens of contracts at the same time. The city did not sleep; the city ate, drank and was merry. Fast money was showcased by the new facades, the shiny bonnets of Lexuses and the magnificent busts of young mistresses. All this noise needed recognition, brilliance, accomplishment, and dominance, if not over the world, then over your neighbours. In response to this demand, we launched a line of gold home fittings, and chandeliers for three hundred dollars apiece flew off the shelves like hot cakes.

"My granddaughter, look, something is going to happen. They're fools, it's money this, money that. All they can talk about is money. And loans? Have you seen the loans they're taking out? It's like they're never going to pay them back."

"Baba, I don't know, really. But what's it to do with us? We're not in debt."

"That's not what I'm talking about… oh well, forget it."

* * *

I wanted to clasp my hands on my stomach like Al Capone, lean back in my chair and say in a tired voice: 'Everyone, these negotiations are over for us; these people are not ready to agree.' Or flip the table over, getting coffee on the floor, the ceiling, and a spatter of someone's brains upon the wall.

I knew this would happen. We vowed from the very beginning that we would not do any business with the clergy. Everything went swimmingly, before we decided to stray from this principle. But no, for two weeks Maryna would not get the idea out of her head: "It's a big order, a really big order..." and then she forced us to come to an interview.

Now some important people, a band of six cult members, were trying to convince me that it was 'unthinkable' the new church in Karlivka could be built without 'this window here', pushing a picture of the altar window of St Isaac's Cathedral in St Petersburg towards me.

"Could you make an exact thirty-metre copy of this?"

"Well, maybe not *that* large..."

If I am not mistaken, it took the German craftsmen three years to make the original stained-glass window. I'm sorry, but even taking into account modern technology, I was not ready to shut down the company for a year and a half or so just for one order.

"You mean to say, then, that you're able to do it, it's just the turnaround that doesn't suit you?"

In fact, we could make anything we wanted, even a stairway to heaven and back. However, I did not want to and would not produce church décor, and we therefore had nothing more to talk about with our esteemed guests.

Our guests, however, thought differently. Maryna stayed quiet for a long time, doing an epic facepalm; Roman was openly laughing into his fist; and I was struggling to stay adrift in this most absurd of conversations. Very gradually, after each time going back to square one, in an atmosphere of general distrust and undisguised contempt — each time re-cultivating my disgust at each one of the six of them — we eventually came to a preliminary agreement.

Instead of making a huge stained-glass window, we would make a 'small' one, three by one and a half. The theme would be a modern take on the Holy Trinity, with some pronounced deviations from the standard iconography. We would submit the initial sketch in two weeks, and upon its acceptance we would receive an advance, which would be one third of the full amount. In two months, we would install the finished window, and would be paid the rest in full.

After consulting amongst ourselves, we proposed such a huge sum to the bishop that he squawked and reproachfully made the sign of the cross. With this sacred gesture began the second round of negotiations. It was here they beat us on our home turf and bamboozled us — whoever has ever had to make a deal with the priesthood will know what I mean. As a result, we agreed on a reduced budget, which still covered our overheads and ordinary income.

As a result, I ended up moving into the workshop until that November. I did not see anyone, I did not follow the news, and I did not read the newspapers. I must have eaten something, for surely you cannot go that long without eating? I had no idea, however, what exactly I ate, and who brought me my plate and washed the dishes. My whole life, the whole world, was centred around my drawing board. The sketches were first drawn on paper, and then Roman took the rolls of drawings and managed to transfer them onto special programs with our IT guys, calculating the technical nuances of the designs, from the curvature of the bends in the glass to the cost of the materials. After this, the whole team moved into the workshop, where we began the fine glass-cutting and soldered the delicate but sturdy structure of the frame. It was on this glass that we tested out our knowhow:

fusing together layers of glass to run together smoothly with one another. According to our design, the window would be east-facing, and the first morning rays should come together in the central figure to form a shining red star.

We were not the only ones to remember the day we took it out of the shop. Together the three main panels weighed over a tonne. In addition to this, not one of them could fit through the door, and so we had to dismantle the wall of the hangar. We had to roll them on logs, like the Ancient Egyptians did for their pyramids, and when we were outside, we had to load them up with a special hoist.

Fortunately, it was not too far from the church, only about twenty kilometres, but I felt every single bump in the road and pothole in my very spine. When we finally reached Karlivka and began our final installation of the window, I was in seventh heaven. Later, the guys laughed about how I, in my state of euphoria, once again introduced myself to the church proprietors, as if I hadn't gone over the finer points of the project with them a hundred times or more.

Installing the window took over fourteen hours, the whole night through till dawn. The next morning, curious worshippers showed up to the church, inconspicuous men smeared with coal dust, women in mourning dress, and the local lay and church powers.

Do you know anything about sunrise in the Donbas? No pale first rays, almost no transition between dark and light. One minute, we were working by night, floodlit by an industrial projector, and within a few seconds we were being blinded by the light streaming in from the street. In the transparent rays of the autumn sun, the figure of the Messiah was lit up with gold, almost stepping out of the glass, and then all the light concentrated at the level of his heart and blazed purple. That is just what it was like... it was like an organ. Yes, it was like an explosive, majestic organ fugue crashing down on you in an avalanche of fifty different registers, right when you are least expecting it, like in the forest or at the dentist's office. It is a pity that I never learnt how to express my feelings properly… I was astounded that my heart was not broken in two by a boundless, unbridled joy. What we saw before us was a masterpiece that had surpassed the work of human hand, and we knew that we were the ones who had created it.

We were paid in full, no haggling on the price, and we received a generous bonus. The priest blessed me as a little extra, and the women took us off for some tea. I readily agreed, wondering if it would seem impudent to ask them if I could take a little nap, if only for about twenty-four hours or so.

The boys, meanwhile, gathered together the tools, the winch, and scaffolding, stuffing them into the van, and zipped off to Donetsk. Having such a large amount of cash on them, they had to go straight to the bank, where the clerks were already waiting for us, and then unload the gear. Only one of the assemblers, Serhii, stayed behind with me and his old Niva car.

I sat down right below the altar, feeling my consciousness gradually slip away from my body. It was a moment of the greatest spiritual triumph, and at the same time, utter exhaustion. The only thing I could manage was to lean against the wall with a mug in my hands, blissfully sipping from it, and admire the hundreds of shades of noble glass, examine the luminosity of every air bubble, every imperfection. Neither the rumble of voices, nor the footsteps of dozens of visitors, or the endless trill of a phone call could distract me from this meditative contemplation. The phone rang and rang, rang and rang, and suddenly, I realised that the guys weren't calling me.

They were ringing the alarm.

* * *

Right at the beginning, when we were still just planning everything, I had a talk with Borysovych.

"Listen, in case, you know… Who do we go to for help, the gangs or the police?"

"Oh, my dear daughter, this is the Donbas! They're one and the same here."

"No, I'm serious. We don't want to hire some thugs for show. We need a real security outfit, one that can react quickly to trouble."

"Komar is the one you need. I planned to talk to him right from the start."

That is how Komar entered our lives. Why he was called 'Komar', meaning 'mosquito' — I had no idea whether it was his surname or just a nickname, but that's how he introduced himself. He was a rather dry man, of medium height, greying hair cut short, which at a stretch you could say was thinning, with an expression on his face as if he was about to shoot someone, or at least swat a fly. Or maybe he had swatted someone yesterday; he had the typical look of someone whose occupation is both 'rough and tough'.

He had some sort of hybrid security firm / sports club / men's club. I was sceptical of the men as a rule, but I had little say in the matter. They charged a small fee for their services, on account of their longstanding friendship with Borysovych — where on earth that bloke got so many old friends from, I'd like to know! One day, some surly sort of people came into our workshop, installed alarms and bars on the windows, sat a few minutes with our IT guy, after which the phones and computers took on a life of their own, regularly hanging up and rebooting of their own accord.

Komar did not like me either, truth be told, and for the first six months of our 'collaboration' he did not say a single word to me, resolving any issues with the men. I did not take it personally at all — I am not that lovable. We worked together like so, nodding at each other the rare times we would pass each other, until we had an attempted robbery. These were local lads, on the hunt for adventures for the thrill of it. They lifted the bars off and broke the windows, at which point the heist of the year was foiled. The response team was there roughly eighty seconds after the alarm went off, who found these juvenile delinquents at the scene of the crime, and then took them off to teach them a little lesson.

This event had both direct material and delayed moral consequences for us. Simply put, the local crime network did not want anything more to do with us.

"Borysovych, let's thank our security outfit somehow. I don't know, maybe I could make them a little car banner with their names on it?"

"Better to do something for Komar's mother. She's an invalid, she's been bed-bound for a long time."

I had a think and then blew some glass into a small panel with a window mount. I then did some active research for the most natural-looking examples of still-life art, and the panel emerged as a weave of cherry branches with the most lifelike and real leaves and liveliest, plumpest, and juiciest cherries I could muster up. For a long time, I did the tedious business of pouring and fashioning the glass for the cherries, with the full effect of their presence coming through — the lads even tried to take one off me and bite into it a few times.

I sent the gift by courier with a note, and then forgot all about it. I heard nothing for three days, and then, on the fourth, Komar came right up to me in my workshop.

"Thank you," he said, in Russian. After a moment's thought, he added, "Thank you", this time in Ukrainian.

That was the first time we talked. Well, talk is one word for it. He could not speak a word of Ukrainian, so he nodded, more than anything, but asked me not to switch to Russian.

"Talk, talk, please. I don't understand anything, but it sounds so beautiful."

He offered to take me on an advanced driving course for

emergencies at their centre, learning how to do handbrake turns and emergency stops and so on. After thinking about it, I agreed, because after learning how to drive, I still did not know how to parallel park, since I had never been taught.

Our timetable was a little strange, given both of our workloads. We would go driving either at night or at six in the morning, training in their luxury cars, or in our company Niva, and only stopped when I could complete the track in under two minutes, ending with a spectacular, controlled skid.

After that, a fragile thread of mutual respect bound us together. I sometimes came to their sparring training, admiring the grace and accuracy of the movements of these trained boxers; their fights had the same relation to regular sporting bouts as that of sharp-toothed jungle felines to spats between housecats. From time to time, Komar would slip into the workshop to mull over one of his usual work tasks — since the sight of molten glass, manipulated by the artist's hand, as it dribbles drop by drop and turns into hundreds of different shapes, could really soothe and enlighten the onlooker.

Now, having received the alarm from our crew, out of inertia I called our security, not doubting that Komar had received the signal before me, and that the lads were coming to their rescue. Judging by everything, our guys had been intercepted in Netailove. It was there where they went off route and turned abruptly off to Nevelske. As we could gather from their GPS, for some reason they had stopped off at an abandoned farm.

"Please, please, please, please let them be alive," I prayed, jumping into the car.

Serhii could only open his eyes wide in shock when I snatched the keys off him and dived into the driver's seat.

"Listen, our lads have been ambushed around Nevelske. You stay here, I'm going to check it out."

"Have you gone mad? You stay here, I'll go."

"Ok, but I'm driving."

"Uh..."

There was no time to say the rest. We were already rushing past the Karlovy Vary motel, then, not slowing down, snaking over the double lines, past the concrete 'ball' of the bus stop on the right and going off-road. We were already close, speeding over the ground and by the pond, without slowing down at the crossing — damn, I did not realise I could do *that!* — and we were flying up to the rusty gates of the old collective farm. From afar we could already hear single shots coming from the tower, like from a carbine.

After the autumn rain, the road had turned into a mud bath, with lumps of mud and clay flying off into all directions, and as an aside I give thanks to fate that we were in the Niva, since no other car would have made it through here. After the last turn, we beheld an epic scene. In the distance, our Gazelle van had hidden itself in one of the hangars. Before us, under the water tower, a foreign 4×4 had got stuck, and behind it huddled a grey Ford. Right next to it in the ditch lay six bandits, who clearly did not know what to do next. I saw not one, two, but three guns — but what for? They still could not lift their heads as they waited for the shooters to run out of ammo.

Naïve little boys. I did not know how extensive exactly Borysovych's arsenal was, but it was enough for a mini war. With Roman next to him too, who, if alive, could hit a bullseye from two hundred metres away — in any case, they could make it until reinforcements arrive.

These thoughts flew by in the seconds between our arrival on the farm and our abrupt entrance right behind the muggers.

"Hold on!"

The car flew up off a hummock as if it was on a trampoline, all four wheels in the air, and landed right in the middle of the bandits, right over someone's back and head. True, I did not even see this; the last thing I remember was a sharp pain from my seatbelt and glass right in front of my eyes.

* * *

"Pour it, pour some more, she's coming back to us!"

"Ok, get out the way, you shouldn't turn her over."

"Shall I inject her? — No, why not? I have a needle in my first aid kit."

"She's breathing, definitely! We need to get her tongue out of her mouth so she doesn't choke on it."

"Use a knife, first use a knife to prise her teeth off it!"

"Hm…bm…"

"What did she say? Quiet, she's saying something!"

"I'll kill you."

I had never been so angry in my whole life. My vision and hearing came back slowly, in fragments, and the first thing I saw when I finally opened my eyes was a forest of hands. Everyone there thought it was necessary to shove their fist in my face, asking me, "How many fingers am I holding up?"

But I did not count the fingers. Don, Oleh, Roman, Borysovych, Serhii, Yurka, and Tolik — it seemed everyone was there. Serhii's split forehead throbbed in front of me, the others were more and less intact. There was Komar too, warming his hands under his armpits. Who was this guy? He even *stands* disapprovingly.

"Tell me what happened."

Like we thought, they were tactically blocked off at the turn-off to Netailove. Just like in the films, the tyres of both cars were slashed, they were forced onto the hard shoulder, and their wheels were shot at. But the bandits had not taken into account that our ex-taxi driver, Don, was fired for his daredevil driving, or that Borysovych could beat anyone at the shooting range. Whilst I'm still releasing the safety catch, he could even hit a bullseye out of his pocket from a distance of ten metres (it was not difficult, apparently. You only have to put your index finger on it right and sort of 'shoot' the gun with your finger).

They did not expect this from our van of surprises. Instead of stopping, the van swerved onto the hard shoulder, snapping off the Ford's wing mirror, and flew ahead, firing straight behind them. By disorienting their opponents, the boys bought themselves some time. A few seconds was enough to slip into the farm in front of their pursuers and to hide themselves in the barn. The battle then turned from an offensive to a positional one. Our boys held on until receiving reinforcements, and the bandits were at a loss, clearly.

Then Serhii and I arrived, and everything fell into place. Miraculously, no one was killed, although three of the six in the 4×4 received serious injuries, so that the security who came after us had to just pick up the wounded.

"What shall we do with them, milady?"

A question with a double-entendre, but I knew the answer.

"Komar, you can't have missed them at some point? They're organised, they've got guns on them and everything. Send them over to your lot, let's see what lesson you can teach them, so that we're never messed with again. The cars are your trophies, take their weapons, they'll come in handy. And find out, please, who's behind this, whether this was their own idea or whether they got a tip off. Can you do this?"

"No problem."

"Don't draw attention to us, if possible."

"Got it. What should we do with the Niva?"

"What about it? The cars busted, as you can see. Someone crashed it, it looks. Hey lads, what are you all standing about for? Salvage what you can, it'll be burnt out soon."

They sorted it all out. After a little while, our security team loaded up the wounded and headed out, leaving their leader behind with us. The carcass of the old Niva burnt out in the ditch, whereas I lay on the hummock and watched the blaze, like Nero over Rome. Roman had a smoke next to me, and Borysovych and Don loaded the Gazelle van, luckily having found a spare wheel.

"Hey Rom, guys, come here. The plan's changed."

"What do you mean?"

"Don't go to the bank. Roman, take the money from the car. Divide it up equally, including Komar, that's a bonus from us. Give Serhii two thousand extra, to pay for the car... Why are you laughing?"

"Listen to yourself. You clocked up 160 km/h on that old Niva on the grass — oh pipe down, Serhii told us — ran over some people, and flew through the windscreen. After all that, could you for once say 'a grand' instead of 'a thousand'? Go on, say 'a couple of g's', eh?"

"My dear colleague, please bugger off."

That day, I did not go home straight away. First, we took the guys back and dropped off the equipment at the base. We agreed that we would all take three days off, giving the lads enough time to hold a wake for the fallen car. Next, Roman had to go to the car wash and clean up his disabled car, which now looked more like a hovercar. The lads then lost their patience and took me to the trauma unit, ignoring my complaints.

The doctor on duty gave me a diagnosis of concussion and prescribed me an ointment for my haematoma. A dark bruise spread out across my face from the locus of the blow, making me look like a panda. My eyelids were swollen and blue; my nose was swollen and I could no longer breathe out of it. The worst of it was that I hadn't worked out yet what to say to my grandmother.

"Auntie Olya, don't you worry, she just walked into a door-frame," Roman began to say at the door when we finally managed to get home, but then he stopped.

My grandmother is sitting in front of the telly, crying. She has been crying for a long time, her face, neck, and handkerchief in her hands were wet through. There is some action film being shown on the TV. A group of policemen in black helmets are beating someone on the ground. The camera then focuses on a girl being dragged up some stairs. A close-up of a bloody face, someone being thrown off a monument, batons again, and blood.

What is going on, is this being filmed in Kyiv? It looks like the
Maidan Square, but it is dark, you cannot see what is going on…
What is happening there?

PATINA

THEY'RE ALL DONE FOR

"My child, so what then, when are your lot going to come kill us?"
I goggled at Valentyna Stepanivna as if she had grown a second head.
"Who is 'our lot' then? Who are you talking about?"
"Your Benderies." [2]
I did not know what to say to her.
For the last ten years, I had been going to my neighbour every week, sometimes twice a week. I would bring lunch, buy her treats or olives, which the old lady would accept with pleasure. She was doing well for her ninety-plus years, retaining (or so I thought until that day) a sound mind and an excellent memory.

She could regale us for hours about 'Hughesovka',[3] where she was born; about Stalino, where she spent her youth; and the city now called Donetsk, and how she knew it. I loved her flat with its piles of dusty newspapers and magazines; I loved her library, where her complete collection of Jane Austen's works propped up an artist's biography of Bosch and a three-volume encyclopaedia of airplane modelling. Her walls, long gone un-redecorated, were covered with paintings from the sixties with their artists' signatures on the back, and on one of the canvases I recognised a collage by the filmmaker Sergei Parajanov.

"Hang on, is that what I think it is? It's not a fake?"

"Of course. His dear Svetlana and I were on very good terms."

Valentyna Stepanivna looked like an owl in her milk-bottle glasses. Her hands also looked like talons as she held her teacup, and unlike other people, she sat sideways on her chair, right on the edge. I loved her, I loved her self-deprecating irony and the stoic way she bore the frailty of her old age.

"My child, could you take me to the shop? I could make it back by myself, but getting there against this wind is just impossible, I would not be able to get out the front door."

---

2   There is a town called Bendery in Transnistria, the breakaway state internationally recognised as Moldovan that borders Western Ukraine. Here, however, *Bendery* is a misnomer for the controversial far-right politician and freedom fighter, Stepan Bandera (1909–1959), who was one of the leaders of the Ukrainian national movement in Western Ukraine. The figure of Bandera has become something of a bogeyman in the national discourse, especially after the escalation of events in 2014.

3   Donetsk has undergone several name-changes in its two-and-a-half century history. It was first called Aleksandrovka; a century later it was named Yuzovka, after the Welsh industrialist John Hughes, who founded several coal mines and steel plants in the region. During the Soviet rule it was renamed Stalin, Stalino, and then finally Donetsk, after the river Donets, which runs through it.

They would call her 'Frau' behind her back, because of how she stood out with her trouser suits and raspberry berets. And now…

All winter I dreamed of putting the world on hold to just think. I once read a story in which the hero lived his life two seconds behind everyone else. This tiny delay was enough to derail him and eventually lead him to suicide.

It felt like I had also ended up in a fantasy novel. Maybe everyone had a psychotropic gas sprayed over them, and I was the only one who was immune? Or was I the one who had gone mad, and so I could not understand the logic of those surrounding me? Was I sleeping, and it was all a lingering dream? Or was it the result of my accident, like my brain had not fully recuperated after the concussion?

Everything had changed. I could no longer recognise the people I had lived with for the last ten years. Moreover, I was afraid of them, frankly.

People began to talk a lot. My neighbours would literally lie in wait for you on the bench under the building. It was impossible to go out and buy bread without someone stopping you umpteen times.

People believed in the Right Sector, Banderites, bogeymen, and alien invasions. Kyiv did not exist anymore; it lay in ruins. American saboteurs had poisoned the water supply, and you could only drink bottled water. The capital's authorities had sent out the order to blow up the mines and flood Donetsk. *'Our boys'* were being fired at on the Maidan square, a Berkut[4] police officer had his eye gouged out. Some people had burst into a woman's house and blew her leg off. Which house? Which woman? Every storyteller had a different version of the story, and the

---

4   The Berkut was a special police force that was dissolved by the Ukrainian government in 2014 after being held responsible for the majority of deaths of protesters in the 2014 uprisings.

story of this poor wretch with a blown-off leg limped from Slovyansk to Horlivka.

Trips on public transport had become a nightmare. No matter
where you went, on every trip someone would come into the cabin with a phone in their hands and would talk incredible loudly,
involving everyone present in the conversation. You would hear
the same stories, and I even singled out a few repeated sources:
there were the elder soothsayers, or 'my daughter-in-law from
Kyiv phoned me', or 'they said so at my daughter's work'.

At first, I would argue with them, but it would turn out badly. Once I was even spat at in my face and shoved out the minibus. After that I would stuff my earphones in, pretending that I
was not there.

On Artem street I once saw pensioners attacking a film crew,
whacking the camera and beating up the cameraman. A few
passers-by looked the other way, and a police squad just stood
there, staring intently in the opposite direction. I ran up to them,
saying something, and began to pull the boy-journalist out of the
crowd of aggressors. The old folks parted in surprise, and then
started on me.

"Who are you?"

"I'm a local, I live here."

"A local? Show us where the Kontinent is!"

"Over there."

"You're lying! She's no local, the Kontinent is over there!"

I was gobsmacked. I knew exactly where this shopping centre
was, since that was where I was headed at that moment. What
was this about, so who were they, then? I then saw a young man
in sports gear approaching us.

"What's going on here?"

"So, look…"

I firmly grab the young man's arm, saying: *"The oldies have
lost their minds. They're telling me that the Continent is by the
Donbass Arena. Don't have anything to do with them."*

I turn around and leave, and no-one stops me. Out the corner of my eye I see that the cameraman has fled.

My work became an island of common sense. Maybe we paid them well, or we were just lucky, but none of our employees had fled on the paid 'one day trips' to Kyiv. We finished the year with orders for the following year, but by mid-February it was as quiet as the grave. Following a week of no orders, we had a discussion and put everyone on their annual leave.

I would go down to the Shevchenko monument a few times, where the Donetsk Euromaidan protests were taking place. I would stand nearby, not daring to join the activists. They were few in number, about twenty people, sometimes fifty, and they stood there like martyrs in the middle of the square. Passers-by would push or spit at them, or just harass them… I grew fearful at just the thought of being there with them, with everyone staring, and I would run away, despising myself for my cowardice.

It was easier on the internet, as I would join patriotic groups on Facebook and on VKontakte, and bravely liked the posts about what was happening. My life in general shifted into virtual reality, since in my real life everything was mystifying and scary. It took me a week to gather up the courage to ask Roman and Borysovych what they thought about the Maidan protests, and fell apart with relief when I heard, "I hope they skewer that criminal Yanukovych."

The day then came when I stopped being afraid, when the fear had gone, and I was left behind with a whole gamut of other feelings. It is probably the same way that the gymnast abandons their fear when they fly towards their trapeze, or how the hunter feels, facing down the wolf with a knife.

By an irony of fate, the date of the birth of the New Me began with that visit to my neighbour. Valentyna Stepanivna came up to our place, which she had not done since Christmas, stamped her feet outside the door and carefully perched herself on the sofa. It was obvious that she had dressed herself up for the visit: she had a little felt bunch of flowers pinned on her grey cardigan; a few rings sparkled on her dry, arthritic fingers. She did not come empty-handed, but with a three-litre jar of *medusa*, or kombucha — that is, homemade fermented tea. It was a wise move: it is impossible to get angry at someone who has brought you homemade kombucha.

"You know, my child, I flew today. In my dream."

"Where did you fly to, then?"

"Into the hall. Down the corridor and to the right. Not very high up, about half a metre off the ground."

"How was that, then? Did you wave your hands about or just flutter them?"

"You won't believe it, it felt completely natural. I was horizontal, face down. I examined every grain of dust on the parquet floor as I flew over it."

Then we looked at each other and burst out laughing. I was bent over laughing, and she was shaking slightly, holding in her false teeth with one hand. At that moment, everything was like before, as if a foreign entity had departed the possessed body, and the puppet was now free of it.

Then we turned on the TV and saw the stream of events from Institutska street. We saw the bodies on the Maidan square; we saw Kyiv's central street, Khreshchatyk, gone dark; we saw the hourly updates of the number of victims. I sat in front of the screen until the evening, and when I stood up again, the fear had already left me.

* * *

We are falling into a rabbit hole. Everything which you once could have relied upon crumbled into dust in your very hands. Reality now parted ways with common sense. I would squeeze my eyes shut and pretend I was not there: someone pinch me!

I am not me — I am a snail, I am an Easter bun, I am part of
the furniture, one of those timeless Scythian stone *baba* statues.
A simple Ukrainian-Scythian stone *baba*.

Three hundred tramps took over the regional government
administration building. They broke into the offices, making off
with televisions, air conditioners, and unused teabags. What, so
when faced with this epic army armed with sticks, gas canisters,
and a week's worth of hangover, the powers that be suddenly flee,
tails between their legs. Are you kidding me?

They let the Ukrainian flags fall so easily, like they were paper decorations, and I could not understand: what, was this
flag, this state, was it all false? Why did the police don their old
St George's ribbons, just to stand there, arms folded? Why was I
laughed at outright when I asked about their oath and the pride
of the uniform?

Why is everyone here at home so calm, no one is lighting the
beacons, no one is shouting, running out into the street in a state
of undress and calling for help?

The city was filled with cars with Russian number plates;
'tourists' who would pronounce their 'o's as 'a's and who would
say 'what' like 'shto' in the Russian way instead of 'sho', stripping
the supermarkets of alcohol; drinking and eating on the lawns;
pissing right in the yards; and our own people just walked by,
heads down.

Never in my life had I felt so alone and helpless. A chasm surrounded me and my grandmother. Neighbours and friends who
would come over nearly every day for tea had suddenly forgotten the way to our flat. Baba Olya became morose; I would come
home in the evening — she would be asleep already, and more
and more often I would rake out empty bottles of wine from the
bin. I did not have the courage to talk to her about it, and she did
not ask where I was going out and with whom.

"Oh Roman, what are we going to do?"

"What to do? The only thing you can do is get out. Don't you see? Everything is going to shit. Get out and take your grand-mother with you."

"And you?"

"Us, we're going to fight, they're not going to get us, the bas-tards."

Actually, it was the right idea — pack up your things, take your grandparents with you and leave this place; leave here while you've still got petrol in the tank and money in the bank — the further the better. I will admit that in my next life I will choose the logical path and run for the hills at the first sign of 'Russian peace'.

Then I went out into the yard, looking at the March puddles, at the black, frozen trees, at the dark railings and garages. At the plastic bag which got entangled in the branches; at the sun above the slag heap, at the oily smoke coming from the power station. I rubbed a fresh burn on my arm from molten glass, and my eyes roamed over the chewed-up carcasses of unfinished stained-glass pieces.

"You're an idiot. I am not going anywhere. Where's Bory-sovych?"

Borysovych and the lads had disappeared down to the mili-tary commissar, which was making lists of people for service in the territorial army. There was going to be some sort of Donbas battalion.

"Roman, you know what? Let's sit down and phone some peo-ple. Let's call our clients in Kyiv and other parts of the coun-try. Let them say what's happening with them? Ukraine has to exist somewhere, no? There has to be solid ground some-where, let's look at where we stand? Another thing; I am part of a group on Facebook where I've been uploading information on the Donetsk Maidan protests. We'll have to comb through all the group members and make a private chat to organise our-selves."

"As you wish, *mein Fuhrer.*"

It was not just a joke, by the way. I once caught a glimpse of his phone and saw that he saved me in his contacts as 'Fuhrer'.

In early March our side held a few rallies which were relatively successful. On the 4th of March up to five thousand people came together, performed, sang the national anthem; passing cars were beeping their horns; people waved at us. I held my pole with its flag and for a second I believed that everything would be fine, that we would change what was happening, that our nightmare would end. We were uplifted and relaxed a little; we stayed together for a long time, planning the details of our next outing.

We had a surprise planned for the next day — we would unfurl a massive Ukrainian flag. Mariia Oleksiivna, a miner's widow, sewed it together in her microscopic flat on an ordinary sewing machine. I could not imagine how she did not drown under the kilometres of silken cloth. When we rolled the cloth up it turned out that we could not fit it through the door, and we could barely get it out the building's entrance.

Families with children had gathered to see the record-breaking flag. The chief of police, some Romanov or other, personally guaranteed that the demonstration would take place peacefully and that the patriots would be protected. The news then reported that we were ten thousand strong — that may be true, but I could not count the number of protesters then. I know only that it was a sea of people, that we were hugging, shaking hands, and I was giddy with relief. There were so many of us all together that we were not afraid to make our voice heard. We were not afraid to sing our anthem. There were young mothers, pensioners, students, family patriarchs and matriarchs, football fans and schoolchildren, old boys from the villages, and fashionable young city 'things'; they all suddenly became related and all one people, although these people had never crossed paths in a previous life. We all became Ukrainians, and carried our Ukraine like an athlete carrying the Olympic torch, higher than the sky.

I cannot say that we relaxed, no. It would be more correct to say that we had not actually steeled ourselves up for what was coming. Most of us had no idea what we were dealing with, who we were dealing with, we did not know what a vile enemy we had on our hands. We had come out onto the square to convince them. They had come out to kill us, and that was that.

When the mass of people suddenly lurched and moved to one side, leaving bodies behind on the ground, I did not immediately understand what was happening. There were far fewer attackers than us — a few hundred — but they were well-trained militants. They did not waste time talking, instead breaking bones and smashing peoples' heads in with clubs and weapons, shooting into the crowd of people, throwing missiles and smoke grenades at people. They did not care who they were attacking — women, children, old people — their purpose was to sow panic, and met no resistance.

At some point I realised that I was falling, and that would be the last time in my life that I would ever fall. I clutched desperately for air, someone's back, breaking my nails as I tried to grab jackets and rucksacks, but it was in vain; my leg got stuck in a gap between the paving stones, and I could already hear my ankle crunching and breaking, but there was nothing I could do. Suddenly, one of the policemen standing at the perimeter and pretending that was happening did not concern them ran up to me. He ran up, grabbed me by the collar like a mother cat would her kitten, and literally threw me under the sanctuary of our flag, into our crowd.

Behind us, I could not see much. I only heard the screams, the groaning, the curses. Someone was screaming his lungs out; someone else was praying. Probably out of fright and emotion I remembered words that I had never specially learnt in my life. I just knew that it was Psalm 91, the soldier's protection: *'There shall no evil befall thee, neither shall any plague come nigh thy dwelling.'* What next? *'A thousand shall fall at thy side, and ten thousand at thy right hand; but it shall not come nigh thee.'* The lines flowed one after the other, and I remembered my mother read it every evening to us, like a lullaby. If I strained just a little, it seemed that I could even recall her voice. Mum, mummy, what were you guarding us from in your prayers?

* * *

The course of events moved so fast that even now, a short while later, I get confused about their sequence. It's all to do with the adrenaline, I think. The rush and the adrenaline filled my being and overflowed, demanding some sort of action. I could not sit in one place. We could not eat, we would barely sleep, we would knock back caffeine pills and sit 24/7 on chat rooms and on the phone. For the first time in my life, I was feeling what it was like to have a nervous episode: when you're shaking so badly from worry that the teacup you're holding tumbles out of your hands; when you cannot speak because your teeth are chattering and your jaw is clenched shut.

I thoroughly prepared myself for the next demonstration. No heels, bags, or rucksacks; hair tied in a bun at the nape of my neck; three jumpers underneath my jacket, which should theoretically soften the blow. There was no point in asking the question, 'to go or not to go?', because I had to be there on the square together with those whom I respected and whom I believed in. Even if we were a drop in the ocean, and even if that ocean was immeasurably far away from us, we would still have to squeeze the last out of us, breathe strength into this fragile stream that will take our waters to 'great' Ukraine.

We saw the rot everywhere. We swiftly realised that neither the administration nor the public prosecutor's office were going to help us. Besides, any form of contact with government officials or a member of the national security network posed a threat to us.

Our people started to disappear. After each rally, the police would detain protesters, and only a small number of these would reappear in court with just an administrative fine. Many were not found at all, and our community's social media platforms were overrun with photos of people who had gone missing. The girls and I would go in search of people at the hospitals; we had to pretend we knew people or butter up nurses and paramedics who would leak information about victims of brutality. The attacks on friends from our circles became more and more frequent. It was not just the organisers of the protests who were beaten or stabbed; journalists writing about the rallies, doctors who tended to the wounded, the girls who would make food and give people from out of town a place to stay were also attacked. Cars were torched in garages and car parks. Children suffered a lot as well: if word got out at school that a child's mother or father was going to the Ukrainian demonstrations, then the child would face the most sadistic abuse.

Riding with a patriotic symbol on your car was another type of trial. If a car with a Ukrainian flag on it stopped at some traffic lights, then a flock of 'aunties' or rabid pensioners, or a band of both, would hurl themselves at it, breaking the doors, smashing in the windows, mirrors, lobbing 'bombs' made of flour, mud, or shit, into the car. After a few such incidents, the amount of 'yellow and blue' cars on the street significantly decreased.

The big event was planned for the 13th of March. In addition to a concert, speeches from Kyiv politicians and church hierarchs were planned. The organising committee was run off its feet; I had never realised that organising rallies was such a bother. Buying fabric for the flags, getting hold of poles for them, bringing equipment to the stage, finding the stage itself — none of the local businesses wanted to associate themselves with us — organising transport, feeding, and finding a place to stay for protesters from around Donetsk, painting placards, taking care of communications, writing releases for the rally, giving interviews, setting up a stream, getting hold of participants for a live broadcast, figuring out the order of events... Our heads were spinning, but we were content amongst the chaos. It felt as though with just a bit longer, we would squeeze them, a few more demonstrations, and things would change. Just look at the *'opolchentsi'*, or ragtag militants, who managed to take over the regional state administration and city administration buildings in just a day. If you looked at the miserable alcoholic feeble mass, the crack-heads and tramps they were made up of, who had slithered in here with the sinful way they were earning their daily wage — just compare them with our bright, rational, strong people! We cheered each other up in anticipation of that day that would definitely come. Good triumphs over evil, right? We were on the side of the light, I guarantee you.

The morning of the day before the rally, someone phoned me on an unknown number. I reply, and at once I hear the voice of our former head of security. To say I was surprised would be an understatement. I had not seen Komar since autumn, and I specifically did not ask after him. He was not among the pro-testers — what did that mean then? True, that was why I had not asked after him. Yet now he was calling me, asking me to meet him.

I did not go to the meeting. I got ready and even put makeup on, and then I decided not to go, changing my mind at the last minute. I asked Borysovych to go in my place, to find out what the 'authorities' wanted from us.

Borysovych called back after a few hours with unbelievable news. It turned out that Komar had brought a whole car filled with batons, shields, and tear gas canisters for our guys. He just muttered: *"So you're not standing there naked"* — and told him to unload it all quickly.

Delighted, Borysovych flagged down the nearest car, driven by some lad called Kostik or something, and filled up the whole car with our new treasures and rushed to our headquarters. They did not have time to thank our unexpected benefactor, as he turned on his heel and left without saying goodbye. He did not say a single word about me, by the way. I phoned him myself, wanting to apologise for my absence, but that morning's number was no longer in service.

We arrived early to Lenin Square, and we had two unpleasant surprises waiting for us. The first was that one part of the square was occupied by supporters of 'Russian peace': there were not many of them, but they had taken up a strategic high point next to the monument. The usual crazed pensioners and aunties with placards saying 'Putin help us' stood at the front; behind them, a throng of other old women. The second bit of news left me completely dumbfounded. Our batons and shields were not there. Kostik came up to the organising committee, hands on hips, and said that he had left the loaded car a few streets away, saying that he could not get access anywhere closer. 'But don't worry!' Everything had been ok'd with the police, apparently, and the protest would take place peacefully — no 'excesses' would be allowed.

Whilst the men were left arguing with each other, I decided to have a look for myself where the car was, and even managed to shove my way out through the crowd. There were a lot of us, many of them holding umbrellas (having learnt from bitter experience, the women had planned to use umbrellas to protect themselves from being egged or from other rubbish that would fly at the heads of the protestors). Manoeuvring my way through the crowd took a while, and I was almost out of the square when my phone rang.

* * *

Oksana and I were not friends. I did not make friends in general, as I had neither the time nor the skill for it, but any friendship between me and Oksana was impossible as a matter of principle. I was tiny and thin, whereas she was three times larger than me; she could fit two fingers around my wrist, with room to spare. I was all knees and elbows, whereas she was all soft mounds;

I was quiet, she was a chatterbox; I would bury everything inside of me, whereas she had no secrets; I never quite learned how to get on with men, whereas she would have one lover breathing down another's neck, sometimes crossing each other on her doorstep.

No, we were not friends. It just so happened that we would eat together. Oksana would come over to eat with my grandma at ours, looking for peace and quiet. Her monologues did not tire me, as I could easily paint with the backdrop of a smooth hum of her endless stories. I would not comment, only nodding and listening. In exchange, my neighbour would praise my work, even my drafts, not letting me throw out any of my sketches.

She had six brothers and sisters at home, as well as her mother, who was killing herself to keep it all together, and a photograph of her father. Her father, a miner, did not come up to the surface one day, and all of our yard gathered together for his wake *in absentia* — that is when you have a funeral, but without the body. I remember them making a widow's pension for the whole family, the amount of offices we had to go around to get it, and how Oksana came over to ours, all solemn. She did not stay quiet for long, about a week, and then returned to her usual self.

I knew everything about her suitors, about her studies at the teaching institute, about the vicissitudes of her quest to find a job. She was one of those rare women who was a naturally gifted teacher. She loved children, the shrieks and smells didn't faze her. She often stayed overtime at work, waiting there late with her last student, and never complained. Therefore, when Oksana announced that she was leaving the school to become a nanny in a family, for the first time in our acquaintance I tried to convince her not to do something.

The new family in question was that of either the sister or some younger relative of Rinat Akhmetov himself. Before hiring her, she had to undergo a thorough vetting by their personal security service, and in the process the girl was so intimidated that she came over to mine and would use hand gestures, scared of letting on too much.

"Listen, this won't end well. You've got to get out of there."

"No, just a little longer. You understand me, the little boy there… He's so scared of his father, of his mother, the bodyguards, everyone. He'd stash sweets in my pockets, you cannot imagine what it is like for him… his grandmother and mother circle over him like vultures, like *'No! Don't ever give your sweets away to anyone!'* He'd cringe and cry, and yesterday I found a sweetie in my bag again…"

And here I was, standing on Lenin square in the company of two thousand martyrs under a barrage of eggs, spittle, and from the one side, and applause, horns, and cries of support from the other, and someone was calling me in desperation.

"Please, I beg you, please, can you come here now! They said they'd kill me if I don't go with them, they said they'd bury me right here, please do something!"

With great difficulty, in between the sobbing and hysterics, I understood that her employers had decided to leave for Russia and told the nanny that she had an hour to pack her things. The little boy had grown to love his nanny, which meant that she was going to Rostov with them — end of discussion. When Oksana said that she was not going to go to Rostov, they told her she could go shove her desires where the sun don't shine.

I thought about the matter. Of course, this was most unfortunate timing. However, when someone in the Akhmetov clan tells you they're going to kill you, then it is best to assume that they are going to kill you. Oksana therefore had an hour, after which we would have to comb the whole of Russia to find her.

"Ok, don't panic. Have you got your things? In ten minutes, tell the bodyguards to load your things, but you go down to the gates. I'll wait outside their place and I'll pick you up. Keep your phone on you."

Making my way out of the square, I flag down the first taxi

I see, and fly off to the family house. We arrived just on time. A gate opened in front of us and out slipped a frightened shadow in a dressing gown and slippers onto the street. We slowed down near the girl — "Come on, jump in!" — and we drove away. We had managed to find a tactful taxi driver, who drove quickly and did not ask any unnecessary questions.

Oksana did not look good. She was swollen from tears, with a noticeable red weal on her cheek, and she was half-naked. Where could we take her, looking like this?

"Do you have any money? Documents?"

"No, I left everything there. My passport, I only have my bank cards, and…"

I do not know whether what I did was the right thing, but I could not think of anything else to do. We arrived at the station, I took out some cash, gave her my jacket and trainers and sat the girl on a bus to Dnipro. I had a contact in Dnipropetrovsk who was the headmistress of a school for orphans; she was a good woman. A few years ago, a sponsor came running in like a headless chicken and renovated the dormitories. Our company installed the glass, and I coordinated all the work through her. A month or two later I went back to visit the children. I noticed that all the decorations were still in place, not a single bracket had been stolen. After that, Stepanivna and I stayed in contact. Sometimes I would draw with her students and was going to take on some of the graduates for work experience, but never ended up doing so. That's why, right now, she was the one who I was phoning, and I asked her:

"Do you need a fantastic teacher, who loves children?"

We quickly made plans: the girl was to be met off the bus, new documents would be made and she would be given lodging at the school. From what I knew of Oksana, I knew that she would cry today, but tomorrow would calm down a little, and the day after tomorrow she would already believe that she was born to work in that institution.

We hugged goodbye; I poked my nose into the girl's solar plexus, and she gave me an affectionate kiss on the nape of my neck.

"Listen, you know, I am so grateful, I don't even know what if…"

"Let's not go into all that, jump in and find your seat. When you get there, phone me."

"I'll miss you too."

I waited until the bus had already left, waving it off for a long time, and then I ran back to the square in her slippers, too big for me.

It was already dark by the time I got to the square. I realise while approaching that things are not looking good. The crowd is not on our side, it is not our people. Shouts, crying, broken glass and plastic underfoot. Everyone is shrieking, and at first, I cannot work out what they were chanting.

"On your knees, on your knees!"

What was that about? Someone over there is being beaten, and I see a dozen young men attacking a man, knocking him down, and stamping on his head. I am sprayed with splashes of blood… God, they are going to kill him! You cannot breathe, the stink of tear gas hangs in the air, and over there rise columns of vapour coming from the smoke bombs. An ambulance comes into the crowd right in front of me, and I manage to follow it. The mass of people reluctantly parts, and we move west, towards the epicentre.

Out the corner of my eye I see the ranks of the armed police, who are sheltered by shields and are just standing there. Where are we going? Ahead the contours of a torched-out bus are visible, and its windows and doors on fire, full of smoke. A group of lads are pressed against its wall, a few bent down, others fallen on their knees, and rocks and other missiles are being hurled at them. The boys are covered in blood, surrounded by a sea of blood, and its iron tang adds to the stench of gas. Finally, the police break through a corridor between the bus and the ambulance and carry a man through to the vehicle. A black stain spreads out on his jumper, and in the background of this stain, his wide face shines bright white. The boy is unconscious, perhaps dead. I look from the side-lines to which way they are bringing him in the ambulance: foot first or head first? I cannot remember which one was the right way if the person was still alive.

I have been barefoot a long time already, having lost my slippers, and it is slippery and wet under my feet. I realise I have to get out, but I do not know which way to go. The square seems endless, wherever you look are shouts, screaming, raging, a massacre. One part of me knows that this is not real, that it is just a bad dream, and we are about to wake up. The other part captures it all like on film, with the tic in my head saying, 'I am a witness. I am a witness. I am a witness.' A witness for what and for whom, lest I now fall? It was a bloodbath.

"What are you standing there for? Get in, quickly, hear me! For fuck's sake, are you deaf?" the paramedic shouts, and I suddenly realise that he is shouting at me.

Without a second thought, I hop into the cabin, and the vehicle whizzes off, drowning out the roar of the crowd with its siren.

* * *

The young man did not make it: he died in the ambulance. Of course, at that moment I was not aware that he was twenty-two years of age and was his parents' only son. The only thing I could see in the vehicle was the doctor's hands. His hands were covered in blood; blood that was almost black at first, and it flooded the stretcher, the floor, and then lighter streaks of it began to trickle towards my seat.

"It's no good; we won't get him there in time!"

But even after it being 'no good', they did not give up, and it was all rather like a rowing race. Yes, they were just like rowers, their backs tilting up and down, the captain counting the rhythm: 'one-two-three, one-two-three'. But I knew then that all this work was for nothing, that the race was lost, and the body that they were working so hard over had become a shuddering, empty shell. I had never witnessed death before, let alone come face-to-face with it like I did then, but I certainly recognised it for what it was.

Then they all stopped. The nurse leaned against the wall, breathing heavily, and the doctor fished a pack of cigarettes out of his pocket and had one right there in the ambulance. The driver reached up and turned off the siren, and the walkie-talkie, which before that moment had been just emitting an unintelligible hiss, filled the back of the wagon with voices.

"Are you hurt?" — they asked, finally turning to me. I could not gather the strength to reply, so I just shook my head.

"Do you know him?"

I don't know — maybe. Where were we going?

Kalinin district, to the department of neurosurgery. I asked to be dropped off right where we are, despite in fact not having a clue where we are and how I would make it home, as I would have to get across the entire city in this state. I didn't care though; I just couldn't stand another minute in this ambulance.

"Ok, but you have to leave your details, you might have to answer questions later. After all, you're still a witness."

I nodded and told them my name and telephone number. All made up, of course, and the doctor realised this, but wrote them down anyway.

The vehicle slowed down; I got out and glanced around. I know this place; we are by the puppet theatre. I realise that I need to get home, preferably without drawing attention to myself, and I remember that I do not have any cash on me. I have a card somewhere — ah yes, there it is, in my pocket. My phone also survived, miraculously. However, I simply cannot muster up the strength to find a cash machine or somewhere to make a call. If I remember correctly, it would be best to cross the street and wait for a minibus going in the opposite direction. Instead, however, I wander straight ahead for a long while, and finally I go into a bar.

The bar was busy, nearly all the tables were occupied, but as luck would have it, I found a spot in the corner by the door. It was warm inside, a TV on each wall, all of them showing the football. I reached under the table for my long-suffering feet, which only had plastic shoe-covers on them (the nurse in the ambulance gave them to me, God bless her) and I ordered a hot chocolate. On reflection I then added some chips, ribs, salad, and a cheese plate to my order.

Bit by bit, the warmth returned to my feet. I tried to move my fingers, as if to move myself. I eat, not noticing how my food tasted and watching the football, the final sixteen of the Europa League, Spain vs Portugal. I supported Spain, while people-watching at the same time. The next group over were a bunch of students having an evening out; their table was so full of glasses that there was no space left for the plate of squid they had ordered and so they were holding it up in their hands, like at country weddings. Further on, a young couple were attentively eating their meal, not looking at each other. At the next table over, there was a birthday celebration, the birthday-girl taking a selfie with her guests.

I felt rather strange; I expected another reaction — at least some sort of reaction! — but I could not find an emotional response within myself. I had become a witness to a great tragedy. What I saw today was something that affects all of us, everyone who lives in this city. Donetsk lay before us, like a great, inert beast that had just had a shot of poison injected right into its spinal cord. Its body was already dying. Soon it would be unable to move, and would only be able to watch as it gets gobbled up by a smaller, but nimbler predator. A long period of agony awaits it, and its peripheral nervous system has raised the alarm, but its groggy head has not yet got the message. In its head, everything is still ok.

I winced and looked around me, eyelids half shut. It was actually better like that, since I found the dim light irritated my eyes. My grandmother once told me about the 'death mask'. It was said that people with a certain 'knowing' could tell if someone was going to die up to three days beforehand, from an imperceptible change in the doomed person's facial features. I was not someone who believed in these superstitions, but this memory came back to me at that particular moment. The whole bar — the guests and staff, all of them — were dead. Their figures became sharper, as if on a flat screen, and the dark and empty spaces between them were no longer so dark and empty. This lasted a second — but it was a second that still happened.

There was the girl, the barista with artfully drawn-on eyebrows, who drags a checked bag across a bridge. The bag is bigger than her, and she has a child in her arms, a boy of about two years old. They get to the end of the bridge, where the road breaks off, and further on they have to climb up a steep incline, holding onto a rope, and the girl ties a small scarf around her chest so she does not fall. They take a few steps without letting go of the bag, but the ground suddenly moves and a deep chasm has appeared in the place where they were just standing.

There was the student, the one cheerfully flirting with the girl next to him, who suddenly freezes and falls forward, three neat holes punched into his back.

There was the robust man over there with a glass of stout. He is stripped to the waist, arms pulled behind his back and tied to a rusty pipe. Half standing, half swinging from the pipe, his whole body is like one big flesh wound. Someone grabs him by his hair, but he does not lift his head, which then flops back down onto his chest.

I wiped my face with my hands. Enough, no more. Apparently, I was finally reacting to the stress, but now was not the time or place to fall apart. I could cry, but it would be better to do that in bed or while taking a hot shower; just not here, in a restaurant. They had a card machine — would they take card? Well, if not, it would seem that today's adventures were not over yet.

I had to phone everyone. I took out my phone and saw that it had run out of battery. I took it behind the bar to be charged, glad of the short delay. For now, we were all still alive, at least only in my head. For now, I could pretend that this evening never happened, that it was all a horrible dream. As soon as I turn on my phone, I would find out the names. Did anyone else get killed, besides the boy with the knife wound from the ambulance? Someone must have, after all; they were being beaten to death. What about that older man, the one who stood in front of the crowd with a flag in his hands… it was like he was using it as a shield — but what could he have done to defend himself with just a scrap of fabric? What protection could it give against the bullets or the stones?

I went to the toilet, meticulously washing my hands and face. I then ordered a coffee as well, savouring every mouthful. My phone had finally turned back on again, and from where it was lying behind the bar, I could hear the messages coming through. Dozens of messages: people were desperate to get hold of me, and I suppose it was not particularly responsible of me, sitting here as I was, enjoying my coffee.

But then the doors opened, and a gang of people burst into the bar. This was not something I expected, seeing them here like this. First to run in was the tousled Borysovych, and Oleg and Don, then dear Roman, helped up the stairs by Komar.

"Hey, what are you doing here?"

For just a second I was swaying in the air, literally hanging off someone's chest. I finally cried; I could breathe again, in and out, and at once I could feel the cold, and the spurs in my frostbitten feet, and the ache in my hurt knee, and my tongue could even savour the food that I had eaten over the last hour. Good God, they were alive? How did they find me?

It turns out the tracker in my phone, which I had long forgotten about, had managed this all by itself, and Komar and the gang were able to track my movements that day. They saw how the square had been cleared out, and our flight to the station, and then how the signal had cut out as the riots flared up on the square. Well, and then I was pushed in front of the ambulance (where I lost my slippers) and my phone ran out of battery. There were all sorts of people phoning the hospitals and police stations in search of little old me, right up until the last minute before my phone got some charge again. Then, when my phone finally appeared back on the network they came here, from all parts of the city, to wring my neck, no doubt.

"Oh, my dear boys, I just love you all so much! Please sit down. I have two important questions — one: who wants some squid? I have a whole plate here. And the second question. There's going to be a war here. Tell me then, whose side are you going to be fighting on?"

IV

ANTHRACITE

A DONBAS TANGO

There's a certain technique you can try
when you want to come to terms with
reality: for each situation, you imagine the
worst possible outcome with the maximum
level of detail. They say it is a good way of
helping you take control over things again
when diagnosed with a severe illness.
I took a few days just to think. For inspiration,
I looked up pictures of bombed-out Grozny,
rereading accounts of the first Chechen war.
Before everything actually happened, I had no
doubt that Donetsk would become an arena for
military hostilities, despite the 'Crimea scenario'
that everyone couldn't stop harping on about.

Firstly, why does no one think that there's going to be a war in Crimea? The peninsula is going to be chewed up and invaded, mark my words. Secondly, although Donbas walks its own separate path, the city is not that separate from what's going on. If something swims like a duck, quacks like a duck, and looks like a duck — then you most likely have a duck on your hands. If someone declares war, threatens war, is gearing up for war, and is bringing war onto your territory — then you will, most likely, have war on your hands.

The most reasonable and logical step would be to prepare for evacuation. I had enough money left for a flat in another city in Ukraine. I found several options in Chyhyryn, up north in Cherkasy Oblast, and planned to take my grandmother there with our valuables, and she could at least live there with her pension until everything here settled down.

This was a first-rate plan. But Olha Ivanivna flatly refused to move anywhere.

"I am 76 years of age; I am not going anywhere."

"Baba, just think about it! When it all starts, everything will be immediately blown to smithereens."

"Let them blow me up as well then. I'm not going."

"Listen, I'm not joking. Who's it going to affect if you die? Think about your heart — your glucose levels! Come on, let's go! There's a nice, quiet flat there. You can wait there a bit, and then you can come back if you fancy it."

"Go there yourself then! Why aren't *you* going?"

I knew why I wasn't going. The realisation came to me on one of my many sleepless nights, as bright and clear as Mendeleev's periodic table appeared one day to the delirious Mendeleev. I wanted revenge. I didn't want abstract revenge, restoring global balance and the general triumph of justice. I wanted real, material payback. I wanted to see one of those people who had filled our streets with their makeshift uniforms, one of those who had invaded and set up base in one of the sanatoriums or recreation centres near Donetsk, one of those who now, at this very moment, was training the *opolchentsi* with their foreign Vologda accents, preparing for a battle in my city. I wanted to see them in front of me, at arm's length, their throats cut. I wanted to see the blood squirt out of their arteries like a fountain, see it bubble with every spurt. I wanted to press my hands against the wound, to feel the hot flesh, the broken trachea, the shattered vertebrae of their cervical spine. I dreamed of just getting my hands on even one of them! Perhaps then, and only then, the emptiness I felt in my chest would go away, and I would finally be able to get some warmth in my bones.

I could not find the words to describe my hatred. The rasping prayers of the ascetic during his punishing fast; the pleading of the epic hero for a drop of cold water in the desert; the entreaties of an orphan who so desperately misses his mother's arms — none of these could hold a candle to my furious invocations of agony upon those who had wronged us.

I was in an ideal position to wage guerrilla warfare. Insignificant and inconspicuous on the outside, but tough and hardy on the inside, I knew this city through and through, I could cross it using a hundred different routes and would still be able to come back unnoticed. I didn't have a husband or children, a fact that previously was considered something of a tragedy, but which now seemed to be a noticeable advantage. No family meant no weakness, no way of blackmailing me. I could go out with just one rucksack on my back, or with nothing at all, and still come up to the surface somewhere or other. I'm not afraid of technology, I love mechanics and schemes — could I not come in handy anywhere?

I did not say any of this to my grandmother, nor to anyone else: these are not emotions to be proud of. So, I stayed quiet.

"You know what? Let's stock up on food. Do you know how to stock up for war?"

My grandmother knew. We raked through all the markets,

buying up flour, sugar, salt, pasta shells, oil; for several days we made lard and tinned meat; we also put together a first aid kit, forming a stock of medicines for everything. We stocked up on candles — from basic paraffin ones to wax church candles and a whole box of aromatic candles for having a bath. Soap, candles, salt, matches. Soap, candles, salt, matches — the list bounced around in my head like a broken record. Shampoo for head lice. Kerosene and a primus, and not just for making food. Kerosene is also useful for getting rid of parasites, and also puts the hounds off your trail. Broad-spectrum antibiotics, amoxycillin, augmentin, furazidin for cystitis. Pads, period products, gauze, and dressings. 'Gold, we also need gold,' whispered an inner voice. 'Sew a pocket into your belt, put it in there. Take it with you.' But I didn't have any gold.

At the time, something strange was going on in the city. The storming of the buildings started looking like a clown parade. Fewer and fewer people came to the weekly *viche*, or assembly, among the 'Dipso Defence', as we liked to call the circus of homeless people and the other clowns who gathered outside of government buildings. Barricades and tents stood empty outside the administration buildings and soon collapsed. At the beginning, the participants of the pickets were paid up to two hundred hryvnia a day, and then their sponsors either changed tactics or ran out of cash, and they were now expected to stand there out of support of the 'ideal'. There were few of an 'ideological' bent there, however. Monkeying the Maidan in the capital, they laid siege to government buildings with tyres and gas canisters, and the more tyres that lay about next to the administration, the fewer people remained on the ground. The city centre residents suffered from the presence of their new neighbours, given their propensity to sleep, eat, and urinate on the entrances of their buildings and steal their rubbish bins.

We also gathered for small rallies, twice holding large events — but to be honest, I went out of a sense of obligation, like going to work, rather than feeling a particular calling to do so. I hope my friends forgive me, but this all felt like theatrics, or some fake wizardry. What could we do in the face of armed militants? Wave our flags at them? Offer them our right cheek?

Like those old protestants on the waterfront. A group of believers would gather there, every day, before the wooden cross. They would kneel beside the pastor, singing their psalms and suffering, like the first Christians. They were attacked by crazed schoolchildren and pensioners along the whole spectrum of folly; guys in civvies would approach them with threats, and these children of God would not react to any provocation. Maybe I'd got it wrong, but I thought that if they had cooperated with our self-defence at least once and turned on their attackers, perhaps their prayers would have been heard?

I remembered how after one rally we were unfurling our flags and suddenly several bodies then living on the barricades jumped out at us. Terrifying, drunken, like wild beasts, they would run up and bite us, a crowd of them running up at each of us.

"Ach, you *kurwa*" — as I was holding the flagpole in my hands, I rushed up to them for a fight, my one and only desire being to get hold of one of them and break that pole in two over one of their stupid heads. Seeing my intention, those chimps stopped in their tracks, and immediately loped off. I even shrugged — oh well, you don't know how terrifying I look when I'm angry! — and I look around to see a dozen of our lot running out to support my outburst. Well then, on we go, and the barefoot wonders run on, bowling over passers-by as they go. I hear them shouting at their handsets something along the lines of, *"-hiiiit, they're going to storm the place! We're under attack!"*

We chased them for a few hundred metres, and then we stopped. Really, were *we* going to storm the building? There were about ten of us in all.

I still regret the decision. What if, back then, we had done it?

* * *

Springtime Donetsk hung in the air, like a soap bubble in the eye of a storm. Or, to make a less poetic comparison, it was stuck like a cow on ice. The fact is that the main events took place in Kyiv and Crimea, in Odesa and Kharkiv, Slovyansk and Mariupol, on the city's ring road and in its outskirts, but the city itself pretended not to be affected.

The cafes and shops were still open, bands were still touring in the city, and the intercity buses were still travelling in. Overcrowded planes flew to Dubai and Istanbul, to Kyiv and to Moscow. Shakhtar Donetsk were still playing premier league matches in the Donbas Arena, nightclubs and restaurants were preparing graduation nights, cinemas were holding a retrospective of British film, and mothers with prams were walking slowly in the parks.

Orders started coming in, and we started work again. It was a trifle, nothing compared to our previous scale of production, but people began to buy lampshades again and held off talk about evacuation. However, the team was reduced by two thirds: only Roman and I, the girls, and some interns were left. The men disappeared from the company, but I didn't ask where they had got to. It was a sign of the times we were in. We learned not to ask questions.

I had a code name for these few weeks of provisional calm: a 'circus'. In every conversation, whenever two or three people got together, you would always hear the same thing: *"When is this fucking circus going to end?"*

Apparently, I was not the only one having trouble adapting to the new reality, but it was impossible to accept those lowlifes in the city centre as the bearers of any sort of power (that's the necessary word, *'lowlife'*). Believe me, even in our neighbourhood, even in the run-down housing blocks, where with the onset of darkness the door doesn't open at all, and in the morning you hear the crunch of a layer of fresh needles under your feet — even so, even there, where the people were really scraping the bottom of the barrel, they regarded these *opolchentsi* in the same way you would look at shit on your shoe.

The general opinion was that this 'circus' would be over soon, that at the top everything was agreed on already and, most importantly, Rinat Akhmetov, the local oligarch, wouldn't allow a war on his turf. He was the lord and master of the Donbas. He appointed politicians who were in his pocket, he commanded the earth and everything in it, even the sky; it was by his almighty will be done that the coal was extracted, water flowed through the pipes, electricity ran through the grid, and we had petrol in our tanks; it was because of him the planes took off from the ground and water coursed through our rivers. And if for some reason the *Master* was the cause of this mess, surely, he would also stop it, whenever he deemed necessary. Would he really just hand over Donbas Arena like that, you think?

Donbas Arena — that was one thing. Akhmetov's obsession with the stadium was well-known, but hardly anyone dared joke about it.

We watched news reports and YouTube videos until our eyes bled. 'In Slovyansk, armed men in camouflage have seized the city police department'. 'The number of victims of the takeover of the regional prosecution office has gone up to 26'. 'The separatists have broken into the premises of the Horlivka Regional Department of Internal Affairs and have smashed the windows'. 'In Kramatorsk the separatists and the police have occupied the city council'. You stand there, a joke, and you think — is this actually possible? A dozen separatist wasters surround a government building and the police come out with their hands up. Shots of them swearing their new oath to the 'people of Donbas'. The shame... I was so ashamed of the men in uniform, I wanted to shout, spit in their eyes. You swore allegiance to Ukraine, you had to protect and serve, so what are you doing, you swine?!

We all then rushed online. Even those who, before all this

started, had no idea what social networks were and what they were for, created profile pages and hung out on chat rooms day and night. It was the only way to exchange news, to find out people's real opinions, because we had to watch our every word in real life. In general, when I ran into acquaintances, I would mumble like I was a mute.

"Oh, daughter, how are you, how's your grandma? How are you feeling?"

"Ah, hm."

"You don't say, for us it's just the same. Are you going to leave?"

"Mhm."

"Well, never mind, God willing, we'll be saved from these Banderites, we'll fight them off."

"Aha."

I also started a blog. To protect myself I gave myself a man's name, using a separate phone with a sim card from the 'other' side. I made a plan with myself that if anything happened, I would just throw away the phone and no one would find me. The phone worked as a portable camera, and I went around three or four polling stations with it during the 'referendum', showing as much as I could on Facebook: the 'security' with their semi-automatics, the queues, the ballot boxes, and the ballots themselves. On the same day, my video was shown by Hromadske, the Ukrainian NGO and internet news station. It was shared thousands of times, and I became a popular blogger. You could say that my blog-pseudonym became a star overnight, and were he a real person, he would have been very proud.

My second secret project was revamping Roman's old Opel.

"Roman, love," I said, turning to my colleague, "we need to make a secret compartment for the car."

What I respect in my partner is his ability to swiftly accept, evaluate, and implement any technical request he was given. After only a week, our 'tank' got a second bottom to it, which could be accessed underneath the back seats. This hidden compartment turned out to be quite spacious, and I could even fit in it if I wanted to — though, God forbid, this was only theoretical. We reinforced the frame and chassis, all the filters and battery were replaced, and the engine was completely taken out and replaced. The car was just as shabby and tired-looking as it always was on the outside, but it would start straightaway, with barely half a turn of the key, and was a much quieter drive. Roman undertook the majority of the work, right there in our workshop, with my help as a runner. After all, this man did have golden hands, and if it wasn't for his disability, I would never have let him go as a specialist.

During the repair process we were visited by Komar and Borysovych. Well, I think it was them, because I recognised Borysovych's feet, and Komar greeted me in a familiar voice. We had just set the protective layer on the bottom of the car; we had to flip it round so that it could cover the hiding box without scraping the bottom of the chassis. Roman was welding the muffler again, welding the whole structure together with the precision of a master jeweller. To do this, it was necessary to crank the car up on both sides and carefully slide the new layer along the grooves on the bottom. We didn't have a pit in our garage to do this, so the car was jacked up, and at the bottom there was minimal space to manoeuvre in. *Hallelujah*! It was my time to shine with my size-zero frame, as any woman with a normal bust would get stuck in this gap. We *petites dammes* have our advantages, especially when we are able to screw the nuts back on in an enclosed space.

"Ahem, what's all this then? My little ones, have you gone mad?"

"Oh, Borysovych, don't sneak up on us like that. Everything's fine, we're just doing some work."

"Roman, are you alive? Can I help at all?"

"It's ok, I can manage. Hang on, give us a minute, we'll crawl out."

"No, it's ok, stay there. Was nice to see you."

I don't know what gesture Roman showed them in the form of a goodbye, whereas I just said goodbye with my feet.

22.05.2014

Then came the day when it all came crashing down on us. The bubble of tension that had been building up all these months burst, sweeping away everything we'd been using to create a semblance of normal life. This was it. We no longer had to think about earning money or making plans for repairs or for holidays. We no longer had to worry about old age and retirement, because we have seen with absolute clarity that we won't have a pension. It was the strange feeling of freedom that those sentenced to death experience: even more strange is the realisation that our fate was completely accidental and also natural at the same time, that it was the Lord's retribution and an incredible, an exceptional honour.

The day had come when one no longer needed to prove anything, when one was left alone with one's own free will, with the heavens, and with one's own conscience.

From that day on, everything was different and filled with a new meaning. In our sleeping and our waking hours, in fear and fearlessness, between the silence and in the fury, in love and hate, I was not alone. I could feel the efforts undertaken by the women doing the same thing under the same conditions. I baked bread; my hands deftly kneaded the dough as if this were their daily work. I washed uniforms and remembered rinsing the bloody clothes in the ice-hole. I went out into the night, and I was like a silent shadow passing along the ground as an unseen shroud, and I knew that I would get there, and I would return by dawn.

There are no words to describe the pain and humiliation with which we went to war. This feeling of helpless despair when uneducated, incompetent, and unprepared men were mowed down, not knowing even where they were supposed to shoot. The depth of shock when we saw how their own commanders were working for the enemy. When we understood that we needed to rebuild all our connections, all our fortifications, that we had no resources, and no government. That what we used to call the government has in fact turned in on itself, and that it has long been paralysed by fear and incompetence.

The sleeping beauty awoke from her centuries-long slumber, removed the cobwebs from her eyes, unwound the crick in her neck, and looked around: "Well I never!". She awoke, putting on her shoes on the go and pulling out something heavy, maybe a big stick, out of a pile of rags, mouse-eaten furniture, and rotten beams, in order to fight off the wolves, which had already come, creeping towards her throat, ravenously drooling, the slobber dripping down onto their chests.

God forbid you should ever live in times of turmoil. But everyone should know what it means to find succour in one's hour of need. To gasp for air, to lie down on the earth. To feel how your blood rises at the level of your deepest, most ancient and buried instincts. How it feels to go down and to spit at hell, being sure that no evil will befall you, because the truth is on your side. Because your kith and kin are on your side. Because the dead are on your side, and the unborn too, here on your right shoulder.

Everyone should see how manna comes from the heavens, how power may raise its head and let roar, when no longer restrained by ancient spells. Everyone should see how here, in the legendary steppes of the Donbas — which actually aren't steppes at all, but fields, ravines, and forest belts — passes a slender figure between the slagheaps and the pipes. How she touches the sky and laughs in anticipation, and from that laughter the earth splits and tears open her bowels, splitting the wires and belching out the tips of Scythian arrows.

Were you not expecting this? Then all the worse for you.

V

TIGER'S EYE

OH, RIBBON AFTER RIBBON...[5]

The day was already scorching, like in high summer. Spring in the Donbas is short — nature here does not see the point in transition periods or in doing things by halves. The green spring shoots immediately acquire a rusty sheen, and by May the light spring breeze has already turned into a gusty and dry, desert wind.We were waiting in a queue of about a dozen cars at the exit out of Donetsk.

The queue was barely moving. Each car was being thoroughly searched; the drivers obediently handed over their documents, opened their boots, and lengthily explained themselves to the *opolchentsi*. Clearly, the *opolchentsi*, our dear dipso defence crew, were in no hurry to speed things up and were enjoying their new powers.

We, however, very much wanted to get going.

"Listen!", I say, grabbing my colleague by the forearm. "You couldn't open the window, could you?"

"It's over thirty degrees outside. The stuffed cabbages will turn sour."

"If we don't get some air in here, we'll turn sour too. Have you not smelt it in here?"

There was a concentrated odour in the car. It was indeed quite the bouquet. The night before I had spent the whole night in the kitchen. All four hobs, the all-purpose cooker, and the oven were on. I made two types of stuffed cabbage: with tomato or with sour cream sauce; I formed hundreds of meatballs, made pancakes, and fried a little fish. Well, 'a little' is a relative term in this case; it was like catering for a wedding. Roman and Don arrived before dawn, bringing oranges and biscuits, and loaded up the car. We put the plastic tubs full of food into cooler bags from Silpo supermarket, covered them with hessian sacks, and I chucked a bag of clothes, a shovel, and a hoe on top. It was only the smell of stuffed cabbage going sour that ruined our disguise.

Our emotions came out on the journey. The day before, the news spread that some soldiers were killed near Volnovakha. At

---

5   The subtitle refers to a famous song by the Ukrainian insurgent army, which fought against the Soviet powers that had annexed Western Ukraine during the Second World War. The song found a revival in the national movements of late 1980s, and since 2014 has been sung by Ukrainian soldiers, with the chorus: *'Ribbon after ribbon, give us ammunition, oh fighters of Ukraine, do not give up the fight!'*.

first, I could not believe it: it seemed so savage, and Volnovakha was already behind enemy lines. I could not piece together the circumstances of the shooting in my head. The city was in uproar, saying the Ukrainian armed forces had refused to fight alongside their people, and for this reason they were blown up by Kolomoisky's[6] militants, and the wounded were finished off by helicopter fire.

"They were forcibly taken to Donbas, their families were threatened, and when they refused to follow orders to kill, vehicles from PrivatBank arrived and everyone was shot!" — that was what was going around.

Rumours abounded, with talk about scores of dead and hundreds of wounded, about a village burnt down by 'the Punishers'. There was only one answer to the question, 'Why would Kolomoisky do this?', and it was:

"We all think that Kolomoisky has gone mad. Tomorrow that Avakov[7] is going to clean out Volnovakha."

Byes[8] then took his turn on the soapbox to sing the praises of this successful operation: according to him, the *opolchentsi* had driven back the Ukrainian army almost all the way back to the Dnipro river. Well, at least we now understood what the PrivatBank cars had to do with things: gangs in Donetsk had hijacked some of the bank's vans, and these and several green armoured vehicles took part in the attack. But that was beside the point. According to the main news channels, our boys spent the night on the side of the road because the local residents would not let

---

6   Igor Kolomoisky is a Ukrainian business oligarch who founded PrivatBank and former Ukrainian politician who spent millions towards creating 'anti-terrorist' battalions to fight the separatist insurgencies.

7   Arsen Avakov was appointed Ukrainian minister for Internal Affairs after his predecessor, Vitaliy Zakharchenko, was dismissed for authorising the use of live ammunition against protestors.

8   Igor Bezler is a pro-Russian rebel leader. The nickname 'Byes' translates as 'Imp' or 'Demon'.

them into Olhynka. One of the locals then rang up the separatists, and our boys were just mowed down in the middle of the night, like skittles in a shooting gallery.

Even if this were not the truth — although this was most likely what actually happened — then you could imagine what sort of mood our soldiers were in and what was going through their heads while they waited on their lines. That was why I thought that we should somehow help them, talk to them, and bring them food. I planned to go alone, but my workmates would not let me, which I was not best pleased with.

I was not afraid of the separatists with their roadside searches because I was convinced that nothing bad would happen to me. But going up to a group of unknown and exhausted, embittered men, who had just lost their friends — what could I say to them? Something like: 'Hello, you don't know me, but I've brought you some meatballs!'? Then they would say... well, I had no idea what they could say to that. Chilling scenarios went through my head, where I would end up barefoot and dishevelled, crying over my rejected meatballs. It stood to reason that I did not want my friends to witness this pathetic outcome to my attempts. I was sure that I would either panic or burst into tears, ruining everything.

Maybe I could say something else, like: 'Hello, I am a Donbas resident, here's my internal passport, don't shoot me!'? ...Oh God — I forgot to put salt on the last batch I made!

Finally, the minibus in front, which had been shuddering at a standstill for about forty minutes, trundled off, and we stopped before the barrier. Three militants came up to us, looking in the window. The driver did not concern them, seeing his disabled sticker and his wheelchair in the boot, but they told me to get out and hold my hands up. I stretched out my left hand, and the patrolman, who seemed too neat and well put-together to be one of the usual drunken louts in the *opolchentsi*, took my right hand.

"Oh, are you going to tell me my fortune?"

(Where do I get these stupid jokes from — and why do they always come out at the most inappropriate moments? I hate myself.)

"Sure, I'll tell you your fortune."

He then held a big lamp with a screen up to my palm.

"That's all, you can go."

We passed in silence, and it was after we had crossed the checkpoint Roman clarified:

"They were from the Caucasus, did you notice?"

"I did."

"Did you understand what he had in his hands?"

"It's a gas analyser, right?"

"Yes. Our guys don't have those."

After Novotroitske we turned off towards Olhynka. I knew this place, coming here several times for artistic inspiration. Limestone, sand, and porphyry are mined here in the villages; water sometimes gathers in the quarries, turning them into un-believably beautiful lakes. We took photographs of one of these lakes for our website: it was a blistering azure blue, with deep, clear water and red mounds of earth standing behind it. I re-member how we placed a few chandeliers on the lakeshore, right next to the water, and did a photoshoot under natural lighting. We did not need to edit the photos afterwards; they turned out perfectly.

My daydreaming about the past meant that I forgot to agree on some sort of strategy with Roman. What would we say to the soldiers? I had no idea.

Goodness, I was lucky I was not alone. Whilst I gathered my thoughts, my partner had already handed the patrolman our documents, opened out on the page with our Donetsk registra-tion, and they shook hands, wishing each other good health. I always disliked that ritual, avoiding handshakes as much as possible, not wanting to touch someone else's clammy palm cov-ered in a film of sticky sweat. I admit now, however, that there is something to it. A few seconds, and vigilance melts into a friendly demeanour, and the muzzles of the rifles pointed at us slightly lower towards the ground.

We ask permission to stop at the roadside and unload the food, as well as talk with the fighters. I look at the commander hesitate, then pull over with us to the side and call over a few men.

I hurry through before they change their mind, pulling out and holding up Roman's wheelchair. I then pull bags and boxes out of the car, taking out the bowls, and I can feel, my skin burned from it even, how hungry the boys are, how long it has been for them since they last saw normal food. But they do not know us in the slightest. Though we are locals and we have come in cars with Donetsk number plates — would you trust us?

Never mind, we would manage.

"Listen, don't worry about any of this, all the ingredients are fresh, I made this all last night with my own hands. We've not come far, we had to stop because of those bloody orcs at the checkpoints, but all the food's been kept in cooler bags. And don't worry! They're not poisoned, I swear to you from the bottom of my heart. Look now, Romchik here will try one right in front of you, just this little cabbage roll. Right, Roman?"

Slightly bewildered by my efforts to convince them, the soldiers were almost hypnotised, their heads following the stuffed cabbage. I approach my colleague, and suddenly he rears his head back like a horse shaking its mane, grabs his chair and wheels away from me.

"I'm not eating that."

"What? Are you mad?"

"Sorry, just I don't eat meat."

"What do you mean, you don't eat meat?"

"I don't, I'm a vegetarian!"

"Really? For how long?"

"My whole life!"

A wary crowd gathered beside us. No one spoke, and without a word I chomped down the measly cabbage roll, the contents of which were already spilling out onto my hands. I finished chewing under the watchful eyes of dozens of eyes.

"Hm. Looks like I over-stuffed them, but they're alright. I hope none of you are vegetarian?"

There was muffled laughter at the back. A second later everyone was roaring with laughter, except for me and the company commander. I had no idea what he must have thought. I thought about the last Ukrainian Independence Day, when the whole team went out and made *shashlik*, and Roman made his signature marinade, with oil and onions, and not a word was uttered about him not eating meat.

* * *

We sat on their lines for an hour. We talked with them while we unloaded the food and then when we collected the pots and pans. I took out my tablet and showed them our videos from the protests with the record-size flag, the winter carols, and the anthem we sang next to the statue of Shevchenko on the square. We told them about the buses arriving from Rostov, about the 'tourists' and those shitty Russian 'Cossacks' joining the separatists flooding the city, about the deaf-and-blind police forces, about the AA meetings masquerading as a national defence league, about Akhmetov's call to arms, and most importantly, about the people who stood with us: real, live people. The boys had hundreds of questions, and I had hundreds of answers. I could have stayed with them until the next day, if only to explain what happened, to prove something to them. It was like I was not just speaking for myself, but for everyone, with only one desire: that they would not desert us, would not give up the fight.

We left with the promise to come back the day after next. I took down their orders, with some soldiers even giving us money for shopping: some wanted cigarettes, some medicines, others their SIM card topping up, and it was really comforting to believe that 'the day after tomorrow' would actually come.

Upon our farewell, I took the hoe out of the car and under the approving glance of the commander I turned over a few metres of earth. What if one of the *opolchentsi* suddenly decided to check us 'dacha-goers'? Our shovel had no mud on it, and the hoe was as good as new.

"It's no matter, though," I tell my partner. "Come on, let's think of a different route. There's no point in driving through the separatist checkpoints, since we don't have a lot on us."

It would have been good if the guys had driven out to meet us and take our cargo, but they did not have the resources to. That was the first out of many thousands of times of hearing the phrase, 'No, we don't have anything', words which would haunt my dreams. The soldiers had no maps of the area, and they didn't know their way around the area. There was also no signal, no intelligence channels, no contact with the locals (though this was probably for the best). They had no first aid kits, no fire extinguishers, no shovels, no helmets. There was no armour for the whole unit, no optics. They had no water and had to go over to Olhynka with canisters and flasks, each time having to endure the hysteria and demonic shrieking of the women there.

"Oh, it's fine, it's worse for our neighbouring unit," they laughed.

Their neighbours were entrenched a couple of kilometres away, in the fields, where there were no villages and no shops of any kind.

"We've been calling them rabbits."

"What do you mean, rabbits?"

"Well over at the farm there they found a pile of cabbage, last year's crop, and they've been living on that cabbage. You know, rabbit food."

That day, my first army contacts appeared on my phone. Uncle Kolya, Ivan Petrovych, Volodya…

"What should I put you down as, child?"

After swallowing down being called 'child', for the first time in my life I said to them, out loud:

"Elf."

It was like a baptism.

When we finally turned back onto the motorway, I grabbed Roman's sleeve.

"Wait, stop here for a minute. How much time do you have, in total? Could you take a few days off?"

"How come?"

"Roman, mate, listen, they don't need us in Donetsk. We're needed in Dnipro."

"For what exactly?"

"Don't slow down. Think about it."

"Oh, I guess. Let's go."

We needed food, not my basic culinary attempts, but proper meals. Bread, meat, sausage, conserved meat, coffee. We needed water, at least a crate of drinking water, and a tank for technical water; and where would they get that from? We also needed wet wipes. Cigarettes too, lots of cigarettes. Of course, no one would let us out of Donetsk with that sort of cargo. It was difficult to get products out there, and prices have gone up a lot.

We needed to find bigger transport, a truck. Money too, we did not have enough, I think. We'll have to borrow some or take out a loan, but that was no issue: I will think of something.

"My daughter, it's people you need. Whenever times get tough, go find people, people will help you," my mother once said.

In Dnipro, I knew people. There was my 'refugee' Oksana, there was Stepanivna, Yuliia Tyshchenko, with whom we held fairs for the orphans, there was the Korniichuk family, and our colleagues from the art fair. We were welcome there.

Hold on. Where did this quote from my mother come from?

I had no more memories left of her! They must be from a film or a book. Well, in any case, we had no other choice, we had to go 'find people', without giving them warning.

On the way I phoned my girls up and asked if we could visit Stepanivna. We informed the headmistress' office, and there was something in my tone which meant she did not even think to refuse.

In all, seven of them came. I stood in front of them and told them what I had seen. It was the shortest and most useless presentation in the world, but Roman added a few words from his part, and then I read out a list of things we needed. If someone had asked us the question, 'Why are you doing this? Don't they already have a logistics regiment — surely they can sort it out?' — I probably would have spat in their eyes, or burst into tears. Or I would have turned on my heel and left, having nothing more to do with this city and its people. Instead, Stepanivna took my pieces of paper and leant over them with a pencil, noting who should carry out each task. Yuliia also called the guys — *"Kotya! I need a truck!"* — and voila, we already had a delivery van, a Gazelle truck.

Oksana then hugged me and said to me: "Write this down. Write everything down on the internet, and put down my card details down to raise money, instead of risking using yours," and handed over her new bank card.

"Are you insane? 'Raise money'? Who is going to give me money? I can't even tell them my real name! How would that look, trying to get money under some picture we've tagged on Facebook?"

"Don't think about it, just write."

That is what she told us to do. 'Just write' — those exact words.

I sat down and wrote it all down. About the quarry with the turquoise water and white sand. About the fact that, for their whole lives, the locals had been selling these mutant crayfish the size of your hand by the roadside. That the guys and I had once combed the whole lakefront but we could not even find a single crayfish claw. I wrote about the unsalted cabbage roll.

(I did not put anything in about our resident 'vegetarian': it was later in the car that he confessed that he hated cabbage, even in borsch, and he burst out with the first thing that came to his head — "You looked so cool with that roll in your hands," he said. "I couldn't restrain myself.")

I wrote about the 'rabbits' that we never saw, and we might never see. I concluded with honesty that the name I had put online was made-up, and that the pictures were taken from the Internet, and that I would not put down my phone number and that people would not be able to contact me. I wrote that I was aware I was asking people to send money God only knows where, putting their trust in some random Facebook account; that it would be unlikely I would be able to upload photos of our aid being delivered, as it would be a long while until the soldiers would let me take a picture of their field camp. That we had only twenty hours to get together funds for the shopping, although I would preferably like to do it in ten. That the point of this post — that I would have never made such a request 'unless…'.

I deleted this last sentence. There was no point in stating the obvious, right?

You would not believe it, but only a few minutes after posting this, Oksana's phone buzzed. Our first donor had put 100 hryvnia on her card with a note on it: 'Fuck 'em!'. Then more and more came on, for different amounts, from 10 hryvnia to the hundreds.

Then we went off to Auchan.

* * *

"'…*give us ammunition! Oh, fighters of Ukraine, do not give up the fight!'*… You know, when I was a kid, I did not know what ammunition was, I thought they were talking about booze!"

"I never knew this song as a kid. I'd never heard it as an adult, either. Actually, please stop singing, my eye's twitching."

"Ok, come on then, you sing, I'll listen. I have to keep talking, otherwise I'll fall asleep and bump into you from the back."

"Hang on a minute, we're almost there. My satnav says we're only three kilometres away. How much does yours say?"

"Our Gazelle doesn't have a satnav. We're using the sun to navigate."

The phone rumbled with muffled laughter and went quiet. I turned it off and opened the window again.

Our little caravan was spending its third night on the road. When we first started loading everything up, everyone but me was asking the obvious question: 'Who's getting behind the wheel?' You needed strong legs to drive a Gazelle van. In the end, we agreed to take two cars ('You'll fit more in that way!'). Roman would go ahead in his car, handle negotiations, and resolve any issues, and I would go behind. In theory, this was no issue, like in the old story about the Hutsul and the bear: the main thing is 'd-d-don't b-b-be afraid!'. Well, that and do not drive too close behind.

In practice, I was hanging from the steering wheel with two hands, like I was holding up a barbell. I had to jump onto the pedal in order to brake. The gear stick was above me, and when going uphill we would stall, only restarting on the third attempt. The headlights were the worst thing about it. I could not quite manage to learn how to switch from a low beam to a high beam: every time I would do so everything turned off, even the side-lights, and the car would go into full blackout.

By the time we took a second trip out, I had already forgotten about our previous spiritual misgivings. All of our fears: how to get off on the right foot, how to approach them, how to address them, what to say — it all lost its meaning. Who gives a damn if it feels awkward! I was beyond caring, I was in so much pain from the drive. Don't speak, just let me lie down in the grass a little!

I fell out of a cabin like I was paralytic, bent in the shape of the letter 'z', unable to straighten the crick in my back. I stumbled over to the fighters.

"Hey lads. Who needs cigarettes? We've brought you all sorts, call your commander."

My colleague and I brought out the maternal instincts in even the surliest of commanders. Without a doubt, the military had to have some instructions for engaging with civilians. We would never have been let into the dugouts and commanders' tents of the NATO army. But the partisan forces of the steppe had different conditions, and we were accepted as one of their own. I do not know what it was that helped us. Was it that we looked just like them: dirty, smelly, grey with dust, in sweat-stained T-shirts? Or was it Roman's innate gifts of diplomacy? Or was it my forty-two-kilo live weight behind the wheel of a huge truck?

Not once were we turned away, detained and interrogated, or asked whether we had some sort of 'mandate' allowing us to go wherever we wanted and bring what we deemed necessary. After handing out bales, pallets, tanks of water, tools, and heavy-duty bags, Roman and the soldiers would lean over the map, plotting a route, and I would doze off behind the wheel.

My comrade laughed: the route led from one dead end to another, apparently. At every unit we took food and water to, they told us to go somewhere else because, they would say, 'We're doing alright here, we'll survive, but over there — it's total fuckery'.

There was no way I could sleep properly. The moment you would close your eyes, you would tumble into the labyrinths of one-way streets and count the endless boxes of food. In Dnipro, all roads lead to supermarkets.

I knew a woman who had the habit of carrying an empty tupperware box in her bag. "So what?" she would say, "I'll go to Galya's house, and she'll have made stuffed peppers. She'll say, 'Oh, I've nothing to give it you in!', and then I'd reply, 'No problem,

I've got a tupperware!'. She'll then say, 'Actually, it keeps better a jar', and I would say, 'Well I've got one!'"

We had suddenly become the proverbial jar, the army's stop-gap. Rumours spread astoundingly quickly that we were collecting aid for the military. The moment the girls would write something on their phones, people would start bringing food and products to Stepanivna. Over the next few days, my favourite question became, 'Do you need…', and my favourite answer became, 'Sure, it'll come in handy somehow'.

"The girls have got you some preserves, some pickles, some jams. Do you need them?"

"We've got some barrels for water, loads, only you've got to wash them out, they had milk in them. Do you need them?"

"You can order tinned meat from army ration packs at the wholesaler. Do you need them?"

I was not sure if people knew what was really happening. Everyone lost their heads and was panicking a bit, but the mix of shock, fear, and anger only spurred us on. It was just that we locals had an advantage: we awoke from our stupor back in March, and we were now running up an escalator that was travelling downwards with all our might.

"How?" wondered my new friends on Facebook. "How are our soldiers going hungry? Where's the quartermaster at then? Why are we selling *you* army tents? Why?"

"That's the thing," we replied. "That's just how it is."

We overtook a convoy with equipment with the overheated and sweat-soaked infantry echelons (who had spent weeks on dry rations). We picked up hitchhikers in army uniform and towed an army ambulance. We followed behind the Ukrainian traffic police with their flashing lights, then turned off-road to field camps. We saw the continuous stream of manpower and equipment, which would spend each night in a new place, breaking down and having no clue what each destination had to offer them. Of course, the logistics corps remained at the rear, meaning that the field kitchens, the fuel tanks, and repair crews were left behind somewhere. People just threw themselves down under the open sky, packing down in abandoned cowsheds on old collective farms or in the ruins of old summer camps, in open hostile territory, just keeping their foot on the brake until further notice.

While waiting for 'further notice', this mass could not remain calm for a second. The camp was practically pitching and tossing like on a stormy sea, connections and teams were being formed, fireteams were forming, people were learning how to shoot right on site, someone was rushing into attack, and others were just circling about, trying to find a peaceful spot to get some rest.

It was then that we first heard the word 'war' being uttered. No one had yet said anything about a war on the television, it still was not in the politicians' vocabulary, but someone traced out the words, 'War's a bitch' with their finger on the dusty bumper of my Gazelle.

It was only by chance that did not get caught up in the mêlée: it was still the incubation period for that year's events; we were seeing the conception of the army, rather than its birth. This was no battle, but the psychological attack before the battle. This was no frontline or one of those 'grey zones' we later had in the country, but a bloody mess, where thousands had come together and were running about in a chaotic mix, losing track of what was going on. The civilian population still clung to its rituals and habits like crabs burying themselves in the sand, digging their burrows to hide in, not noticing that the water has already receded by several kilometres, and that in the distance, on the horizon, stands a wall of water that will soon wash away the shore and take the island with it.

* * *

We had to return via back country lanes all the way home. It was long, although peaceful, with no checkpoints. We had to do so because none of the *opolchentsi* would ever believe that we had been at our dacha, because no-one could ever come back from a trip at their dacha as dirty and smelly as we were.

In the cabin, everything was grey with dust — the bodies, clothes, the blankets on the back seats, Roman's wheelchair and a forgotten biscuit box. We did not talk, we even had the music switched off, because even thinking was too hard, let alone speaking. However, there was one topic that was still niggling me.

"Listen," I finally dared to say. "How did you become disabled?"

"What do you mean?"

"Why can't you walk?"

"Are you serious? You don't know? No, you can't be for real! You've even startled me; I was dozing off!"

"Well, you shouldn't be; you're the one driving. What's so funny? I've never asked you before."

"Were you never curious? You had countless chances to find out from people."

"I wasn't going to ask them behind your back! I'd feel uncomfortable. Will you tell me how?"

"There's not much to say. I was being stupid. It was all just pure stupidity."

"Did you have an accident, or did you fall?"

My colleague was quiet for a few seconds, and then briefly and clearly laid out the situation. He was right, after all; it was a stupid situation.

He was a young graduate of the Donetsk National Technical University, had been a safety engineer of all of about five minutes, and got a pre-diploma internship at the Skochinsky mine. But instead of doing what everyone else did — get someone to sign his forms and take it easy — he wanted to go down the mine. The mine's administration did not understand why, and for a long time tried to dissuade him. Eventually they gave in and let him go down.

He went down the mine, and the first thing he saw was that the methane sensors had been switched off. Panicking, he swore like mad and turned the sensors back on, at which point the sirens went off, because the readings were off the scale. They brought the miners back to the surface, people were fired, the management were giving a dressing down, and the workers were circling him like wolves, because they were not being given shifts.

The next day was just the same. He came to his internship, changed, and got in the lift. There the lead taskforce was waiting for him.

"They said to my face, 'You idiot, where do you think you're going? Turn back, or there'll be trouble'. I wasn't going to do that; I was young, a terrier."

"So, you went down the mine?"

"Yeah. That day I got caught in a collapse in the shaft. Not a big collapse — a localised one. A rock to the head, and then a shovel to the spine."

"Did you see who hit you?"

"Nope. I immediately collapsed. They thought that I was dead and didn't try to recover me. They were going to fill the shaft in. Borysovych found me and pulled me up, then took me to the doctor. After that I had a long treatment, I was in bed for six months, after which my hands started to move, and I worked on my rehab. Two months after that I could sit up."

"What about your studies?"

"Nothing. I was taken off the course, and never finished my diploma. I went on disability benefit."

"Listen… didn't you want to find out who did it? Maybe you can still, somehow."

"There was a gas leak there a week later in the western shaft. Thirteen men died, from *that* shift, by the way, as well as Borysovych's nephew. Three dozen more were injured. Now there'd be no one to question. What can I say? It was my own fault, my own stupidity. You can't go against the system, especially not here, in our ends."

"I guess."

We found it hard to talk after that, and we fell silent, each of us in our own thoughts. Roman, checking his inner satnav, managed to get out of the labyrinth of detached houses. I would have been stuck there a long time; all the streets with their miserable little houses all looked the same to me. I was sick with fatigue and the lack of sleep, my eyelids burning furiously — it felt like with each blink my lenses were scratching my cornea. My eyes filled with blood, like a vampire, and started weeping.

"Why are you torturing yourself? Take your lenses out!"

"Where can I put them? I've forgotten their box. I can't see anything without them."

"What do you need to see for? We've almost arrived, we're turning into Kyivskyi district now. Put them in a bottle of mineral water at least, you can rinse them in solution when you get home."

That is what I did. I took out my left lens (which felt like it had grown onto my eye), and I barely raised my hand to my right when I froze, a pillar of salt.

The picture that we were met with will be forever etched into my memory, because whether I want to or not, I will never forget it. We turned onto the avenue by the district hospital and saw that it was completely empty. We were the only ones on a usually crowded main road. Except for the huge army truck driving headlong at us.

It was being chased by a low-flying helicopter: it was flying so low, in fact, that it almost touched the tarmac. I could clearly see its big black nose, its jagged bottom, white flashes of gunfire aimed at the truck. I could hear my own screaming, Roman was braking like mad, but we were hurtling forward, the KAMAZ army truck swerved on its side, and we were still advancing on it. We move to the right — and they swerve right; we swerve left, and the truck also jumps into the left lane. Literally a second before colliding with them — half a second — when I could already make out the driver's face, its ten-tonne trailer hits the kerb, flying vertically, holding for a second, and crashing onto the verge. It then rolls, like a giant, unrestrained comet gone haywire, demolishing everything in its path. People tumble out of the back of the truck, right from under the wheels, out from under the enormous meatgrinder. God, how many of them were there? They were Russian soldiers, not ours, I could see their green uniform, and then just a mash, just a mash of body parts. A severed hand with a watch on the wrist falls on our bonnet; everything around us was covered in blood; pulverised corpses were scattered for hundreds of metres around, wherever you laid your eyes there were chunks of flesh. These pieces of people's bodies were as small as the chunks of meat you put in your goulash. This was the precise word that came to mind at that moment — 'goulash'.

I suddenly realise that I can no longer breathe. It is like I have forgotten how to do it; my chest will not rise. I try to chew the air, swallow it like water, but it does not enter me, it gets stuck in my throat. I remotely understand that I am about to suffocate. I pull on my companion's sleeve, and he whacks me on my back with all his might. I finally take a convulsive breath, then cough for a long time. My seat is wet, I cannot understand — what is that? My water must have spilt... I gesture to Roman in that moment — "Don't stop! Let's go, let's get out of here."

We start in reverse, not looking at what is behind us, then we turn around, and put the windscreen wipers on, cleaning the glass of blood, and the berry scent of the screen wash and the stench of blood stings our noses. I do not want to think what is beneath the wheels, or what the car itself looks like. We fly away from here, so that no one can stop us, so that no one can see...

Without turning his head, Roman takes the bottle out of my hands, takes a big gulp of water and immediately spits it out onto the floor.

"Apologies. I just drank your lens."

VI

AMBER

THEY HAVE DISGRACED US, AND THEY HAVE BETRAYED US

No-one was home. I glanced in my room, then went into the bathroom, throwing my clothes straight onto the floor. I went to turn on the light, but the power was out. There was no water either, hot or cold. I pulled my phone out to call someone, just to hear someone's voice, to not feel alone, but the black screen did not come to life: it was out of battery. I washed myself using water left in the kettle and fell upon my bed. Maybe the city had been overrun by orcs whilst we were away. That, or aliens. Or maybe I had fallen into a parallel universe. Maybe I was asleep and it is all just a dream?

Whatever it was, I did not have the strength to think about it. One day, we will be delivered from evil (on that day, our pizza will be delivered too). But right then, all I could think of was sleep.

But I could not sleep. I was awoken by voices, footsteps, a clatter. Something heavy was being dragged across the floor; I heard something fall with a crash.

I jumped to my feet, pulling on my dressing gown. The door swung open, and two people entered the room. Before me stood a thin, lanky boy in camo trousers and jacket, and your average 'opolchenets vulgaris' wearing flip flops, and my very own grandmother peeking out behind them.

"Oh, you're home? Sorry, I didn't realise. Boys, bring it in, put it by the wardrobe."

"Baba, what's going on?"

"Later, later. Vanya, dear, put the boxes over there by the wardrobe. Thank you so much, you've made an old lady happy. Tell Petrovna I said hello, I haven't forgotten my dear relative, God save her. Yes, the bucket goes in the kitchen, put it in the fridge. Let's settle up, boys."

The boys brought several heavy-duty bags into the room, flour in one, and sugar in the other; I didn't look through the others, but Vanya said that there were pasta shells too. A box of apples sat next to the bags, as well as a barrel of oil. There was also a plastic bucket chock-full of bags of spices — pepper, paprika, vanilla, and dried yeast. There was also a crate of canned fish, mixed together with bottles of shampoo, toothpaste, and little caramels. Vanya at last brought in a bundle stuffed with packs of baby food and a sack of cabbages.

Finally, the whole group shut themselves in the kitchen with my grandmother for a couple of minutes, after which our guests left.

"Baba, can you explain what is happening? What was that?"

"Glad to see you too. Welcome back."

"Yes, but…"

"My daughter, listen." Olha Ivanivna immediately scmewhat shrank, hunched over and sat on the edge of the bed. "There's been a lot going on here. As to this," she said, nodding at our stockpile of food, "the *opolchentsi* robbed Metro supermarket. They took it apart. The next day already they were taking goods away. Some of them are sleeping there, eating there, shitting... Others are selling things off on the cheap. That one was Petrovna's grandson, he's a bit more educated than the rest, hobnobs with the commander. Petrovna and I have known each other for a long time. You know her, we go to Easter mass together, remember? She's the one who sent the boys over to me. They've given me a whole granary; it's a bit overwhelming, actually. I paid 200 hryvnia for the whole thing, look at us, happy as Larry!"

"Baba, but all of it's been stolen. What do we need it for?"

"It's stolen, yes. If it comes to it, I'll ask them again; they can bring more. And you will accept it and say thank you. Do you think the boys have got anything to cook? Or eat, for that matter? What if the food runs out, God forbid?"

"Baba, calm down."

I went up to her, sat next to her, and poked my nose into her bony shoulder.

"Don't worry Baba, everything's fine. Well done, you did everything right. If they can, they can bring more."

"Really? You understand me? During the war, my mother, your great-grandmother that is, stole a heifer from a farm. I was only small, but my late sister told me that they survived because of that meat, they were starving. Back then they were being heavily bombed; the whole family was hiding in the cellar, and the mothers were tiny back then, as thin as you are now, and climbed out of the cellar and ran into the village. We all thought we'd gone mad, then burst into tears when we saw them come back late at night leading a calf along with them."

"Baba, listen to me. I think what's going to happen to us is going to be worse than what happened in the war then. I also think you should leave here, like we planned. Come on, while we have the chance, eh?"

"No. I'll say it again, not at my age. I don't have much time left, as much as God will give me, but I'm going to die in my own home. There's nothing for me in a foreign land. Don't ask me, and don't try to persuade me. Go by yourself if you want, and only when I already can't walk and can't move, then you can take me then wherever you want, headfirst or foot-first. But I'm not going anywhere while I stand on my own two feet."

We fell silent, closing the unpleasant topic. I did not want to argue. We all make choices, and sometimes all that we need to do is to accept and respect others' choices. My choice at this point was to fall asleep. For the first time in my life, I couldn't feel either my arms or legs — my body was literally numb. I pressed on my calf, saw the impression in my skin, saw the red marks from my nails, but I couldn't feel anything. The artillery fire out the window hurt my ears. Something was going off near the airport, but I couldn't care less. I did not care, I just wanted to sleep, to die — well, sleep at least.

"Baba, let's speak about this later, I'm dropping off right now."

My grandmother sat with me a bit, and then she took herself off to Petrovna's place. They decided that my grandmother would stay there for a while. They would be safer in a private house, and if something happened, they could hide in the cellar. It would be more fun in a two, less scary that way.

I curled up on my bed, feeling the force of gravity within every cell of my body. My arms and legs momentarily hurt, but I would not have changed my sleeping position for all the chocolate in the world. It was the sweetest feeling, imagining myself in a quiet boat, enjoying the coolness and smell of clean bedlinen. There was no shabby city here, no roads, no windows, no people. I was alone in my shell, I could hear the thundering outside the window, but I did not care. I breathed rhythmically, losing track of things with every exhalation. Breathe in — one, two, three, four — and the terrible truck was no longer in front of my eyes. Slowly now — two, three, four — and it was never there. I held my breath to the last, till my ears blocked up — it's a dream, just a dream — and once again I was breathing deeply. I then visualised a thin golden thread being pulled out of my chest. This thread wound itself around my body, looping around me, creating an impenetrable cocoon. No one but me could get inside, and I could stay inside of my secret golden cave as long as I want, my whole life if I wanted. I did not care if there was anyone knocking outside. Go away; I'm not home.

However, the obsessive banging in my head does not stop. I open my eyes, listening — there it is, someone is knocking like mad at the door. I freeze, hoping in vain that our unwelcome guest will grow tired and leave. The rhythmic banging stops for a moment, and then the attack begins again on the door and doorframe. Did they find a stick or something?

"Next time use your head as a doorknocker, you idiot! I'm coming!"

I get up, with difficulty, and stumble into the corridor. I open the door, leaving it on the chain, and I see a familiar face in the darkness of the stairwell.

"Hi. What are you doing, have you gone mad?"

"Oh, hi. *Why wouldn't you open the door?*" — it was Klyotsyk, the local legend who brought hell to the neighbourhood. He was bladdered. Auntie Masha said that this bloke was dropped on his head as a child. Whenever there was any trouble, some street clashes, fighting, some hubcaps had been stolen, or a dustbin had been set on fire, you knew that Klyotsyk had something to do with it. No matter how often he was caught, no matter how often he was beaten within an inch of his life and would spend months recovering, he was always fine. He would lie low for a while, and then once again, like nothing had happened, he would be riding around on a car with no number plates and pawning phones.

"You're all I need now. What do you want?"

"What would anyone want from you? Listen, is your grandmother here? Go downstairs. They're taking over your neighbourhood tonight, they're coming over here now. I've been asked to pass on the message to you to head down to the cellar, or even better, fuck off somewhere for a couple of days."

"Who asked you to tell us?"

"Old man Pykhto. That's it, I'm off, see ya."

The lad ran downstairs. I stood there a second and then ran into the kitchen. I open the window — ah, there he was, sweetheart, phoning someone right under my balcony.

"Yeah all's good, she's here. Yes, everything's fine, only she's as grubby as hell. Something's wrong with her eye as well, got blood in it... That's what I'm saying, red eyes... That's fine. I told her. Yes..."

"Klyotsyk!" I bellow from the balcony. "Stay where you are, I'm going to throw this bin on your head right now. I'll give you a bloody thumping!"

"Ha-ha!"

I close the window, lock the door and once again fall upon my blanket. I remember the warning for a second and think that I might actually need to go down to the cellar, but I pass on the idea. I do not have the strength. I will sleep here.

Then I hear a light rap on the door.

* * *

I would have never opened the door if I had not burst out laughing. After all, who am I to fight the Universe, if all its forces had mobilised with the single goal of parting me from this bloody sofa? It was meant to be. So what if my guardian angel, poor thing, puts on a fanfare and pulls out all the stops to prevent me from having a kip? Perhaps Klyotsyk was not intoxicated after all, but was standing before me like a herald of the Apocalypse.

"Hi."

It was Maryna who was herald of the Apocalypse this time. We stood in the doorway like lemons, mouths agape, looking at one another. I cannot imagine what she must have witnessed at that moment, whereas I found myself staring at the Donetsk Venus.

Wherever it was our former PR manager had spent the last few months, it clearly suited her. She was perfectly coiffed, with a smooth seaside tan, and shimmered in my hallway in her golden dress like the Firebird; diamonds sparkled on her fingers, and even her miniature golden sandals twinkled with rhinestones.

"My eyes can't stand it! I have to sit down. Put a bag over my head so I don't go blind with awe."

"Well we better stick a whole blanket over you, you shouldn't see anyone looking like that! Have you been in a zombie attack?"

"Yeah, nice to see you too."

"Hi there, dear."

Maryna hesitated. It would have been appropriate at this moment to have a hug and a kiss, but I understood why she hesitated, and prudently stuck out my hand.

"Don't even think of touching me. I've been on the road for four days. I've just got back, and the water's out."

"Really?"

My guest turned and went into the bathroom. Strange; why did she never take my word for it? And why was I almost not surprised, when the tap hissed and gurgled at her touch, giving forth a stream of nice clean water. There was even hot water, by the looks of it.

"Go sort yourself out, I'll wait. Is it alright if I sit in the kitchen a bit? This is really important."

"Sure. We are like yin and yang, you and I."

Whilst I soaked in the shower, Maryna managed to make coffee, prepare some muesli, and make some little sandwiches with pâté. The coffee did not surprise me, after all, my grandmother and I must have had a box of it lying around, but where did she get the pâté from? It amazed me, the ability of this woman to make herself at home anywhere, with the maximum level of comfort. Stick her on the North Pole in just her swimming costume, and within a few minutes she would be drinking coffee under a fur blanket with the penguins nuzzling her feet.

If you are a fan of black humour, then you would find the reason she came quite funny.

Maryna flew off to Egypt with another one of her Ediks or Vadiks. Who it was is beside the point, we were used to her panoply of suitors: as she said, 'Every girl my age should have a Vadik' (or Edik or whatever it was). There were other tourists on their flight with them, since there are always people who do not concern themselves with politics or 'temporary inconveniences', even in Donetsk. They had to return via Kyiv, however, because Donetsk airport was where the war started. Shit happens.

The problem was that her Mazda was still in the parking lot next to Donetsk airport and Maryna very much wanted to get her toy back.

"Are you joking? You've left your car at the airport? Doesn't it cost three hundred hryvnia a day to park there?"

"Six hundred."

"Well, you did always like the sweet life… What now?"

"Would you come with me? They promised they'd help me take the car out, but I'm scared."

I daren't even ask why she had not got her Alik or Pavlik to help her. It was too obvious…

"Do you want to go now?"

"No, they said after seven."

"Are you mad? Who's leaving the house in the evenings nowadays?"

Still, close to seven, I changed, threw on a jacket, put on some glasses (no more lenses!), and we left. I will not make excuses, nor will I put it down to my own naivety. Now, I would not have done what I did; but despite the marathon of upheavals taking place in the spring of 2014, we still did not take the war seriously. I was curious, for instance, about what was happening at the airport.

I was unaccustomed to seeing the city so empty. We did not see a single car, a single living soul. Even the dogs were hiding — the streets used to be full of them. During the summer, the hot tarmac spread a little and bounced underfoot. We could have walked down the middle of the road if we wanted, but we still stuck to the side of the road, hugging the bushes. We were silent, for the most part.

"Who's your next of kin? Have you sorted it out with anyone?"

"I've got one, from the Ukrainian side."

I slowed down. It was only subtle, but our side did not refer to our army as 'Ukrainian'. It was just the army — no clarification needed. We called them fighters, soldiers, whereas the separatists called them *'boys'* in Russian, alongside a dozen other epithets. As a rule, we avoided any abbreviations which the Russian TV channels now used to refer to our region. It was as if saying this previously non-existent 'D-R', short for Donetsk Republic, out loud, would mean this phenomenon would become less shadowy and become more substantial, as if every mention of it would reveal and fix it onto our side of reality.

"Did you get hold of anyone from the other side?"

"From the DPR? It's more difficult, I mean, they left today; there's no one. They were flustered at first, now they're stepping down, saying there's no one in the regional administration."

"Maryna, let's sit down a second."

We sat down on a bench under a shelter, conveniently hidden from the pavement by a lilac bush.

"Listen, I hadn't asked you. How do you feel about the recent events?"

"What do you mean?"

"About what's happening in the city. Whose side are you on?"

"No-one's. I think both sides have messed up; they're stuck in a rut. Let the politicians work it out and leave us out of it. I don't want to get involved in it, it's not for me."

"Would you not call this a war? That we're being attacked?"

"A war — with whom? Against whom? Is Ukraine really going to fight against Russia? It'd be like an elephant facing a gnat — they'd only have to spit and we'd be washed away! What difference does it make having more than one passport, anyway? Russians are good people, what, am I supposed to attack them if they're not sharing at the top?"

I was fuming; you could have practically lit a cigarette off me. I just broke a twig off the branch and rubbed a young leaf between my fingers. I could not get used to the idea that the abbreviation 'DPR', for the 'Donetsk People's Republic', had entered our lives. Even yesterday, no one had ever heard of those letters, heard of any 'republic'. Yet today people were saying it, talking about it as if it was a legitimate player in this game. I had that feeling again, like there had been a shift in spacetime and the people around me start having memories from a parallel dimension, and you realise that your reality and their reality are now two different realities altogether.

"Ok, fair play. Don't take this personally, but I'm not coming any further. It's not my day, clearly. I've changed my mind, sorry, go call up your Vitalik."

"Hold on, wait!"

Maryna grabbed my hand and I noticed how strong her fingers were. I would definitely have an imprint of her fingers on me; I get bruises instantly.

"What are you doing? Let me go already."

"You think I don't know anything? About what you're doing? Who is going to protect you? No-one's going to shelter you."

"To be honest, I don't really care what you know. We're not going to have a fight in the middle of the road, are we? Go back to where you came from. So long."

"Of course, you're the saint here. There's only two sides to the story: yours, and the wrong one, right?"

Maryna finally stepped back and I backed away from her, rubbing my hand. Each second it felt like the distance between us was increasing by the kilometre. Just a few words, and the girl in front of me was standing on the other side of the Grand Canyon.

"For some things, there aren't two sides to the story. No matter how hard you try, you can't turn black into white. And don't tell me that you can't tell shit from chocolate! Maybe some of them, yeah, but you can't think every gangster you come across is a normal person."

"Oh yeah? Well, what about your Komar? You know that he's joined the *opolchentsi*?"

"What?"

I was baffled. My momentary bafflement became a momentary victory for Maryna. Now she was satisfied.

"Never mind, you go find out, I won't bore you. You're the clever clogs here, you know everything! Tell me, why is that? How come the lads chose you, hovering around you like you're smeared with honey? Are they blind, or stupid? You're nothing, you don't have anything, no tits, no pussy, they're all circling round you like the Holy Grail's about to open. Or did you put a spell on them?"

"Yep, I put a spell on them. Maryna, let's end this ridiculous conversation, otherwise I'll put a spell on you too — I'll curse you with seven years of bad skin. Goodbye. By the way, I'm firing you."

I turned around and walked off, not looking back, although I was tempted. I was curious: was she still going to the airport? We were right next door; we had almost reached the cemetery.

Three months after this conversation, Maryna handed over my address to the DPR blacklist, and half a year after that she moved to Rivne, where she had a successful small business selling children's clothes. We never saw each other again.

* * *

My feet took themselves to work. I had to think in a calm atmosphere, and I cannot think of a more calming spectacle than a drop of molten glass at 600C in a mould.

It is not so difficult to guess that for a woman of my age, being single is a bit of a sore spot. Maryna hit the sore spot, as much as her imagination would allow her. However, she did not hit the bullseye.

Look at me. I am almost thirty, and I am single. I do not have a boyfriend, a suitor — all my short list of brief encounters could be totted on one hand, and I only had sex more than twice with one man, the rest of the relationships falling apart after the first attempt. I have never made a man breakfast; I have never been brought coffee in bed — or to the table. I have never been on a date, like in a film, with flowers and a trip to a restaurant. In fact, no one had ever given me flowers, not including the yearly bouquet on the 8th of March, which they would hand out at work.

I do not know what a family 'scandal' is, I have never had to plan a trip with someone or have a shared budget. I have not had a single episode in my life that might be called romantic. Where other people had passions, tenderness, the textbook butterflies in their stomachs, what did I have? Work, it looked like. Stained glass, lamps, the sharp and razor-like edge of just fired and correctly cut craft glass, fifty shades not of grey, but of cobalt and tempera, adjusted for the angle of falling light. Surely this was not very much, and no work could ever feel the void of feeling incomplete and would not warm the cockles of an old maid's heart (let's just call me that, eh?) on the cold winter evenings? Surely, I would have to suffer from the bottom of my heart? The thing is, I am not suffering. I exist, as you can see, as a happy old maid.

Maybe it's because I never had a loving family. The sort of family where I could see myself becoming a wife. I rejected my childhood memories, it did not work out with them, and after my move here to Donetsk I witnessed dozens of family dramas, from quiet instances of adultery to rowdy lovers' tiffs, where the TV gets thrown out the window and it ends in a blood-soaked stairwell (blood which I ended up having to mop up, because the originators of the blood did not think to clean up after themselves). Lots of vodka, lots of hate, lots of screaming in front of children, and very little love.

We had a lot of wife-beating in our building. During the week it was fine, but on Friday, it would begin. The shouting would start on the other side of the wall, then underneath us, dishes would start flying, something heavy would thump on the floor, a man's shouts with such hysterical, feminine overtones that you could not make out the words, drowning out a woman's shrieking. Then there would be a few hours of quiet, and at night the next act would follow — a desperate squeak of the bedsprings.

When I was young and naïve, I would run to the rescue. The neighbour would be crying out frantically, making an inhuman noise. I would go to my grandmother, but she would just keep making porridge and act like she could not hear anything. I would go upstairs to Tolik's place, and bang on the doors. The screams would subside after a minute, and the head of the family would come out.

"What do you want?"

"What is going on at your place? I'm calling the police. Where's Natasha?"

Then Natasha would leave her room, leaning on the wall, with a split lip, blood trickling down her chin and dripping onto the floor.

"We're fine, leave."

"What do you mean, fine? I see you…"

"What are you, stupid? Piss off, you cow."

"Fair enough."

I would not see the woman for about a week, and then I would

see her in the yard like nothing had happened. We would say
'hi', she would send my grandmother her regards. She would pop
over to ours quickly after that for a coffee, or to show off her new
embroidery, or to discuss the latest TV show. I would not mention the police again.

This was one of the more violent ones. You could get lost
amongst the silent tragedies. How many times had I lent 'just
a twenty until payday', because the husband had drunk away
last month's wages, and there was no more to buy milk for the
kids? How many times had I seen the mournful women's march
to the mines on payday, when the women would rush to snatch
something for the family, before the cash would fall into the
hands of her fine fella?

What about suicide? Here, suicide was considered almost
a non-event, it was not news for long. 'The cucumbers started
coming up', 'Pork's got more expensive', 'Oh, Vasya's hung himself'. In every third building someone had hung themselves, and
they, by the way, are laid to rest in the common cemetery because if they were taken to the cemetery for suicides, then it
would outgrow the confines of the consecrated territory.

I honestly have tried to imagine what my husband would look
like. This is a fashionable thing to do nowadays. They call it 'vi-
sualisation'. You draw or download photos off the internet, stick
them on a wall in front of your eyes (in my case, I would probably have to stick it in my workshop) and wait until the thing you
have projected happens in real life.

There I was; I honestly tried to visu... visua... — oh, never
mind, it's a difficult word for Ukrainians to pronounce — I drew
him, basically. Other than the basics — that he should be a man,
with arms, legs, and a head — I could not get any further. I do
not believe that we have 'another half' to us. The whole idea
of a 'half' is like we are inferior, like have been found wanting.
Maybe, just maybe, there is a man on this earth who would need
me. Who would want to do his own thing while I do mine, and

then we eat dinner together. Who would want to sleep with two duvets, because I do not share mine. Who would have his own money and I mine, although we would still share. Who would want children with me, precisely from me, with my personality and hair colour. With whom pregnancy would not begin with, 'Oh no, there's two lines', but with an open and honest conversation. Who would worry, and not know how to begin, and then would say, 'Let's have kids!'. Who would never in his life, under no circumstances, call me a bad word — because I know myself; I would leave in the clothes I stood.

I know that I am a bit weird. So, should my 'other half' also be a bit weird? I do not want that. I do not like weird guys; on the contrary, I would like someone who was uncomplicated and straightforward. Someone, for whom 'yes' means 'yes', and 'no' means 'no'. For whom a 'no' today will also be a 'no' tomorrow and the day after. I would like predictability. In general, I don't trust fate. Whenever someone says that everyone has their own destiny, the sceptic in me awakens. Firstly, the number of people on this earth is odd, and even if everyone on the planet was paired up, there would still be a loner left at the end, and that may well be me. Next, if you put the time scale on the y axis your geographical location on the x axis, what are the chances that your perfect man will find himself in your place and time? What if we passed each other by thirty years, because what is thirty years on the scale of eternity, and my ideal man has just been born, or, conversely, has just started his pension and gone to live at his dacha and started beekeeping?

Lost in thoughts like these, I got to the garage, and was very surprised to find people inside. The workshop was teeming with life.

On the upside-down drawing board were piled up a barrage of beer bottles and a mountain of dried fish skeletons: common roach fish with cleaned out and salted bellies. There was also a salad of hastily-made salted young cucumbers with radish, some sausage, and a half-empty bottle of Khortytsia vodka (well, or half-full; the optimist should always say 'half-full').

Borysovych sat there, frozen, a cucumber between his teeth. Next to him sat Roman, looking deranged, like he had just seen a ghost. Don held a glass next to his mouth, wavering over whether he should inconspicuously drink it or put it back down.

"Hi boys. Don't pay any attention to me, today's just one of those days."

"Uhh… hi? What are you doing here?"

"I'm here to think. Just think… Borysovych, you know the old joke about the Tsar, Peter the First? He was brought a report: the cannons were not set off for various reasons, which they listed, but reason number thirty was because there was no gunpowder. That's the situation I'm in right now. I can name ninety-nine reasons why I've never got married, but the hundredth reason is because no one's asked me. I have no idea why. Listen, can I grab you for a minute? I need to talk to you."

In abject silence, Borysovych put his cucumber down on his plate and we went out of the room, the rest of the room goggling at us, wide-eyed. Even the dried fish were ogling us, it felt.

* * *

"Borysovych, a little bird brought me the news today that Komar has joined the separatists. Have you heard about this?"

He did not even have to say anything. I knew he had heard.

"Slow down," he said, reading my expression. "Slow down, we're not even sure. There are rumours going around, but what does that mean? There's a lot of disinformation going about at the moment."

"Borysovych, if you want me to preserve even a crumb of trust and respect for you, you're going to give me a clear and thorough run-through of everything you know."

"There is nothing to run through. About a week ago, a separatist department was seized. Then there was a rebuttal in the news that the police force was working normally. I phoned them a few times, but the boys never replied. But they released a video on YouTube yesterday. Have a look for yourself."

We went over to the table, and Borysovych opened up the desired page. In the video, near a brick building — maybe it was the police state department, I do not know, I wasn't there — there were policemen in navy uniforms lining up. A middle-aged man in Russian frog camouflage was making a speech in front of them.

"Line up! Order! I wish you health, comrades!"

"Greetings!" — the response from the rows of navy blue.

"We thank you for your service… from this moment, from this very minute, Aleksandr Viktorovich is named head of the police service. All his orders are to be followed without question. At this moment, your task is to withdraw the police officers. These are normal, loyal people. You will answer to us. Your task is to protect public order, to prevent the seizure of buildings… In order to distinguish yourself from the other police officers, who have not yet sided with the people, I ask you to tie the St George's ribbon on your right epaulette. Are there any questions?"

A timid question from the back: "Where do we get a *ribbon*?"

"The ribbons have not yet been provided."

Fin — end of story.

"Ok, make it full-screen. So, our guys are there, then?"

"It's the separatist HQ. Look here, the camera is passing over the façade. See here, 00:32, you see two people there? The guys answered our call, when the alarm went off. Maybe you don't remember them, but I know. And here…"

"I see."

Komar stood second on the right. The image was out of focus, it was of his profile, but you could tell it was him. Here again, he was swearing allegiance to the separatists. I wonder if he'd put his ribbon on his epaulette yet, or not.

"Why, Borysovych, do you know why? It's such a betrayal."

"I don't know. I still can't believe it. I believe my eyes, but I can't believe this."

"Were you in contact with him."

"Until very recently. He was one of us, he was sound."

"Can you see who they're swearing to?"

"I wish I hadn't. Listen, you, change your phone. Don and I have sat here for two days, he reinstalled all the computer software on your computer too. You'll still have to change your phone."

"I will. Let's go to the kitchen, pour me a drink."

"Let's go, my daughter."

You cannot trust anyone in life, except yourself, and even then, not always. How many times had I had faith in the wrong people? It had never felt as disgusting and painful as now. But in the end, what am I fighting against? Komar had never promised me anything, we had never made a blood pact. I was expecting a certain type of behaviour from him, but I had made it up — what did he owe me?

Oh captain, my captain, what have you done?

It was time to think constructively about this. We would probably have to move the workshop from this address. We would have to let people go, without endangering them. Finally, I would have to deal with my phone.

The most amazing thing, it turned out, was how many important contacts I had: the job took several hours. Then, I lit the furnace, waited for the temperature to reach 800C, and then I threw my phone in. I thought it would be much more romantic to throw it into the river Kalmius, to wash this all away, so to speak. But no matter; fire would also do. In any case, I would not have made it to the river right then anyway.

I fell asleep right there in the workshop, on the old, squished sofa, covered with a worn-out old Carpathian throw. The throw prickled mercilessly and reeked of cats; every spring in that sofa squeaked, every movement throwing up a cloud of dust, dried paint, and crumbs into the air. I did not care a jot, however. I slept for thirty hours straight without waking and did not have a single dream.

VII

SILVER

NEVER SAY NEVER

Throwing my phone into the furnace was
a very, very bad idea. Do not do it, ever.
I would have to get used to it: as
each event unfolded, this city
would turn over and reveal
a previously-unknown side
to it (a bit like showing
me its backside, right?).
Yet I would still remain
totally naïve, because on each
occasion I would believe that
things could not get any worse.
I stood by Forum supermarket on
Artema street, like a spy with their own
personal arsenal of spy gadgets (that is, my
bank card) and I was reflecting on what
I was witnessing. The once-busy square
was now completely empty. No cars
in the carpark, no old ladies with
their wheelie shopping bags
at the bus stop, no-one.

The shopping centre was closed, it seemed. On the right, however, under a dazzling red sign in the style of the Pixar film 'Cars', life was bustling — and blood was flowing.

About a hundred people gathered near a private cashpoint. At first, it was an orderly queue. Then something happened, and the crowd broke up into several groups of belligerents. In the middle, in the epicentre, two or three people were beating each other up. The fight was so vicious, that people were having their ribs and jaws broken and blood splattered the audience. The spectators would take half a step back, but then would immediately move forward again, not so much attracted by the spectacle of the brawl as by their desire to get to the cashpoint.

Today was my third attempt to take cash out. In total, I had stood in a queue for over seven hours, with no results. The card machines both at Kontinent and Mahnat supermarkets had run out of notes right before my eyes. Rumour had it that there was still a working cashpoint at the train station: the one I was at right now, at Forum supermarket.

While I was asleep, Donetsk was cut off from the mobile phone network and from any banking facilities. PrivatBank, Oshchadbank, and even the smallest banks had shut their branches. Account-holders and clients were met with closed shutters and blinds. It was announced that this was a security measure, supposed to last a couple of days in all, and on Monday services would be running as usual. However, no-one really believed this.

Those who were used to accessing money with their card — like me, for instance — were left in a sticky situation. You could still withdraw money on your card from ATB bank, and there trailed a queue of people, several kilometres long, stockpiling grains, salt, and tinned goods. I did not need food supplies, however; I needed a phone.

Phones had to be bought in cash, and SIM cards could not be found at all. First it was the mobile phone network MTS that ceased to operate in the city, then Kyivstar, and then people completely lost their way. As a result, there was a rush of demand for SIM cards from both operators, and replacement cards were being sold for three times the price. That is, in order to put 30 hryvnia on your phone, you had to cough up 100 hryvnia to give to the reseller.

But the queue for the phone shop would be the next step in this quest; for now, whatever the case, I had to source some cash. I only had 50 hryvnia left in my pocket, and I would have to pay at least 30 hryvnia for a taxi home. Even then I somewhat doubted that anyone would be heading in our direction; I had to walk seven kilometres to get to the centre.

I can't be sure when the fracas all started; I bet some pickpocket caused it, but the chaos worked in my favour. While everyone was distracted, I slid past as their backs were turned, almost right up to the wall. After that I clung to a chubby lad who bulldozed his way through the crowd. I stuck to him as if on a leash, and bit by bit my battering ram and I managed to push ourselves through to the coveted window. Everyone was taking out a thousand hryvnia at a time and the cashpoint was quickly running out. With this amount of cash, it is imperative to find a safe way out through the crowd, without drawing attention to yourself.

My thousand hryvnia was not enough for a phone, but I made my peace with this fact. The plan was to head down to the station, as maybe there I would be able to get the rest. If not, well, I would just go and sleep again, and maybe then everything would settle down somewhat.

I sat down at the bus stop. There had not been any trolleybuses today — do they even exist? Sooner or later, they would have to come. A few pensioners were waiting there too, clearly also optimists like me. In any case, it never hurt anyone just to sit down and think a bit.

How quickly people's behaviour had changed on public transport! If before I was the only silent one, an island buffeted by the endless waves of conversations, interruptions, and gossip, now everyone else sat in silence too. Passengers would speak very quietly, right by their companion's ear, lowering their voices in certain places. Even the most mundane of conversation topics took on a dramatic emphasis, like at the theatre. Against this background of whispering, with its many hidden meanings, any loudmouths and provocateurs were now especially audible. A distinct Russian accent added a jarring dissonance to the trolleybus's polyglossia. I could tell what it was from the softest murmur, from the first word someone said, from the first instance the speaker would pronounce the letter 'e'. This foreign way of speaking grated at the ear with its cloying pretentiousness. The simplest question made the speaker sound like they were getting hysterical, as if they were complaining about something and threatening you at the same time.

However, it was not worth getting held up. It was already seven in the evening, and either I went home on foot, or I would spend the night here under the bus shelter. The way home was about ten kilometres, no public transport was running, and as for hitching a ride — there were no idiots about for that. Of course, the best thing would have been to phone my friends and ask for help, but what are you going to do. You're on your own now, Mata Hari.

With some regret I got up and made my way north, staying back a little from the road, which was still empty. About an hour later, when I felt that I had already covered about twenty kilometres, but in fact cannot have been more than three, I caught up with a couple on the road.

A man and a girl. He was in green camouflage and grey trainers, holding a rifle at his side. You could see his hand in black cut-off gloves holding the butt of the rifle, which had a pink rubber band tied around it. The other hand was lying on the girl's neck. He tickled her neck as they walked, a bit like how we sometimes scratch puppies or kittens at the scruff of the neck. The girl recoiled from these movements, helplessly shrugging her shoulders and slowing down, but his heavy palm would not let her stop; he gave her a shove, and almost falling, she trotted next to her companion, getting tangled in her skirt.

At some point, the girl looked back, and I saw that she could not have been more than fourteen, a schoolgirl. And so, there we were, the three of us on a never-ending street: me, a girl scared half to death, and her armed escort.

Well, that was it, essentially. Detached and calm, like in a film, I realised that I was about to die. The wise thing to do would have been to stop and hide amongst the labyrinth of small, detached houses in this part of the city. The only sensible thing to do would have been to let them go ahead and count to ten. That's right: wait. Wait, let them go ahead! 'Wait', I said! Wait, what are you doing?! Arrrrgh!

"Aaaaaaaa!" I screeched like a madwoman, loud enough to burst your eardrum, *"Anya, Anya, wait, hold on! Anya!"*

The couple in front realised that I was shouting at them and stopped. The separatist cocked his weapon and pointed his rifle at me, but I ignored it and ran at him, screaming bloody murder, trying to raise my arm with my fistful of notes up higher.

"Anya! What are you doing, your mother's been looking all over for you! She's been to the commander's office; everyone's been looking for you!… Thank you, thank you so much! [this was to the bearded *opolchenets*, who lowered his weapon and for a second almost lost his composure]. *Look, take it!"*

I stuff my thousand hryvnia into his hands, and he automatically takes the money. It was lucky that the cash machine only gave out fifty-hryvnia notes, as they made up a nice little wad of cash.

"Take it. It's so good you've found her. Thank you so much, I'll take her home from here, it's not far…"

I grab the girl's arm and pull her with all my might; she is wilting, little trooper, as the two of us run into the nearest

alleyway. The turn off is only a couple of metres away, then ten
more or so; left, right, left, and here is a hole in the fence. Let's
hope the owners of this garden don't have a dog... Come on,
crouch down!

We huddle in the bushes in someone's garden and lay quiet as
a mouse. He has not fired any shots. Is he chasing us? No, by the
looks of it. There are no streetlights around here; it is hard to see
in the twilight, but the street seems to be deserted.

The girl next to me suddenly began to tremble and mewl, just
like a puppy. I hug her with all my might, hugging her to my
breast — well, to my ribcage. It was only then that I realised how
thin and dirty she was, and how badly she smelled.

"Shhhh, settle down, it's ok. He's gone, there's no-one else
here. There, there!"

"Where do you know me from?"

"I don't know you."

"But how? You called my name..."

"Are you called Anya?"

"Yes."

"You won't believe it Anya, but I just guessed."

"Then who are you?"

"I think I'm an elf." An elf who has had a knock to the head,
clearly, and left without its last penny. "Anya, tell me, do you
have a phone?"

To be honest, I need not have asked. The girl had no phone on
her, just like she had no purse, no gold chain, nor a pair of her
mother's earrings. The girl was very, very unfortunate. Yet, on
the other hand, today was the luckiest day of her life.

Anya lived with her mother in the Smolyanka neighbourhood.
This meant that we would have to go by all the back alleys and
side streets all the way to the other side of town. Oh, my poor,
poor legs!

"Does your mum at least roughly know where you were taken?
Are they looking for you?"

They were. They had been looking for her for eight days already. For that whole time Anya had been locked in a cellar. Anya was fourteen years old.

Lord Almighty, I do not want to hear the rest.

* * *

I had a colleague who could talk about his future family life for hours. His most cherished dream, right from primary school, was getting married. One time I could not hold back:

"Vasya, can you tell me, why do you need a wife?"

"Oh, you won't understand. Look, I come home from work, knackered, hands covered in engine oil, I can barely drag my feet off the ground. I get to the entrance of the block of flats, open the doors, and at home *dinner's ready*!"

This 'dinner's ready' was said in caps lock, with such delight, that it immediately made you think of a bowl of borsch with soured cream, filled right to the top, so thick that the spoon stands up in it: and stuffed pancakes, and potatoes with *salo*[9] and onions, and a plump homemade poppyseed pie… you cannot argue with pie! Dinner being ready: that is the standard foundation for marriage.

I was sitting in the kitchen, writing a report on our volunteer spending on Facebook, and at the same time I felt myself a truly happily married woman, because in the kitchen was a clanging, squeaking, and frying, producing dizzying aromas which penetrated all corners of the flat. Every minute I was being brought either a meatball to try, or some stuffed cabbage rolls; the next, an ice-cream sundae with nuts. Everything was made in industrial quantities, in various vats, basins, and tubs; all in a cleanly and an orderly fashion. And with the perfect amount of salt and pepper.

Because now I had Tetiana.

---

9   A Ukrainian delicacy of raw-cured pork fatback.

Tetiana — or Tanya, for short — and I got to know each other on that fateful night a fortnight ago, when Anya and I finally got back to mine. After hanging around in the bushes for a short while (well, not for a short while in fact, but until the middle of the night), we decided to go to my flat, and from there get hold of Anya's mother. It was quicker to get to mine, in any case.

While we were lying underneath the shelter, the girl, snivelling and stuttering, told me their story: the children's story. It was a case where your classic childhood antics had ended in tragedy. Three teenagers, Instagram stars to be, took a few selfies in front of the occupied Ukrainian Security Service building. Of course, they took a picture of the building too — it looked really cool, after all! All three of them were arrested, at first almost officially, but then the soldiers found photos and videos from one of our Ukrainian checkpoints on one of the kid's phones. They also found a bracelet with the Ukrainian trident on it.

I tried not to listen to what happened next. With all my might, I conjured up a huge field of wheat with cornflowers. The birds were twittering, the ears of wheat rustled in the breeze — and there I was, in the middle of the field, watching the clouds. Shhh, everything will be alright. I'm not here, I'm not on this street, I can't hear anything. Shhhh…

"Seryoga was the most beat-up out of all of us. They were kicking him; blood was coming out of his ears and his nose. He began to vomit up blood, and then they dragged him down the corridor. They told me to crawl on my stomach and wipe the blood from the floor with my clothes. I didn't want to, but our interrogator hit me a few times, and I fell down. He said that us 'khokhols'[10] need to be taught basic hygiene. He laughed."

"And you?"

---

10 *'Khokhol'* is a word often used by Russians as an ethnic slur for Ukrainians; alternatively, many Ukrainians call themselves *'khokhly'* as a form of ethnic self-identification, to differentiate themselves from Russians.

"I did what he said. There were people in some offices there. One woman went to fill up a kettle in the sink. She said hi to him, well, you know who. And then she stepped over me and carried on."

Cornflowers and ears of wheat. Think of the corn field. Shhhhh…

The last couple of kilometres were the hardest. For starters, we crouched down in the grass at every movement, whenever it felt like there was someone in front or behind us, and we hid until everyone who happened to pass was out of sight. Secondly, I had a particular disability that I hid from everyone in vain: night blindness — I completely lost my sight in the dark. If I could see well enough during the day thanks to my contact lenses (their prescription was −7 for each eye, and had to be adjusted with glasses), then at night I completely lost 3D vision. That's why it was no surprise that the moonlit path which I was following so confidently turned out to be a ditch full of water, which I tumbled into, to Anya's terrified 'oi', almost breaking my neck.

It is clear that God has special providence for fools, for we did not come across a single separatist patrol and, it seemed, no-one paid any attention at all to a couple of lonely ladies on the empty streets in one of the most crime-ridden neighbourhoods of Donetsk.

However, at home, behind windows blacked out with rugs, we were met by a real party. Well, that, or a wake.

Everyone was there. Roman and Borysovych were smoking in the bedroom. Oleh and Don were bending over the bed, where a map of the city had been put up and was covered in marker pen. Some lads I did not know were looking through my email on my personal laptop. How did they work out the password?! Olha Ivanivna was calmly playing a game of solitaire and was the only one, it seemed, who was unsurprised by our arrival.

If it could be measured on a scale of one to ten, where one would be the final scene of *The Government Inspector* (where they famously 'break the fourth wall'), and ten would be the re-action when Mathias Rust illegally landed his plane on the Red Square, the reaction to me and Anya's arrival would have hit twenty. Essentially, everyone was completely lost for words, and only Roman could utter something like 'Heeeey!', pointing his finger at us.

My grandmother put her cards away, got up and hugged me at arm's length.

"Well then, you old devil!" she said to Borysovych. "I told you that the girl would be all right, she's made of sterner stuff than that. She'll not go wrong."

"Oi kid, gimme your neck!" Borysovych said to me. "I swear, I'm going to put a chip in the back of your head."

"Oh, fuck the chip!" That was Roman. "Where have you been?"

It took a little while to explain the situation, and a little more time to put the terrified girl in the bedroom, wrap her in a blan-ket, give her a cup of tea and get her mum's phone number. The girl actually knew her mother's number by heart, which aston-ished me. I had never in my life learnt a mobile phone number by heart, not even my own.

They entrusted me with phoning her. The woman immedi-ately picked up the phone after the first ring — something that only a mother who could not leave the phone out of her sight would do.

"Hello. Is this Tanya?" I had to ask, just in case.

"Yes, it is!"

"Listen, don't worry, everything is ok. We've found your daughter, she's safe with us."

"Who are you?! Where?"

"Hang on, I'll explain. I'll give the phone to your daughter; you can speak with her."

They did not manage to speak, however. Anya burst into tears — *"Mum, mummy!"* All those listening also started cry-ing. There was not a dry eye in the house, and Oleh came up to me and hugged me so hard from behind that he almost smothered me.

Everything then settled down. The guys took the girl home. The interns were sent back to their accommodation with Oleh. I was washed, fed and put to bed. Roman, who according to Baba Olya was 'running up the walls' while I was gone (personally, I do not approve of those types of jokes in regards to a person who is paralysed), lay down on a folding chair, whereas Baba Olya and Borysovych went to the kitchen to blow off some steam. Borysovych was a fan of Captain Morgan, and although Baba Olya made fun of his 'bourgeois' choice, even so, there was still a bottle of rum with a black label in the cupboard.

Tetiana came early the next morning. She was a tall, curvy woman, who once upon a time — it could have been a week, or it could have been ten years ago — was a beauty, and she collapsed in tears on my shoulder. Peering from behind her shoulder stood Anya, scrubbed-up and looking a little refreshed, and she was also blubbing.

The girls did exactly what I and any other sane person would have done in their place. They fled Donetsk with one suitcase between the two of them, leaving behind their flat, school, and a job in a prestigious restaurant. They did not know a single person beyond the confines of Donetsk Oblast, and they did not have a penny to their name, as Tanya had either sold or given away everything valuable that she owned in order to buy her daughter's freedom from that cellar, and they went off by train, happy to be alive, without thinking about what tomorrow would bring.

I thought that we had parted ways forever, but after a week I found Tanya once again standing at the door, with no daughter and with no suitcase. She briefly informed me that her daughter was safe, and that she herself was going to live with me.

"I'm a cook. You need a cook, don't you?"

"I do. Come in."

* * *

"Have a woooonderful holiday today!"

My neighbour thus greeted me at length, opening her arms for a hug.

"What holiday?"

"Putin's just announced the independence for the people of the Donbass. What, haven't you heard?"

"This is the first I've heard of it."

"Well, that's it now. We can say that we're part of Russia now."

She shuffled on, falling heavily on both feet, gasping because of her chesty cough, there with her calico dressing gown, thick calves, and poorly-dyed grey hair. In two months, Auntie Marta would be blown up by a bomb at her *dacha*, where she was digging up potatoes. They say that her foot and a piece of her scalp were all that was found of her in that two-metre wide blast crater, so they buried her in a box. They found courgettes from her garden launched half a kilometre away by the explosion.

* * *

"God bless you, our sons!"

An old granny in the queue baptises two *opolchentsi* who were huddled behind us with a bottle of vodka.

"Bless you for protecting us. I do feel sorry for you! I'm going to church every day to pray!" They mutter something and go towards the exit, and the queue stays silent. She carried on: *"You do feel sorry for them, and for us — for everyone!"*

I rush outside without buying anything. I still cannot choose anything I want to buy; even the supermarket shelves have become foreign to me. For years, I would fill my shopping basket automatically, my hands reaching independently for the milk, the ham, for the biscuits. A delivery of fresh chicken comes to our local shop at nine o' clock in the morning; the pork and mince would be delivered in the afternoon. During the daily sale, one of my three favourite types of yoghurt would be reduced. Sadochok juice, triangles of Chumak tomato paste, President cheese; hundreds of familiar goods, and the loss of each one of them from the shelves niggles you, like a stone in your shoe. The haste with which supermarket chains rushed to replace Ukrainian goods with Russian ones just looked like a clumsy attempt at washing the blood away from a crime scene. They must really fear Ukraine, then, if they are ready to wage a war against Ukrainian soured cream…

* * *

"Hi. Can you come here? Me and the girls have got a load of jars of preserves for you."

Of course I could come, even though a city 'curfew' had already long been in place. They said that people are already being detained for being out late, and you had to be careful, but I could not bring myself to abide by their rules. As such, I end up driving up to an old Khrushchev-era apartment block when it is almost night, as it is already dark. The girls — whom I do not know — are out there waiting for me. Barely exchanging a hello, they hurriedly take the packages of jars out of the entrance to the apartment block. I start to help, walking up to the entrance, and I see a whole arsenal of preserved goods, clearly ransacked from the whole block. There were jams, *lecho*, compotes, canned meat, stock for borsch. Between three-litre vats of preserves and little pots for baby food, there were hundreds of jars in total. The four of us spend over an hour loading the car up, cramming the boot with them, piling them up inside up to the roof of the car, wrapping them with newspaper and clingfilm. I stuff the jars underneath the seats, wrapping them in rags, piling them up in tiers from bottom to the roof of the cabin. I push the driver's seat so far forward that my knees are jammed in, and we stick an extra batch of jam behind it. After getting in my seat, when I have already started the ignition, the girls try and give me another bag to put on my lap. The bag is full of homemade *salo* and

a little pouch of money, almost 2000 hryvnia to go towards the
war effort.

* * *

"Listen, one of your friends called. The youth camp has written off a bunch of sleeping bags, they can give them to us. Do you
want to pick them up?"

True, we had a real shortage of sleeping bags, so even old Soviet ones would do. We rushed off with the guys to what used
to be the Pioneers Palace and in four trips took away hundreds
of sleeping bags. Heavy ones, solid, like big cotton quilted blankets; to us, they were prized possessions. Our new treasures
were rather dirty and smelly, some got at by mice, and well-
stained with years of use. We could have taken them to our fighters as they were — it would still be better than sleeping on bare
earth — but I did not want to do that. I decided that I would have
them all washed and cleaned, but as only a few of them could fit
into any establishment at one time, a laundry job of this scale
would have taken years. Baba Olya consequently went round
the neighbours, bringing a few sacks to each flat, saying that we
needed help. Astonishingly, no-one refused, even the neighbours
who did not have a washing machine. At the end of the week, on
schedule, the sleeping bags were brought back to us freshly laun-
dered, and one activist even sewed a few designs on her sleeping
bags: the Russian tricolour flag, Orthodox cross, and the inscrip-
tion, *'God is with us, Russia is with us!'*

My grandmother found me standing there as they once found
Lot's wife, a pillar of salt looking at the embroidered sleeping bag.

"Baba, can you explain this to me?"

"Oh, it's no bother, just fold it up nicely and no-one will see.

"Baba!"

It turned out that Olha Ivanivna had told everyone that we
were laundering sleeping bags for the *boys* from the separatist
section.

"Well, what are you going to do? Beggars can't be choosers you know!"

* * *

I always used to buy my supplies from the first manufacturer I would come across; at a stretch, I would buy from the first wholesaler. If you have patience to spare, however, you can find the supply source for a fair price, which you can reduce once or twice over.

When we started buying stuff for the army, we tried to go down the same route. The girls rushed to the nearest military surplus stores, whereas I took to the computer. That is how 'government liquidation' entered our lives: we would source military warehouses in Germany, the States, Poland, Czech Republic, and the UK selling written-off military gear.

"Girls," I would say, "shall we trial this first, find something small and useful that we don't have yet?"

Funnily enough, our side had nothing. Boots, kneepads, army jackets, flak jackets, helmets, binoculars, tourniquets, bandages; there were hundreds of outposts in the field where these things were absolutely non-existent.

"Listen," said Oksana, sending us a link to a Kharkiv site. "Look, people here are ordering eyewear from the US. Let's get some ourselves, every second wounded soldier comes in with an eye injury."

"Alright then. What's this — facial armour? What does that protect against?"

"If only I knew…"

New goggles cost 800 hryvnia apiece in our military warehouses. In America, they went for 70 hryvnia each, with a discount if you bought a thousand or more. However, first you needed to win a bid, which, to take part in, you needed someone with a US social security number. Next you had to find someone who could go to the warehouse in the middle of the desert there and pick up our purchase, and then deliver it to the post office to send it to Ukraine. Next, you had to agree with a delivery service to give a discount on transportation and customs clearance in Ukraine. From there, it would be easy to get the delivery from Lviv to Dnipro and distribute it from there.

At each of these stages a large sign glowed in neon letters, saying, 'Are you crazy?' Stop getting ideas above your station, things don't happen just like that, not without acquaintances, experience, or even anything at all! We had no money, after all. Where were we going to get these 70,000 hryvnia from?

"Do you know what we've come up with? We've decided to put what we're doing on mumsnet and parenting websites."

"Hang on, *what* websites?"

"You know the ones, where mums discuss childrearing, pregnancy, breastfeeding, preeclampsia, you know the one."

"God, what did you post on it?"

"We said we're collecting money for masks. Like you said, 70 hryvnia per mask. We thought of a promotion, like, buy one for yourself and get one for a soldier, too. Cool, right?"

As a result, our first thousand goggles were paid for by all these mums and neurotic yummy-mummies. These were the very women you hear about in the dumb-blonde jokes, residents of the most vanilla chat-forums with profile pictures of cats, bunnies, and angels.

'Our little munchkin is already six weeks old!'
'Happy anniversary to me and my husband!'
'Would you look at the state of this cat! He's sat on the baby!'
'What are you supposed to do when your ex gets in touch???'
'Request for army goggles for our men, urgent collection!'.

Bombarded with orders between 50 to 100 hryvnia, I urgently called around churches in the Ukrainian diaspora. Well, who else was I supposed to call? The church communities had their own Facebook pages, the odd contact details. I called, wrote, and begged like never in my whole life. Well, even if I had never got a penny for free (having only ever been paid for work) I had still never begged like that before. There I was, beseeching and pleading with strangers, without rehearsing what I was going to say first, and people actually believed me. They found cars, extra pairs of hands, and volunteers who would go to the warehouses, load up, send the gear off, and even contribute to our cause.

Our goggles arrived in boxes sprinkled with sweets, bags of coffee, vitamins, and they had also sent us medical gowns and masks, as well as adult nappies.

"I don't get it, what are the incontinence pads for? For snipers, or what?"

"You are a funny one. They're for the hospital."

In the process of this procurement we gained several overseas contacts, and almost everyone whom we dealt with wanted political information, asking, 'What are you doing? Why? Who is at war with whom?'

"Tanya, this is madness. They don't know the difference between us, you know, between Russia and Ukraine. They think it's an internal conflict, that we're fighting amongst ourselves."

"Who gives a damn."

Tanya was not listening. She and Borysovych were playfighting over the borsch in our kitchen, where there was already not enough space to breathe at the best of times.

"What do you mean, 'Who gives a damn'? Come on, put that beetroot down! Tanya, you realise that no-one is going to help us? We're being trampled on here, no-one is going to intervene, and we're being swatted like flies. Don't you care why us flies are fighting between ourselves?"

"Stop nagging, I don't care. Would knowing change anything for you? For us?"

"Well no."

"There you are then. It is what it is. Look how your lot spent twenty years in the woods hiding in dugouts and nothing came of it."

"What do you mean, 'our lot'? Who?"

"Well, Bandera's lot."

"Oh, and why are you not saying 'our lot' then?"

Tanya sighed, took off her apron, and sat down opposite me, shoving aside a chopping board littered with onions and potato skins with her elbow.

"Because they're *your* lot. Here, it's always been like we're part of Ukraine, and at other times it's like we're looking through the window from the outside at what you're doing over there. There's the *kutia* Christmas puddings, Christmas carols, *vertep* puppet shows. *Vyshyvanka* shirts, the Ukrainian language and traditions… It's sour grapes, it's like we want it all, but also find it all hard to swallow. If someone here tried to start a *vertep* show here, he'd be laughed out of town. We've always thought that all this Ukrainian stuff just isn't for us. Do you remember when President Yushchenko decided to divide us into different nationality types? Do you remember how people here really believed in them? It's because here, if you say you're Ukrainian, everyone points the finger. We're *khokhols*, not Ukrainians, that's all we're allowed to call ourselves."

"Hang on, how does that work then? You're Ukrainian, Borysovych, the lads… You're not *khokhols*! You speak Ukrainian, after all."

"We speak it with you. I was worried at first about opening my mouth, I had to consciously find the words, and then I managed to speak it without any problems. You remember the bleating and mooing when we first tried to speak it with you."

"Oh, come off it, you weren't *bleating*."

"I'm not so sure. Should I tell you how my grandfather ended up settling here?"

"Tell me."

"He served in the state paramilitary security service after the war. He was ordered to guard this one poor blighter; it was a viciously cold winter, this prisoner was freezing, and he asked to warm up in the dugout. My grandfather felt sorry for him, so he let him go. But this guy took off. He managed to escape the dugout, basically. My grandfather looked at what happened, and then decided to run away too, because in the morning someone would have to be shot, either this young boy, or some old man in his place. And where was it everyone ran off to? They came here, to the mines. They took anyone who came, here, anyone who was healthy and could bear standing in water up to their knees in the mines. They would give out documents that my grandfather had 'lost', apparently, and they put his name down as 'Petro Tonkal'. That's where the Tonkals come from, but who he really was, where he was born, his nationality, his surname — no-one knows to this day, since he took his secret to the grave."

"Ok fine, but that was then. But what about now? Who do you feel you are?"

"Now? I feel that we need to survive and fight off these Russians. Then Ukraine will accept us for what we are; we'll come in handy for her then, deaf, dumb, and with no memory. Then we'll learn your carols, they're not going anywhere."

* * *

I was hardly *living* on the internet then, but I was posting at least two or three times a day. Facebook became an outlet where I could post under a fake name. I wrote every time that the name I was using was fictional, that I did not exist and never had done: the only things that existed were Donetsk, the war, and that we were stuck in the middle of this city like flies in amber, and these short missions out to military positions was perhaps the only thing keeping us here during such a time.

I tried to report to our donors, as we were sent funds, and quite frequently at that, although I was always subconsciously afraid that they would ask us to transfer the money back. So, I had to make reports… but what could I show them? Pallets of stuffed peppers and meatballs in the kitchen, photos of big cooking pots out on the field, in the grass. Piles of uniforms: Ukrainian 'oak' camouflage, German Bundeswehr and British pixel camo, Czech underwear and T-shirts (which were four hryvnia apiece! We took them by the load from a Polish warehouse. They were a little holey, a bit faded, worn a little thin — but what did that matter? They were discarded as rags, and still others just disintegrated. We were given T-shirts in bales from Poland, in huge stripy bags, big enough for me to get into, with space to spare. That was how I found myself coming back to square one: I once vowed never to carry bags from the bazaar like our 'tinkers' of old did, and just look what happened…).

The first bulletproof vests arrived. At first, they were black police vests, which were only really effective as psychological protection, and thereafter came Italian, German, and Israeli armour. Our friends in the diaspora bought the first batch in Italy and transported it by lorry to Chop. They managed to bring it over, but they could not get it across the border, as customs would only let it through as commercial cargo. We were stuck, that was it, we did not know what was happening…

I snatched the phone, and said to the border officers, "Guys, this is for your men fighting in the anti-terrorist operation, do you not understand?"

It was like talking to a brick wall: they would not let the shipment in or back out, it could only stay in the customs penalty area.

It was good that old Roman was there.

"They're not the ones you need to call," he said.

"Alright then, so who were we supposed to call then?"

"I don't know who. Borysovych, however, he knows who to get hold of. Wait."

How were we supposed to wait? We were about to get fined, or the shipment was going to 'disappear' completely, and then where were we supposed to find it?

"Wait."

The lads made a few calls, had a cigarette, then called around again. After an hour, around thirty men with valid travel visas in their passports turned up at the border crossing; thirty smugglers turned up and *'solved'* the problem, thirty Transcarpathian millionaires turned up and each carried the vests across the pedestrian border crossing, and each of the customs officers averted their eyes. The old gypsy, Zhora, made two trips on his own two feet, and almost died of the *'strain'*, as he happily and breathlessly reported when they loaded up the lorry on our side of the border.

That evening, we flew off to Dnipro to meet our priceless cargo, and then by the morning we were delivering it to various army lines, five pieces per troop, solely for the use of combat missions.

We filmed the armour on our phone, hiding the faces of the soldiers, and the last batch the lads put on right in front of us, jumped into their vehicles, and headed off into the mix. I then lit a cigarette for the first time in my life, and Roman took funny photos while I was on the floor from coughing so much. I have these photos on me to this day, but they were not suitable for our donor report.

In general, we did not have much that was suitable for the report. By and large, we did not see the army as such. The oldest commander among our contacts was thirty-year-old major Vovchik from Ochakovo, turned almost black from the sun, exhaustion, and lack of sleep, whom we gave some bandages on a flying visit. The rest were — well, we would have said *opolchentsi*, if that word were not associated with those shits on the other side. They were *haidamaks* (Ukrainian Cossack paramilitary), guerrillas, Cossacks — but not an army.

Sometimes, I dream that I am standing in a field in a thick fog. White tendrils of fog flow underfoot, obstructing my mouth and eyes. I am alone, and at the same time not alone. To the left and right of me, men and women walk past, silent and focussed;

they go one by one, or in groups, with machine guns and rifles. They do not stop, they only slow down. In each group going past there are more and more of them, and I am in a desperate hurry. I put something in each of their hands: some get cigarettes, others sandwiches, or a muffler or a magazine. They take them without looking back, and they dissolve in the gloom, and I dare not linger there; time is short. I do not see any faces, merely arms and backs, arms and backs. This is how my army was; this is how I remembered it. Arms and backs.

* * *

The magazines were a complete nightmare. Getting the magazines ended up being a real saga, I will tell you now. Whenever I get asked what Donetsk was like in the early summer of 2014, the only comparison that comes to mind is of a lonely wife being beaten and raped by her husband, yet who will not open the door to the police, answering with a 'We're fine, please leave!'. At first glance, we seemed fine. So what if a few buildings were seized by gangs? Well, and if they have blocked off a couple of streets? These were just temporary difficulties, the barricades have been up in Kyiv for three months, it was nothing. The mayor's office reported daily on uncovered crimes, public transport was still running, the courts were still hearing cases, the street sweepers were still sweeping the streets, the newsstands were still selling newspapers. As a rule, you could still get anything you wanted in the city, albeit for a little extra.

The soldiers asked us to hurry up in getting them magazines, that is, clips for their semiautomatics. As if there were enough semiautomatics to go around anyway, and disposable ammo was hard enough to get hold of as it was. That was just how it was: someone would get shot, their ammunition would fall to the ground, it never got recovered, and then it was lost forever.

We promise to try and locate them, but then Borysovych says,

"We've got them! Right here, in the army supply warehouse, you can get 'bananas' for twenty hryvnia each."

"What do you mean, from the warehouse?"

"Directly from it."

"In Donetsk? Aren't these warehouses for our side? You mean to say that charging their own men for supplies?"

"Bingo. You're the queen of asking stupid questions today. Come on, the lads and I will head off, and you wait here."

"Wait here? What! I'm coming with you!"

"Stay at home. Otherwise you'll start asking questions."

"I promise I'll be silent as the grave! Just tell them I can't speak. I'm coming with you; I can't miss this."

The warehouse was a sort of covered-market-type hangar next to a former military unit in Lenin district. It was business as usual for the military settlement up until a month ago even; then, after a couple of attempts to storm it, it was now wholly unclear what was happening behind the high concrete fence. The barbed-wire iron gate was locked, no equipment was visible, and most of the windows had been smashed in. When we came up from the back entrance, however, they were waiting for us. A man in camo looked out and nodded at a side door — come on, quickly.

"Long live Novorossiya!" — Borysovych greeted them.

"God bless the Donbass! Bring up your car and let's go, I've prepared everything for you."

In addition to clips, they had got together some canned meat for us, dugout brackets, mufflers, and oil that we were low on. There were also army tents for 3000 hryvnia each, and we took four. On the shelves lay assorted army belts, flasks, some other junk, and boxes of grain, all in bulk.

"We've got an inflatable rubber boat; do you need it?"

Unfortunately, we had to say no to the dinghy.

We drove back without a word. The filling on my wisdom tooth had fallen out, and, for the first time in many days, I did not know what to say.

* * *

"Hi, can you have a look? We've got a letter from America; I don't understand what he wants."

"Come on now, what do you need? Have you not stuck it into Google? Put it into Google Translate."

"It just comes out with some mumbo-jumbo. I think that he's asking us how cold it gets in winter."

"It's Craig from eBay, we bought some ammunition belts off him. Yes, I see. He has a batch of winter boots, good for temperatures up to −40. He's asking if we want them for the winter. Look, they're snowshoes. Thirty dollars a pair."

"Yeah but, why would we need winter shoes? Tell him that it's +30 degrees right now, do we really need those boots?"

"You don't think we'll need them?"

"Fat chance! We'll be all clear here by winter."

We never bought those boots, which we regretted, of course. We worked with Craig, however, for a long time after that, right up until he sent me a batch of sapper blades instead of assault vests. Can you imagine the shipping costs to Ukraine?!

'My dear friend,' Craig messaged me, in English, 'I do have one question.'

'Go on.'

'The Russians are buying the same stuff as you are from our store. Uniforms, ammo belts, boots. Are you not going to have problems on the battlefield, if both sides are dressed the same?'

'Don't worry, my dear friend,' I replied in English. 'No problem.'

VIII

CORAL

MY CUP RUNNETH OVER
(PSALM 23:5)

"Get up, you hear me, get up! Quickly, wake up!"
If anyone wakes you up like that in the summer of 2014,
first you fall on the floor, and only then you open your eyes.
"What's going on? Are we going down to the cellar?"
"No, look, look!"
Tanya shoved the laptop right under my nose.
"They've taken back Mariupol! Our boys
are there in *Marik*, they liberated it today!"
Are you familiar with the feeling, as though
an immense weight has been lifted off your
shoulders? It feels glorious, just being able to
crunch your back and stretch your spine.
"Tanya, so that's it, right? Our boys are advancing?"

Our boys are coming. Our boys are coming! *Our* boys — how bloody good does that sound? We fell upon the screen, watching the scenes over and over again, especially the bit where a dozen separatists in tracksuit trousers were having their noses shoved into the mud. My God, did this mean the ones here would be sent packing soon? Our boys could not just stop at Mariupol. Soon these local crap-hat generals were going to be rounded up and put away. If only this could have happened back in March!

"Tanya, shall we go see the guys, find out what's going on? Let's stick a barbecue on, grill some *shashlik*! What a day!"

"Oh, go on then."

Tanya and I were lucky. We didn't just complement each other; we completed each other. She was like the yin to my yang: no wonder they say that one man's gain is another man's loss. Whatever I lacked had been bestowed upon Tanya in miraculous proportions: she had luscious curves, and a bosom you wanted to just nestle in. She had absolute confidence in herself and her rights. She had what would be more politely referred to in books as 'sex appeal', whereas my grandma would call 'slutty eyes'.

At the same time, she was a cynic. She did not expect anything good to come from the world on principle: every word she came across was met with suspicion. She believed in having an 'iron fist', and when it came to dealing with the local separatists, she did not believe in a carrot-and-stick approach — it was more like a stick-and-stick approach. In contrast, I would falter, get embarrassed and try to explain myself; for her, all of about three words were enough to dot the i's and cross the t's. The first time we met, she gave me a brief summary of her life story so that no more questions would come up. She was born in a village near Volnovakha, a town in Donetsk Oblast; she married young, straight after school. As men go, he was alright, but he became decidedly not-alright whenever he drank. One time he tried to strangle her when she was pregnant. Tanya turned around and walloped him with a frying pan so hard that his nose went back into his head. He never got up again after the blow; Tanya was charged with murder and was given a minimum sentence, serving four years in prison. When she was released, she sold her mother's house and bought back her daughter, who was living with Tanya's parents-in-law at the time. At first the child did not recognise her mother, but they gradually managed to get along and moved to Donetsk, restarting their lives from scratch. Everyone respected Tetiana, including our block's 'committee', the local young offenders, shopkeepers, and the guards at the checkpoints. The lads from my warehouse would often come to visit, and once, with my very own eyes, I saw Borysovych tickle her under the ribs while lifting her up off the ground. He immediately got an elbow to the head, followed by a packet of *pelmeni* from the freezer to nurse the bump on his head. During all the years of our acquaintance, none of them had ever thought to tickle me like that.

It just so happened that Tetiana started joining us on our trips. Of course, Roman was against it, but the God's honest truth is that we were rather 'colourful' weekenders, just me and him — we stood out. That is why we agreed on the following: our *dacha*, or little cottage in the country, was in the direction of Kurakhiv, and only there. Whenever it came to going east or south, I would either go alone, if it was not too far, or with Tanya.

Now we were 'vegetable traders': the perfect cover. The guys managed to find a beaten-up 1993 Renault 'Kangaroo' van which went for a song, and we loaded it up with onions, carrots, greens, seasonal berries, which we got on the cheap from farmers anxious about the current situation, and took them all to Avdiivka, Khartsyzk, Horlivka, Makiivka, and Yasnuvata, depending on the route plan. You could have hidden an elephant amongst these vegetable boxes, but even when we were passing through the checkpoints, we were never searched. Tanya's leopard-print leggings, costume jewellery on her fingers, her blonde curls tied up with a flirty satin bow, and that familiar 'slutty look' all gave the militants the signal, like, 'Come on, we're one of you, off on a ride — don't upset us *'girls'*!'

We loaded ourselves up, circumnavigating the problem areas. There was a group on Facebook which posted the coordinates of separatist checkpoints and their location in real time, posting things like:

278. Blown-up bridge in Halytsynovka.

271. New checkpoint in Donetsk, Primorskaya street, at the turn off to Khoroshevo.

273. Donetsk, at least one grenade launcher located in the bushes underneath the electric pylon, information still reliable as of one hour ago.

Updates followed every hour. No matter how run off my feet I was, I would enter fresh data into the group myself. The Yandex traffic app would also give helpful updates: whenever there was a checkpoint, if every car was checked, traffic would slow down, and a snake of cars would build up. For us, an ordinary sat-nav and a traffic map were enough to successfully circumvent any danger.

Even if we got searched, there was nothing on us that was a cause for worry. Well, apart from the vegetables, pasties, and cabbage rolls, of course. Maybe it looked like us girls had too little on us to be taking to market? Even then, there was nothing incriminating on our phones, something I took special care over. I would immediately delete any numbers after incoming calls; I knew the most important numbers by heart, and my address book was filled with contacts (in Russian) like *'2 l of milk for Tuesday'* and *'cabbage 4 uncle Grisha'*. I immediately uploaded photos and videos onto my home laptop, and if there was any 'compromising information' on my phone, then it was hidden in a sneaky little folder which, without knowing the name, could only be found with hardware diagnostics (thanks to Don's computer wizardry).

The core of our volunteer group remained in Dnipro, though

the girls had left the residential school. One day, they were visited by a delegation of local 'dignitaries' who offered them accommodation in the centre of town — in the Jewish cultural centre. Without hesitation, they agreed, and now Oksana would sit on the phone and sort through ammunition under the curious gaze of children with their little ginger side curls. The people who came to visit the centre (which felt like) one hundred times a day were surprised at first by their new neighbours, but everyone soon got used to it. It was just a sign of the times: Crimea and Rome had fallen, everyone was living cheek by jowl, the rabbis were serving in the Right Sector (a far-right nationalist paramilitary movement), and civil activists were sleeping on sofas in the synagogues.

A day later, we drove by Dnipro, loaded ourselves up to the brim, and quickly rushed off to the Ukrainian army positions, where we threw bales and boxes of uniform at them or gently unloaded cases with binoculars and optics and hurried home, covering the seats with a tarpaulin and empty banana boxes.

Everything was going so well, so it was very, very unfortunate that we managed to get caught out by one little detail.

* * *

"Tanya, stop, we're lost."

"Calm down, we can't have got lost. We're nearly home, this is our neck of the woods."

"Stop."

We had been driving in no particular direction for seven kilometres already. In a situation like ours, seven kilometres is a lot. To our left stretched endless rows of crops with sparse undergrowth. To our right, the fields of young sunflowers turned into fields of maize; not a living soul was to be seen, neither oncoming nor behind us. Evening fell.

If I were writing a horror story, then this short phrase, 'Evening fell', would have been intended to make the reader's hair stand on end. Well, that or make the reader's toes curl, which was happening to me right then, because when the sun begins to set, we become a target. After dusk we would become easy prey, the bottom link on the food chain, a nice bonus for anyone with a rifle, as they could now call dibs on an as-yet 'unclaimed' car, delivered by God unto the needy.

From time to time, I restarted the satnav and checked my phone; in vain, since there was still no network coverage. A lone dot blinked on the screen in the middle of a field, as the satnav showed no roads or directions. Tanya unfolded the map once more, trying to determine our location. However, the landscape which stretched before us did not correspond in any way, shape, or form to the marks on the paper. According to our calculations, we were supposed to have gone through Mezhove and joined the highway after Makiivka. What most definitely was not on the map were the miles of maize fields intersected by a cobbled road.

We drove through the fields on a wide, two-lane road which should not have been there, and it was paved with quarried stone. The second we felt the wheels give out a solid 'brrrr', instead of the usual whirr over the ground, we braked so hard that we nearly went through the windscreen. The paving was old, and had contracted over time, but it was surprisingly neatly fitted. I had seen something like it before in Lviv, and also in Kyiv, where we were taken on a school trip. These were no modern, prefab factory slates, but hand-hewn stone, which was fitted together so flush that even a razor blade would not pass through the join.

"Did you know that we had this sort of thing here?"

"Are you joking? I've never even heard of it."

I could not sit still, turning around again and again, before turning to face behind me. The road seemed to melt away behind us, engulfed in a thick fog that sank upon it, not like a solid wall, but in wispy horizontal strips that parted in the air like eggwhite in milk. Fogs like this can make you believe in unicorns. We sailed through this milky calm like the Flying Dutchman;

even if I were lacking in any sort of imagination, I still would have said that this was not about to end well.

I thought about the last 'valve', as we called the checkpoints, when we gave the boys cigarettes, a tub of homemade sausage preserved in lard, and a case of mineral water. I also thought about how they received us quite absent-mindedly, rather practically, rather than their usual gratitude:

"Ah, what do we have here? We'll have that then."

Thinking back, one of the soldiers might have had a chevron with an eagle on it, and now I think — well, what if it was an eagle? It was the symbol for the Berkut, the special police unit known to torture Ukrainian citizens. I thought about the local taxi driver at the exit, shouting at them because they would not let him pass, whereas we were waved on through, and they even gave us some basic directions. Only there never was a left turn after two kilometres.

"Stop! Oh, damn, stop! Crap, it's too late, they've caught us. You'd better pray now."

The road took an abrupt turn, and we burst onto a separatist checkpoint, practically landing on them. For a moment there was still hope that it could have been one of ours, but even in the dusk it was clear that the flag on the checkpoint had three stripes, not two. We had arrived.

"Quiet now, don't panic."

We automatically slowed down, turned off the headlights and the lights inside the car. I kept my passport and documents in sight, opening them up on my Donetsk residence permit for convenience's sake. Tanya would be the one to speak, as I would be too afraid.

"Guys, don't shoot, we're just lost! We were taking our goods to the market and then got lost!!", shouted Tetiana as soon as we stopped at the DIY barrier.

We had three — no, four — barrels bearing down on us. We were lucky that we were not shot right there by the entrance.

"Get out the car; hands behind your head."

A while ago, back in May, I asked Borysovych what we should do if we ever got captured.

"By yourself, or with someone else?", he asked.

"How about by myself?"

"If you're by yourself, cry. Just burst into tears straight away, till there's snot bubbling out your nose, until your whole face is swollen. When they beat you, try to pee yourself immediately. And cry."

It's easier said than done, bursting into tears. The tears did not come; from fright, clearly, because this was no ordinary checkpoint. We had four Chechens aiming their weapons at us, on a road that did not exist.

It was either Jamil or Shamil who undertook the interrogation, I did not catch the name. He asked us in broken Russian who we were and why we were allowed through the Ukrainian side, since no one else was allowed on this road. Muddling her words from the nerves, Tanya explained that we were not up to anything at all, that we were supposed to be carrying vegetables from Donetsk to three locations today and got lost on the way back. We did not know why they let us through, she explained; maybe it was to mess with us. We had asked them the way and then they told us, *"Go straight ahead"*.

As an alibi, we had a folder with invoices in it. Being paranoid, I take these things seriously, and before every mission I print out a route list and the necessary receipts, all with stamps, signatures on various forms. The lads had made me around twenty different ones, mostly from ATB supermarkets. What else? Our phones had been wiped, and we did not have any tablets on us. There was nothing in the car that would suggest any military involvement. There were two dirty cooking pots, but that could easily be explained, there were boxes for cucumbers, and a plastic tub for the berries.

"Huh, what?"

I had got lost in thought and had not heard what they were asking me.

"I'll ask you once again. Where did you turn off after Zuyevka?"

"Zuyevka? What do you mean? We didn't go through Zuyevka."

"Well, she says that you did", he said, pointing at Tanya.

"Well, I don't know, she knows better than I do, she's the one driving. We were supposed to come out on the other side, towards Donetsk. I'm telling you, we're lost, the satnav broke."

"Give me the satnav."

I handed it over in a flash, knowing that since the recording function had been disabled, it could not have tracked our route. We turned it on, and 'Solomon Samsonovych', the voice of the satnav, did not fail us. What a guy.

"Goddammit!", he thundered, in Ozzy Osbourne's voice. "Holy shit, I can't find any satellite connection. We've crossed into the bloody combat zone."

"What the fuck?!"

"Sorry, that was an accident, we just installed a programme where the satnav speaks in different voices. It couldn't find any signal, not for a while now, something's broken."

"Oh yeah?"

Shamil slowly pulled out a knife. In general, he did everything particularly slowly, that was how he spoke, and moved, as if he had an eternity in reserve. The knife was huge, like a machete, and in one swift movement, the Chechen clove our Solomon in half. Then he turned to Tanya.

"I am now going to cut your right breast off with this knife. Then I am going to play football with it, all over the Donbass. You got me?"

It was at this point that I burst into tears for real and threw myself onto Tanya's neck, because that was the point where she lost it. She did not give two hoots about his threats, to put it mildly.

"Now you listen here, you evil little bastard! I'm going to

smash your face in, and fucking kill your wife!" — that was our Tanya.

"Don't listen to her, she doesn't want to do that!" — that was me.

"I'm going to kill you, you bitch!" — from the paramilitary.

Then the phone rang. At the sound of it, every living thing in a hundred-metre radius froze and stared at me. To cheer Don up, the day before I had asked him to record a 'rough and tough' ringtone for his contact on my phone, that none of my other contacts would have. Don growled, said *"Go on then"*, and took my phone away for half an hour. As it turned out, the phone now was playing the sound of a muezzin calling people to morning prayer. When I first heard it, I had to sit down.

"Yeeeeemeeeeheeeuuuuummneyeheeee!"

"What is that?" asked the disorientated *ikhtamniet.*[11]

The ringtone repeated itself.

"It's for me. They're phoning me back at the warehouse."

"Answer it", he said, pointing his knife towards the speakerphone button.

My dear Roman had called, and I had saved his number in my phone as 'Proletarka Warehouse'.

"Hello, how may I help?"

There was the shortest of pauses. One time, before the war, the lads had asked me why I did not switch to speaking *russki* when anyone ever addressed me in Russian. Jokingly, I answered that was my little code. If I ever got kidnapped and my kidnapper was holding a knife to my throat, I could warn my friends by speaking in Russian. Surely, he could not have remembered? It looks like he had, our little genius.

"Girls, where have you got to? Why haven't you reported to

---

11 Something like a 'little green man', this term is used pejoratively for Russian-backed paramilitaries based on Ukrainian soil. It comes from the Russian *'ikh tam niet'*, meaning, 'they aren't there'.

any of the delivery points? Why is the car not at the warehouse? What's happened to the berries? Where are you?"

"I'm sorry boss, they've stopped us in…"

A blow to the hand, and the phone flew onto the ground. The militants sat us under a tree and went to search the vehicle. Tetiana sat there silently, wound tight as a string. I kept on blubbering. Was it worth even stopping now, when I was doing it so well? I was not sure if I would be able to start bawling my eyes out again. I put my head on my friend's lap for comfort, and her trousers soon darkened with tears. As far as I could tell, my nose had completely swollen up, like it should be.

"Forgive me."

I barely heard her through my sobbing.

"Forgive you? For what?"

"We won't make it out of here. I've left the stickers in the car."

I used to think that the phrase, 'speaking with a dead man's lips', was just a metaphor. It is not, in fact. It refers to that sensation when you speak and your lips move, but you cannot feel them.

"Where?"

"Stuck in the sun visor."

A week ago, we received a delivery in Dnipro, a box with national symbols in it. Bracelets, flags, ribbons, coloured blue and yellow like the Ukrainian flag, alongside black and red scarves, bandanas, and bumper stickers, after Stepan Bandera's flag. There was also a roll of stickers in the shape of a heart, with the logo, 'I help the Ukrainian army' on it. We were even joking about them, that having them on us was akin to suicide. Tetiana wanted to take a few of them to Donetsk, to surreptitiously stick on pensioners' bags on public transport, which I categorically banned her from doing.

We handed out flags at the military positions; they were practically tearing them out of our hands. The military equipment of the Ukrainian army often had no identifying markings, and after several incidents in which they had opened fire on their own side, the boys were begging us to give them flags, or at least something blue and yellow. Bracelets and other souvenirs also went like hot cakes, but the stickers had to be thrown away. After all, we were not *that* desperate to get ourselves killed.

Yet now I was not so sure.

I sat up straight and wiped my face. The tears instantly dried up. I did not think it would end like this. I wonder how many millions of people had said the same thing to themselves before they died. It is probably the most popular 'endnote' out there.

"Tanya."

"God, oh God, oh God, forgive me."

"Tanya."

"Huh?"

"I have a grenade in my jacket. I can… right now, you understand? Just for us, that's a guarantee. Or I can throw it at them, there's only four of them, but there's no guarantee of, well… What if it doesn't reach them? Then it'll just end up being a very long end for us. Let's have a think, when they come back together."

We fell silent, watching the car. After all, what was the hurry? The separatists were pulling boxes out the back and had brought a jack to take the wheels off, then went to the boot. I had forgotten how much rubbish we had accumulated there. Oh, they found my pink makeup bag, I had been looking for that, and my hoe. The broken carcass of my poor old truck glared at us, and it was obvious that it would never leave here.

Suddenly one of the goblins stood up, a bottle of my cherry wine in his hands. I wanted to make a classic homebrew with the first cherries of the season, but I simplified the recipe that I had found on the internet. I stuck the cherries in a two-litre plastic bottle, added some sugar, a little water, but instead of leaving it in a cool, dark place, I wrapped it in foil as 'thermoregulation', wrapped it up with some duct tape to keep it together, and stuck it in the spare wheel compartment. I assumed that the cherries would ferment more quickly from the constant, uniform movement, and the warmth of the car. In theory, the bottle should have been taken out after three days, but then I forgot about it. How long had it been on us? It cannot be alcoholic any longer — it would be more like a nuclear bomb by this point. And now this monkey is about to detonate the bomb.

"Stop!" I screamed in Ukrainian without thinking about the consequences. "Stop, don't touch it! It's about to explode! *It's about to explode!*" I added in Russian.

A second, and then everyone was on the floor, apart from me and Tetiana. Another second, and we were on the ground, with four rifles fixed upon us. A third second — ugh, why am I so unlucky?

"It's just wine! It's gone off, you mustn't touch the bottle!" I tried to say, at the same time recoiling away from the muzzle aimed straight at my stomach. *"It's wine!"*

Shamil lifted me to my feet in one motion and shoved me towards the boot.

"Open it."

Jesus, Mary, Mother of God… OK, fine, fine. Breaking my nails, I took off the duct tape and foil and tried to take out the cork. The lid was stuck tight. Was it hot in here, or what? There I was, hands slipping on the plastic, damp with nervous sweat. I tried to turn the lid, to no avail.

By that point, Tetiana could not stand it any longer, saying, "Let me try!", took it, and in one go twisted the top off the bottle.

The second she did so, a stream of red lava burst forth. Who knew that a two-litre bottle could have so much potential? We could have made a dozen films about a chainsaw massacre, and there would have still been some of that liquid left. In a flash, the car, the tree, the maize, the separatists, and all of us from head to toe were covered in blood the consistency of syrup — anyone who had not dived for cover. In fact, no one had taken cover; on the contrary, they had all come to have a look at the free show we were putting on for them.

The witnesses to the Big Cherry Bang froze, stiff as a corpse, and said nothing. A juicy, cherry spirit hovered in the air, and the last drops of cherry rain fell upon the grass. This would have been an ideal moment to throw the grenade, but I stood there, then ran about in circles like the rest of them, hoping to the very bottom of my heart that this was a dream.

Yet at the very next second the moment was lost, for we found ourselves no longer alone at the checkpoint. Two military trucks came down the turn-off, just like we had done before them.

* * *

It became very crowded around us. I understood that the commander of the militants who had stopped us had arrived. Even the Chechens could not explain what was going on here, although who could?

I watched the scene as if I were out of my body. It is said that this is a form of psychological protection, where the amount of stress which you undergo within a certain time frame becomes too overpowering, and you suddenly realise that all is vanity, vanity of vanities, and that nothing matters in the face of the Universe: not your miserable little life, its duration, or your last thoughts.

The timespan of my existence went from years to seconds the moment I put my hand in my pocket and fingered the metal 'tendrils' I found there. The pull ring slipped onto my thumb, like a wedding ring.

Well, what are we waiting for? urged an inner voice. Don't be afraid, it's not going to hurt. Yeah, you've got it. Here, let the boss come a bit closer, we might be able to get him too.

Maybe a UFO will fly in too and whisk me and Tanya off to a safe and well-fortified spaceship. I will count on a miracle till the very end.

In the meantime, the commander was barking at the local militants. That or he was just talking to them, you could not tell with the jarring language they were speaking in. Soon some of the separatists started unloading wooden boxes out of the military truck, and the rest turned to us. A few of the men took out their phones to take a selfie, with us in the background. A few others just gawked at us, like monkeys at the zoo.

"Come on, come on! We gotta capture this!" rang about my ears.

"Hello, girls."

Who was this old bloke? Before me, in a tarp flak jacket with no chevrons and a strip of red duct tape on his sleeve, dirty, stubbly, smelly, and a little older, stood the commander of the goblins. It was Komar. Oh, my dear Universe, you certainly do have a terrible sense of humour.

"I wasn't aware that you sold cucumbers."

"I wasn't aware that you spoke Chechen."

"*Khan kha.* It's Avar. My mother is from Dagestan."

We fell silent. It was one of those pauses which last a lifetime. I had no idea what to say to this man. Should I ask him how he was? Perform an exorcism? Spit in his eyes?

"Why is it that every time I think of you, I always think of cherries? And now we've got ourselves a cherry jam."

"It's wine. But I don't think you need to be thinking of me."

"Yes, you're right. But I see no reason to detain you. Get yourselves out of here immediately, you've caused too much trouble. And take your hand out of your pocket."

"With your permission, I'm going to keep it in my pocket. Tanya!"

Tetiana did not need to be told twice. In an instant, she was in the car, without even a backwards glance at the boxes left on the road. I snatched back my passport and documents that Komar held out to us. It was time to get out of there.

I would think about this incident tomorrow; on Monday; after Christmas. The gods were probably getting bored and wanted to make a little fun for themselves. Who am I, not to laugh at their jokes?

Tanya did not speak. She drove, clenching her teeth, with only one pair of headlamps on. She was staring intently at the road and repeatedly shrugged her right shoulder as if trying to drive away an invisible fly.

Nobody stopped us after that, and we got back on the main road about twenty minutes later. Before turning off, before anyone would see, we slowed down and threw out that roll of stickers. Then we joined the flow of traffic, got stuck behind a lorry, and overtook a minibus. It was an ordinary civilian *marshrutka*, with dirty windows and a banner with the logo 'Shakhtar Donetsk' on the windscreen, ferrying people to their evening shift.

It was only then that I sat back on my seat and felt that I actually had a back. My friend also exhaled.

"What do you think… Does this make any sense?" Tanya said.

"What we're doing, you mean?"

"Yes."

"I don't know. Actually, this probably doesn't make any sense at all."

"But we're not going to stop, are we?"

"Me, no, definitely not. We don't always choose the paths we walk on."

"Some of them choose us, right?"

"Yes. But Tanya, I'm on my own here. You have a daughter, so think carefully whether you need this."

We then drove on in silence, and I thought my companion was finished with the conversation.

"They raped my baby girl in a basement, three of them at a time. I took her to a psychiatric hospital, in Vinnytsia. We'll be there for another six months, at least. She's having panic attacks."

"I didn't know."

"No-one knew. And don't tell anyone either, ok? Listen, let's sing something. Here's one: *The rye ripens, ripens…*"

"Come on, I'm tone deaf and I can't sing."
"Don't care. *The glad guests...*"

The rye ripens, the reapers reap,
The glad guests head on home...

CARNELIAN

LOVE AND STUFFED CABBAGE ROLLS

In Donetsk there was once a psychic who also worked at the city's Hospital No.1 for infectious diseases as a health assistant (actually, maybe it would be better to say there was once a health assistant who also did psychic readings). Auntie Zina was in the circle of my grandmother's closest friends, and regularly went to her Saturday seances where they would dissemble, at length and with gusto, the polished bones of every inhabitant of our district. When in the mood one time, the old lady told us the secret to her success as a clairvoyant: reading people's medical histories.

Before her sessions she would read her clients' patient notes (which indicated their age, marital status, and diagnosis) and this would greatly increase the accuracy of her predictions.

"You mean to say that extra-sensory perception doesn't exist, that it's all a lie?"

"Well, not quite. It's both a lie and not a lie. It's that you see one thing and say another."

"How's that?"

"Take death, for instance. You can tell straight away when someone's going to die soon. But are you really going to tell them? Or, look at photos of dead people; it's like the portraits of the dead have faded. Alive people will shine in their photos, they shine in a certain spot, near their head, whereas the photos of other people have turned dark. It's clear that they've all followed different paths, and these faded ones no longer exist on this earth. Or it's like their arms and legs have been eaten away in the photo, dissolved, do you see?"

"No."

"Never mind, you'll learn. It's easy to tell apart the dead. It's harder to read the living. They come to you with their troubles, and you just know that no-one else is to blame for it all. They're the ones who are to blame, they've made their own bed and now they have to sleep in it. But is this what they want to hear when they come to me? I have to make something up! I feel sorry for them, especially the women. They're all unhappy. They're knocking at the wrong doors leading to the wrong places. Some woman will come to me, wanting to get married to this particular man, and I look, and say, 'He's not the one, he doesn't want you. Why chase after people who don't want you? No good will come of it, you're only going to cry over him, you'll become an old nag, you'll bear sickly children…' But who's going to hear this? No-one will listen."

How many years had it been since then — ten? Zina, short for Zinaida, was already long gone, having died in a fire. A few flats in her building went up in flames; two whole families died from carbon monoxide poisoning. The official inquiry put the cause of the blaze down to a faulty boiler, but people around said that the witch was the one who set the fire.

She had been forgotten already. I still don't believe in fortune-tellers, looking for that clandestine medical history file in each one of their predictions. I do not trust photographs.

Nowadays there are a lot of photos around Donetsk. I go to the bus-stop to read the latest notices. Every lamppost on Panfilov street is covered all over with posters of missing persons; walking beneath them was like walking past a grotesque cavalry parade, spears held high, under the stern gaze of dozens of eyes. Young and old, male and female, the posters of the missing were pasted one on top of the other, each one with the words: *'Have you seen this person? Not seen at home since…'*.

Look, this old man looks familiar, and I am sure I have seen that girl before… The stacks of notices were updated every day, some photocopied, some written by hand, others printed in colour and made up like proper advertising posters.

The faces on the posts turn white and fade away within the day. If by morning their facial features are still clearly discernible, by evening the faces become a pale oval, framed with hair… Auntie Zina, I know what this means, but I still don't believe you.

The city was full of rumours about 'death lists' for Ukrainian patriots, but hand on heart, I doubted their existence. I believe that people were being taken off and killed, not because of any list, but out of envy, or due to a loose comment. Maybe the victim became the unwitting witness of an unfortunate event, or got a new car or a new phone. I say this because the guys and I were leaving Donetsk twice a week, and I saw no blockades, no 'red' or 'white' fronts like in the Civil War a hundred years ago. The Ukrainian authorities had left, the Russians still had not arrived, and whatever had formed in the interim did not live up to the status of a republic, not even a banana republic. And why would the local mafia need any lists of people to kill anyway?

Even before the war the police had not been very helpful. Now, they were totally absent. Formal criminal proceedings had to go to Mariupol, but what was the point? No-one was going to chase anyone up, neither through official channels nor through old connections. Moreover, the old connections had all been lost, thanks to the mud that had bubbled up from the bottom of the mire, wiping out our old systems. It's like when someone 'finds' some nice new wheels somewhere — that was now our reality. You 'find' the car in the field, wipe the blood off it, and ride it back home, to your mother's and neighbours' delight.

Just yesterday, an acquaintance from a Kyiv insurance company called to investigate the situation as well as have a long-distance shoulder to cry on. Over one hundred of their vehicles had ended up in Ukraine's 'grey zone' near the conflict and could not be brought onto unoccupied territory. What should they do?

"Nothing; hide them. Just let them sit in some garage, it'll blow over soon."

"You think it'll be over soon?"

"Without a doubt."

Oh, how I wish I was actually without a doubt. It is just that active people and passive people do not get along. Passive people were happy to put up with these posts covered by funeral shrouds of missing persons' posters. These were the uneasy people stepping into a bright future as a Russian citizen; they owned the shops now accepting roubles; they put up with the hot ashes of a 'drained' city; they had in the drawer a set of keys for thirteen flats whose owners have asked them to water the plants till they return. The active people, like me, were not happy with this and hoped for something better. It can't last *that* long. That would be unfair.

It was not a metaphor, calling it a 'drained' city. I have always had a hard time with metaphors, like my Ukrainian teacher, Halyna Stepanivna, told me, who said I would be better off 'taking minutes, not writing stories'.

At first, children and men started disappearing. Public places fell silent and empty; the grass in the stadium grew tall without footballers running over it every week. The markets and newsstands closed; the bread stall on the corner lasted the longest, until the day finally came that instead of bread, we saw only shutters in the window. Cars disappeared, and even taxis stopped going through our neighbourhood. You could walk right down the middle of the highway if you wanted, backwards and with your eyes closed. Still, the lonely pedestrians kept behind the railings on the kerb, scuttling from shadow to shadow.

I was burdened with a dozen new responsibilities: drawing water from the pump, as much as possible; filling up buckets and casserole pans as a reserve; going round the houses I was acting as caretaker for, turning on the lights, opening the curtains, treading the path from the gate to the door, so it looked like someone was living there; and feeding the cats.

We now had seven cats and a slobbering bulldog called Bucks. Bucks was afraid of doors, the sound of the toilet flushing, laughter, and sudden movements. He would involuntarily shit himself from fright, which would end up frightening him even more, and then he would skitter around the flat before huddling on my feet, after which he would keel over on his side and play dead. As such, we could now only walk slowly and evenly round the flat, like when you're wading through water, and Tanya would place the saucepan lids on a special felt square to muffle the clang of the lid.

Several neighbours who had gone away for a few weeks brought us their pets to look after, and I did not refuse them (don't ask me why). I wanted to say, 'no', right up to the last minute, but for some reason I said, 'yes'. I need to go to a psychologist to work on my boundaries, clearly.

Alongside the cats and dogs, which were at least quiet, I would host a crew of my grandmother's confidantes, who conversely never shut up. My Baba Olya had practically moved into her companion's detached house, where they, the four Mohicans, made a shelter in the loess and now spent their days awaiting the shelling, drawing pictures of bullets and scaring each other with horror stories. Whispers started going around that Donetsk residents were now no longer eligible for Ukrainian pensions. No matter how much I tried to convince the oldies that there was no way that this could ever happen, that their pensions would persist like a golden statue to Chairman Mao, they would not listen to me, and panic ensued.

We could not work out what to do with our workshop: close it? Move it? Where, and how? It was not a pair of socks you could chuck in your rucksack and be off with it; we had heavy equipment. The machinery was expensive, too, and I had not paid off the loans for it yet. What is more, who needed our glasswork anymore? Plywood was now in demand in this city, not stained glass. Once again, what could we live on? Our reserves were not bottomless: we could last a month maybe, but what next?

'Get out of here!', screamed my conscious and subconscious awareness.

'Just wait a bit,' whispered the devil on my shoulder.

Meanwhile, we divided the shop into two parts: we moved the equipment, crucibles, and drawing boards into one half of it and locked it. The guys set up an automobile service station in the other and did everything, from changing number plates to a complete re-servicing of vehicles, no questions asked. Even when lads brought in — at first timidly, and then more openly — cars to us with obvious signs of combat damage, or paid for spare parts with cases of duty-free whisky from the airport, or even when they brought us work in the middle of the night and took it away by dawn — no questions were asked.

Roman became one with the lathe. He would fashion dovetail joints, mufflers, mounts, brackets; he did everything under the radar, sometimes for soldiers that we knew, and sometimes for people I had never seen before, who would sometimes turn up in person with money for the metal, or instead send us silent couriers with a package in their hands.

At first, and second glance, this all looked like a Brownian motion. Everyone was buzzing around, flitting between panic and apathy, hope and despair, stubbornly sticking to their habits and rituals. Time to come to work; time for coffee; time for a cigarette break; time for lunch. Even when the next garage over was shot at and went down in flames, we still stopped for lunch.

There is an old Japanese saying: 'Quickly is just doing something slowly without stopping'. Things were not going slowly for me. I was doing everything on the hoof; with things sometimes not going to plan and leaving me furious. My favourite phrase during the July of 2014 was: 'Sorry, I'm going as fast as I can'. I wanted to believe that we were approaching the finish line, although sometimes doubts crept in: 'What if we were just going in circles, like this is some bloody hamster wheel? What if this isn't a matter of weeks, but of months, or years?' 'Phew, hold your tongue…'

Sometimes Borysovych would grab me whilst I was on the phone, taking it off me and sitting me behind a bowl of borsch, which I would eat right to the last drop, under the hypnotising gaze of that old tyrant and of Tanya, her arms akimbo. Those two had found a common language in cookery, and they made a tasty borsch.

* * *

I could hear the creaking of the old swing from afar. We had grown so unused to sounds from the playground, that I straightaway recognised the drawn-out squeaking. Who was causing it? Should I go look?

A figure of a woman was perched on the swing, and it was immediately obvious that she was too big for the child's seat. She literally spilled out of its iron frame, which mercilessly dug into her flesh. The woman, however, paid no attention to the awkward way she was sitting. In a melancholic manner, she would push off from the ground, fly up a metre, then brake with her foot against the railing, and once again stick her heels into the ground. Whoosh — scrape — squeak. Whoosh — scrape — squeak. She obviously was not embarrassed by the fact that the swing had woken up the whole neighbourhood.

Hang on — that's Lida, our favourite milkmaid! We would buy milk and cheese from her every Saturday. It was Lida, who stood out from the other market sellers like a seagull among pigeons. It was Lida, who always had a snow-white tablecloth, a clean apron, and disposable gloves. She would be sold out of milk within half an hour, since a queue of regular customers would always gather at her stall before she turned up. Her kilo-blocks of cheese were neatly numbered and initialled for each of her customers, and every jar of soured cream was decorated with a little rose carved out of butter. Our cheese was labelled 'OI', after Olha Ivanivna, and, if she was in a playful mood, Lida would draw a shamrock on it, alluding to my 'elvish' origins.

For a long time, we merely exchanged hellos and a few words about the weather, until one day I was running late by a whole hour, and she waited for me. I then helped her bring in the empty vat to her car, and we sat with a coffee and got talking.

It turned out that our milkmaid had lived practically her whole life in Donetsk and was as far from being a village girl as a qualified interpreter and translator could be. She had a prestigious profession, a swish flat, and unquestionable authority within the translation and interpreting sphere. When it came to her career, everything was going swimmingly. When it came to her personal life, things were hard: her status meant an empty bed, weekends in front of the telly, and New Year celebrations as the only singleton in her friendship group.

There was nothing wrong with her — she was just unlucky. She either came across married men, or people in open marriages, or people who just wanted a companion who would pay for their own meals in the restaurant and to pay for their half of the holiday. She thought to herself: 'I should get a cat, or adopt a cat, what else can I do now…'

Her and Petro's relationship took off practically before her eyes. One day they are meeting in a seminar, her sat in the booth and him working as the sound technician; the sound keeps dropping off the headphones and she keeps having to interrupt and repeat the translation. The next day, Petro is already waiting outside of her office with a bunch of flowers. Three days later, he proposes and takes her to meet his mother, who says that 'she has never met a girl like Lida in her life'. The mother was 'very friendly', apparently.

"It was like I was hypnotised; you get me? That's how fast everything moved. We had a wedding, Petro paid for everything, and the guests were mostly from his side. Only my goddaughter from Kharkiv came, and some colleagues. I asked my girlfriends, but for one reason or another none of them could come: one was on holiday at the seaside, another had broken her leg. When I threw the bouquet, I didn't see a single familiar face; only strangers."

After a week's honeymoon the newlyweds moved into Petro's place, in a village near Donetsk. The cottage and the estate formally belonged to his mother, and though she lived with her son, Petro was considered the homeowner.

It was a large, two-story house, but it was in need of repair.

The wedding money went on making their 'nest': the young couple painted the ceilings, stuck up wallpaper, changed the windows, but there wasn't enough for a bathroom and new furniture.

"No worries," said Petro. "We'll take out a small loan, we'll pay it off easily."

They took out a small loan for the kitchen, then another for the bedroom furniture. Then the opportunity arose to buy off the twenty acres of land behind the house; then they paid for the installation of gas pipes and a well, because the water in the village was often switched off at the mains and had a distinct metallic taste. Then the mother got ill, a stroke or something, and had to undergo expensive tests at the regional hospital.

A year later their oldest, Bohdan, was born. A wonderful little boy, happy and inquisitive, but unfortunately, he had coeliac disease and so had to go on a strict diet from an early age. The child needed plenty of care, so Lida did not come off maternity leave. She had to forget about translation. Moreover, three more children 'came along': Olenka and Mariika, and the younger one, little Serhii.

In a family meeting they decided to sell her flat from before she got married. The resulting funds were enough to pay off their debts and buy three purebred cows, ten Vietnamese potbellied pigs and two hundred ducklings.

"The land will always provide," said Petro. "Besides, no-one can go hungry when *salo* and milk is around."

They had no problem feeding their charges, and the plot around the house grew into a whole hectare, which they ploughed and sowed with beetroot and potatoes. (Oh, and don't think that Lida was the only one in charge of the garden — from time to time they would hire helpers, sometimes one, sometimes even two!!) The animal husbandry, looking after the house, the kids, and the household — that all fell on her shoulders.

I am ashamed to say that I gave in to my curiosity and went to visit the 'farmers'. I wanted to see what it was like there, in the house that had swallowed up a flat in Donetsk and ten years of this woman's labour. I also had to see the pigs; I could not miss that.

As Lida said, the mother-in-law was very friendly. She did not leave us alone for a second, telling us long stories about Petro's childhood with gusto. Lida was constantly having to excuse herself and go out, popping back in, and never finished her coffee. Plastic tubs of slop from the school canteen were brought in, which they would buy on the cheap. The tubs had to be emptied, washed, and returned to the delivery driver. The oldest two then ran home from school, and the father brought the youngest home from playschool. Petro sat next to his mother, pushed a bowl of grapes towards me, and then started peeling them with his fingers, removing the skin from every grape.

"Ah!", laughed Larysa Viktorivna, that is, his mother. "Our Petro doesn't like the skin; he peels everything, cucumbers, tomatoes, peppers, everything."

I then got ready to leave, and Lida hurried off to the evening milking. Each cow provided around twenty litres of milk a time, three times a day. The fresh milk would be stored in the pantry, where the cream was also left to turn sour and where the curds would be separated, churning out fresh cheese.

"Lida, listen," I said, before I left. "Don't take offense at this, but what is going to protect you and your children?"

"What?" Lida looked at me, and I could tell from this look that we would thereafter no longer stay friends, though I knew I would still deeply respect this woman. "Here's the thing: I look after everyone here, the old crone, and Petro too."

I did not go back to the village, but Lida and I would still catch up. The mother-in-law was still unwell, Petro was still working at the company, the cows kept breeding, the plot kept growing, and the family too: after little Serhii came little Kolya.

We had not seen each other in recent times: Lida had not been at the market for half a year already. I was too busy to give her a call or go visit. Yet now, in the middle of the night, I find her right here in our yard — which, by the way, had been under shellfire.

"Good Lord! What are you doing here? Where are the children? Are you hurt?"

The creaking stopped, and two eyes looked up at me. If I were a poet, I would have said that they were eyes of true despair or something fancy. However, in our more prosaic world, I saw them as the eyes of a beaten-down dog whose tears have dried up, wondering only how best to tie a noose over the swing's crossbar.

"They threw me out."

* * *

"They didn't say anything to me, you get me?" she explained. "I never thought it could even happen. Everything was fine — Petro went to work, I did the chores, and his mother was in bed. Suddenly, my husband comes home from work before lunch, a time he never usually does. He says something to his mother and they leave the house, just waving at me, saying, 'See you in a bit!'. 'In a bit' means 'in a bit', right? What else would it mean?... They weren't gone long; three hours maybe. They come in and call me into the hall, and my mother-in-law says:

'Here's the thing, my daughter: I've sold the house and the farm. You have to understand that when the Banderite partisans come they'll kill us all. You've seen the horrors on television... Basically, my daughter, we're going to Russia, beyond the Urals, I have relatives there, they've invited us to live with them.'

'Who's we? Petro? Petro, say something!'

Petro said nothing. He stood there, then muttered something under his breath, like 'Sort yourselves out!', and went into the kitchen.

'Larysa Viktorivna, I'm not going to Russia, and neither are the children.'

Larysa Viktorivna sighed a solemn sigh: 'Well, see for yourselves. I'll pray for you'."

Lida continued: "Can you imagine, she said that she would pray for us?! She then went off to pack her things with her son. I was left with the children, and we had to find somewhere to live the very next day, and I couldn't work out what to do. My head was as empty as a drum. I was pinching myself, asking myself if it was a dream. Then some neighbours were heading to Donetsk, and I asked if they could take me. I was trying to make a plan, maybe I could come to you and your grandmother's, we could talk. I don't have any friends, anyone… I came and saw the lights were off. So, I sat here on the swing. Forgive me, I don't really know why I'm here and what I want from you. Leave it. I'll go…"

"Stay," I replied. "Where are you going to go? You need people: whenever something bad happens, you should go find people. And don't look at the bar of the swings like that! Promise me, you won't look at a crossbar like that ever again. Shall I tell you, why?"

"Why?"

"Because if you hurt yourself your soul will be stuck here forever. No-one will be able to see you — you can see everything, but you won't be able to talk to anyone: you can't speak or get out the way. You'll be hanging from these swings for all eternity: till the end of the world, till after the swings are gone, till after Donetsk is gone too, when everything has been submerged by a great flood, and you will be tied to this hole here, like a dog tied on a leash. Is that something you want?"

"No."

"Amen, sister. Let's go have something to eat, and let's think how to get out of this shitty situation, or at least get something out of this…"

"…out of this shite?"

"You *are* vulgar, Lida. We shouldn't say shite, but 'life situation'. Come on, get up, you're squeaking like a rusty trolley. I have some *Napoleon* layer cake in the fridge. Let's hurry before it gets eaten."

* * *

We came in quietly, so that we wouldn't wake anyone up, and went straight to the fridge. The first thing I did was get out the bucket of fresh, home-grown eggs. We were lucky; we bought them half-price, although Tanya grumbled that we could have bought whole chickens for that price.

"Take this," I said, putting it in front of her. "Take them one by one, and squeeze each one as hard as you can, just crush it."

"What for?"

"Lida, that's just what you need to do. Put as much anger into each egg as you can. Pretend you're crushing eyes, instead of eggs. Try it."

Lida sat down hard on the stool and stopped a moment. Then she slowly reached out, took one egg and held it for a long time, thinking. Suddenly it exploded, spattering in all directions, ricocheting off the cupboards and all the casserole pans. Then again, and again, and again. She did not stop, squeezing them with all her might, tearing the yolk with her fingernails, smeared in it up to her elbows. The eggs blew apart in her hands, the shell flying out like confetti; the woman finished off the remains with her feet, mercilessly stamping on these budding chicken embryos. She howled, laughed, and at the end roared like a wounded she-bear, a noise that was terrible in its ungainly fullness, in its despair. I said nothing, wanting to become part of the wall, not letting a single movement, a single breath, reveal my presence. Only fools would try to distract a woman when she has gone for the kill.

She knelt on the floor in a yellow mass. She scooped it up with her hands, immersing herself in it, warming her hands in it like a huntress warms her hands in the entrails of a freshly-killed wolf. Finally, she came to, and it was only then she noticed me, it seemed.

"Thank you."

"No worries. Go clean yourself up, the water's running today. I've left some trousers, a T-shirt, and a towel. Go wash up, and we'll throw away these old clothes. You run in; I'll clean up."

There was a lot to do, but no matter: we would manage. The main thing was she did not put a noose around her neck today; she will have a bath and go to sleep instead. Tomorrow will be a new day.

We will need to find somewhere for them to stay. These sorts of blows can knock you off your feet, but when you are a mother of five, you have to get back-up. It will be painful, and she will cry herself through more than one pillow, but her children will be her support. They will survive together, help one another, and study, make their own families, and give birth to grandchildren. Only I will have to make that decision for her, because she is not able to do so today: she is alone, like a child, and she will go wherever you take her.

That is why I reached for the phone right in the middle of the kitchen, sitting in a puddle of egg that was drying before my eyes. It had dried so hard that I would not be able to chip it off with my teeth.

"Good evening, Borysovych. I haven't woken you up, have I?... Ha-ha. I will very much need you tomorrow morning, around five. You, and maybe three or four of the guys, the trusty ones. I'll need the truck too. I'll tell you what's going on..."

* * *

We arrived at their house at dawn. As I thought would be the case, after her bath the evening before, Lida fell upon the guest sofa and fell asleep, the sleep of the dead, and I did not hear the squeak of single bedspring. All seven cats lay around her, meaning I had my first good sleep in a long time, as I did not have to shove hairy little bodies off my chest all night.

In the morning, we were tempted not to rouse our guest, leaving us to do her dirty work ourselves, but I rejected this thought.

What would now happen when we cross this bridge would stay with her for the rest of her life. It would be a bitter memory that would poison the coming years, and would last a long time with phantom pain, but this was her chalice that she must drink to the last. Or not, we will see. Sometimes I get people wrong.

Lida opened the door with her key. No-one was there to meet her, as everyone inside was sleeping. We waited by the car. The woman was gone a long time, more than an hour, although the light shone through the windows of two rooms and we could see some movement. Then they came out: first Lida, with an infant in her arms; then Petro, with a rucksack and the smallest boy; finally, the three older ones, a bag for each of them. Little Bohdan pulled a suitcase on wheels, and the wheels got jammed in the grass. Larysa Viktorivna was the last one to slip out the house, and she stood there on the porch, wrapping a red towelling robe around her.

Lida sat down beside the driver, not looking at her husband. The children settled on wooden seats in the body of the truck, and Petro hesitated, not knowing where to put the baby, and in the end put him in the cabin.

"Alright, time to go," she said.

"Lida, are you mad?" I replied.

"What do you mean?" she said, looking at me in surprise.

"Right, let's write this off as a momentary lapse from the stress. You're leaving the house which you lived in for how many years? Ten?"

"Twelve."

"Twelve years, then, with five children on your hands and all you've got is hand luggage. Come on, let's take your things with us. We'll move you over comfortably."

"I don't need anything. I've taken all I need."

"Maybe you don't need it right now, but believe me, a bed and a TV never hurt anyone. Isn't that right, Petro?"

Petro clearly did not expect this turn of events. I had begun to get used to his way of speaking without opening his mouth, although I did not listen to what he said. You needn't pay attention to a man who has just thrown his five children out of the house with his own hands. Besides, four robust young men and an aggressive-looking Borysovych were standing behind me, who had already suggested burning this whole place down to the ground.

I expected Larysa Viktorivna to throw herself in front of us, but she only wrapped the robe tighter around herself and stepped back, pursing her lips. My grandmother called this type of mouth, a 'chicken's arse', and, if needed, I could shoot just as dirty a look back at her.

I sent the boys into the house to take what we needed. I thought that these pilgrims needed dishes, bedding, a washing machine, a fridge, a cot and a children's bath, toys, two bikes for the children and one for an adult, a laptop, a multicooker, and dozens of other things which caught our eye and which migrated into boxes and bags that we prudently had brought with us. We hurried with all our might, so as not to prolong the painful process for Lida, especially since the children in the truck began to whine, and the cows in the barn started mooing from the pain of not being milked, which made her suffer even more.

When the truck was full, I returned to the children and their mother, who was crying softly, watching the collapse of her life's project.

"You think I'm a fool, don't you? Do you think I really didn't know who I was living with?"

"You knew, of course. How could you not?"

"I knew all about him, from our first months together. Understand me…"

"You stayed because of the children?"

"Yes, but not in that sense. I did not stay with him *because* of the children — I got together with him in order to have any. They're so wonderful, they were all wanted; I was expecting them and loved them so much… and love them still. Who would I have had children with? I was already thirty when we met! He thinks he's won, that he's got the upper hand. God, they can take all their crappy possessions with them, the walls even, only let me take the children. If he hadn't handed them over, I wouldn't have gone anywhere. I would have gone with them, right to the ends of the Earth, even to those bloody Ruskies."

"You don't need to go to the ends of the Earth. I stayed up last night; I think we've found you a place to live in the meantime, in Kremenchuk. We'll go now, we'll show you."

"Why Kremenchuk?"

"Why not? It's a lovely city, you'll see. You'll like it. There's a great park there, and a river, and lots of jobs."

"What river?"

"The Dnipro! How's that for a river? You can go swimming."

"Hold on, but I don't have anything, bar a few thousand hryvnia on my card."

Always a fan of theatrics, Borysovych appeared at the window, having been eavesdropping at the door.

"Here," he said, holding out an envelope, "Take this. Your relative has shared the proceeds from the sale of the old hacienda with you. It'll definitely be enough to get you going."

"How? They're not the sort to pay you back; never, not in a million years!"

"That's because you don't know how to talk to them. You can reach anyone, if you know where to knock. Come on, let's get out of here."

At this, we set off.

* * *

It was all quiet in our garage, but I knew for a fact that Roman was there. This was because I had already checked all the other places that he could be in.

"Roman, love, can you hear me? Open up, I'm coming in!"

It was difficult to crawl in, because the door would only open twenty centimetres or so, no more. I squeezed in, once again thanking fate for my small stature, and found our genius with a sheet of iron in his hands. He grudgingly nodded at me, looking over the bullet-ridden plate.

"Hi. Do you know what this is?"

"Is it from a bulletproof vest?"

"Yep. Do you know what I used to puncture it?"

"A fork?"

"Almost. This hole was made by a Makarov pistol from twenty metres. This is from ten metres, you see? You could put your hand through the hole."

"Well, not my *whole* hand, maybe two fingers. Shoot it one more time from up close then give it to me. I'll make a nice base for a lamp out of it."

"If I shoot it from up close, you'll be making a lattice-work lampshade out of it."

"Where did you get it from?"

"This is the armour that our side has. I borrowed it from the boys to test bullets on it. They're given this like it's first-class gear, but it's actually third-class gear, fourth-class, if that's even possible. It's like psychological protection. There's more. Look."

Roman turned the plate over and slammed it against the heavy lathe. A dozen pieces were left on the table, the sheet having shattered like glass.

"It just crumbles into nothing. It goes straight into the body alongside the bullet, so you take in a load of fragments. The shrapnel shoots off in all directions."

"Have you let the boys know?"

"Yes, but what's the point? It's a drop in the ocean."

We fell silent for a bit.

"Did you want something?"

"Yes. I need to stay on your sofa tonight. If possible, I'll sleep now. It's bedlam at home."

Roman laughed briefly, puffing his cigarette.

"I know. I thought you'd come here earlier; we even made a bet with the boys on how long you'd last. If it means anything, I believed in you, I put it at five days. You've lost me three beers."

"Piss off, I've not slept since Tuesday, the baby's teething. I'll just sleep here, ok?"

"Go sleep already."

I would have even slept on the floor, since it was quiet and no-one cried on the other side of the wall. It was not that I did not sympathise with Lida and all her misfortune, but I thought that one day all my guests would leave, taking the cats and Bucks with them, and I would be left at home alone, able to freely walk from room to room, lie with a book on the floor, or grab a small porcelain cup, roast some coffee in a special frying pan with some grated garlic left on it, making only one portion, adding some caramel to the brew... and this could all take place in silence, without a single word said that day. Fanciful dreams of solitude beckoned me like the Holy Grail beckoned the pilgrim, and took flight.

I could not turn this family's life back into what it used to be, but I could help them with their future. My desperate cry for help on Facebook was answered by thousands of people, and the mass of sympathetic and even merely interesting comments had grains of something constructive in them. Lida was offered several options for housing; we turned down distant and depressing villages and offers to come live somewhere with 'no need for documents', and we settled on a little house in Kremenchuk, which I liked from the beginning. The mother of a friend of a friend had died, and it was very unfortunate, of course, but this friend of a friend had agreed to give away her mother's house for half the price if we could pay in cash by the end of the week and was waiting for us to prepare the necessary documents. The rest was a trifle, really: transport all their treasures, including the children, beds, and bicycles to Kremenchuk. Just the thought of the move made my eyes twitch. I could not drag it on any longer, however, and tomorrow we would start packing our things.

In the meantime, God save Roman and his couch, I will sleep in the workshop, where no-one can bother me till morning.

* * *

At first, I dreamt of a river; black, and deep, not like the shallow streams we have in these parts, with a black pine forest lining both banks. A whole flotilla of rafts was coursing down the river, and people were standing on each of them. They passed me like I was not there, not turning their heads, focussed on something important ahead which magnetically drew them towards itself.

Then I fought with a dragon; the large and lumbering beast blocked out half the sky, and I attacked him with a short sword, knowing that we were at a stalemate. He could not catch me, but I could not pierce his iron belly either. We collided and bounced off each other with a crash, and I desperately tried to keep two thoughts in my head: the first being that two people were needed to kill a dragon, it cannot be done alone; the second being, 'How would I poison it?' Should there be a chemical corrosive catalyst?'

'Eureka! I'll pour hydrochloric acid on him!' — I guessed, a moment before waking up.

"Oi, Roman!"

"Shush, what are you shouting about?" said Roman, raising himself up off the floor.

"We'll poison him!"

"Who?"

"The dragon. Oh, wait… it was a nightmare. Sorry, I woke you up."

But what was that? Although the dragon remained in my dream state, the sound of metal clanging remained in my waking state, and grew even louder. The walls of the garage were vibrating from the noise, like from an earthquake. It sounded like someone had tied a hundred sheets of metal to a chain and was dragging it across the tarmac, sparks flying.

"Let's run and see."

We dashed out of the workshop (it was good that I had fallen asleep in jeans and a jumper), and I quickly pushed Roman's wheelchair out onto the road, towards the source of this cacophony. We understood that it must be a procession of heavy equipment, maybe even tanks, and that could mean only one thing: our boys had entered the city! Finally, the offensive had begun, and this protracted nightmare could end. We could not believe that this intervention had happened in total secret, that no-one had let it slip. They were pressing in a ring around Slovyansk only yesterday, and the day before we were with scouts near Kramatorsk, and now they were already here, in our city.

"Jesus, my heart's about to burst! Let's take a breather, I can't run like this... Or not, don't stop, let's go, I can't miss this! I'll remember this for the rest of my life, my dearest Roman, what joy! I'm not crying, no, but let me hug you! My God, we've been waiting for this, why have you stopped, come on!"

We bounded out onto the avenue like we were raving mad, and I fell onto my knees in a bush on the side of the road, gasping for breath.

"Here they go! Look at them go, the beauties, my little bear cubs! Look how many of them there are, it's a whole army! Look, it's the commander's car with the flag! Over here, look, we're here! Our dear boys, I've waited so long for you!"

I am so happy. Dear God, how may I endure it and not just die of happiness here, right here on the tarmac?

"Glory to Ukra..."

A heavy hand clamped over my mouth, and I choked down a scream. They are here, right next to us, the first and second cars, and I finally see what Roman saw from afar. A flag. A pirate flag with a navy-blue cross on a red field. There is no blue and yellow on it. There are people in armour, waving their hands in response, and I push with all my might in an attempt to get up, to not be on my knees before them, and I bend in two from a sharp pain. It pierces my stomach and chest like a bolt of lightning, exploding somewhere behind my chest, and the bile rises up out of me and ends up on Roman's feet.

"This acid is disgusting," I thought, and for the first time in my life, I fainted from grief.

07.07.14

What did the city look like under occupation? You would not believe it, but no different. It looked the same as when it was unoccupied. Buses still went, people were still about, the shops were still open. Traffic jams at rush hour, and markets on Sundays.

Only now, when you tumble out of a July bus, 'sweating the seven sweats', as they say, you bump into soldiers. They politely let the passengers off, and then ram themselves into the cabin, using the butts of their rifles to push themselves in.

You grow used to walking along with your head down, looking at the tarmac under your feet. That, or you tilt your chin up and look at the roofs about; anything not to look at what is in between, twixt earth and sky, where rifles are all your eye catches. You see the safety clasp off and you stop dead when you see them casually turn towards you, following the line of fire across your chest, and you cannot help but wonder, 'Why is everyone so calm?'.

Why is no-one hitting the ground, head in hands? Why are they not swerving away from them as they walk? How are they able to pass through these clusters of green, practically nudging through them with their shoulders, not slowing down and continuing their conversations?

"Why are you stressing? They're not going to bother us, and won't bother them. It doesn't affect us, you get it?"

I needed to adapt to life in these new conditions. At first, I could not decide whether I wanted to even live anymore. I said to myself a hundred times that my value as a person and my personhood did not depend on external circumstances. What is inside is what counts, never mind other people's opinions. This acute longing, the hole in my chest, feeling orphaned — these were all the result of my personal problems and my unjustified expectations, and thus were my issues to deal with and mine alone. If the world happens not to live up to your preconceptions about it, then change your preconceptions, not the world.

Nobody called. None of the soldiers, although I hardly expected them to. Well, maybe I did a little, somewhere in my being, maybe a word or two along the lines of, 'We won't desert you'. However, my noble Ukraine said nothing, as if listening to itself ask — 'What's it like to lose a hand?' Was I just deceiving myself, and we in fact were not a hand, but an appendix? Were we gangrene, rotten flesh, something it would do better without? Maybe those who kept shouting that there was no-one here worth protecting were right? Was this grey land, generously ploughed and sown with bones and iron worth the blood being spilled to save it? Maybe the only thing left was to flee this plague house, and abandon the fools stuck here. I see the joy among my fellow citizens who hold up these pirate flags on every corner, I hear the words that we are now a 'republic'. If they are a 'new republic', then who am I as part of it? What am I to do alongside these 'republicans'? Run away without a backwards look. One ought not to seek the righteous in the steppes of Sodom — here every man is for himself, and no-one is for 'us'.

> *I peer into our tomorrow:*
> *'Tis but shadow and gloom*
> *And gloom and shadow, shadow and gloom,*
> *But gloomy water and a forest of doom.*

Vasyl Stus[12] — that old scrap-metal poet from the firepit knew everything about Donetsk, the old prophet: he was not afraid of any of *them*, he defeated them all with his glory, in a sense — but what was the sense in his victory, when Vasyl Stus is dead, and *they* are alive, their children are alive, and their grandchildren walk the streets? What would I have said to him, had I had the opportunity? Would I have told him to back down: back down, give up, live a normal life? Raise your son, run for the hills, to a safe place in the country, go fishing. Keep your head down, save your gene pool. Life will go on.

Well, or not.

Stuff your 'place in the country' up your arse! If I had ever met Stus, I would have told him to kill them all! Tear out their eyes, their throats; your death should be on the battlefield, where they cut you into twenty-one pieces, but your enemies should wet their deathbeds at the very thought of you. You should die in a way that no-one, not even those vermin, would dare say you had ever hung yourself. Sit up and laugh, laugh in their faces. Even if Ukraine no longer is around you, and all that is left is boundless and bare, even if it has become the lone and level sands of an Egyptian darkness, Ukraine will live on in your head, because Ukraine — is you.

I will 'back down' all right, you sons of bitches. I will 'back down' in such a way that you will tell your own godforsaken great-grandchildren to come after me.

---

12 Vasyl Stus was a Ukrainian poet and active dissident whose work was censored by the Soviet regime for his political views. He eventually died in a Soviet labour camp.

X

MILL SCALE

DEADHEADING

"Lida, get out from under
there. I have two pieces of news
for you, would you believe."
Lida was scrabbling on the floor,
trying to crawl out from under
the couch. Four children's legs
and a tail stuck out next to her.
"Hold on a second. Bucks is stuck,
he doesn't want to come out."
"I can empathise with him.
Go to the kitchen, kids, I've
got you some peaches."

199

The children flew out the room, and my friend and I sat on the sofa. The dog lurked beneath us, categorically refusing to leave his comfort zone.

"Lida, we're not going to get out of here by car, definitely not with all your things, or they'll demand so many bribes off us that it'd be cheaper to throw all this junk away."

"What do we do now, then?"

"We have to pack everything and take it to the post office right now. I know the manager there, he told me on the sly that this is the last day you can send anything by post. Basically, we have to send everything now. We'll then make our own way by train or bus, as it looks."

"Alright then. Let's go."

I am always surprised how quickly and submissively adults do what I tell them, and at the relief they feel in transferring the responsibility for decision-making onto me. The time for marvelling at this phenomenon would have to be saved for later, however; for now, the woman was busy getting the little ones ready, and my grandmother and I packed the boxes up. I did not know how many pieces of luggage they would allow us to take, under what conditions, and what Lida would do if her property did not make it to its destination. Then again, Lida herself might not make it to her destination, and it was better not to even think about that possibility.

We did it all in an hour. You would have thought that we had been burgled from the looks of the place, and even Borysovych gasped when he saw the bombed-out house with the mountains of clothes, pairless socks and torn boxes. I did not give him a second to look around, however, shouting:

"Hurry up! Throw it in the car, let's go! We don't have a second to spare!"

The sight with which we were met at the delivery office defied any stretch of the imagination. The warehouse was being stormed by a thousand-strong crowd; the queue stretched back roughly three hundred metres from the entrance. Who *wasn't* there? There were pensioners with bales and bundles of wares, old men carrying prams and car wheels. One woman, in tears, was stuffing mink coats into heavy-duty construction bags, whilst her companion packed them together with brown scotch tape. Someone was carrying office supplies and a huge, sixty-inch-screen television. Bundles of books and pillows were lying on the roadside, and someone had thrown out an anticue floor lamp. One girl's arms were breaking under the weight of a pallet of baby romper suits: *"Please, let me through! I've invested all my money into this, I've taken out loans on these! I can't leave them behind, please!"*

"Vova!" I yelled, catching sight of my acquaintance, the manager, around the corner.

Vova was squatting with a cigarette, visibly wishing the earth would swallow him whole, but I did not give up. Vova owed me like the land owed the collective farm (I say that tongue-in-cheek) that is, he owed me five hundred dollars since even before the war, and my moment of reckoning had come.

"I am well aware of what you're dealing with and I get it. But you should get that she is a mother of five children. Five, Vova! They don't know anyone on the other side. They have to bring their things with them, the children can't sleep on bare earth."

"How? Tell me, how? My lorry's been here loaded up for half a day already, and it can't leave. How am I supposed to get it there without a driver? Do I get behind the wheel myself? Everything gets shot at, you understand? My last vehicle came back without hubcaps, all shot through the body."

"Let's not panic, shall we? Borysovych!"

Borysovych nodded.

"I'm giving you Borysovych, he'll get you out. In return, you'll take our boxes for us."

"Sheesh... Alright."

I don't know what surprised the man more, my change into

Ukrainian, or his own reply in Ukrainian, but, unexpectedly for me and for him, he nodded.

We drove out three blocks away and waited for the lorry. By joint efforts, my pilgrims' belongings were loaded in, some in the back, some right on the manager's lap, so that dear Vova was left with minimal breathing room and a total of about twenty centimetres' space to move his hand about. Some other boxes were thrown out into a ditch right there, an act about which I am still ashamed to this day. Borysovych jumped behind the wheel, adjusted his money pouch at his stomach, and set off without further ado.

A few hours later, the news reported that militants had seized the warehouse of a major postal delivery office in Donetsk. At nine the next morning our delivery arrived in Dnipro, but it was only then Borysovych got in touch.

"You know what, Borysovych? Get home, Tanya's upset."

"Is she actually?" he muttered into the receiver.

"You are an unscrupulous, ragged old tomcat. She's upset."

"That's good. That's really, really good. Tell her to keep crying, I'll be there by evening. Only I'll have to drop this nitwit off, he's been a pain in the arse the whole way here."

"In what sense?"

"In a literal sense. Don't ask."

* * *

"Mariika, have you got it all? Repeat it to me!"

"I know it, it's fine."

"No, one more time. What's mummy's telephone number, in case you get lost?"

"Zero five zero, four four three… um… zero seven zero seven."

"Fine. Olenka, your turn."

"I know it already!"

The little one rolled her eyes.

"No, you don't. What should you do now?"

"Hold your hand and not let go."

"Well done. Bohdan?"

Bohdan grunted.

"Lida!"

"Don't worry, me and the baby are clamped onto you, I'll rip that clasp off your clothes in a sec. Stop panicking, you panic more than me!"

"That's because you've always had five children, whereas I've only recently adopted you all."

For the hundredth — nay, the thousandth — time, I was regretting that I had not taken the men with us, because right then we had to fight. We had gathered on the platform to wait for the train. New arrivals pushed us from behind, and an immovable wall stood before us. In front, people were wheezing, crying, and howling; someone here was getting trampled on; someone there cracked a rib. We and the children were being squeezed and mangled in the crush of human bodies, with no way out. We thanked our lucky stars that we had managed to send our things separately and were now making our own way with a small rucksack, because the people who had come here with suitcases and bags were faced with a choice: either leave them here now, or die in the stampede under the weight of their own bags.

Tickets were not an option. No-one knew when the train would finally come and where it would take us. We took the little ones by the arm and held them above our heads or on our backs in order to win them a few millimetres of life. I was punched in the side, and though the rucksack softened the blow, for a second I believed that my back was broken and that I would keel over there and then. A boy with a cage in his arms shoved past me. In it was either a pet rat or a hamster, and the boy tried to keep hold on it but could not manage. When the cage fell at his feet and broke, the boy dived after it. I could not see behind the mass of backs to find out what happened to him next.

The crush intensified from all sides when the train finally

arrived. The frantic crowd bowed back away from the wheels, and by some miracle we slipped a metre forward and ended up almost right next to the door. The conductor hung off the steps, and without a second's thought I shoved Lida into his arms.

"Help us! We have children on us!"

Bohdan and the children jumped in after Lida, and Serhii and I were the last to be pulled in. Other passengers grabbed onto our legs and by the hem of our clothing, and were it not for the conductor, I would not have kept hold of the folding steps and would have succumbed with the child.

The next moment, we were running down the dark corridor and took the bunk by the window. My arms and shoulders were covered in grazes, and blood was running down my temple from where someone had grabbed my braid, tearing out my hair and some flesh with it. The children were no longer crying, but were mewling softly from fear, like kittens. I hurriedly felt along their little arms and legs, fearing most of all that I would find a soft spot where there was a broken bone.

"Climb onto the second bunk, quickly!"

Passengers were still rushing in from below, so getting on the second bunk was a chance to save ourselves. I moved from the second to the top bunk and settled the two girls next to me, awkwardly tugging out a jacket from the rucksack and putting it behind them. The main thing was that no-one would fall on us up here, and a little bit of air reached us from the crack in the window. All the windows in the cabin were boarded up with plywood. A couple of inches were left open at the top, letting in waves of soot, heat, and the foetid stench of the station from outside. Your whole body got immediately covered with dust and sticky sweat; sweat gathered in puddles under your feet and tummy, and every movement was accompanied with the squelch of plastic as it stuck to bare skin.

The train stood there for a long time, more than four hours, although the doors were locked almost straightaway, which cut off only a tenth of the rabid crowd. I could see from the crack in the window how the platform once again filled up with people and how the mass of people swayed from side to side. Someone climbed onto the roof of the carriage and I could hear the footsteps clanging above my head. The crowd set upon our window several times, but the men inside jumped to the rescue to stop them smashing in the glass.

It was quiet in the carriage, despite the dangerous crush, and the adults stayed silent. Going to the toilet or walking down the corridor was not an option. We very quickly began to ration water, passing it to the children and animals for a few sips; well, and to pour a little on the face of someone who was dying for it. Cats and dogs sat under nearly every bottom bunk, and their cries, which mingled with the howling of children, were almost the only interruption which broke the depressing silence — apart from the woman on the bottom bunk who would periodically cross herself and say a prayer.

We set off at last. I have never travelled like that, neither before nor since. We either crawled slowly along, at the pace of a drunken turtle, or we suddenly burst into a mad gallop, so that the measured 'tuk-tuk' of the wheels turned into a continuous, rapid 'tra-ta-ta'. The train would then brake sharply, meaning we would scrape our knees and elbows, drawing blood, trying desperately not to fall on any children. There were no stopovers and no ticket or document checks. Moreover, I had no idea where they were taking us. It could have just as well been to Kharkiv or Simferopol. Judging by the sun, we were still heading west, although several times the train stopped, jolted, and then went backwards, which meant I completely lost my sense of direction.

This could have been a mass grave on wheels. If we had been shelled, no-one would have got out of there, and a fire in one carriage would have spelled doom for the others too. 'Mother of God, mother of God, mother of God...' the middle-aged woman repeated below us, without stopping; to try and interrupt this monotonous whispering, I turned to the girls and began to tell them a fairy-tale I knew from a manga strip.

"Once upon a time there was a girl called Yuzuko. She was a beautiful and gentle creature who had one peculiar foible. She always said exactly what she was thinking, and that always got her into trouble. And so, one time…"

Yuzuko, my childhood love, went on one adventure after the next, and I soon noticed the girls were not the only ones listening to our fairy-story, but the bunk next to us and the one opposite, and I even heard a request to raise my voice from the one below.

"Itsuki-san, I would gladly marry you, and become lady of this glorious castle, the never-ending rice plantations that stretch to where the sun rises, and the enchanted cows whose horns hold up the sky, and whose hooves wake up the thousands of springs of the Xing-ju every morning. But I still cannot forget how I once saw you and your bare behind running away from a single, lonely bee…"

"We've arrived! Fellow passengers, let's leave in an orderly fashion, no rushing, we've arrived!"

At this, everyone burst into tears at once. They shouted, started talking, shoving each other, and lit up right in the carriage. I lowered the girls to the ground, then hopped off myself, and I was deftly caught by an uncle who gave off the scent of nuclear-force sweat, tobacco, and smoke fumes: "Well done, little one!"

To our utmost joy, we were in Dnipro.

* * *

It was like I was in a backwards dream. You know those dreams when you are walking naked down the street, and everyone is staring at you? Now, however, I had the feeling that everyone else was undressed. I just wanted to poke every one of them, make sure they were real. The poor children barely had time to turn their heads: 'Look, look, a flag! And another, a Ukrainian one! And a traditional *vyshyvanka* shirt! Look, a Ukrainian trident on the building, a huge one!' The blue-and-yellow and the red-and-black symbols flickered before our eyes; these Ukrainian colours were everywhere — on fences, lampposts, and cars. The place was teeming with dozens of soldiers who walked in and around the station: they were Ukrainian soldiers, and I saw Lida crying, smearing the dirt from the journey around her face.

"Good Lord, we made it! Where do we go from here, with the children too?"

"What are you shouting about? Everything's fine. Where do you want to go first?"

"To the toilet. And McDonalds."

"On we go then."

We went to the toilet, then to McDonalds. Then my girlfriends from Dnipro came and met us, and everything fell into place. If you asked me now, how many times in my life I had ever felt happy, I would put at the top of my list the moment when Lida and I said goodbye to each other. There we were sobbing on each other's shoulders, next to the pre-paid minivan going to Kremenchuk, as the driver poured a six-litre bottle of washer fluid onto the road.

"Come on, you should get off now. The children want to sleep, lie them down on the seats."

"Can you not still come with us? Let's go, we'll make a new life..."

"...and raise a cow?"

"We can get a cow! I worry about you; I think there's nothing for you back in Donetsk."

"I don't think there's anything in Donetsk for any normal people anymore. But where would we find normal people anyway? They don't get on with us lunatics."

"Promise me you'll come visit?"

"I promise," I promised with as much force as possible, knowing that I was lying with just as much force. "We'll see each other again."

XI

GOLD

NOT BURIED, BUT SOWN

"Eat, my daughter, eat," said the old soldier gently, pushing the bowl towards me. "Eat, you need it." Well, I have been told my whole life that I 'need' to eat, but my constitution is such that no matter how hard I try, whatever I 'need' still results in a size zero. Though I really was hungry (when did we have breakfast?), I was not hungry enough to give in to a tasty salad of instant noodles with canned meat. The noodle broth had made a chemical reaction with the fats pretending to be first-class beef and the surface of the bowl of food was covered with a hard, grey film.

"Uncle Kolya, I cannot eat that. It's terrifying."

The soldiers tried to hold back their laughter.

"But you weren't afraid of coming here in the dark?"

"That was an extraordinary event, a *force-majeure*."

"Well eat then, my 'majoress'."

Do not ask how I ended up in this army sector and where the group that was supposed to meet me went. If anyone in the future gets their hands on the chronicles documenting this war, then the first three scrolls could easily be titled *Chaos*, *Anarchy*, and *Courage*. There was no clear front, and boys from both sides were jumbled together. If we tried fighting according to the principles of those damned cinephile commandos — shoot first, questions later — then we would have caught each other in the crossfire long beforehand.

So, there I was, sitting with the guys in an abandoned dacha, having dinner, when two men come out of the bushes with some binoculars in their hands. There was a fifty-fifty chance of them being on our side. Shadows flew over to meet them; a short conversation followed and they parted off in different directions. Phew. Looked like they were on our side.

I had waited eight hours at the bombed-out petrol station. The scouts were supposed to pick me up as I was bringing them binoculars and sights. The squad had not come out to the agreed spot, and I finally returned to the base. It was lucky I came across one of Uncle Kolya's rat packs with the foppish label 'Dandies' written on it, since I had already crossed paths with those particular dandies from Lviv and therefore was not afraid when these fighters blocked my way with whooping and whistles.

"Have you gone mad? Where are you off to? You're heading into artillery fire, there's a fight going on that way. Oi, turn back!"

"Yes, I'm heading to the base!"

"The base is gone, turn back."

So now we are having dinner on the terrace of a lavish cottage. An enormous oak table is littered with the remains of fish from the nearest lake, watermelon rinds, and used teabags. Uncle Kolya sweeps it all on the floor to make room for our plates. There is no light, no gas, and the boys have set up a camping stove on a luxury barbecue. It is clear that the place's former owners loved wood and iron, and I could see by torch beam the grapevine fence, the skilfully-wrought iron railings on the first floor, and the lush engravings on the wooden gazebo.

"Look at the chandeliers here! You've never seen anything like it. Come, I'll show you, they're fit for a palace."

"Alright."

We entered the building through the dark entrance. There was a huge living room on the ground floor. The windows were now blocked with sandbags up to the ceiling, and the Italian sofas and wardrobes were piled up in the far corner to make a barricade.

"Look at the toilet! A proper throne."

The toilet bowl was fashioned in the form of a sphinx, with huge gold columns for legs. There had long been no running water in the toilet, and the seat of this monumental throne was covered in a brown crust. It was better not to dwell on its origins.

We went upstairs to the first floor and looked over the marble floor and the nursery, full of motifs after Formula 1: red, white, and black chequered walls, a cot in the shape of a car, and autographed posters of famous racing drivers on the walls. Then there were the chandeliers: a massive, three-tiered chandelier was hung in the playroom and the master bedroom; the children had an avantgarde construction from glass and chrome, whereas the parents had a cascade of crystal droplets. The crystal beads that had been shattered by shellfire crumbled and creaked and underfoot, and I picked one up that had miraculously survived.

"It's pretty, right? They have expensive taste. What couldn't they afford, I wonder?"

"It's pretty, yes."

Bronze with patina, pressed jasper and red crystal. My work.

We finished this order before the war, making only one model of each chandelier per my sketches. We had to look in the living room, where there should be a flower wreath with nine edges to it. I then remembered who the client was. He owned a car dealership; a rather busy, older fellow who haggled ferociously — not over the money, but the time it would take to make his order. He needed it 'for yesterday', since his wife was giving birth, and he wanted to surprise her on her discharge from the maternity hospital. If you really wanted to know, they were expecting a boy, their firstborn. They had been undergoing fertility treatment for twelve years.

"Do you know what happened to the owners?"

"*Niet.* I dunno. They were just some separatists. Listen, we'll put you in the attic, ok? There's a bed there, a mattress behind the chimney, it'll be the safest place. Is that ok? The lower floors'll get shot at."

"That's fine, thank you."

I was too shy to ask where the toilet was, so I decided to wait until morning. It was quiet behind the chimney; the bricks muffled the sound of the battle. The noisy machine-gun fire which erupted here and there around the whole village was nearly drowned out here. In any case, no-one would find me. That was what I was hoping for, at any rate.

I did not notice that I was drifting off as I clutched one of those crystal droplets in my hand. I then had an unpleasant awakening, with someone literally pulling me out of my sleep by my leg. I opened my eyes and saw two figures above my mattress. A tall, thin soldier stood behind a shorter one, who was shaking my ankle with all his might.

"Hey, what are you doing? Alright, I'll get up!"

I rubbed my eyelids, putting my lenses in place, and got to my feet. Surprisingly, there was no-one there.

"Hey, where'd you run off to?"

Oh well, time to go downstairs. It was quiet inside the house and out in the yard. There was only one soldier by the door, rocking on his chair.

"Where are you going?"

"I don't know, I was woken up by your lot. What happened?"

"Which soldiers? There's no-one here, everyone's out on the line, the junior ones are changing over."

"How? There were two of them. One was tall, the other short, he nearly dragged me down here by my leg."

The lad jumped up and went white as a sheet; I could tell even in the darkness.

"What the... Two of our soldiers died yesterday. Vitka and Batya. Batya was about here, up to my shoulder, and Vitka was lanky. That is, tall, not lanky, he always corrected people when they called him lanky; he was tall."

"I see. You know what — let's go somewhere else. Is there anywhere to go?"

"Yes, next door. There's a garage with a bunker."

"Let's go to the bunker."

The fighter nodded. Neither he nor I wanted to talk. We quietly made our way to the neighbouring garage and sat there till morning. When dawn arrived, the boys took me back to the highway. I left the binoculars with them.

* * *

"I have a nose for it. I've been doing this for twenty years. You know how it feels? I can look in a minibus of civilians crossing a checkpoint and I can pull the right man out. Do you know how many snipers I've caught?"

"Hmph, I'll tell you which one's the sniper, it's obvious," I said.

"What's obvious? Let's have a bet, then! Show us who the sniper is. Don't tell her, boys!"

The boys put down their spoons, with a faint cheer at the prospect of some light entertainment. Spectral shadows danced behind us, and we clustered like moths around the only flame, warming our hands against the trench light. The tent was sheltered on an abandoned farm, and it was the safest place to hide out in the surrounding area — the bushes around the perimeter were criss-crossed with tripwires. The soldiers on guard outside would then fall on their sleeping bags without undressing, and then fall asleep half in the open, rifles still in their hands.

Alright then, let's take a look. A pair of twins in striped army vests, blonde-haired sunflowers with dark blue eyes — definitely not them. Too alive, restless, walking one after the other, like a tail after its dog — (or dog after its tail?). Jokesters who loved clowning around, they will either die together or both of them will live on, to their mother's joy, and they will get married to another pair of twins, and no-one would ever tell the brothers apart.

There was the stern lad, with big biceps. His was pure sinew that grows underground with a drill, a rock hammer, and buckets and wagons of coal. It was obvious that he was a miner. He was uncomfortable above ground with his back to the open air, and I did not need any clues to tell that he was either a mechanic or a driver.

Then there was the former teacher, one of those who never stopped being one. He was either a maths or a geography teacher, as well as a tourist and amateur enthusiast. He had spent his whole life pulling difficult teenagers out of difficult families, caring for them, cleaning them up, delousing them, getting them off sniffing glue, teaching them how to fight, how to go one-to-one with a bear, and how to light a fire with only one match. He went to war by his own accord through the recruitment office, and one day just appeared on the frontline with three wolf cubs alongside him. They were the only ones with proper combat jackets and combat boots, as well as razor-sharp stilettos on their chests, small but wieldy, sharpened and well-weighted to the hand, so that they could be drawn in one motion. A fireteam, what else?

Then there was the sapper. Who was he before the war? An IT or computer technician. Sedentary work, Minecraft, and fighting with tanks purely on the mental plane; two children, summer holidays at the seaside, and fishing at the dacha. He could be the sniper, but I see a professional Leatherman on his belt: we bought these multi-tools and I was aware where they had got them from.

Besides, I knew exactly who their sniper was. I recognised him straightaway by his characteristic gaze with which he sussed out me and Roman. Only professionals look at people like that, at once both at you and at the horizon behind you, calculating the possibility of enemy ambush and picking a place to form a line. His age checked out too, since there were no better marksmen than people just over the age of sixty. Then I silently held up my mug and saluted the phlegmatic uncle, and in response he 'cheersed' me with his tumbler carved out of a shell casing. I bet he carved it in his spare time.

"No, that's not fair. You already knew, right?"

"Oh, come on," Roman remarked. "You know who you're dealing with here: she's a witch."

"What, really?"

"What, you don't see it? Whenever we visit you, everything dies down, gets all quiet, like we're on holiday! The moment we leave, the shelling starts up again. It's like that on all the army lines."

"That's true! It's awesome. Why don't you live with us then? You know what sort of woman we want here? A calm, fearless lady. And one who can cook."

"Great, nice one boys, you've gone and given away my hand in marriage without me knowing. Where's my prize for the correct guess then?"

The platoon commander was confused for a second.

"You can have a grenade, if you want."

"No, thank you."

"The trousers, then. We'll give you some vintage trousers, they don't fit anyone here."

"*What* trousers?"

The boys at the table were already roaring with laughter. Amidst this banging and drumming I was ceremoniously handed a pair of quilted cotton trousers the colour of yellow bile, with a high waist and clasped together by four buttons. The rotten cotton wool squeaked from old age, and the crotch bore the stamp: '1937'! Hang on — was that their date of birth?

"Oi look, it's like they're tailored just for you. When we were issued them, we thought they were for children or something. These won't fit any of our fighters, not in length or waist."

I was already trying on this 'novelty', and therefore did not immediately catch what he said. When it finally filtered through, I froze, one leg already in a trouser hole.

"What do you mean, 'issued'? Issued for what?!"

"That's the uniform we were given. Their documents said they were valid as army trousers, so they're accepted and signed for."

"Fine, the size is a problem. But what about the time of year? They're winter trousers!"

"What's the point of more summer ones? You'll blink and it's winter already. We now have Shrot who's *responsible* for them. He signed a load for the whole squadron. The other big men will take them, but you'll come with more trousers, alright?"

"Stop, don't force yourself into something that small. Just write a report that they got lost."

"For everyone?"

"Well, it happens. Tell me," — this was to me — "my *volunteers*, could we get some uniform off you? Fatigues, ideally, at least for these three lads. They had to crawl along the ground for two kilometres yesterday, their elbows are torn to shreds."

It was possible, in fact. They could get uniform, shoes, and a thousand other items from us, from helmets and condensed milk to cars and ammo. I do not know exactly how many people bought and sourced goods for us, fulfilling any orders we asked of them. I had at least three hundred people directly corresponding with me alone, not counting the donors who transferred money towards our advertised list of requirements. Within a few months, we had managed to do something that can take years in peacetime: we had built ourselves a reputation. If I found out that even a penny of the money meant for the soldiers was going into someone's pocket, I would have bit off my own hand, but no-one even thought of dipping into the collected funds. We stood there, like pyromaniacs next to a giant bonfire, throwing more and more fuel onto the flames. Bulletproof vests? Stick them in. Camouflage nets? We'll knit them. Tyres, stretchers, medicine — put it all in. Food? We'll take it. Do you need water, timber, brackets, diggers, cables, generators? Hand them over, don't slow down!

We did not dare think that this was a job for the nation's absentee logistics regiments. We did not dare think about how no other army in the world fights without any armour — batting away the fire from BM-21 Grad rocket launchers with a pair of trousers from 1937. We knew that the enemy was everywhere, that we could trust no-one. No-one but these boys, who take a nap for a few hours, get up, get some cold pasta and water down their necks, shove magazines and grenades straight into their pockets, and go on a raid in battered trainers. You can trust no-one but yourself, and I know myself. Nothing but your eyes and hands, nothing but whatever you can carry and hand out personally, nothing but this indescribable feeling of power, when your strength is at its last, and you fall, and fall, and suddenly you are picked up, given a moment's rest, and infused with the resource which you need to carry on.

If this is not a patriotic war — a Great war — then I do not know what is.

* * *

"How about this: no deviating from the plan. There and back. No turning off, no stopping anywhere, and we'll spend the night at the base."

"Or what?"

"Or… I want to watch the football, you got it? Don't I have the right to do that once in a blue moon? The girls got me some beers and smoked fish."

"Well, if *the girls* have got you some beers and smoked fish… Alright, we'll do as you command."

Roman gave me the side-eye to see if I was kidding, but I was serious. It was a short task, bringing the artillerymen terrain plans and repair kits, which meant a trip through the occupied zone.

"But let's get pizza for the boys. We'll get it to them still warm: how many of them are there?"

There was no room to swing a cat at the Italian pizzeria, the only decent place in the whole city. All the tables inside and on the street were busy. What was going on there?

Ah, the World Cup's on. People are out enjoying themselves.

"OK, three pizzas to take away then, please."

I checked the speedo: not far to go, the roads were empty, and I knew every hole in the road. The artillerymen were already waiting for us, and it all looked promising. I could even remember the key points about the program which I had to make sure the gunners were aware of. The terrain plans had three types of maps, from old standard-issue ones to modern ones, and separate algorithms for each type of weapon. I began to list all the program features but stopped, noticing their sceptical smiles. Oh, let them figure it out themselves, if they're so smart.

I switch to the soldiers. The photographer in me is roused, and I take a few expressive photos for a competition on the Discovery Channel. That is, for a Facebook post. I take pictures of their hands, because I cannot take photos of any other parts of them. Hands like theirs are perfect for dramatic photos, with the dirt under their nails, broken bones, burns, and impressive calluses. I ask the boys to bring me something brutal for the photo, like some shell cases, and they pull out a hammer and a homemade kettlebell. I tell them that this was for witness reports, and Roman laughs:

"Don't listen to her! Next she'll bring you special Korean gloves to soften your skin, and you will end up looking like priests with their silky-smooth hands."

Ha-ha, very funny.

The boys were entrenched in a pine forest. The dwarven pines honestly saved their lives by sheltering them from view, and the fresh scent of pine resin masked the smell of weaponry. Our feet sank up to our ankles in the sand, and if I closed my eyes we could have almost been by the seaside. How long since I had last walked through a forest! How terrible it was, too, that my grandmother and I had never once seen the sea!

We drank up our coffee with the soldiers, and the pizza was a hit. Roman and I were approached by the quartermaster, a calm and commonsensical fellow, who I did not hear utter more than ten words over the whole evening. He never asked for anything, but I liked the way he dealt with logistics. He kept a prudent supply of food and had dug a food store into the ground, instead of having a refrigerator, and the men did not sleep on the floor but on wooden bivvies. It was the only unit where they did not eat any old bully beef, but got proper canned meat from Kharkiv.

"Girls, I have a request for you, if I can."

Roman took the word 'girls' on the chin and nodded.

"Here's the thing: I'm going on holiday. You couldn't send my things by Nova Poshta postal service, could you? I've packed a bag and put this address here on it. I can't carry it there by myself."

"No problem, we'll send it tomorrow."

We said a brief goodbye and left, with only half an hour till the football and dried fish. After only a few kilometres, my companion slowed down.

"Listen, is something niggling you as well?"

"Sort of. Let's open it carefully. You stay there, I'll run and get it."

I bring over a box from the boot, cut off the layers of scotch tape, and we burrow inside it. Everything seemed fine: changes of uniform, old boots, some jumpers, a T-shirt, waffles, and sweets. Where was he sending waffles — Pyriatyn? What, were they out of waffles in Pyriatyn? Oh well, what's next: trousers again, new trainers, an infrared camera…

"Bugger."

"Shit."

"Well then, let's go back."

We were allowed back in without having to say the password or show our documents. Something about our facial expression told the person on duty at the checkpoint to stand aside. Roman stayed in the car, while I went to the commander in the tent. I politely asked permission to enter, and just as politely placed the box on the table and explained the situation. The three soldiers smoking there got up and disappeared behind the door, and I was left alone with the commander.

"Coffee?"

"No, thank you. Will you take care of it?"

"We will."

"What will happen to him?"

"He'll get what he deserves. It's our business now; forget about it."

I held out my arm, then left. He was absolutely right, this grey-haired chap, who did not take hold of my hand in farewell, but my forearm, which was how we shook hands amongst our allies. It was their business and theirs alone, and it was not up to anyone else to poke their nose in other people's disciplinary methods.

My poor Roman was quiet, and I drove slowly, paying tribute to his deep inner turmoil. In the end I could not hold it in.

"So, did you see what happened? What will they do to him?"

"God, I thought you'd gone braindead there back in the woods. Thought you'd never ask! Yeah."

"So… What will happen to him?"

"I won't say."

"Well, keep yourself to yourself then. I'll ask Borysovych later, you're one hundred percent going to tell him. Well, where now? To the football? The second half's already started."

"I don't really fancy it now."

I then slammed on the brakes. We stopped abruptly on the empty road and froze, craning our necks to the sky like children watching fireworks for the first time. BM-21 Grads were firing over to the left of us. Rows of red and yellow comets left a bright trail over our heads and disappeared beyond the horizon. We had stopped beneath a giant, shining arch, and it was the most dazzling illumination I had ever seen.

"Let's get out of here!"

Pedal to the metal, we reach the town in a record thirteen minutes. We park next to the same pizzeria, where there were still no empty tables. The waiters were still run off their feet, the group celebrating a birthday at the table in the corner were still raising their glasses, and the lovebirds were still occupying the red couches in the smaller room. I grabbed the waitress by the sleeve:

"Can you tell me…?"

"*Yes?*"

"Do you feel like there's a war next to us?"

"*Well no, not really.*"

"Three pizzas to go then, please."

* * *

I hate calls in the middle of the night the most. I also hate when Oksana calls me at night, crying into the receiver, and I cannot piece two words together.

"We, oh my dear, we…"

"What?"

"Don't worry, everything's ok."

"Spit it out!"

"*Our Radio*, a radio station phoned, and…"

"I have to stop you there; what radio?"

"I can't remember. *'Russian'* Radio, or some Russian schlager station, something like that…"

"And?"

"They want to buy for us, as in, not us, but you, well, not you, for you to take to the fighters…"

"Breathe. Try one more time, or I'll hang up."

"Thirty infrared cameras!"

It was not a joke. One radio station dipped into its own coffers and bought a batch of infrared cameras, to distribute among the volunteer groups supplying the Ukrainian army. I was not aware of the criteria for handing them out, but a few of these goodies reached us, or rather, as Oksana aptly remarked, me personally. Or rather, not me, but my Facebook profile.

So, how do we prove to them who I was?

By some miracle, they knew that a woman was in charge of my profile, although I looked a little different to how they imagined, apparently.

We met in a maize field near Dnipro. It was easier for me to go by the back roads in the fields and for them to turn off a kilometre away from the highway, so they would not get caught at the checkpoints.

The radio station sent two Jeeps full of people. We sent my own good self and our beloved Opel. After lengthy consideration, I did not take anything with me, not even a companion. I covered my hair with a headscarf and put on black tortoiseshell glasses. Before leaving, I looked in the mirror, and ended up taking my glasses off.

The young men bashfully asked me to upload a sentence or two onto my profile as proof of who I was.

"No worries," I said, and wrote, 'Putin's a fucking scumbag'.

That post received more than three thousand likes, by the way.

However, I finished them off when I reversed the car into the maize field and dived underneath the car and opened its hiding place. Could I not keep the valuable cargo in view? Thirty little cherished boxes were neatly stowed away, and only the rows of maize knew where I had put them.

"Is there a way we can contact you directly?"

"Write me a private message. I will definitely answer. If I can. As for witness reports, I will not disclose any data or photographs. However, I will send you a photo of each box's delivery. You have done a great thing today."

"We're fighting a common cause. Do you really live in Donetsk?"

"I do."

"How do you get out of there? We need to get one person out, but she can't, not by the usual route. She's on the death list."

I took a deep breath, getting ready to talk about 'death lists' and similar urban myths, and then exhaled. No, it was not worth it. If I let them down by honestly telling them that, in most cases, you can just get the bus to Dnipro instead of galloping across minefields under cover of night, then they would take away the thermal imaging cameras off us out of disappointment.

"Tell her to get in contact with me; we'll think of something."

"Thank you, and good luck."

They were good guys, sincere too. One made the sign of the cross over my back. But working in a Russian radio station? I could not do that. However, I have not compared people to myself for a long time, not since I stopped trusting people. Which is why we now did the following: the burner phone with the broken SIM card was thrown into the bush, following correct procedure. They can always write to me instead. What else? No-one went into the car, I made sure of that. However, I would still go see old Roman and get him to make sure that no-one had stuck anything to the car's undercarriage. The infrared cameras might have a tracker in them, so it would not be a bad idea to go bother Don for him to check. If he gives the all-clear, then I will believe in miracles.

* * *

"It's all good, you can take them. The equipment's clean."

"Are you sure? Are you absolutely sure?"

I did not wait for an answer; besides, Don was not going to answer. All my thoughts revolved around distributing the devices. These ones would go to the airport; another two here — no wait, five here.

We met with the fighters at the airport at the beginning of July. Well, 'met' with is the wrong word — they caught me in the hangar, where I came desperately hoping that the boys would not shoot me without warning.

We did not realise it straightaway, but the fighting in the airport would last a long time. No one thought that it would take weeks. We heard the gunfire going constantly, but we did not run over there with food or water.

"Who gives a monkey's about that," said Tanya. "They eat like horses; they'll gobble both you and the cooking pot up. As if they need our stuffed cabbages."

This was true. They did not need our stuffed cabbage; they needed information. You cannot fight in a city where you do not have the eyes and ears of the locals. In an ideal world I would have gone behind the line, got to know the commanders, and offered my services. In our reality, however, it would be cheaper and less trouble just to put an advert in the newspaper, saying, 'I am so-and-so, I'm leaking information about the *opolchentsi* to the Ukrainians, my address is…', if you know what I mean.

As such, one day, I put on some plastic clogs, wrapped myself up in a chiffon robe, pulled a panama hat right over my brow, and blended into my surroundings. I looked like a typical pensioner, a prime specimen of the geriatric tribe. The only strange thing was the hoe in my hand. It would have been better to drag along a wheelie shopping bag in the other, but I cannot walk dragging one of those, as they cover my legs in bruises. I could go anywhere looking like this. No one would pay me any attention: not the separatist patrols which combed the neighbourhood, nor the women handing out bread. I passed the hangars unbothered and dived into a hole in the fence adjacent to the bus station behind the airport.

I was afraid of going to the airport itself and sat down on a bench in the old departure lounge. I was thinking I should tie my headscarf onto my hoe and wave it out the window as a flag, but then rejected the idea: it would be easier to accidentally hit an old hoe-carrier.

I did not wait long, maybe twenty minutes, until three soldiers came in.

"Hello. Why are we sitting here, who are we waiting for?"

"Hello. I need to see your commander."

"Hey lady, is that how it is?"

It took half an hour to call over the commander, since the fighters seriously wanted to send me back where I came through the hole in the fence. Finally, the officer arrived, who had clearly just got tired of listening to the racket over the airways.

I know exactly what is the first — and second — impression I make on people. 'What the hell?' is their normal reaction. Yet the thing is, in peacetime I would never have thought of imposing myself and would have shirked away from the limelight. Now, I would not have even dreamed of turning back. The stars had obviously aligned: I was hungry, grumpy, and tired beyond belief. All I cared about was business. As such, I skipped over the usual rituals of greetings and establishing who we were and got straight to the point.

"Whatever. We can sort you out with eye protection, medicine, communications, ammunition, do technical repairs to a reasonable extent, and can report enemy movements of manpower and equipment in the surrounding areas."

"Um… Are you kidding? Which areas?"

"One second."

I had a tablet that was tied against my stomach. Well, honestly, I could hardly carry it in my hands — I was carrying the hoe! I clamped it between my legs and unfastened my buttons. The fighters stared, like they had never seen a belly before in their life.

"What are you doing? Stop that immediately!"

"Excuse me? I'm getting my tablet out… Look: we're here. See these streets here, and here: we can guard them continuously. This area is blind, you can't get heavy machinery through there. You can see everything from the cemetery here, there's a good view from the tower. There's also the yard on Spartak street? The orcs have put their machinery there; I've marked down the coordinates for all of them. As of yesterday, they had three BMP amphibious fighting vehicles, two BRDM-2 armoured patrol cars, and one tank. By the looks of it, that's where they hide their 2S9 Nona gun mortar."

The commander lit a cigarette, looking at me with a particular interest, like an entomologist at a small insect.

"Let's sit down, and you can tell me one more time, this time in order. Firstly, though, who are you?"

"We're just people; Ukrainians. I think you need our information. Take it, use it, trust it. Do with it what you want. I will leave this tablet with you; I brought it for you anyway. Here's the charger. Here's my contact number and call sign, you can get through from your side. Besides, we also have a small automobile repair station and a workshop, if you need repairs or metalwork; swing by."

"Where are you from though? Don't try to fool us with that 'local' nonsense. No one speaks like that here."

I silently pulled out my passport and showed my residence

permit. I then carefully buttoned myself up, once again put on my panama hat, and hunched over. When I lower my shoulders and buckle my knees a little, at the market they all start calling me, 'babushka'.

"Thanks for this talk. I'll wait for your call."

They never called.

About a week later, a taxi slowed down next to me with a large plastic aeroplane on the roof. It scared me, since an unknown car is never good news; if you have quick reactions, you can pull away from the road and run away, with a high risk of getting a bullet in your spine.

"Hi, don't you recognise us?"

"*Niet, sorry.*"

"Why aren't you with your hoe today?"

I look round — it can't be!

"How did you end up here?"

"Don't ask how we found you. Get in, let's go. Show us your workshop."

That's how we started working with the soldiers. The men established contact with Roman and Borysovych, sometimes handing over a list of requirements to be done 'yesterday already'. I did not object to mediating and understood that, in our world, nine times out of ten, men choose to interact with other men. In this unspoken hierarchy, women are given a place in the kitchen, and who does it really worry that I am the one who scopes out and buys the weather stations, combat jackets, and tourniquets, totting up in my head the details of both the suppliers and each order. Roman would then go to them, wipe his hands respectfully, talk, and have a beer. War is a private men's club. Women just get caught in the crossfire.

I would later see the conspicuous Daewoo Lanos with a plane on it in various areas of Donetsk. I would not be surprised if the boys were actually using it for a side-hustle as taxi drivers — I would have done the same in their place.

* * *

We visited this village at the beginning of May. Then, the gardens bloomed and the streets were drowning in a white haze. The fruit tree blossoms hung in the air like fog, and magnificent flowerbeds lay in front of every house. The housewives had an intense rivalry about who grew the best tulips.

And yet here we were, in July, when the blossoms had formed into crisp little apples. We drove in to drop by but did not drive far through. The only street was blocked by a battered water tower, which had fallen across the way as a giant roadblock. There was no way round, and the village stretched out like an intestine along the roadside. There was also no-one to ask how to get through; there was not a soul to be found.

"Hang on, I'll find someone."

"Don't trouble yourself. Can't you see what's happened?"

"What?"

"Look at their gardens and vegetable patches."

The vegetable patches were left unsown. The ploughed field was overgrown with pigweed and orache, and in some places the weeds had grown higher than your waist. The garden plots were abandoned, which meant that there were no people here.

"Oh Lord, let's get out of here. Turn around."

Roman carefully reversed, trying not to clip the hard shoulder, and we flew out of that village like a cork out of a bottle, without looking back. But where were we going? We were the only ones on the open road. Throw your eye to the left — ploughed fields, throw your eye to right — maize. A dusty minibus came headlong at us, deftly avoiding the potholes. It suddenly braked, the driver's window parallel with ours. The window lowered, revealing a robust grey-haired man in all-black, with a large gold cross hanging at his chest.

"Father, could you tell us: is this the right direction to Krasnogorovka?"

"Of course not, my son," he answered in his bass voice.

"Uh..."

"Follow me, children!"

We drove after him.

That was the first time in my life I saw a bona fide chaplain. Strangely enough, we lagged so far behind him that there was a half an hour interval between us and him entering Krasnohorivka.[13] The town itself was just as deserted as many of the other settlements we had gone through today. Here, shop windows were also broken in, empty plastic wrappers were also flying around and getting stuck to the spruce trees, and rubbish was strewn everywhere. The brand-new rubbish bins had long been overflowing, and every turn in the road opened onto another landfill. However, in the middle of this wasteland — so, by the statue of Lenin, like in every town here — there was an unexpected oasis.

Our aforementioned minibus was parked there, and next to it stood a queue of maybe a hundred men, no less. They stood in a disciplined manner; no-one was shoving or fighting each other. People were swiftly dispatched humanitarian aid and disappeared in an instant to neighbouring apartment blocks. The chaplain was handing out two loaves of bread each and a bag of groceries.

"Roman, look!"

I jab my companion's forearm, but he does not react.

"Motherf...!"

"What?"

"Look at the road. We're done for: we've only got one spare wheel."

I looked closely, and my blood ran cold. The whole road was liberally strewn with shrapnel. The roadway was covered by an

---

13 Note that the Ukrainian title of Krasnohorivka would be pronounced differently in Russian, i.e., Krasnogorovka. Many places in Ukraine have different names in Ukrainian and in Russian.

iron carpet. There were fragments smaller than your nail and larger than your forearm, some straight, some serrated, and we had no chance of getting out of here without puncturing all our wheels. Every fragment had razor-sharp edges which could easily slice through a car tyre.

"But what about him?"

I nod at the chaplain.

"How would I know?"

"Well, wait a second. I won't be long."

I carefully get out of the car, taking care not to step on anything that would pierce the sole of my foot right through to the bone. I stand at the end of the queue: the others give me a sideways look but say nothing.

"I heed you, my daughter."

Give me a break — *'daughter'*? He is hardly older than I am, only he has bags under his eyes.

"Bless me, father. Bless our journey onwards. And if you could, so we arrive there in one piece."

He put his hand on my head and held out his cross for me to kiss. I stuck my nose towards the cross, genuflected, and then ran back to the car. Was it worth having the sign of the cross made over me? Oh well — it is what it is already.

We made our way out of Krasnohorivka without puncturing a single tyre.

XII

MICA

THE ART OF BREATHING UNDERWATER

"Baba, are you serious?
You're talking rubbish."
"Tell me, do I ask much of you?
Have I said a word to you
about all your doings? Have
I ever told you off for it?"
"Tell me off, if you want.
But I'm still not going. Who do
you think I am — a mobile
pharmacy? Or a vet?"

My grandmother turned to the window. We had been quarrelling for an hour; it was our first quarrel in many years, and I was not ready for it.

Olha Ivanivna *only* wanted me to rush off to this village, some Zasypne or Nasypne or other, some place off-road in the steppe where you have to get there on horseback, and only across dry land. Her friend from prehistoric times lived there — a friend whom I had never laid eyes upon — and she urgently needed a whole load of medicines, supposedly for her knees and head, as well as dietary supplements, homeopathy cures, Furosemide and Clonidine.

That was not all, however. The woman from Rozsypne had also asked her to buy her some ducklings. Not many — just one hundred in all. And, what is more, my grandmother had managed to get hold of them. Did you know that they sell ducklings in Donetsk? I did not; not until the door opened, and the baffled taxi driver brought in three boxes full of yellow lumps. The ducklings quacked. My grandmother huffed. Tanya guffawed.

"Let's all calm down. I'll go, but on the condition that this will be the first and last time I do this. Next time, I'll give you the car and you can drive yourself to wherever you want to go. Do you have any instructions for me?"

"Instructions?" asked my grandmother, businesswoman-like, the tears drying instantly on her cheeks.

"Well, on how to look after them. How do I feed them, water them?"

"No need. Petrovna will manage by herself. Just make sure that they don't get too hot or cold. Don't put on the air-conditioning and don't open the window."

"Bingo."

I found myself greeting the sunset on the remote back roads of Zhdanivka, Khrestivka, Petropavlivka, and Stepovyi. I could not go along the highway since the way through Shakhtarsk region was closed off. Besides, it turned out there were either two hamlets called Rozsypne on the map, or one of them had been split in two by the railway, meaning there was a separate route to reach each side of the village. Finally — and predictably — I could not get any signal on either my phone or satnav.

I checked on the ducklings every ten kilometres or so. They fell silent, which I found suspicious, and laid their heads on one another. I had no idea whether this was normal for ducklings. Were they unwell? Did they need a drink? How would I give them a drink? I could not pour water on them from a bottle, that was for sure. Maybe I could make a little bowl and put it on the floor for them to drink from — but then I would have to release the little birds from their boxes. I could not imagine what our Gazelle would look like with a hundred ducklings wandering about in it. Roman also wouldn't be best pleased, I bet.

I doubted I was going the right way, but I had no one to ask. The closer I got to the destination, the fewer people I saw about, and I had not seen anyone for the last hour. It was like these were grave villages. I did not see a single oncoming car, a single dog or chicken on the side of the road, not a single light in any of the windows, and it was strange that there was no sign of any military activity, as this was deep within hostile territory for both our side and for the separatists. Truth be told, the peasants living here had never surrendered to anyone; they have always lived here and will live here another thousand years, regardless of who is in power. From here it was just as far to Kyiv as it was from Moscow. Here, people's gardens were many acres in size, and to this day they sow potatoes with a hand-drawn plough, and in the evenings, they watch the only channel available on the TV.

There are also pits everywhere here. The contraptions that, at first glance, looked like chicken coops over in the fields turned out to have a rustic-looking hatch and a winch on them. Bucket, shovel, rock hammer: these comprised the local lads' basic arsenal. Whatever you dig up is yours, pure and honest. They say that the rich veins of ore can earn you up to a thousand hryvnia a day. However, if, by some stroke of bad luck, you get stuck underground, no one will rush over and dig up your land. They say in the best-case scenario a widow will be brought a few thousand hryvnia at the funeral. In the worst and most likely scenario, the shaft gets covered over with earth, so that no trace of it is left.

But now was not the time for cracking jokes… Where would I find this Petrovna? I would have liked the chance to ask someone. If I had got my bearings right, the ducklings and I had found the right village. Only there was no one there to meet us.

* * *

"Lady, hey lady! Wait, please; I need to ask you something!"

The woman by the well stopped and reluctantly turned towards me. I hopped out of the car and ran over to her, in order not to miss the first living soul I had encountered for the last forty kilometres.

"Can you tell me if this is Rossypnoe? How do I… Oh, Lord."

There was something wrong with her face. Her lips were totally bloodless, without the slightest hint of colour. Her face was a solid white canvas, punctured by dark, bottomless eyes. Her pupils were dilated, like a junkie's, though this girl did not look like a junkie — she looked like your average village girl, with thick calves, a faded woollen housecoat, and a little cross on a chain sparkling at her chest.

"Dead…"

"Who's dead?"

"Dead, all dead."

She looked at me as though she had only just noticed me, and suddenly grabbed me by the shoulder. Her fingers were an iron vice clamped to my body: that was how strong they were. If she had grabbed me by the neck, I would not have made it out of there alive.

"Let me go! What are you doing? Let me go now!"

I resisted with all my might and walloped her on the knee, which caused the vice to loosen for a second. In one bound I leapt onto the road and tore away to the car. However, something made me look back.

The woman was still standing there, holding her hand in front of her, and the lower part of her face was trembling. I felt like it had suddenly gone very cold. She was trying to say something, but her lips were not obeying, and only deaf tones made it through her clenched teeth. Was she having an epileptic fit?

I started getting anxious. I probably had to sit her down on the ground, or even better, lay her down and wait until the fit had passed.

"Quiet, shhh… It's ok."

I took hold of the woman by the waist and began to stroke her back.

"Let's sit down, shall we? It's ok, don't be scared."

She stopped shaking as suddenly as she had started, turned to me, and said in a calm and normal voice, without a trace of hysteria:

"People fell from the sky. On my barn. They're lying in the garden. Naked; they're all naked. There are legs everywhere…"

She started shaking again. What should I do? She was high: there was no other explanation. Where on earth would she have found drugs here in the wilderness? It must be something synthetic since she was having terrible hallucinations. She was breathing evenly, with no irregular movements. Should I leave her here? A car might hit her, if someone other than me drove past… I tried to entice her into her yard, hoping she would obey me, since I could not move her by force.

"Come on sunshine. Don't cry, honey: it's all a dream, a horrible dream. It'll all pass now. We'll go home and put you to bed under the covers. Come with me, come on! Let's get you some water, I'll dig out some Corvalol and make some tea. Come with me, dear, just a bit more. Come on."

Trying to comfort her like this, I led my unexpected companion across the road and opened the gate. I hoped there were no dogs in the yard, as there was no way I could get away from them. The woman walked like a sleepwalker, leaning all her weight on me, but she was still moving forwards. Suddenly, her body twitched, and I felt her every muscle tense. She held her hand up and pointed at the tree in front of her. I glanced in the same direction.

On the roof of the brick barn right in front of us hung a girl. Her legs and the lower part of her had fallen into a hole in the roof and the sharp edges of the roof slates had cut her in half. The upper half of her torso, from her breast upwards, was hanging against the wall, and her long blonde hair was caked with blood. A navy-blue bone was poking out of the place where her shoulder should have been, and she had no arm.

I stepped back once, then twice, and then I saw the dog. The big shaggy hound was sitting on top of a human foot in a trainer.

I would like to be able to say that in the moment I held my nerve and reacted appropriately to the situation. Truth be told, I couldn't hack it. My mouth filled with sweet saliva, my knees buckled and turned into cotton wool, and I literally felt my entrails rise up into my throat and stop me breathing. I abandoned the woman in her own yard under the hanging corpse, and ran off to the car in a panic. I tore off, leaving skid marks in the mud, and fled from the village.

I drove for about 20 kilometres without seeing where I was going, not looking back. I lost the front bumper in a ditch, something was rattling at the back, and the steering wheel was veering off to the right, but I did not care. Even if this Gazelle had to run on flat tyres, there was no way I was stopping. If it came to it I would have run away on my own two feet, following where my eyes took me, as long as it was away from here.

When a checkpoint appeared in front of me, for the first time, I did not care which flag was flying on it.

"Stop, I'll shoot! Where are your documents? Are you ill or something?"

I held my hands over my head and slid out of the car. I understood exactly what they were asking me for, but I could not work out which documents I had on me and where I had put them. My eyes searched out the flag and I tried to count the stripes on it, but without warning, and with a very inconvenient timing, I had stopped being able to tell the colours apart. Everything around me turned black and white, then grey. My ears were ringing, and the ringing turned into an unpleasant, high-pitched noise that sounded like a thousand mosquitoes had suddenly appeared. Then the light in front of my eyes went out and I found myself in total darkness. In those last few seconds, I marvelled at how simple dying was.

* * *

I have lost consciousness more often in the last six months than in the whole of my life before that, and it was already becoming a bad habit. It was as if a fuse had blown and my whole system had switched onto emergency mode in order to avoid circuit overload.

The border guards were sitting at the table in a good-sized house on the edge of a village. It had a large hall with enough space to take off your shoes, a kitchen with a Calor Gas cylinder and a real traditional stove with a sleeping ledge on top of it, and three walk-through bedrooms with heavy wooden doors, which were painted blue. The boys had got themselves a TV with a DIY antenna which only received Russian TV shows, and right now were watching the show *Wait for Me.*

"You hang on there, my daughter, we're going to have dinner now. I make a divine borsch, you know that? Anyone who tries it can't eat anything else!"

I nodded, agreeing without questioning. I found it so pleasant, lying on the old, squashed chair with the delicious smell of frying onions coming from the kitchen, stroking a cat stretching out on my lap, and I felt totally and utterly drunk as a lord, as they say, revelling in my pleasure.

Before this, the soldiers had poured me some water and listened to my story. I paused for a while, choosing my words, repeating myself like the woman in the village — 'dead, dead' — but the boys quickly understood what was going on. The oldest soldier, nicknamed 'Granddad', hugged me and put a canteen with homebrew into my hands. I drank it in one gulp, not tasting the alcohol but feeling the wave of warmth rushing through my chest to the bottom of my stomach.

"More, please!"

"Drink up, child."

We then went into the house, and were already on the threshold, practically nodding off, when I remembered the ducklings.

"Please, let the ducklings out! They're hungry."

"What ducklings?"

"In the crates."

It looked like that was the second time I gave them a surprise that day, and they opened the car. The slightly mucky ducklings visibly cheered up in the open air, and the boys gathered a whole tribunal to decide what to feed them. Luckily, a neighbour came by and sorted everything out. A place nearby dealt in boiled eggs, and the ducklings were snapped up by the potential poultry farm like an unwitting swimmer by a shoal of piranhas. They then took the boxes with the birds in return for a bucket of milk and several links of homemade sausage. I did not object: seemed like a fair exchange to me.

Granddad was then unhurriedly coursing between me and the frying pan, upon which he was sautéing the borsch ingredients. He was talking the whole time, but I was only half-listening, nodding off here and there.

"So, my daughter, it's all happening at the top, the fighting, and we're the mugs who are cracking our heads together. The politicians from America and Russia aren't letting on what's actually happening, and we're all just pawns in this. I'll tell you now, there's not going to be a war. Everyone's out here, spooking each other and then retreating — no-one wants a fight, not really."

"Are you serious?"

"Why not? Can't you see how everything's been wound up? It'll unwind in the same way."

"But people are dying, so many people have been killed already!"

"Well, the boys can rest in peace. But I'll say now that it's not worth us fighting with Russia, it'd be better for us to come to an agreement with them. Because no matter how we go about it, they'll grind us into dust. What are we supposed to do, naked and barefoot, against Russia?"

"What can we come to an agreement about?"

"Aye, if it was up to me an' all, I'd bring about order straightaway. Look here," he said, pointing towards the window. "We're here, and their border guards are over there look, all of a kilometre away across the ravine. I know each and every one of them, they come here on Saturdays to the *banya*, you know, our hotel with a sauna — The Adele's its name. We go fishing over by them see, there's good quarry further on. Who am I supposed to fight against? You think they want war? You think my brother-in-law wants to shoot me?"

"What brother-in-law?"

"He's the head of their dugout. He's also one of us, a *khokhol*. We studied together in Kharkiv, then I became godfather to his son, Volodya. When this all kicked off, I phoned him up, saying, 'Hey, buddy, what, you think I'm a fascist too?', and he says, 'Nah, I don't believe in that stuff'."

"Do you know what though, you're still out here digging trenches because your brother still shoots at you without thinking."

"*Nah*, you're talking rubbish. Nothing's going to happen here, they'll get scared and scatter. And the dugout? What do I need

a dugout for? You should see the mighty cave I've dug for myself
here. I hacked it out of the rock myself, when I first came back
from military service. We've only got soil for about a metre and
after that it's shale. Have you heard of this sort of thing?"

"What's that, did you live in it?"

"No, although my grandfather did. Many people from our village lived like that, that's how we did things — it's like they went
to work in the mines and came home to their own mine, like
'working from home', you could say."

I fell silent. It was not the right moment to argue. They kept
me warm and fed me. The branches of the apple tree were tap-
ping against the glass; bees were buzzing outside the windows
and chickens were clucking. A cat, which gave birth yesterday,
was purring on my knee, and the boys had put a box with four
ginger kittens in it on the table.

It was all very homely and peaceful. The children outside ran
down the street and went up to the soldiers without a crumb of
fear to ask for a can of condensed milk or a handful of sweets.
The grannies were sitting on the benches outside the little cot-
tages, waiting for the herd to come in. The cows would be driv-
en in in half an hour, at which point Granddad would bring over
fresh milk. I was spending the night in the house on a feather
bed with a wooden frame with big 'pinecones' on the corners,
which you could neatly screw off and back on.

Who would it hurt if I start trying to prove something? Only
myself; no-one else.

"Well, everything's ready, let's eat. I'll call the guys and go
down to the cellar, I've been pickling some tomatoes in a barrel,
we'll try them for the first time."

"Let me go. I want to see your famous stash."

"Come on. Only be careful going down the narrow steps. The
barrel's to the right of the door, just as you go in. Here; take this
bowl, lift the lid, put it back and then use this rock to clamp it
back down."

"Alright."

I wanted to get a bit of air. The midday heat had already passed, and it was that short period before dusk when you could still see outside, but you could smell the flowering Matthiola. The village lived and breathed its usual evening routine. The bucket rattled at the well, as the cattle were lowing and the crickets were chirping. The large grey dog in the yard turned its head in my direction, decided that I was not worth a barking at, and dozed off again.

"Lie down, little dog. I won't disturb you; I'm just getting some tomatoes."

The cellar was really first-rate. The neat stone steps brought me no less than three metres down into the ground. It was quiet, cold, and clammy down there, and it smelled of brine. Inside were jars of jam and conserves; rows of jars of *lecho* and spicy *adjika* sauce were hidden amongst the cobwebs in the deep. If there were mice there, then they were extremely well-behaved, because I could not detect even a hint of that classic mousy smell down there.

I leaned over the barrel of pickled tomatoes, pulling at the heavy wooden hatch, and at that very moment the first explosion took place.

* * *

I had read about shock waves before, but even in my nightmares I could not have imagined what it was like to feel one live. I would at least like to have been morally prepared for it, if you can be prepared for something like that.

The sensation is probably akin to crashing into a concrete pillar at full speed. That, or belly-flopping into the sea off a seventy-foot cliff dive. A battering ram flew into my chest, pulverising my ribs, and I was flung across to the far wall. This was not a question of seconds, but milliseconds: there I was, standing with the tomatoes in my hand, and then, suddenly, with no transition whatsoever, I find myself lying on the hard ground with planks and jars falling on top of me, and I can neither breathe nor cry out, my mouth gasping for air like a fish on top of the ice. The terrible sound burst my eardrum, and then I stopped hearing anything but a continuous droning. Something trickled down my face, getting in my eyes: it could have just as well been blood or jam; I did not feel any pain.

Black smoke billowed in from outside. The smoke quickly filled the cellar and rose to the ceiling. Realising that I had to get out, I crawled towards the light, but did not dare climb the stairs. There was at least a chance of salvation, even if the hole filled in, whereas above ground there was no chance whatsoever. The earth shook and sagged from a series of explosions, and then a projectile hit the ammunition warehouse.

It looked like a nuclear explosion, or maybe a solar flare. I saw the firestorm whirling over me and felt it singe the hair on my head. My back was unbearably burnt, and I instinctively rolled about on the floor to put out the flames.

I do not know how long the shelling lasted. I guess it's like the people who come to see the end of the world probably couldn't tell you how long Armageddon lasts for. Seconds? An eternity? I fell to the ground and could barely breathe, due to the wall of hot dust that burnt my lungs. Granddad was not lying: the cellar really was hollowed out of rock. The stone walls shook and buckled, but they held true.

I waited until the last, burying my face in a damp mash of tomatoes. At some point I felt myself roasting alive, like the legend of the old Cossack, Baida Vishnevetsky. I needed to get out.

I crawled upstairs, and each of the fifteen steps was like my personal Golgotha. My legs would not obey me; I could not lean on my palms, and my arms were bent out of shape, like they belonged to someone else. I had to heave my chest onto each step and tighten my knees to propel myself upwards. The floor was swaying, the stairs shook, and I could not see a thing in the dark, apart from the flashes far off in the distance.

It all then stopped at once — both the shelling, and my protracted climb. I fell on the surface of the earth and rolled away with the last of my strength. The house and the apple tree were on fire: the windows I had just been looking out of were already gone, and the wall was lying there in a pile of bricks. There were only a few railings left standing from the fence, and a crater the shape of a funnel was left in the place where the barn and the dog had just been. I saw the burnt-out skeleton of my car. I saw the black snow in the air, wondering somewhere in the back of my head — 'Why was it snowing in July?'

Snow fell: everywhere you cast your eye, big black snowflakes lightly falling all around, and I began to shake from the cold.

All around is silent, like a TV on mute. The branches on the trees are silently being shot off, and gravel and small pebbles are falling around. It's like I have a big fish tank on my shoulders instead of a head, and I'm looking at everything like a fish through water.

Suddenly people lean over me, a man and a woman. The man is very similar to Granddad, and I am glad that the old chap was alive, even if he is a closet separatist. He doesn't have a scratch on him, and his clothes are like new. Where did he find the white shirt from? I don't know the woman at all; slim, with a mousy brown ponytail on her head, she's also dressed like a doctor in a white coat. Both of them are shouting something at me right in my face, and I see their lips moving, but I cannot make out a single word. I prop myself up a bit onto my elbows in order to see better, and with an effort I turn my fish tank head. My eyes are stuck together, they are so thickly crusted with blood, dust, and tomato pulp, and I try to wipe each eyelid with my fingers. I cannot work out whether I have my lenses in or whether they have flown out from the force of the explosion; I cannot focus my vision.

"Here, quickly, there's a child here!" someone yells, right behind me.

I get on my knees and get on all fours to look at the child, but I cannot see anyone.

"Lie down, lie down! Don't move!"

Are they talking to me?

"I'm not a child," I reply, because I thought it was important for them to know. However, I answer them in my head, because the external manifestation of that thought comes out something like 'Eeeeah'.

"She's alive! Quickly, to the car, I can't see who's here! Be careful of her back! One, two, three, up! Find her vein!"

Someone takes me by the hand and lifts me up, pressing my face to a hard combat jacket. I want to say that everything is ok, they don't need to rush, I'm not in pain, but I change my mind. Talking requires effort, every word requires so much work, and I'm busy. I breathe, inhaling through my nose, exhaling through my mouth, trying not to use sharp movements, and I am still trying to follow the fish in my aquarium.

"Girls, hold on tight. We're swimming out of here."

MIRRORS

CANDLELIT WEDDING[14]

The following week has not been retained in my memory. I am not even sure it was a week, because time ceased to exist. I *was* aware of the fact of my existence. There was a body which I inhabited, and which I could leave for short whiles. There was a wall in front of my eyes, and I understood that it was a 'wall' and it was 'white', but I forgot the words that signified this.

I could see the bed, myself on the bed, and the drip stand. A doctor in scrubs would pop in, shine a light in my eyes, flick through my patient notes and test results, add something to my medical history, and then the nurse would go out and come back with new vials of drugs. Some girls would come in and leave me oranges and yoghurts. The cleaners were constantly mopping the floor, pouring water out of the still-clean mop bucket and putting out new bin bags. There were also people there who, at first glance, had no connection to hospital goings-on. Two or three of them would sit on top of the blanket and talk quietly amongst themselves, not paying attention to me. They would drink tea, open and close the window, and laugh. One granny in a sports hoodie and black skirt was knitting a scarf and did not stop to sleep or go to the toilet. I would fall asleep — there she was, sitting by me — I wake up — still knitting. I tried to say something to her, but the old lady did not turn her head in my direction.

Then another doctor appeared. It was not the one who would usually come in, but a lithe man with slightly balding, grey hair. He stopped in the middle of the ward, and barked:

"What is this mess? All visitors out — now!"

They made their way out: a woman with a baby and a young soldier. The last one to stand up was the old lady with the knitting, who wound up each ball of yarn, unhurriedly gathered her needles, and suddenly winked at me.

The doctor, meanwhile, did not miss a beat.

---

14 The subtitle of this chapter refers to a dramatic ballad by Ivan Kocherha, *Candlelit Wedding*. The play, set in the sixteenth century, dramatises a fight between petty craftsmen and the ruler of Kyiv about their right to burn candles so they could work by night. The hero of the story is Ivan Svichka, whose name translates as 'John Candle'. Kocherha said that the 'candle' the story refers to was the 'burning light of love and torment, extinguished by one unjust man and triumphantly relit forever by the might and the will of the many'. (Andrianova, N.M., *Ivan Kocherha: literaturnyi portret*, Kyiv, 1963)

"You've been lying here out of it for too long. Yes, we're changing your dose. Look here, we are stopping this and this and this —
I want 0.5 of this in six hours, and we will stop it completely in the morning. It's time to wake up."

Who was objecting to it? I had not asked for them to put me asleep at all.

I slipped out of sleep, like a foot out of an old worn-out sock. There was no-one in the ward. Rain pattered on the window; there was the sound of the ambulance sirens outside. I looked at my hands, then held my legs up next. My hospital gown clung to my thighs; I had no underwear on beneath. I carefully touched my head: my head was in one piece; that was good. Instead of my usual braid, I felt bristles. Was I bald? I had to look at myself.

The mirror hung above the sink. Without breathing, I turned onto my side and lowered my legs to the floor, pressing my toes against the cold tiles. Nothing hurt, only my eyes had misted over from my long period of convalescence. I had another strange feeling, like there was a gap between my brain and my skull, and it was snugly filled with something else. I felt the presence of something new; for some reason I felt strongly that I had to get to a mirror. Let's see, maybe I would not recognise myself at all? Then we would have to move to Plan B, whatever that may be.

But it never came to Plan B, because I was caught by a nurse, one of the three who took turns in the ward.

"Good Lord!" — she exclaimed, clapping her hands together. *"Anatolievich is a genius! Only where are you going my girl, you can't do that!"*

"It's ok," I coughed in reply.

I felt like I had been screaming for a long time, loudly at that, and I was now hoarsely scraping over broken vocal cords.

"Where are we? What's the date today?"

"The twentieth. And you're in Dnipro."

"The twentieth of what?"

"July. It's your third day here."

"What's wrong with me?"

"The doctor's now going to come and explain. Lie down," she said, gently pushing me towards the bed. "You can't stand up."

I feel my body. I think I am hungry. When do they serve breakfast? How do I also make a call from here?

As if reading my thoughts, the woman suggested:

"Do you remember your name? Should I give you a phone? Maybe you could phone your relatives?"

I am sure I remember. Who should I choose? Baba? It's a bit early for her, my grandmother does not appreciate people calling before lunch. My Roman? Not yet; he will have a go at me for trashing his car. Tetiana then. Tetiana is an early bird, she definitely will not shout at me.

"Hello, Tanya? It's me. I haven't woken you up, have I? Can you pick me up?"

"Huh? AAAAAAAAARGH!"

An absolutely inhuman, physiologically-impossible shriek broke the silence. I started, the nurse dropped her mug, sirens went off in the distance. What was the matter?

The discarded phone came to life in a second: I look at the screen and I see Borysovych's number, although I could not be sure in my condition. I take the call and listen to the string of the filthiest insults I have ever come across.

"You little... I'm gonna... right out the ground..."

"Borysovych, just talk to me! Have you gone mad?"

"You little..."

"Give the phone to someone else please. Who's with you? Oleh, my Roman, the girls?"

"Who are you?"

"What do you mean? Maybe *you're* the one with concussion, not me! What's wrong with you?"

The silence in the receiver lasted an eternity and an hour, and then a totally different voice, old and infinitely tired, croaked:

"My daughter, is that you?"

"It's me."

"Where are you?"

"In Dnipro, at the hospital. Why?"

Another pause, and then, very quietly:

"Well who are we burying right now, then?"

* * *

Funerals are not like weddings: you can't call them off, even if the deceased has either risen from the dead or changed his mind about dying. Furthermore, my funeral — good God, I never thought that I would write these words — turned out to be quite a crowded one.

The nurse, being a kind soul, gave me her phone and gave me the office Wi-Fi password. Then I read through my Facebook page, alternately closing my right then my left eye so I would stop seeing double.

The first thing I saw was a photo of my real face, instead of my old avatar. It was a portrait from pre-war times, from one of our old catalogues. After that was a short obituary, which included my full name, and hundreds of posts from friends and acquaintances in mourning. My page was swamped with images of candles and bouquets, and all the posts about the collections, purchases, and delivery reports went on and on, into the abyss.

To top it off, there were photos from my actual funeral, which were practically live uploads. Here was the white, closed coffin, covered by a pall, standing out amongst the crowd like a three-tier cake. My girlfriends were there by the coffin, swollen from crying; Tanya's black guipure lace headscarf had slipped to the back of her head and stuck up almost vertically, like a traditional Ukrainian *ochipok* headdress. There was a close-up of my grandmother, the fine sliver of her lips dividing her face in two. I saw dear Roman, the guys, and recognised Borysovych's back. I had to enlarge one of the photos to the max, because it looked like Komar was sitting on a pew with some soldiers — I just couldn't believe it.

Like any normal person, my first wish was to put a stop to this ugliness: change the password, stop any further posts in the group, give some refutation, some sort of explanation at least. But my finger hovered a millimetre from the screen. No, a story about the death of a little-known volunteer was one thing; a tragedy, but still a usual enough occurrence amongst all the other deaths that had happened this summer. The story of me rising from the dead was totally another thing. They would never let me forget this: I would have to tell this story of my miraculous dormition and divine resurrection until the end of my days. I am not against fame and glory, of course, but not at that price. As such, I just changed the page's picture back to my old avatar, took down the photos at the cemetery, and deleted the most emotionally-charged messages, especially those by the profiles of real people. I had nothing to replace them with.

Meanwhile, the hospital was buzzing, like morning rush hour at a train-station. For some reason, I thought that hospitals were supposed to be a haven of peace and quiet, but here, peace was a long-forgotten memory. Every minute, patients were being wheeled down the corridors, someone would be knocking at the doors, and some relative or other would be poking their nose into the ward, looking for their loved one in the trauma or surgery unit. The doctor came in and explained at length the nature of my polytrauma, but the only thing I only managed to take away from this was that I was not allowed to stand up, bend over, cough, or sneeze for three weeks — and I needed complete rest! Of course, the first thing I then wanted to do was sneeze, and my poor rib winced from the sheer pain of it, as if my whole body had become one pain centre which had just been jabbed by a hot poker. The chaplain then came by and said a prayer, followed by some girls on volunteering duty who brought yoghurt and a box of marshmallows. After them entered a small woman with the sort of blissful expression on her face as behoves only Jehovah's Witnesses and Amway salespeople.

"Do you want me to massage your head?"

"Huh?"

"Acupuncture, it's good for the pain. I work with patients here every day."

"No, thank you."

"Why don't we try anyway? You'll see, you'll like it! It's not expensive at all."

"Get your hands off me!"

The lady stood back, offended by my refusal, and then had some words with her posse outside the door, removing me for good from their list of potential clients (I would have said that this voodoo crew had put a 'black cross' over my name, were this not a poor attempt at black humour).

* * *

They did not cancel the wake, but simply got up from the table and left to clarify the situation. My grandmother, in that same old black skirt, coiled as tense as an African black mamba, sliced through the blockade of nurses like a knife through butter, paying no attention to the objections of the staff. Borysovych, Oleh, and Tetiana went with her. Stepanivna and Roman flew in after them, Roman clutching a funeral wreath made from fir branches and carnations.

The door of the ward slammed open, and everyone stopped in their tracks. I sat there with a marshmallow in my gob; the ward nurse froze by the drip stand. Tanya gasped aloud, and gently swayed back into Borysovych's arms. My grandmother nodded to herself, went over to the bed, and began to feel the nape of my neck, my back, and my arms. A second later, my nose was firmly imprinted into Stepanivna's bust, and I desperately fought for air. Borysovych said something which I could not make out and downed a glass of water. Old Roman took out a cigarette, which he chomped between his teeth without lighting it. He handed over the wreath to the bewildered nurse, who placed it in the sink.

Every story has its logical explanation, and mine was no exception. I was taken away in an ambulance out of the fire zone by volunteer paramedics. They were sure I was a child (hello there, genes and my −AAA bust). The wounded were taken to Starobesheve, and from there everyone was taken together by helicopter to Dnipropetrovsk, although I do not remember any of this. Similarly, I do not remember them wiping the soot, blood, and pickled tomatoes off me and stitching me up. By some miracle and by the providence of God I ended up without any serious injuries, not counting my concussion, broken ribs, and head wounds.

My bag, which contained my phone and papers, did not go up in flames as might have been expected, but remained under a table in the ruined house. It was found there a few hours later, when it was turned on and the phone began to ring without stopping. The bag's owner was identified by the phone and passport and, what's worse, a skeleton was found in my car. We never found out who it was. Perhaps one of the kids there had climbed in to play with the controls. Perhaps one of the neighbours had dived in there in a desperate attempt to shield themselves from the shrapnel; I never lock the doors and always leave the key in the door.

That small border hamlet lost seven people that day. Of the soldiers who never managed to finish their last meal of borsch, four perished. Grandad took a direct hit from a 122-mm shell from a rocket launcher, and all that was left of him was collected in a bucket. My Roman and Borysovych arrived there in the morning; they told them everything and showed them my ducklings. The boys took the body and drew up the documents in Dnipro — I did not want to hear what happened after that.

"Baba," I rubbed my cheek against her small hand, "Baba, fair enough that *they* believed I was gone. But why did you think, you know, I…?"

"It's a war, my daughter. The war has changed everything, you can't find anyone's next-of-kin anymore, everything's changed. I don't see you anymore. Now the dead — and the undead! — are piling up."

Tanya and Stepanivna were sitting by my feet and weeping. Tanya was bawling like a small child, whereas Stepanivna mumbled a prayer of thanks to God: "Jesus Christ, Lord our God, keep me eternally at Thy side, and let Thy Righteous Blood…"

"Say a prayer to grant us additional mental powers," asked Roman. "I heard about that one, the priest read it to us in church."

"Did it help?"

"No, not in the slightest."

At that everyone burst out laughing: me, the girls, and even Borysovych.

"Listen, people, you don't have something to munch on? I'm as hungry as a wolf."

At the mention of eating, Tanya's eyes welled up as she whispered her response:

"Here, have this. I took it with me, just in case."

She handed me a Tupperware box full of *kolyvo*. She grabbed the traditional funereal porridge from my wake.

* * *

I was transferred that evening from the ICU to a normal ward, and I realised that I would not get any rest there. The old lady next to me, a former ambulance doctor with sixty years' experience, came to from anaesthesia. She started talking before she even opened her eyes, and did not stop. I listened to her family history, from her grandchildren up to the generation before her, with plenty of details about a certain promising grandson, then a detailed report about a trip to Yugoslavia in the sixties, and received a great deal of advice about diets, rehabilitation, and how to find a husband. She filled the pauses with lines by Pushkin, such as *'By the sea stands a green oak tree'*.

Borysovych put up with this racket for five minutes, after which he leant over and muttered something in this woman's ear, whereupon she stopped, mid-sentence, like a toy with the batteries just removed.

"Borysovych, you're a saint, thank you."

"Any time."

The day before, we discussed my situation. We would not give an explanation about the death of a volunteer, and our group would continue to work. I would come back to work under a different name and would do essentially the same thing as before: upload lists of requirements for the army, reports, short accounts of what was going on, and photographs. We would explain what happened in private messages to trusted friends, but we would not make it general knowledge.

The last thing we were left to deal with were my documents. After our initial euphoria, we realised that the only thing I could produce at a checkpoint was a death certificate. We could technically annul it in a court and put me back on the list of the living, but no-one knew how we could do that whilst being registered in Donetsk. What, was I supposed to ask the separatists for proof of who I am for the Ukrainian courts?

We took a shortcut instead. When the separatists started taking over official buildings in Donetsk, the first thing to go were the passport desks. These good old traditional Soviet offices had no security and were full of blank documents that no one thought to rescue and take out of the city. Empty passports started appearing in bulk on the black market, something our Borysovych felt very uncomfortable about. They said on the news that the numbers of these passports had been annulled or entered into a database of lost documents, but people in the know just laughed.

"Borysovych, why didn't you just tell me you bought them?"

"What for? There's a lot I don't confess to."

The guys were beaming with pride. They shone like copper kettles, utterly pleased with themselves. I had the ideal passport in my hands: not new, a little worn, with two photographs in it. On one, a round-faced teenager in an ironed blouse looked out at me, on the other, a serious 25-year old woman, that is, Viktoria Stepanivna Storozh, born in 1989.

"Why 'Storozh'?"

"Me and Don thought of it, he wrote it down. It's symbolic, no? Storozh, it means 'watchman', and you do guard over us on all of those missions of yours."

"Got it. And then Viktoria, that's for victory, right?"

"That's after Stepan Bandera's daughter. Patriotism, right?"

"You do chat rubbish in your old age, you know."

"It's fine, you'll be this person for a bit, then when everything 'simmers down' we'll sort ourselves out."

We really did think everything would 'simmer down'. Like a shagreen skin left out to dry, the 'anti-terrorist zone' of Ukrainian army operations contracted every day, and the isthmus between the Donetsk and Luhansk fronts, which were falling apart before our eyes, was growing thinner and thinner. It was clear that Odesa would hold firm; Kharkiv did not fall to the separatists; Kherson and Mykolaiv pushed out the separatists, and Dnipro was ablaze with all shades of the colours blue and yellow. Neighbours who had rushed out of the warzone in a panic were starting to phone us up and find out what was going on so they could come back. How much longer could they stay away? Summer had flown by unnoticed, and the first of September was breathing down our necks; it was time for the children to go to school. They could not stay at the seaside forever — the holidays were nearly over.

My grandmother and I worked on our resettlement arrangement.

"Think about it," I said to her. "What if someone sees my photo and works out I'm your granddaughter? What if they dob us in? Let's take you to a safe village, you'll stay there a few months."

Baba was not having any of it.

"Firstly, you look nothing like yourself in that photo, no one has ever seen you look that beautiful." She was bang on the money there. "Secondly, the graves won't allow it."

"Huh? What graves?"

"If you live as long as I do, you'll know which ones. I not only have to think about the graves here, but the ones over there, too." She pointed a finger towards the earth. "Over there, where my mother lies in the ground. And my mother's sister, and my godmother. Not my father's grave — that's your great-grandfather — since he fell in the war; we don't know where and when. But my mother is buried there, and my grandmother too, rest in peace, near her in the old cemetery. They'll bury me there, too, which is only right. You aren't just fighting for the sake of it. You're fighting for your land. And our land is only ours if we support it on the ground."

Oh, Baba. You've packed your bags for your journey to the other side too soon. With a backbone like yours, you will be burying many more of us first.

PLEXIGLASS

TEMPERING METAL WITH A COOL FLAME

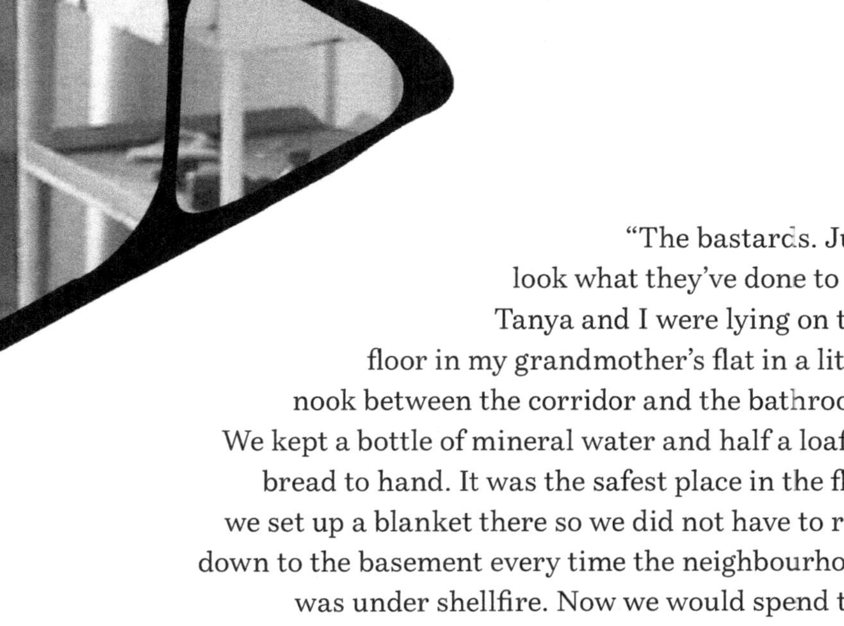

"The bastards. Just look what they've done to it!" Tanya and I were lying on the floor in my grandmother's flat in a little nook between the corridor and the bathroom. We kept a bottle of mineral water and half a loaf of bread to hand. It was the safest place in the flat: we set up a blanket there so we did not have to run down to the basement every time the neighbourhood was under shellfire. Now we would spend the night there, sometimes together, and sometimes I would sleep in the bath if left home alone.

We were huddled over the dim screen of my mobile phone, which within the hour would be out of battery. It would have been a good idea to turn it off since we were not sure when we would be able to charge it again, but the internet was our only source of entertainment that night and the only bridge between our perverted world and the normal world.

"What are you talking about?"

"Look! They're selling my flat!"

We were reading the ads under the *'broshenki'* section on a Donetsk online forum. A *broshenka*, from the Russian word *'brosat''*, 'to throw away', or *'broshennyi'*, 'abandoned', was a flat which belonged to refugees or to people from Donetsk who, most likely, would never return home. Recently, there had been a boom in carpets, appliances, and furniture at our online second hand sites: they all went for a song, being sold at half or a third of their actual value. Everything was paid for in roubles, for *'pick-up only'*.

Tetiana's flat was being sold according to all the usual marketing principles. Here you had *'discounts for real buyers'*, *'ready to live'*, and the fair warnings that *'all deals are formulated under DPR law'* — and lots of pictures. Tetiana swiped through the pics, looking at her bedroom, children's room, bathroom, and kitchen. The 'seller', who looked like they had Buryat ancestry, showed off the new plumbing, solid wooden cabinets, and the television.

"Oh, they've already taken out the washing machine. And they've run off with my Thermomix!"

"What's that?"

"It's an expensive food processor. I saved up for it for a whole year: me and my baby couldn't afford to go to the seaside that year. We should have gone on holiday after all. Damn, would you look at that! They've got my sheets on the bed. They're sleeping on my bed!"

"Right, give that here. It'll break your heart."

I took the phone away and closed the page.

"You don't get it, I'm not whingeing. I just want to remember it.

Give it here and I'll take a screenshot. The page has the contact number of that arsehole who's selling it."

My friend went on the site once more, but the homepage had refreshed and we saw a new ad:

'Souvenirs from 'the plane'. For connoisseurs and collectors. Makeup, men's and women's clothing in good condition, toys, papers. Price negotiable, discount for wholesale buyers. Confidentiality assured.'

"Oh my God. Is that what I think it is?"

"Yes."

"Surely we must have hit rock bottom by now?"

"Not in this town."

Tanya turned off the phone and put it away, taking out a pack of cigarettes from under the pillow and lighting one up.

"By the way, I wanted to say I'm pregnant."

* * *

I decided to light our last candle. Let it burn out, I did not care by this point: I had to look properly at Tetiana.

"God, would you look at your face! I knew you would react like this," she said.

"Are you sure?"

"What do you think?"

"I'm gonna kill that old imbecile. You're excused for your temporary lapse of sanity on account of the hormones, but what on earth is he thinking? Why are you still here?"

"Well, where am I supposed to be?"

"I don't know, the moon? Come here..."

I crawled over the barricade of pillows and cuddled my friend. We lay there, as if floating on a raft over the abyss. Outside was the thundering and whistling of war: somewhere in the distance, rocket launchers were busy firing shells and there was absolutely no guarantee that the next one would not fly into the flat and hit us. The noise even hurt my teeth and pressed on my diaphragm.

My heart pounded, not in my chest, but right in my throat, and we sat and wept in the midst of this hellish scene. I do not know whether it was from happiness or fear, or something in between, but the floodgates opened and tears washed over us...

"Borysovych knows, at least?"

"He doesn't know a thing. I haven't said. No-one but your grandmother knows. She guessed."

"I'm not surprised about Baba; she can tell straight away if someone's pregnant. I should have done too... Turn to the light."

Tetiana really had changed, and if I had not been so self-centred, I would have realised immediately. It is impossible to miss a pregnant woman: she is like a standard-bearer in a crowd, holding a huge torch over her head. Future motherhood changes her facial features; even if she does not show yet, it is like an invisible sculptor has rubbed out the old lines that trace her features and drawn new ones on a living figure.

"But you're going to tell him?"

"I don't know. We've never seriously discussed the future. First he starts pulling my leg, then I his, and then we start bickering. And he says all the time that he's an old bachelor."

"Tanya, we know Borysovych is a crook, and that he's wily and unscrupulous. But he's not stupid. Would he lose a woman like you? Never."

"You think so?"

"I know so. Unless the old goat dies of a heart attack from the shock first."

"No worries, the old goat has strength enough for ten. He's as tough as old boots."

"Well, you would know."

We burst out laughing, as though this was the funniest thing we had ever heard. Then we fell silent, watching the glare from the glow on the ceiling: a fire had started in our district. I then fell silent, because I had 'cockroaches' in my head, as my grandmother liked to say, and women 'with cockroaches in their heads' are awfully quiet. Each cockroach represented a thought, and you would have to wait an eternity before they would agree amongst themselves.

One shouts: "This is a shitshow!"

Another one corrects it, saying, "Don't swear. It's just a difficult life situation."

The third one says, "Confucius said: 'God forbid you live in times of change. While pregnant.'"

The fourth: "Do you think I'll be godmother? I would like to buy the baby a little stuffed lamb as a present and knit it a christening gown. And get it a special photo album, with angels on it."

"We need to get her out of here."

"Tomorrow morning, get her out!"

"What about the father? Why doesn't he sort it out and take her away to Volyn? Our countrymen will surely take her in."

"It's definitely a girl, she's got a dimple above her lip, on the side where it's a girl."

"Just shut it!" — I shouted at the voices in my head, putting together the prevailing opinion: *"This is a shitshow."*

Perfect, classic, Confucian.

* * *

Only the Thursday before Tetiana and I were walking around Dnipro, eating pizza, riding on the tram, and looking at the unfinished Parus building, upon which activists had painted an enormous Ukrainian trident, sixteen stories high. During my illness I had become unused to people and cars, to shops, to the door handles at the shopping centre even. Everything looked so bright and wonderful, as if washed clean by the rain.

I walked the streets like Artyusha, the old loony who served five years in Prison No.152 and came out completely mad, drooling over schoolgirls on public transport, leering at them with an *"Oh, giiiiirls..."*, dribble running down his chin — it was revolting. That was what I was like, a loony stopping and grabbing

Tetiana by the arm every other minute: 'Oh, look, a sale! Oh, ice cream! Oh, look at that car!'. I marvelled at the children at the playgrounds, the broad arbours of the trees stretching over the train tracks, billboards with new adverts, cash machines with no queues, SIM cards freely available on sale, and Ukrainian flags. People were just walking, laughing, talking at the top of their voices on the phone, sitting at the bus stops, looking like they had nowhere to be… The streetlamps were working, restaurants were open, and the café terraces were rammed, with pop music blaring out the speakers. At first glance, it was like nothing had changed and life was just like before the war — only now there were more soldiers.

Even I, who knew this city inside out, including that hidden side of it where we found aid and supplies, pooled money and rallied people to get shipments together; even I, who knew this city's warehouses, pharmacies, and garages like the back of my hand; who went through its construction depots which gave 100% discounts and took off tens of thousands of hryvnia from orders for the army; even I was lulled into a false sense of security at this illusion of peace and leisure. It was like how silicone lips and sparkly manicures can create a false image, the false eyelashes preventing you from seeing the intelligent gaze of the person looking out at you from the glossy magazine cover.

After that, we returned to Donetsk. I thought travelling from free into occupied territory would be different to what it actually was like. Even if there was no hard border, I expected at least stop signs, roadblocks, barriers, and some intensified checks, and fidgeted with my new passport, wondering whether I would slip through the net of searches and interrogations.

There was nothing like this at all. We passed untroubled through the villages, roads, and sunflower fields of our native region. We were ordinary Ukrainians: a little tired, a little stressed perhaps, but no-one was particularly interested in us. There were too many of us in the minibus; we had to push to get out, treading on people's feet; some people were wilting in the heat. Even so, we calmly passed through the checkpoints with not so much of a glance in our direction from the soldiers with assault rifles.

Then followed a few kilometres of the so-called 'grey zone', which looked more like a patchwork quilt, as God only knew who controlled these fields and plots and where lay the boundary between free and occupied land. We had turned from citizens into collateral, and, like in every war, the losses to the civilian population rounded up into the thousands. We could only put our hopes in the driver's skill and his connections on both sides of the frontline. I wanted to believe that the bloke knew what he was doing, and that the women at the front would devoutly stifle the chatterboxes on the bus, hissing, *"Shh, don't distract the driver!"*

After Kurakhiv, conversation faltered, and we arrived at the first separatist checkpoint in silence. They were not interested in us here either; one militant looked through the window, exchanged a few words with the driver and waved him on with a 'Go through!'. Perhaps they thought we would get searched later on, or perhaps they had finally got tired of this protracted comedy of errors, and they no longer cared who was coming in and out of Donetsk and what for.

I had not been at home for two weeks, although it felt like years. I felt as though during this time another batch of aliens had landed and had once again taken over my countrymen's brains.

There were whole districts in Donetsk where everything was *'harasho'* (i.e. 'good', in Russian), yet where people were being shot at a mere kilometre away from you. It was a mystery to me how there were swimming pools and gyms still open in the city; concerts and cat shows were being held; posters for events were put up; and public maintenance workers still planted roses and swept the streets. I think that this is yet more proof that the Donbas represents an anomaly in spacetime. My fellow citizens and I found ourselves inhabiting parallel universes — only for some reason I could see them, and they could not see me.

The dramatic inhumanity of my fellow townspeople was depressing. The word for it is 'dehumanisation', right? The stable, well-fed areas of the city with running water and electricity were not the ones which took in our refugees from the north, washed them, gave them a bed for the night or even just something hot to eat. Those who could, left. Those who could not leave were then left worried about where to park their car so it would not get stolen, how to seal their doors and windows off from burglars, but they did not think about us on our exodus from the areas of the city under attack: they barely even remembered we existed. *"Wow, you've got it rough up there!"* — they would merely say.

I knew we had it *rough*, but what do we do next? If Donetsk was becoming the country's ghetto, then we were becoming a ghetto within a ghetto.

My building was not one of the lucky ones. A shell flew into the one of the building entrances last week, and the third floor burnt down. Miraculously, no one died, but it was after this the people who had held onto their flats until the very end left. Only a handful of residents were left in our apartment block — mostly pensioners in a deep fugue, propped up by their TVs. The neighbours set up a bomb shelter in the cellar, stocking up on water and candles, and put bunks in there. It could accommodate about three dozen people, but I made the decision with myself that I would not step foot in there; if only because going underground would make me panic.

The morning after the first shelling, I sent Tetiana to live at Borysovych's place.

"Let her go and sort herself out," I thought.

Knowing the old bloke as I did, he would make sure Tetiana would be sent packing to the motherland in a flash. Even if not, she would still be safer at his than here.

After she was gone and I was left home alone, I turned my phone off and lay down in the flat to think a while. They say the human brain is a most powerful tool, able to squeeze out traumatic memories and insert something less traumatic in their place.

"Do it then," I told myself. "Go on, squeeze them out. I am creating the ideal conditions for doing so. Those big cabinets in the corner, go use them to hide terabytes of memory. Just leave in their place a field, a great field of wheat for me. Make sure I see this meadow every time I go to sleep. I am happy to listen forever to the rustling of the ears of corn, to how the earth cracks under the ripening grain. I want to fall backwards, backwards into the wheat, and to hear an invisible lark singing in the sky above."

* * *

If I had had the chance to spend that summer in a cryochamber instead, I would not have hesitated for a second. I would have written on the door: 'Thaw me out when it's all over!' and gone to hibernate. But this 'over' was only a pipedream.

I would not have got up off that divan were it not for the seven cats in the house, which would not let me lie in bed. My grandmother took Bucks with her, and the kingdom of felines was bequeathed to me. As such, the next morning I nevertheless got up, took a twenty-litre cauldron outside and cut down an acacia tree for the first time in my life. The green sapling did not burn well; still, I got a fire going, brought the water to boil, and cooked millet porridge with stewed meat. It was almost like *kulish*, the old Cossack dish they used to eat on the hoof, but it had no *salo*, no mushrooms, nor onions. Lyudmila, who lived on the other side of the building, came over to investigate the source of the smell of smoke. A couple from the flat above came down, as did a few invalided neighbours, and we then counted up our 'assets' and 'liabilities', so to speak.

Amongst our assets were the cauldron of stew, the pump in our yard where we could safely draw water, my first aid supply, and my blood pressure monitor. Amongst our liabilities were:

three people who were bedridden, one of them diabetic; nine people who were invalids, but mobile; and a mother and children on the eighteenth-floor. We had no gas, electricity, water, or phone signal, but there was still internet. Ambulance services and taxis did not serve our district.

A well in the yard with an old oak table, a rusty swing, and some sheds also created the illusory and illogical feeling of security. It felt safe here, and no-one really wanted to leave in order to find 'freedom'.

Our building had always been a bit secluded. Firstly, in contrast to our neighbours, we had a closed courtyard. When the district was first being built, the house had no sewerage and the residents had to scamper out to use the outside toilets, and water was drawn from a pump. The place was completely revamped after Ukrainian independence from the USSR, with bathrooms being installed in the building and gas pipes fitted, but the wooden sheds that used to be the toilets were not taken down. They were divided between old-timers living there who turned them into barns or garages, or as one family did, kept a goat there. Gradually, our own little 'industrial estate' expanded, what with the neighbours ploughing up and sowing an allotment on the wasteland behind the garages, putting in new corrugated-iron storage shelters, and accordingly moving the fence a few dozen metres back.

There were two ways of accessing our yard: either through the central gate, or through an inconspicuous opening behind the allotment. We welded the iron gates and fashioned a lock for them. We had the idea of organising a night watch, but never found anyone willing to do it. Plus, what would a bunch of helpless pensioners do against armed terrorists? We had enough trouble with our own neighbours, who once tried to chase the orcs out of their yard who had brought a Nona self-propelled gun in to fire on Ukrainian lines. People were shot by gangs without a second thought, and we would then go to the funerals to honour the victims; sometimes of three people who had been shot in one go, buried in closed coffins.

It was not clear what we were sitting and waiting for.

"Who's to blame?"

There was only one answer to that eternal and classic Russian question among our neighbours:

"The Ukropi" — after that fun little play on the Russian words for 'dill' and 'Ukrainian'.

"What do we do now?"

There was no answer to *that* question. We agreed that everything would soon be over, and for now we had to just pray and endure it. In the end, either the *Ukropi* would enter the city, which was unlikely; or *'our boys'* from the separatist side would take Kyiv, and everything would settle down. That, and Russia would invade, of course. Russia's second coming was awaited like manna from heaven, and I never even tried to convince or persuade my neighbours otherwise. I would make my porridge every morning in silence; I would hand out the bowls of stew to anyone who wanted it, in silence, giving the scraps to the animals. I convinced myself that I had to treat these people like they were unwell or intoxicated, that is, not to trust them one bit and not to rely on them for anything. God willing, this will end soon, and they will somehow be cured. Well, that or shot; I did not care.

I did not have the strength to walk long distances. Or even short ones at that, since I had made a decision in the manner of King Solomon not to rush around anywhere, to sit at home instead and wait for a solution. I had no problem when it came to food: I had various grains and pulses, *salo*, and potatoes. That, and the supplies from the refugees who handed me keys for safekeeping, saying to me directly:

"Take whatever you need, eat anything you can see. We can't take it with us anyway."

Hence, like Robinson Crusoe, I would bring a whole warehouse home with me, each time blushing and mentally thanking my absent benefactors. Pasta, sugar, flour, jars of preserved vegetables or jam, hardened biscuits and crackers, canned food — everything that was needed here more than there. War quickly deprives us of our everyday conventions.

Few of our refugees thought they would be gone for long. The majority of them just grabbed a rucksack and a pair of suitcases, and went away for 'a week or two'. They left their furniture, pictures, souvenirs, toys, children's drawings, fridge magnets, crockery — all the things that we seem to inconspicuously acquire and that bind us to a place like thousands of capillaries bursting with blood.

Lyudmila and I went around the block twice a day: peeking in the attic and shining a torch in the corridors to check for any strangers. Lyudmila was the only mother with children left in the block. (Sheesh, I'm not going to delve into her story too. All I'll say is, the father of the family was arrested. The family already paid his bail a second time — we sent them money for it. Now they are just waiting until the father is set free. I am almost certain that they are waiting in vain, but I cannot say it to her face). We go on the hunt for food together, because if you do it alone, it's burglary; when you are with your neighbour, it's an expedition.

Have you ever seen a house that has been abandoned without notice? The houseplants are the first to die. The women still held out hope for their little orangeries as they fled: practically every flat had a bucket with strips of bandages feeding the flowerpots from it. The flowers would lay under these soaked strips, from which water would drip down and feed them. The water did not last long, till the end of the month or so. Then they lived on the memory of water, as long as they could. The geraniums immediately withered and crumbled into dust, whereas the cacti and orchids lasted until July; now, in August, everything had dried up.

The house also stinks. Almost every flat had something edible left in it, something left uncooked on the hob or gone sour in the fridge. Imagine what a two-month-old borsch smells like! One woman forgot her laundry in the washing machine, and the rags rotted right in the drum. When I went into the flat the stench hit me in the face, and we ran home to get respirators.

The house also gets covered in dust; cobwebs spring up everywhere; mice and cockroaches move in; bats settle in under the roof, hinting to all of us with their presence to go away: 'Your time is up!'. Stairs begin to creak, never having done so before. Something goes bump in the attic, and light flashes in the abandoned windows. You comfort yourself with the thought that it is just the flash of headlights from the street, but at the same time you know that there are no cars on the road.

The first entrance to our block stank, but to a greater degree than the others. With every day the sweetish smell of rotting flesh grew more and more noticeable, until it was unmistakable what it was. What had most likely happened was the owner had locked their dog in the flat in the panic of leaving, and it had then starved to death.

"Let's go have a look," I say to Lyudmila. "We'll open the door, clean up, and dig around, since I already have flies the size of horses flying around my flat."

"Let's go, then."

We quickly found the source of the stench. It came from Borys' flat, the local drunk who took to the bottle after the death of his mother some years ago. In May he went to fight the 'junta'. I never saw him go, but my grandmother said that he was roaming about the yard, absolutely plastered and touting an assault rifle.

"Oh, look, it's open. Shall we go in?"

"I don't know, I'm scared. Shall we call someone?"

"I should at least open the window to ventilate the place, otherwise we'll be gassed by the fumes."

We looked in and called from the entrance, but no-one answered. Lyudmila then stumbled into the bedroom and immediately flew out. I wanted to look, and she pushed me back, saying,

"Don't go in!". But there was no way you could hide what was
there.

The corpse had melted all over the bed. The hermetically-
sealed room had heated itself up like an oven in the summer
heat, and everything that was once flesh and blood had disintegrated and diffused across the room, corroding the mattress
and the parquet floor. In fact, Borys — and it *was* him, judging
by the remains of the green camouflage uniform — had turned
into a skeleton. Everything around it — the ceiling, the walls,
the old-fashioned wall cabinet, and even the windows — was
plastered with muddy stains. If it was blood, then it must have
flowed in streams, like in a slaughterhouse.

"Let's get out of here — run!", I said, grabbing Lyudmila.

"But, there…"

"It's none of our business!"

"Maybe we should call the police? Or the military police?"

"You mad? Forget that."

That evening, I called old man Vasyl, and we dug a shallow
grave behind the sheds. We then returned to that awful flat and
took the remains out right on a blanket. If we had a gas mask,
I would have worn one, but instead I just wrapped my face in
a towel.

The four of us threw Borys into the earth and stuffed him
in with shovels. We hesitated — ought we say something? — but
neither I nor the old man could find the appropriate words.

That was the first night in many weeks when I was not awoken either by the explosions outside or the cats jumping on my
face. All because I got out a jar of my grandmother's moonshine
just to clean off my hands, but then mechanically drank a whole
mug of it. It went down like water into parched earth. The last
thing I remember was thinking whether I should limit myself
to two gulps, or to have a third one. Then whoosh — and it was
morning already.

My grandmother distils the best moonshine in the district.

* * *

I could not say that week was only a tragic one. There were also happy moments.

For example, old Stepa was taken into our cellar / makeshift bomb shelter. God forgive this sinner for laughing at another's misfortune, but this news will warm my heart on the cold winter evenings.

She was the first to hang a DNR tricolour flag on her balcony, and then a Novorussia flag with a cross on it. Stepanida was the one who distributed invitations to the separatist referendum around people's flats. She was the one who raved about the higher pensions and the wonders of Russian medicine, about *'a normal, wealthy country, and not this backwards Khokhland'*, a play on the words *'khokhly'* (a slur for Ukrainians) and 'Holland'.

"Even the Americans are going to come and work at our hospitals. My sister got her teeth done in Moscow with her health insurance policy, they now shine like mirrors. And all for free! You could only dream about that sort of thing over here!"

She was the one who led the distribution of Rinat Akhmetov's humanitarian food parcels and hired girls to work in their centre (you spend five days packing food parcels, and on the sixth you get one for free). Then her car also got stopped and searched by the separatists. She had more than thirty bottles of oil with Ukrainian labels on them, condensed milk in plastic tubs, and boxes of biscuits in her boot. No matter how much she swore to God they were hers, no matter how much she tried to convince them that they were humanitarian aid, they would not believe her.

'You're giving supplies to the Ukropi!' — and that was it. Most likely, the militants' sweet tooth got the better of them, and it was a nice car, not all beaten-up.

They held her at a factory for three days. They would not let her sleep, did not feed her, kept her in the cellar, and finally threw her out in the clothes she stood in, without her car, money, and papers. She came home dirty and tear-strewn, wanting to say something, yet though her cracked lips would move, you could not decipher the words. She could not get into her flat without her keys, but one of the local old boys cut through the lock for her.

"Oh no!" I say, *"How terrible! Are they really targeting their own people? You were fighting so hard on their side! Oh, how insulting!"*

"Oh, go shove it up your arse."

Those were the first Ukrainian words I ever heard from her.

* * *

That day turned into a surprisingly quiet evening. It was stuffy in the flat, so I went downstairs and sat on the tree stumps. There was a brief moment of calm in anticipation of twilight, when everything around went soft and blurry, when contours and outlines lost the sharpness of their edges. It smelled like Matthiola out. The sounds of the city, of the war, had died down; you could not hear the cars, or the clang of iron. I clenched my eyes shut and listened to the evening birdsong, the first time I heard it that summer. I then started singing myself at the top of my voice, just for myself and for the night bird.

> *In the cherry orchard*
> *Where the nightingale sings,*
> *I begged him to go home*
> *He wouldn't let me go…*

After some time, I realised I was not alone. Two people came up from the cellar, and a neighbour pulled up. Everyone was quiet, as all of them did not want to spoil the moment. I shuffled over on my seat, they sat down, and at first timidly, and then more confidently, picked up with their voices.

> *My daughter, are you all right?*
> *Where have you been all night?*

Why, your braids are undone
And your cheeks wet with tears!

We sang and sang some more, without stopping. How did I know all the words — the others too? We sang the folk songs and Ukrainian classics: 'She Walked through the Garden', 'Halya', 'Wherefore Did My Love Leave Me?', and 'Chervona Ruta', and 'The Hutsul Girl Xenia'… More neighbours joined us — the whole block, it felt. No-one hurried down to the shelter: no-one dared move. I did not see people's faces in the dark, I only felt the tears run down my cheeks and the trembling of my voice, and the same trembling and cracking in the voices of my neighbours. For a moment, I felt sorry for them, and me, and for this shabby but familiar yard, which had already changed irreversibly from what it once was. We were like penguins on an ice sheet drifting abroad the seas, and the ice was melting and cracked beneath our feet.

"Listen, listen to me!" — suddenly I felt a slap on my shoulder. "Turn around!"

In front of me stood Lyudmila, out of breath.

"What?"

"I've just gone to see my mother, and a huge dove flew right out in front of me on the way. It wasn't one of our usual pigeons, but a white, purebred dove — it was glowing! It flew at me like a comet, before swooping over my head and soaring into the sky, fluttering its wings. I stand there and he hovers above me, not flying away. Don't you think that's a sign?"

"It is."

"It's a positive sign, right? Is it telling me my Petya will be back with me soon? That he's ok? Tell me!"

She grips my shoulder so hard that the bruises will not be gone till autumn, shaking me, and my poor head rings like a church bell.

"Just say he's alive! Say it!"

I embrace her, saying nothing, and she howls into my chest.

AQUAMARINE

HOURGLASSES

That was the last night
I spent at home, although
I never would have known that
morning. Everything was just like
usual. Sometime around seven I lit a fire
and pulled out the Dutch oven. I had already
grown fond of this Dutch oven, forgetting already
that once we used to cook on a normal hob. I felt like
I had always gone around smelling of smoke,
with greasy hair under my headscarf and
a black rim of dirt under my nails.
A little later people started crawling out
of both our cellar and the neighbouring one to
get water. A brief exchange of news: whose house
got hit, is anyone injured? Everyone was intact,
though one wall was shattered into pieces.
Then my phone rang. I did not immediately
register what that sound was; I had got so
unused to having any phone signal.

"Hello, my dear Roman."

"Oh, hi. Listen, can you come to the office and get yourself out of that hole of yours?"

"Hey, we're not a hole, we're an outpost! I'll come now."

"Please, it's important."

Right that moment, I took off my apron, washed myself under the pump and ran to work. Well, not quite; I popped home first and took some cash and my passport with me. As I was leaving, I bumped into Lyudmila and stuffed my keys into her hands.

"Feed the cats, ok? I won't be long," I said.

It is unbelievable how difficult travelling is when you can only go by foot. Is this really only eight kilometres? It was five minutes by car — no time for a backwards glance. It is three hours by foot, especially on feet unused to walking.

At around the halfway point, civilisation appeared. The clean dustbins were the first sign. We, in contrast, had not had bin lorries coming our way since July. To deal with the stench the old boys and I had to sort the rubbish, burying any organic matter and burning the plastic. Here, it seemed, people were cleaned up after.

I then passed a working supermarket and right next to the workshop I watched the street workers digging a flowerbed for a long while. Pinch me! We were being bombed by night, but here they were planting flowers like nothing had happened!

I stopped again, this time in front of my office. I burst through the new gates like a battering ram, pushing the sticker that read: 'Under the protection of the Ministry for State Security of the Donetsk People's Republic', which was stuck on our entrance. The same stickers adorned all the windows.

"Greetings, friends. Or should I now say that in Russian?"

Four pairs of eyes looked up at me in an obvious state of confusion.

"What are you on about?"

"I'm talking about our new security."

"Oh, that… Forget about it."

There was a wall of smoke in the room, making my eyes water. The ashtray on the table had long been overflowing, and the lads had started putting cigarette butts in a sugar bowl I had made. Roman reclined on the couch, straight out of one of those old paintings of opium dens. What was he doing? Was he meditating, or what? Borysovych was pacing from corner to corner, smoking one cigarette after the other. Oleh and Don were standing over a laptop.

"Alright, listen," Borysovych stopped in front of me. "I'm talking to you as a fighter right now, not as a woman, alright? If you want to kick and scream at me, do it a bit later, in a few days."

"I'm listening."

"Komar didn't abandon us. He was working with our side, and very effectively. He leaked us valuable information: lists of people, documents, army locations, and lots more besides."

"He was working for us?"

"Bravo," Roman piped up. "Cutting right to the chase."

"He was spying. It was going to your funeral that burnt him. He got spotted there. They got him a week ago. The whole of the last week we've been trying to find out where he is and what's happened to him. We only managed to get him out yesterday and take him to the hospital. He is now in intensive care, but under guard. But this is just a breather for a couple of days."

"So, he needs to be taken out today."

Borysovych nodded, more at his thoughts than at me.

"That's what we need to do. We have a plan, but we need an ambulance and a woman to play a nurse for it."

"You've got a woman, that's no problem, but what about the ambulance?"

"The problem is, we don't have one."

"Dial 03 then."

Roman started coughing on the couch. As if I did not

immediately realise he was laughing! I do not like his cough. He'll cough up a lung next.

"Well, that's one solution. We'll tell you all the details of the plan so you can look at it with fresh eyes, maybe you can think of something. Only," Borysovych paused — "you understand that this might be a trap, and they're waiting for someone to come after him, in which case we won't get out alive."

"So, we have a fifty-fifty chance of making it?"

"My daughter, our chances were always fifty-fifty."

I came right up to him, stood on my tip-toes and breathed into his ear so no-one else could hear.

"Why didn't you tell me earlier, you imbecile?"

"I couldn't, I swear. I gave my word."

* * *

In any situation you cannot understand, just close your eyes and look ahead. This is you. This is your immediate future, for a second or two. Then this is the flow which carries you towards your destiny, and which you can neither change nor turn around, but which you can negotiate with. This is how the surfer negotiates with the wave, straight out of his wildest dreams. This is how the weather-beaten horse rider negotiates with the mountain of sinew beneath his saddle. This is how the mother in labour negotiates with the pangs of childbirth and gives birth to a son. This is how the hand negotiates with the grain lying in the damp earth, which will then grow a green shoot.

To change the hand one is dealt, to turn one's luck at a really critical moment, one must be extremely honest. One must say, 'I am that; I am a grain of sand on the ocean shore. I may not be able to stand against or contend with the goliath that stands before me, but today I shall take what I can from the ocean, and it will pump its waters through me. Because I am asking with my blood right, which carries within it the eternal molecule of the primordial sea'.

Because behind me loom the shadows of women who have walked before me, and their traces and my own footsteps have become one. Because behind me is the longing of the she-wolf who has led the hunters from her lair. Behind me rustles the maize that beat my mother's brow as she ran into the oncoming shadows. Because behind me is the ashes of that fire, and only now can I remember who that woman was who died in that fire.

The stream of destiny that ran before our feet shuddered and quivered like a drawn bowstring before the archer releases his first arrow, the string digging into his fingers, his impatient shoulders growing weary with the strain.

"Don't worry boys. Don't panic. Everything will go fine."

"You think so?"

"I can guarantee so."

* * *

First, I got washed and dressed. There are things you can only do with clean hair.

Goodness, how forward-thinking we were to install a proper bathroom in the workshop, and how glad I am of my habit of leaving spare T-shirts and trousers where they might be needed, including at work.

Whilst I scraped the soot off me and washed my hair again and again, the guys got together. For months now, I had not intruded on their affairs and had not asked questions. As such, their new fatigues, assault rifles, and the holster with a pistol which Borysovych tied above his knee should have surprised me, but they did not. Little surprised me anymore. I had no time to be surprised. I waded into the fateful stream, pulling out positive outcomes for me and the guys. I also made sweeping motions, sweeping away any obstacles before us with an imaginary broom.

Some unknown men joined us too. They drove up in a brand-new Landcruiser with 'holey' number plates.

"You got your papers on you? Show us."

Borysovych took out a burgundy card with a two-headed eagle coat of arms on the front. The newcomers passed around the certificate, meticulously twisting, smelling, biting it to check, and were eventually satisfied with it.

"It'll do. It's good quality."

Of course it is! If I understand correctly, our Oleh had not produced anything of bad quality for quite a while.

We went together to one of the abandoned houses belonging to one of the neighbours whose keys lay on my desk, waiting for their owners to return. Only Roman did not join us. He would cover us from behind with his Opel, and if anything happened, he would stall his car, cutting off our pursuers. Well, that was our plan.

While we prepared ourselves, I called an ambulance and wailed into the receiver.

"Come, please come! My child is choking, his grandfather is giving him mouth to mouth! I beg you to come now, we'll pay, petrol, for the call, just come! He's only eight, I'm his mummy, here's the address... He has allergies, he needs an injection now! *Help us!"*

Either it was just one of those days, or pre-war standards of medical care were still maintained in this neighbourhood. Maybe we were just lucky, but the ambulance arrived within five minutes. We heard the sirens from afar, and I ran to the gates to greet the medics.

"Here, here!" I waved my hands and opened the gates. *"Drive in here!"*

A young medic and a nurse ran out of the van, the driver staying inside. We went into the building, where loaded barrels were already waiting for the ambulance brigade. Everything happened very quickly; less than a minute and we had the uniform and medical supplies on us, and the doctor and nurse were on the couch, bags over their heads. Now for the driver.

"Come here!" I ran over to him. *"Come here a minute, the doctor's asking you to help take out the stretcher."*

The driver got out of the cabin without even taking the keys out of the ignition and followed me.

"What the..."

That was it. I did feel sorry for them, honest. I leant down and whispered in the girl's ear:

"Don't worry, everything will be fine. They'll let you go."

The nurse sobbed.

One fighter was left to guard the medics, whilst Oleh and Don had already connected their laptop to the onboard navigator. They work extremely effectively — literally a few clicks, and they're in. I would have only been able to turn on the programme within that time, whereas the boys were already done. The ambulance would register as being at this address for as long as necessary, and then it would 'go' to whatever address it is given. The radio reported to the base that the team was treating the child on the spot. The dispatcher accepted the message and disconnected.

We jumped into the ambulance and rushed off to the hospital. The next half an hour went second by second. Seconds had never lasted so long in all our lives. A black car hung on our tail, which we could not shake off.

* * *

We were let into the staff-only area without any questions. Borysovych waved the ID card through the window, and they lifted the barriers. We lined up, shielding ourselves in tortoise formation in front of the No.14 building. The 'guards' were the first to open the car and opened the doors for Borysovych. Two went ahead, followed by Borysovych, three covered the sides, and I came out last, with the medical bag in my hands. The bag was actually very heavy, but no one thought to help me.

Two *opolchentsi* guarded the entrance, and they rose cautiously at our appearance, but did not raise their weapons. Borysovych poked his ID under their noses without slowing down, and the guards jumped back. One was left scratching his head, wondering whether he should call someone.

Once in, we were invisible, and people stubbornly avoided noticing us. If we accidentally caught a patient or a doctor's eye, they would momentarily avert their eyes. The cleaner with her mop inhaled, about to say, 'Where are you going on this wet floor!', but even she thought against it. Disregarding the lift, we took the stairs to the first floor, with one fighter holding back on the ground floor.

Ours was the last ward along the corridor. Two people were chatting by the door, and at least one witness was inside. I slowed down next to the nurse's station and told the confused nurse, *"Patient in ward thirteen, quickly."*

The ward was tiny, barely able to fit two beds, and once we had all squeezed in, there was no space at all. The ward had a strong smell of blood, urine, and rotting flesh, but the barred window would not open.

A separatist was sprawled on top of the sheet on one bed in shoes and camo. At our appearance, he propped himself up with some effort, emitted a boozy belch, and lay down again.

A body was lying on the neighbouring bed. I stopped, hypnotised. I restrained myself from covering it with a shroud. It was like the man in front of us was divided into two parts, the boundary running through the middle of his torso. Pale legs were marked here and there with sharply-defined burns; his groin and thighs were covered in dozens of round welts, the size of a penny. From his diaphragm upwards, his neck and arms were one dark bluish colour. All over was one solid haematoma, as if he had been dipped upside down in a tub of blue ink.

He was barely left with a face. His shattered nose was held together by a plaster splint, a tube was inserted between his swollen lips, and the man was breathing heavily, rhythmically breathing out pink foam. His roughly-sutured wound stretched from his chin, across his left eye, to his hairline, which was crusted over with blood, and his eye was totally welded shut as one black eye. However, the wounded man could see with his right eye, and he checked out the guys, Borysovych, and then rested upon me. It was impossible to identify the patient: he could have been any age, height, or even race.

Whilst I looked around, Borysovych gave brief instructions to those present. He spoke completely differently to how he did with us, the Ukrainian way of pronouncing 'h' and 'shh' disappeared somewhere, and even his intonation changed.

"Prepare the wheelchair, we'll take him out now."

"We haven't been warned about this!"

"Don't worry, we're not waiting around."

The separatist was clearly hesitant, not knowing what rule to follow, when we heard a categorical order from behind the door:

"I forbid you to touch him. It is not allowed."

At these words walked in a small doctor with short ginger hair. She held a paper file in front of her, as if using it as a shield, and clearly was not going to back down. In a moment the winds had blown in our favour: now the separatist was not arguing with Borysovych, but with the doctor, finding himself on our side of the barricade, so to speak.

"Yes? And why is that?"

"He cannot be transported. He will not live more than three hours without medical attention."

"That's fine," said Borysovych, taking the doctor's arm, *"that's enough time for us. We don't need more than that. Come in!"*

"I forbid it!"

"Oi darlin'!"

'Our' separatist on the bed had come back to life somewhat.

"I'm the only one forbidding anyone around here," he said. *"Got it?"*

A stretcher rolled through the door. The boys took the sheets, on a 'one-two-three' moved the patient and pushed everyone to the exit. We went out of the corridor. The doctor said nothing, collecting her thoughts, and I noticed that she was not a redhead, but totally grey, with badly-dyed red hair.

The old separatist still tried to call someone, getting out his phone and waving at us to stop: "Wait!".

Then an explosion went off on the floor below. The walls shuddered and the plaster flaked off; the stairwell and corridor were filled with smoke, women were screaming, and people were tearing out of the wards.

"What are we standing around for?" Borysovych barked at the *opolchentsi. "Run!"*

At the command, 'run', everyone did their own thing, the majority running away from the fire, to the stairs at the end of the corridor, and only our separatist suspected something.

"Wait, hang on!" — he cocked his assault rifle.

The thickset uncle next to me who looked like a bus driver stepped forward and held up his hand. There was nothing threatening in his movement, it had no hidden power — it was the same way you would put a hand towards someone you recognised in a crowd. But the separatist went quiet from this simple gesture, released his weapon, and clutched his chin. Something black was sticking out the middle of his neck, jammed into his jugular fossa. For a second I thought one of our fighters had stuck a badge there. Then, without a single rattle or sound, like in a silent film, the separatist keeled forward, was picked up by four pairs of hands, and was taken into an empty ward and laid onto a bed.

"Out."

We hurried over to the emergency exit. I held the drip stand and did not let the medical bag leave my hands, which hit my calf with every step, causing me pain. We went down unhindered and left through the side door, which was open, because someone had shot through the lock. Shouts and shots were heard from the end of the building, but we did not see what was happening there.

The ambulance waited right next to the building. We loaded it up and tore out of there, weaving between the old and new buildings of the regional hospital. My boys fell behind, and I found myself in the womb of the ambulance surrounded by unfamiliar men, not including Borysovych.

We were mercilessly tossed around at each turn, like in a centrifuge. It was impossible to stay put on the narrow seat; I had to hold on with my hands and legs in order not to fly out at each turn.

I did not know how to help the wounded man. I still could not equate this worn-out body with Komar. He was probably in a lot of pain, as the old Fiat vehicle had no suspension, and we felt every pothole. I took my robe off and placed it under his head. I then leaned over and whispered right to his lips, not caring what we looked like from the side and what the fighters thought about us.

"Light upon light, water on water, Earth on Earth, good on good, here are white bones, here is yellow fur, put a bone on his bones. Mountain after mountain, stone after grass, fish after water, stand, bones, upon bones, veins upon veins, blood upon blood..."

"A knife. Quickly."

I hold my hand out to the 'bus driver', and, without questioning, he places the sharp blade that he had just used to stab someone into my hand.

I clench my fist, not sparing my hand. Blood seeps over my hand, and the treasure drips generously on the body on the stretcher. I draw a wide line from his chest to his groin. There is no better conduit for our thoughts than blood. Blood is always an emergency line, a direct link to the inside of our world, the very first channel of communication in the history of civilisation. Where prayer needs days, and divination takes hours, blood delivers answers in a second, and there is no blood like now, willingly let by a hot blade.

"…*Blood on blood, shadow on the la-and whence it came, wherefore it came, from the crags, from the steppes, from the caves, from the waters, from the roads, from the valleys, from the thunder, from lightning, from fi-ire, from the wa-ter, whence you came, go there, so that no-one saw when you came, so no-one saw where you came out of…*

…Blood on blood, vein upon vein, rib upon rib…"

"Komar, don't you dare die! I won't let you; you hear?! Come back, old Cossack. You know my voice, you see the way, you know who I am here next to you. Come on, come back to me."

Maybe I imagined it, but his breathing levelled off, and the pink foam stopped forming on his lips. His cold hand grew warmer, by ten degrees, and barely perceptibly, but the trace of a pulse trembled within his fingers. It was quiet in the cabin. Everyone was sitting and looking at me, and I was eternally grateful to the men for not asking me any questions.

"My daughter," said one of my companions. I almost winced at the unusual address, since up till now the only Borysovych could call me 'daughter' in that way. *"You can't carry on with us. We'll run into trouble, it's dangerous. Don't worry, he'll find you. He held on for seven days, he's out the woods now. If the commander hears that we put you under fire, he'll skin us alive. Hurry on, now!"*

I looked at the commander, who seemed to feel better. He even gestured at me to take the tube out of his throat, as he was trying to say something. But no matter how he tried, I only caught an incomprehensible gurgling, something like '…barkal… erkulei…'.

The car stopped, and I jumped out. I knew that they would be able to leave the city without a single shot being fired, but I did not object. It was too soon for me to flee Donetsk; I had to look after the cats.

Would he find me? And where was he going with my sacrifi-
cial blood on his chest?

Поворо
НЕ
MED

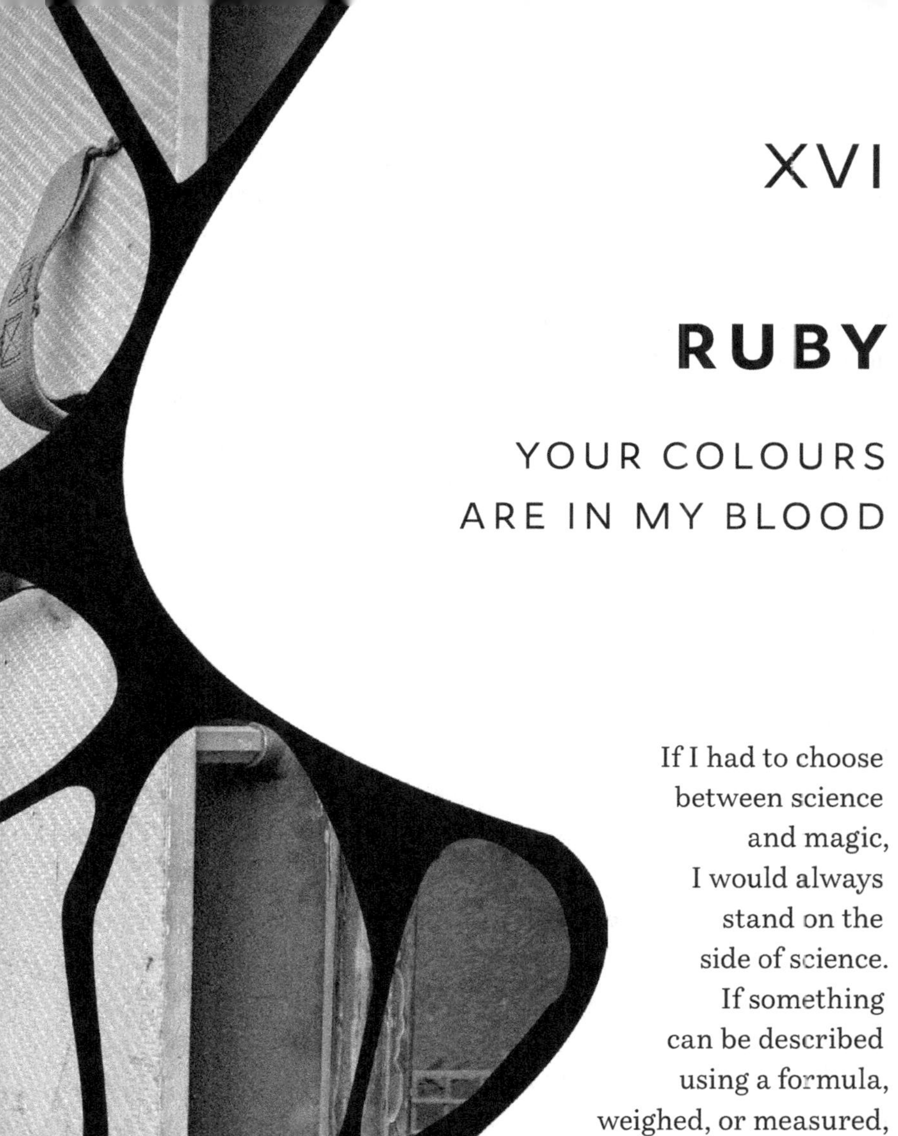

RUBY

YOUR COLOURS
ARE IN MY BLOOD

If I had to choose
between science
and magic,
I would always
stand on the
side of science.
If something
can be described
using a formula,
weighed, or measured,
then it would make
more sense to perform direct
measurements on it than to look
for a hidden bottom to it. If glass melts
at six hundred degrees Celsius, then you might
pray, nurse it, or dance around it all you want, but the
glass will not melt at four hundred degrees. Well, unless you
add some iron oxide, andfiddle with it a bit, and do what my
great auntie used to say; 'tart it up then chuck it out'.

However, there is one thing that has a chalk circle drawn around it, that science cannot cross over. It is something that we recognise exists, but we cannot classify or control. Coincidence, serendipity, luck, chance, destiny — call it what you will. If you happen to be standing by a plinth and a brick then falls on your head, according to all the laws of dynamics, you were in the wrong time and place. But what were the forces which put you in that place at that time? What stopped you from moving half a metre to the side? Physics will give you an answer to the 'why', but who can answer the 'why me?'.

After all, there are people who have it easy: a house, a job, a family — small children with smaller problems, and bigger children with bigger problems. They have got their lives together: the dacha, the garage, the yearly summer holiday. You look at them and sigh, wondering: 'Why can't I live like that?'. How many times have you sworn to yourself not to get involved, not to look, not to stick your nose in other people's affairs? Yet still, somewhere in the world, the battle between good and evil takes place, and on that spot the earth cracks open and the rift always — always! — runs between your feet. No matter how hard you try, the ground always splits beneath you, and you are left dangling by a thread over the abyss. Then everyone around you turns and waits for you to decide which side you will jump onto.

This story has only a little more left to it. Going through my memories of what happened, I would ask myself again and again: 'At what point should I have given up? Where was the last point which we could have turned off, instead of ploughing on ahead and ignoring all the signs?'. And every time, I take myself back to that day.

…A hole gaped in the fridge. Its jagged edges curled over, and the torch's beam caught the shards that had been soldered to the wall. Broken glass crunched underfoot, water was leaking from the ceiling, and instead of kitchen furniture, there was just a pile of kitchen fittings and lumps of concrete…

"Hi, can you come over? Your place has been hit."

The voice in the receiver seemed only moderately agitated. This was a familiar tone of voice, from before the war, a mild warning between the neighbours at the dacha, to the tune of: 'Hi, Ivanovna? You better get back here, someone's in your yard.'

I got up quietly so I would not wake up old Roman and Tetiana and went outside. Yesterday Borysovych had gone off somewhere, so we spent the night just us three.

It was the darkest part of the August night, the hour before dawn, when one's eyes are blind and see nothing at all. I lit a cigarette outside, breathing in the smell of smoke alongside the perfume of the night, the apples, the dew, and the powerful odour of my unwashed body.

We gathered at Roman's place the day before. His was the only inhabited house in his ends: his neighbours on either side had disappeared, and we figured it would be a good flat to use as a hideout for a few days. Why a few days? Because the idea had gone around that Donetsk would be taken back by Ukrainian Independence Day, the 24th August. Upon what confidence, under what basis, and upon what authority this rumour was grounded was an unknown, but I kept catching myself planning my future of a 'before' and 'after' Independence Day. We awaited that day like a child waits for Christmas, although we kept our hopes to ourselves.

Each of us openly admitted that we had to get out. Yet we would not leave; we circled about like vampires chained to a crypt. I did not have the strength to leave myself, feeling that I would not manage the trip. The distance to Kyiv or to any place in the 'Motherland' seemed insurmountable, like going to the moon.

Roman categorically refused to entertain the idea of evacuation, alongside all other proposals. Living with him was getting unbearably difficult. He would use all sorts of language against me and the guys whenever we brought up his constant coughing or him needing to see a doctor, and he truculently smoked cigarette after cigarette, running through our tobacco supply at an alarming rate.

Tanya spent day and night in the toilet, suffering from severe morning sickness. In her brief moments of reprieve, she would stuff something down her throat, drink some water, and once again would be doubled over the bucket.

"I'm throwing up more than I can eat — where's it coming from?"

Borysovych got hold of lemons from somewhere, since she could only get respite with lemon in her mouth. She would even drift off with a slice between her teeth, begging us to shoot her and put her out of her misery. No matter how much Borysovych and I wanted to get her out of there, we could not work out how technically to do it — should we drug her?

I had no contact with my grandmother, although one time I went to see her. In Roman's attic we found an old camping stove from Soviet times and a little kerosene. I took it over to the old folk and Olha Ivanivna deftly set up this device and even boiled a kettle on it. Surprisingly, the old ladies had settled in well to their cellar and even refused to leave.

Now, there was the matter of my apartment being hit. What inappropriate timing! In any case, God forbid, nothing valuable has been left there, I have my documents and my cards with me, my rucksack, laptop… The cats. How could I forget about the cats?! The cats are there, my neighbour was feeding them. Oh, Christ. Damn, damn, damn.

* * *

I did not wake anyone up and did not leave a note, since it was much easier to slip through the city alone. I crept out of the yard and ran, hiding behind the street fencing. The main thing I had to worry about was falling or twisting my ankle. I said a prayer under my breath as I went: 'Protect us, O Lord our Saviour; God help us sinners, do not forsake us…'.

After my concussion I began to forget the simplest things. For instance, I spent two days trying to remember the word, 'ketchup'. It was the same with prayers: I could not remember the words to the Lord's Prayer. It ended with the words *'For thine is the Kingdom, the power and the glory'*, right? Or was I imagining things?

I did not go straight into the building, and waited between the garages for half an hour. There had been a fire the night before and our flat and the flat above had burnt down. The part of the building between the two front entrances suffered the main blow, which meant our kitchen had crumbled into our neighbours' one. The front wall had fallen down, and the red tiles of the kitchen were visible from the street. Our neighbours' kitchen was decorated in red and black with gold fittings. They were awfully proud of their European-style renovated kitchen, having taken out loans for the equipment, their plasma screen, and German refrigerator which also had an ice dispenser. While renovating their kitchen they came over to mine for design advice, bringing colour samples; I would suggest something and they would do the exact opposite, and would come over again and ask:

"Stools or chairs?"

"What about the bar?"

"Should we build an arch?"

Eventually, the load-bearing walls of the Khrushchev-era flat were demolished, and the kitchen and living room and corridor were combined into one space, with a sauna set up in the bedroom. The sauna overloaded the building's electricity circuit, and whenever Tolik went for a dip after work the light would go off in the whole building.

I finally decided to go inside. At least the stairs had not collapsed! Everything around was covered in dust, but the doors were still in place. It felt so strange to turn the key in the lock whilst knowing that the flat behind the door was no more. I stepped over the mountains of rubbish — everything that was once mine and my grandmother's property, turned in an instant into a pile of junk. The entrance to the small room was blocked off; a partition had fallen into the big one, and the blast wave had broken apart the furniture, shattered the parquet floor and radiators. Everything that was not broken had burnt down. I knew that no-one would have survived, that this house had turned into a grave for the seven cats, and it was only a lucky coincidence that we had not joined them.

There is nothing left for me to take even as a keepsake, and so I turn around and… I turn grey. Right in front of me stands Basya, one of our feline wards, a snow-white Siamese which I could never quite find a common language with. She would not eat the food I gave her, meaning I had to open a reserve tin of pâté especially for her. Basya had to have a separate litter tray and would not share a toilet with the rest of them. She would never let me pick her up, covering me in scratches at any attempt to stroke her.

That was the first time in my life I had seen a ghost.

"Basya."

My mouth had gone dry, and my dumb lips could barely move.

"I didn't mean for it to end up like this. Forgive me."

The spectre came up closer to me and rubbed herself against my leg.

"Miaow."

I sat on the floor and burst into tears.

* * *

That day was unusually roasting, even for that summer. By eight in the morning it was already thirty degrees in the shade. I could barely drag my legs along, sweating profusely. Having the cat in my arms felt like I was holding a pot-bellied stove, and I had a burn brewing where her little body was held against mine. Basya's luxurious tail had turned into a grey rag and hung down almost to my knees. I was like Da Vinci's 'Lady with an

Ermine' — though my once-pretty kitty now looked more like a mangy flea catcher — as I had the same beatific facial expression as the women in the portraits the great master was so famous for.

We did not go over to our neighbours; I did not want to see anyone. Nowadays, the further you stayed away from people the safer you were. We carefully went down the stairs, noiselessly tiptoeing down so that the whole construction did not fall down on us. I quietly opened the door, where I bumped into Lyudmila going into the building to get something. She froze as she saw us, hand raised. I was not in the mood to say hello, barely nodding, and went on my way. As I turned the corner, I looked back. The woman stood there, unmoved, hand still raised as if blessing us from behind. Interesting; clearly, I was not the only one who saw a ghost that day. (I am tired of playing the role of the living dead. I'm reminded of the son-in-law in that old story of the Hutsul and his hated mother-in-law, who keeps miraculously recovering from certain death: 'Mother, surely now it's time for you to rest?').

The journey back took a few hours. I felt like I was wandering through the desert, wading up to my knees in the sand, and I would never finish this Sisyphean journey. Back then, before the war started, I would not have given a second's thought to ask someone on one of these blocks for water, but now there was no question of that. If you need to know what the Apocalypse looked like, imagine this: no industrial ruins, no scenes of floods or terrible fires, but the empty rows of blocks on the outskirts of Donetsk.

The district hadn't merely died: it had dissipated like sand in water, with whole streets disappearing off the map. Everything here was in ruins. The buildings were huge whale carcasses left on the beach to ruin by the sun and by vultures. The owners of the houses leave at night or early in the morning. The windows are already broken in by noon, and piles of junk appear behind the fences. A pile of rubbish on someone's property signalled a *carte blanche*, a free pass to break in. By evening the house has been opened like a tin can. The people living next door are the first to turn up with their cars — the same people the previous owners had spent their whole lives with! These were the people they drank with on holidays, who were godparents to their children. The neighbours take out clothes, appliances, hack out taps and sockets, as well as air conditioners, if they have any. Or they are preceded by organised marauding gangs, who pull up in a van and take everything, right up to the doors and the window frames, stripping the iron off the roof. The destruction is completed by scrap metal hunters, who rip the frames off the walls and fencing, take up the old linoleum and parquet, cut out sheets of drywall, and hoover up the rest with the least value. Three days — a week, maximum — and a bare husk is all that is left of someone's family nest. That's not the end of it, however. The end comes when someone eventually turns this ransacked house into a toilet. I cannot explain this act. Every room in these houses is plastered with shit. Why do people do this? Why not use the trench dug in the yard for this very purpose? No; someone just has to go and defecate in the kitchen.

* * *

I heard the shots from afar, from about 500 metres away. Short rounds of automatic fire, series of six to eight rounds. From the first shot my legs gave way, not in the figurative sense, but in the direct sense, when your knees suddenly sag lower than you are used to, and your gait turns into one of a legless drunk. Falling to the ground and clinging onto the fence, I stumbled over to my dear Roman's yard.

"Protect us, O Lord our Saviour; God help us sinners and do not forsake us…"

Not us, please, not us, I beseech Thee. I ran, rushing down this last street at the speed of a battered tortoise, wondering whether it would be worth falling on my stomach and crawling on my elbows to get there any faster.

When I finally arrived, there was no one by the house, and a wave of relief swept over me like a shower of golden rain. Clearly, I had to thank God for His mercy. I was hearing things; the noise was an echo coming from another block, and it was fear that made me think it was for us. I will go straight to the doctor tomorrow to prescribe me something for my nerves.

I let my arms fall, and my half-smothered cat falls onto the floor. Sorry, kitty; I will bring you some water, just wait a moment. I open the gate. Roman has a fortress for a house, you cannot see anything from the street, the two-metre-high fence is overgrown with ivy. I catch sight of a body on the threshold.

I walk forward as if hypnotised, although the voice in my head screams right in my ear: 'Run away, foolish girl!'

Roman lies face-down, his right hand thrown forward in a feverish attempt to reach something. He has no weapons next to him, but the porch is littered with shell cases; there are dozens of them. My eyes search unconsciously for his wheelchair, but it cannot be found anywhere, as if some miracle came to pass — 'and the blind saw, the deaf heard, and the paralytic picked up his bed and walked'.

The body was laced with bullets: his head, spine, legs. I didn't even have to turn him over to ascertain he was dead. Then I heard a noise in the house itself. Someone was there.

Quietly — telepathically — I open the door and squeeze inside. I crouch down completely and scuttle down the corridor to the master bedroom. There, the corridor makes a sharp turn; Roman still joked that his mother had especially designed it so that his father could not navigate the corridor when he came in blind drunk. I look around the corner and witness the whole scene.

There are three of them, three big men in Russian frog camo and canvas boots. They are focused on making mincemeat out of the woman lying beneath them with these boots. They are out of breath, and their wheezing is superimposed on the cracking of bones and a wet chewing sound. There is barely anything left of Tanya, and I reassure myself now that she was already dead by the time I did what I did.

I take the grenade out of my pocket, pull out the ring and hurl it into the room, straight at the feet of those three.

* * *

The smoke settled and silence fell. The silence rang in my ears; it filled my head. Nothing broke the silence, not a single external sound.

I went into the bedroom and thought about how I would clean all this up. I thought about how to separate Tetiana from the rest of the flesh here, for it would be wrong for all of them to lie in the same grave.

This was the moment Borysovych called.

"*Dotsya*, my daughter, hi. Please forgive me, child, but I have very little time left. I'm calling to say goodbye."

"Where are you?"

"I'm on a slagheap. I went to do a reconnaissance mission, to check on something. I found their warehouses here, daughter. There are shells and explosives, thousands of stacks of them."

His voice cut out, and I could hear other noises in the receiver. Before the war, I would have said that it was the sound of the crack of a whip upon water, or fireworks. But not now, obviously.

"Are they shooting at you?"

"It's fine. They're utterly terrified, everything here's going to be blown to smithereens. Don't interrupt me, ok? I'll give you our coordinates, they're going to hit my location, and I won't have time to tell you otherwise."

"Speak, Borysovych."

"Don't abandon my Tanya now, will you? Look after her and the baby, I beg you. I couldn't get through to her; tell her I love her so much. And that I'm really sorry, and that I will still be with them, maybe as an angel, or someone else, but I'll be there. Tell her not to cry over me for too long: she should move on, and be happy. Tell her that there's no-one else like her on earth, and that I regret nothing."

"I won't abandon her. I promise."

Tanya's blood stopped flowing and started to clot on the floor. A round onion lay in the puddle; I reached out to pick it up and only then realised that it was an eye.

"Tell Roman to forgive me. Daughter, it's my deepest sin, I punish myself for it every day. I was the one who hit him in the spine that day. It's all my fault. I was so stupid; it was only when the rest of our gang of miners died that my eyes were opened. Tell him this betrayal of mine is the only thing in my life I would change. There's never been a moment I didn't regret it."

"He forgave you, Borysovych. He's next to me, he can hear you; he says he forgives you."

"Really? Christ, forgive this old fool. And you, daughter. I know about your mother; I know what happened to her…"

This was no explosion. There are no words for this in any human language. The earth crumbled, swept flat for dozens of kilometres around. A mushroom cloud rose over the city, and that day all the Russian sites wrote that Ukraine had set off an atomic bomb near Donetsk. Half the sky was ablaze with a crimson glow. A cannonade of smaller explosions then went off, detonations from the rest of the ammunition not yet set off by the first explosion. Oil tanks caught fire, and hundreds of pyres were lit that day. The clear day turned to night, and red ash was falling, falling overhead.

OUTRO

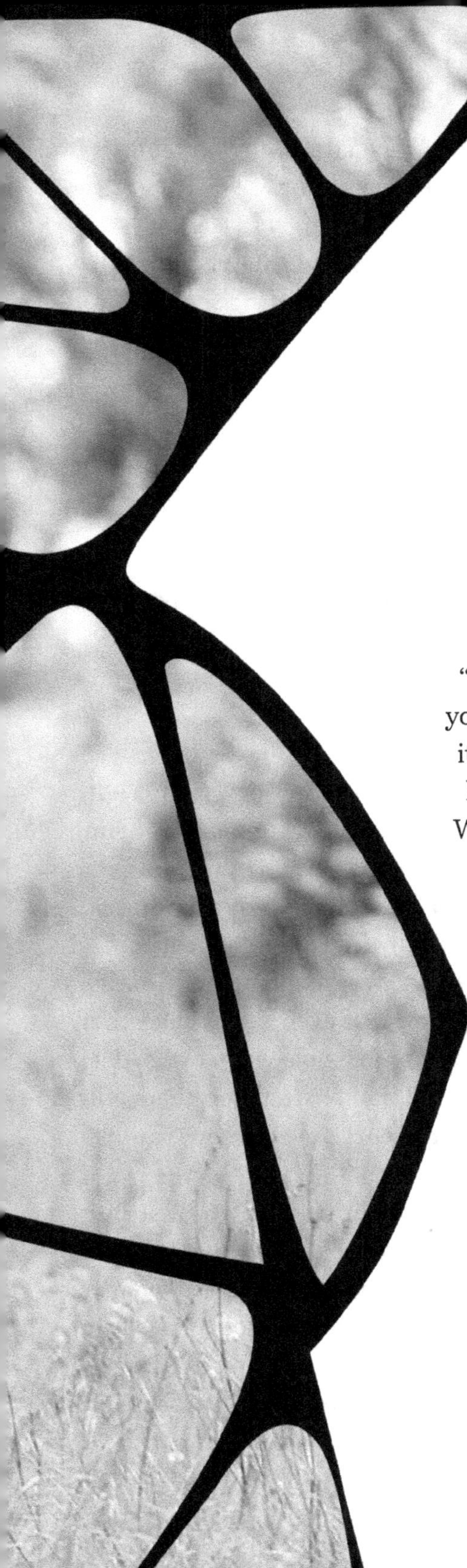

"Madam, what sort of story are you spinning me here? I told you, it's not allowed; I cannot let you leave with an underage patient. We are responsible for her care." The three of us were sitting in the physician-in-chief's office with its high ceilings and arched windows, remnants from the Tsarist era. The doctor, a middle-aged woman with rubies in her ears, clearly wanted to strangle me. She was not to blame, I suppose; I had not washed in three days, and my trousers, combat boots, and camouflage rucksack were covered in a thick layer of dust.

"Anya, do you have your things?" I asked the girl, who had not said a single word throughout the conversation.

She nodded.

"Well, go get your things, and Dr Sofia and I will have a talk."

Anya left, just as silently as she had been sitting there. I waited until the oak door closed behind her, so heavy it did not let a sound out into the corridor. I turned to the doctor.

"Listen, I'm presuming that your profession means you can read people well. Let me tell you briefly about why I am here and what I intend for this child, and then we will make some arrangements."

"I warn you — I have very little time."

"It's fine, I won't take long. Here goes… I met Anya before her mother. This is how it happened…"

* * *

…There was no shovel in the house, so I cut the ground with a knife and hauled out the earth with a bucket. This took a long time, until the middle of the night. I placed my friends into one grave, and then went to the other side of the plot and dug out a hole for *those* three. I gathered all the remains I could find in the house — knuckles from fingers, fragments of bone, hair — everything I could find. Before that, however, I searched their pockets and burned their documents. The hole wasn't very deep, no more than a metre in depth, and I had to stomp on them with my feet to stuff the bits in. I scattered earth over it and trampled on it to flatten down the earth.

I then went back to my friends. I didn't want to just bury them and leave it at that, without saying anything. It wouldn't be right. So, I drew water from the well and washed myself over the grave, washing my hands. I said a prayer instead of a priest and blessed the ground. There is no cross there, no sign at all; but I remember where they now lie, and one day I will show the child.

* * *

"I promised to look after this girl, standing over the body of her mother. Therefore, would you tell me, please, under what grounds can you deny me this?"

The doctor thought about it, and I did not rush her. This conversation was a mere formality, frankly. I had two train tickets in my pocket, and we would be spending the night in Kyiv.

The doctor's office looked out onto a splendid view of the hundred-year-old manor grounds. The paths were strewn with yellow leaves, and I wanted to spread my arms out wide and fall backwards into the autumn piles of leaves.

"But what will you do with yourselves?"

"What? Oh, don't worry about us. We will live."

…The leaves rustled underfoot in just the way I expected. We went across the park, wading up to our knees in the fragile ochre and crimson foliage, leaving two wide tracks behind us.

"Come on little one, catch up."

I gave her my hand, and her slender palm reached out trustingly in response.

"Let's walk a little longer, eh? We have some time. We can go get pizza."

Then my phone rang. I look at the screen and recognise the number. One of my contacts was now available.

Yes, live. Above all — we will live.

01.09.17–23.12.18

TESTIMONIALS

In March 2014, some sort of unbridled bacchanalia engulfed the centre of Donetsk. For the first time, I started seeing strange people who stood at crossroads, talking about how the western regions of the country have so much and yet work so little, and how hard the miners toil and how little they get for it. The 'Banderites' were cruel, and greedy, they said.

"That's not true! I go to Truskavets, near Lviv, every year. I know there are good people there!"

The crowd looks at the miner with disbelief, and only his size and formidable appearance stops them from objecting. I quietly stand next to this rational-minded man in support.

Later the mob set upon the regional state administration building, breaking in the windows. The Ukrainian flag was torn down, the Russian tricolour flag put up in its place.

On the Monday afterwards I brought my child to school and encountered the hostility of a grandmother of one of my daughter's classmates. She told me about how she had been raped as a child by a soldier in Stepan Bandera's guerrilla army. She went on to tell me that I would be in trouble soon, as her son was a policeman, and that I had no business being in Donetsk with my 'Banderite roots'.

The only thing that reassured me back then was the brand-new Ukrainian flag hanging on the front of the school. That was the school headmistress, feared and respected by all, loudly and convincingly asserting her stance.

On the 4th March 2014, a mass patriotic protest took place in the city. Several thousand people from Donetsk had come together in protest of the chaos in the city and the calls to join the separatists. One post on social media led to many reposts, which led to a gathering of interesting, successful, and beautiful people around the Intercession Church. It would be impossible to convey the atmosphere there. We sang the Ukrainian popular song

'Chervona Ruta' and the national anthem. The next day, even more people came and joined us. Activists who had been on the Euromaidan in Kyiv brought a giant flag, which they placed on the square. Unexpectedly, my daughter and I found one American among the crowd, the pastor of a Protestant church. He said that the embassy banned him from going to rallies like this and asked him to get his stuff together and prepare himself for evacuation.

Our group of patriots started to recognise each other, but we did not exchange numbers for practical reasons. For example, there was Anton, who had his own printing press, and printed us information leaflets. There was Irynka, who would cut out stencils by night, which we would take with cans of spray paint and spray on tarmac, on bus-stops, or on buildings the following: *'Donetsk is Ukraine!'*. There was Olenka, who had her own real estate agency. We could gather there to organise our protests and discuss counterdemonstrations. There was Sasha, who was friends with ultranationalists and would tell us which ones were in the police and how we could use that knowledge to avoid getting caught. There was a Georgian family who lived in a remote area of the city, where it was very quiet and you could hide everything you needed in the cellar of their large house. Afterwards, I would go to their neighbourhood and I would see Russian Federation special forces wandering about. They were not even hiding it: they had not even taken the chevrons with the image of the Russian Bear off their uniforms.

But that was later; for now, we were riding on the wave of euphoria from our actions, from the night sabotage raids, from the fact that a whole load of volunteers were queueing up at the military enlistment office, from the news that a Ukrainian Donbas battalion was already in the works and the boys were more motivated than ever before: we were preparing for something new. Diana promised us a stage; Serhii was supposed to lead a prayer for Ukraine. We bought up gas canisters as self-defence, the head of one of the police units took away the rubber batons and truncheons. The preparation was excellent. There was no way we could become a target! It was time to fight back.

However, it did not quite work out like that.

Before the rally started, one friend phoned me saying that she wanted to leave the city as soon as possible. Her 'master', for whom she worked as a nanny, had decided to take her twin wards abroad and was forcing her to accompany the children. She was afraid, they threatened her, and they would take away her passport in a foreign land, effectively turning her into a slave. I decided to leave the rally, ran after my friend, and sat her on the bus. I could only have left for about an hour, but by the time I returned to the square, it was obvious that something terrible had happened.

Buses and trolleybuses were passing by unawares. However, Lenin Square was doused in smoke. The explosions of bangers and firecrackers were deafening. The crowd was roaring; shattered glass was everywhere. I went towards where the stage was supposed to be, as if in a thick fog. From afar, I saw a bus and a group of boys who were on their knees, spat on and drenched in green dye. There were several bodies lying motionless. The bandits began to disperse in pairs, probably rather frightened by what they had done. The ambulance rushed in, and I came in from the side, which is how I got to the epicentre of events. The paramedics brought in anyone who was unconscious first, and then started to grab and stuff the van with anyone covered in blood, until it was completely full. The police only pretend to serve and protect.

I was home already by the time I heard about Dmytro Cherniavskyi's death. At the hospital, a relative of one of our activists would pronounce two more young men dead. This was the starting point of the war in our city.

After that, a small crowd was permanently gathered at Lenin Square. I went to lay flowers at the place where Dmytro and the unknown two fell. The whole trolleybus was discussing the events. Someone was talking about the members of the far-right nationalist group, the Right Sector, who had arrived by bus and provoked the fight. I did not restrain myself and began to protest that there were no Right Sector goons there, only our fellow Donetsk residents. Some bright young fellow shoved a binder right in front of my face and asked me to come and act as a witness. I refused, saying that I had to pick my daughter up from school and that she was waiting for me there. Of course, he accompanied me right up to the building, but my intuition told me that he had no idea about the other exit to the school. I told the security that I was going up to the second floor and slipped under the stairs out onto a completely different street. From then on, I would have to stay quiet on public transport. Who was it, and where the hell had he come from?

Soon there were more and more of these funny sorts of people in the city. Brown coats, clumsy shoes from the nineties, and fedoras. They would take pictures in front of supermarkets and shopping centres and would say to someone on the phone, in Russian, *'Oh yes, this really* is *Europe, it's so beautiful!'*

It was obvious from their pronunciation that they were not locals, or even from Rostov, just across the border.

On the 17th March 2014 the 'With a Prayer for Ukraine' rally took place. It was organised very seriously, unlike anything that had been seen before. Mounted police, thousands of law enforcement officers from other regions, speeches by politicians, including Oleh Lyashko (the old head of the Radical Party). A student from Lviv came up to our group of protesters. He was astonished that people were coming out and intended to fight and asked to sign our flag. Everyone signed it, adding slogans like *'Donetsk is Ukraine!'*, and *'Glory to the heroes!'*. I wrote, *'Help us, please!'*.

On the 28th April 2014 the 'Automaidan' came to Donetsk. It seemed they had not quite realised where they had ended up. Near the Shakhtar Donetsk stadium some locals had gathered in their cars.

"We'll put on a good show! Ukraine has to see how much you're fighting for it here," they said.

When the procession went past the regional state administration building, a brick was thrown at the cars. It was good that few people knew about the procession, because the consequences could have been much worse. We never saw or heard anything more of the Automaidan.

The last rally took place that same day. It was a march. Maybe people were not risking it anymore, because the police had clearly shown which side they were on, but the 'ultranationalist' Shakhtar Donetsk supporters had decided to come together *en masse*, and they were indeed the driving force. Those lads were clearly not afraid of anything. They walked at the head of the procession, with women and children tailing them. Suddenly, well-armed young thugs in masks jumped out of the blocks we walked past. I turned and saw a wall of police shields in the hands of separatist thugs.

Panic broke out. The crowd of patriots splintered into different directions. The 'ultras' were walking and singing far away in front. Our people were being picked off one by one, beaten till they were unconscious, or till their body was lying in a bloody puddle. I fled, several blocks away from the slaughterhouse, and caught my breath; I walked a few blocks further and went to the shopping centre. People were out shopping without a care. Through the window I saw people still running in a panic. We had once again lost the fight. Now was not the time to take a picture for the press, but to arm ourselves properly. Of course, there were lots of journalists that day from the BBC, UNIAN, The Weekly Mirror, and so on, taking photos, each bloodier than the one before.

The days and nights were infinitely long. Bad news was constantly reaching us from various channels: the Donetsk Republic flag was hung from the Donetsk Airport; photos of activists were downloaded off the Internet and stuck on the walls of the regional state administration with the caption, *'Time to eradicate the traitors of the Donbass.'* I had a search for myself, but Google did not come up with any photos — it was good I did not look like me in them at all. I was in almost every photo from the Euromaidan or the protests in Donetsk, but I was almost completely concealed by someone taller than me, or I had my back turned. After that, it would be wise if I changed my style of clothing. I was lucky when it came to my name: there were thirty people who had the exact same name as me on *Odnoklassniki*, the social media site, alone. What can I say? Even my mother-in-law had the same name and surname as me; a friend of mine did as well, and her mother-in-law. It was a popular name.

Checkpoints were set up around the city. Buses with members of the Right Sector would never be able to get in, though I may have wanted them to. The Ukrainian comic opera *A Zaporozhian Cossack Beyond the Danube* received a standing ovation in the Opera House. People were quite literally crying and clapping for much longer than before, which was nonsensical for a city that was known for being so dry emotionally — yet here, talking about 'politics' had become more and more dangerous.

We had gathered a small, private patriotic group on social media, which was our source of all the city's news and where we would put our comments. Since April we had been constantly meeting soldiers in the METRO supermarket near the airport. They were a very different sort to the dubious personages which circulated the square and around the regional state administration building. They stood in a queue, politely letting families and children pass. I would like to believe that they were *ours*, but they stayed silent and I was too embarrassed to speak. On the other side of Donetsk, beyond the checkpoints, we were sure that the Ukrainian army was there. Our hopes blossomed, but were still ever so fragile.

On the 9th May the conductor of the opera was nearly beaten to death for conducting a performance of the Ukrainian national anthem. There were more and more professional soldiers in the city, which was clear from their straight-backed military posture and their uniforms. Many people were waiting for the referendum on the accession of the Donbas to Russia. Our handful of activists had been putting up stickers with a very strong adhesive with the captions, *'Putin is a terrorist'*, and *'Russia will close the mines'* and so on. They were practically impossible to tear off, and there was a chance that they would get people thinking.

That mortifying referendum took place on the 11th May 2014. There were ten times fewer polling stations than usual, and by noon there were enormous queues forming outside them.

"Have you been there yet? Hurry! I've been telling all our neighbours to go vote, and they all refuse," an old and persistent neighbour barked at me.

"Yes, we already voted at the Planetarium, where they set up a temporary station. We ticked the box for joining Dnipropetrovsk Oblast, not Russia. We have nothing special here; only coal and McMay mayonnaise. You buy your food from ATB-Market, I'm guessing? Look: Oleina oil is produced in Dnipropetrovsk, and pasta there too. The supermarkets Amstor and Varus only moved here from neighbouring regions."

The old lady was taken aback. I felt that she was ready to vote for her whole family, even the dead ones, for the same thing as us. Later that evening we went to our protest section, and it was sad and empty.

The fighting was only taking place in Slovyansk, but on the morning of the 22nd May 2014 we heard the news that Ukrainian soldiers had been attacked in the Volnovakha region. Many of those boys died or were wounded. Doctors we knew sent us messages asking to bring them civilian clothes. Many full ambulances were brought to Donetsk. This war blew away all the slogans that were bouncing around in my head. It was clear that we were not fighting back and did not know how to.

There had never been so many posts in our Donetsk Facebook

group. The collective brain tried to decide: 'What do we do now? Are they going to leave us to our own devices?'

We made the decision to go and find the lads who had survived and convince them not to desert us.

On our way out of the city we bought lots of oranges, and at the last moment I threw a box of biscuits into my shopping basket. For the first time at a checkpoint I did not see a bunch of alcoholics and society's cast-offs, but a perfectly-disciplined unit. They checked the hands of all the drivers and adult passengers for calluses left by using weapons and any remnants of explosives. We drove on and tried to remember every twist and turn in the road as the passengers checked the maps. Not straightaway, we still found the unit that suffered the misfortune. They were practically children. Dirty, frightened, with low morale: they said they were being annihilated. It felt like the Earth stopped turning for an hour. So many months of our struggle disappeared into an abyss. We treated the boys to oranges, and they swallowed them whole, peel and all. We felt so sorry for them. Maybe it was for the best that they were retreating. We had survived thus far, so we would fight on anyhow.

I will probably never forget the 26th of May. My child was doing dance classes right near Putyliv Bridge. It was a fine day; I went outside, and a helicopter flew past me, firing right onto the ground. I rushed to the road, and saw several cars and an army truck flying off towards the airport. I could not see what was inside. Maybe weapons; could it really be carrying people going at that speed? Before that, we already knew precisely that the airport was the island of Ukraine in the city, and that today the henchmen of the Chechen strongman Kadyrov, Putin's crony, had lost their patience and had decided to have a little punch-up. Fighter aircraft were circling over the city, and it was clear that they were repeatedly setting off surface-to-air missiles from various slagheaps, but the heat missiles were not hitting their targets. Every day, I was learning so much about war...

The women in our patriotic group had started going out to their summer houses: summer had arrived. Their dachas were actually located in the free areas. They brought back from their trips lists of essentials that the Ukrainian fighters needed: uniforms, boots, and food. I baked nut bread and little buns nonstop; the men marinated meat. We collected and prepared eclairs, layer cakes, meatballs, fresh fruit and vegetables, and even borsch. The logistics services frequently forgot about them for extended periods of time, so the soldiers had to buy themselves packet noodles and cigarettes, because what else could they afford with their wage of 1800 hryvnia, which even at the time was less than 100 dollars a month? As such, like us, they waited for their orders and learned how to survive in the steppe.

We bought bricks of cigarettes and plenty of water at the petrol stations near the exit by Avdiivka. We spun long yarns on the spot to the surprised traders about why we bought so much stuff. People were almost out of real money, as a few cash machines were still working in Donetsk, but they were filled up with money quickly enough.

On the 5th of July militants from Slovyansk, headed by Girkin, entered Donetsk. They 'liberated' the city from Nova Poshta postal service and PrivatBank for good. Deputy minister Tuka's helmets were stuck forever in one of the central branches of the courier services. After this we would have to have all our parcels sent to the town of Vuhledar, on the unoccupied side. This was actually very convenient, since we no longer had to risk bringing army uniforms into Donetsk. The main thing was that there would be no extenuating circumstances or shelling (which had to be expected) to prevent us making the last minibus back.

Upon my return to Donetsk I would frequently see the BM-21 Grad rocket launchers firing at Ukrainian military positions. The land around them had become scorched earth. My land.

One day, one of our Donetsk volunteers disappeared. He dropped me off near the supermarket after one of our routine trips. His car was stopped in Putyliv district, one block away from home. They found photos of our trips to Zenit in Dnipro on his phone. Ukrainian servicemen smiled in the photos. Our fellow volunteer was stuffed back in his car and forced over to the cemetery. Then their little game began:

"If you can get away before we count to ten, then you're in luck. If not — we bury you."

He managed to get away, but one of our most trusted cars was lost. Although this was a trifle in comparison — he was alive!

Luckily, I was not in any of the photos.

Maybe I was not there at all, and it was all a dream? Every day I would see photos on social media of volunteers in military uniform carrying goods to 'the most dangerous positions on the front'. I was persuaded to take out stickers saying *'Donetsk is Ukraine!'* and *'I love the Ukrainian army'* from my bag, and in their place, I asked some of the Right Sector guys to put a grenade in there. The city was constantly booming, with my house right next to a slagheap where soldiers were based and a little further down was a parking lot where lots of new army equipment was being brought. It was only a mile or so from my house.

Once I came back to my neighbourhood from the airport and I saw that half of the buildings were lit by bright fires, and mine seemed to be drowning in a gaping black hole. I saw my neighbours near the entrance.

"The shelling stopped not long ago", they said.

An electrical junction box had blown up opposite my window, and plenty of flats were destroyed. I had got used to the fact that my house had not been hit by any shrapnel for almost the whole summer, and I opened my door in one confident motion, took off my shoes and stepped in. Glass crunched underfoot.

I turned on the lamp. It was as if a tsunami was rushing through my kitchen. I started looking to find what it was that was big enough to fly in and blow up here. A beam of light fell on the refrigerator opposite the window. There was a gaping hole in it.

FAKENEWS! FACEBOOK SKETCHES

ROMAN MALYK

Episode 5
2014. Spring. Luhansk

I drive around Luhansk making my deliveries as calmly and carefully as possible. When I come across any separatist militia cars, I hug the side of the road and pretend I'm not there.

I'm overtaken by a Jeep. Some Russian chanson music blasts out the windows.

The Jeep is festooned with St George's ribbons from the Russian military.

The Jeep overtakes a parked car with separatists inside. One of them waves the Novorussian confederacy flag out the open windows, shouting, "Russia's with us!"

Suddenly, the car with the separatists starts off. It chases the Jeep and pushes it towards the hard shoulder. I pass their cars with care. I see inside the open Jeep. The whole of the inside is covered in Novorussian flags. The driver and the passenger are all smiles. One of the separatists is saying something to them. I notice their smiles slowly begin to fade.

I am travelling back the same way fifteen minutes later. The Jeep is gone. The driver and the female passenger stand forlorn on the side of the road. They are no longer smiling. The passenger fidgets with the Novorussia flag in her hands, looking lost.

Episode 3
2014. Summer. Luhansk

My brother-in-law's car barked. Well, 'barked' is the noise it made — it won't start.

What should we do? We could dig around under the bonnet of an old Zaporozhets or Zhiguli, no problem.

But it's a flashy Toyota. We'll have to reboot-reload-refresh-re-whatever the computer.

No screwdrivers here. We needed an expert.

Where? Who do we call? We needed phone signal. My brother-in-law took his phone, and instead of getting a taxi, got his neighbour to take him to the eastern parts of the city, where you could find mobile signal. He started phoning around various numbers and received the following information:

1. Workshops, auto repair stations and mechanics specialising in Toyotas are currently not in Luhansk due to the instability of the region.
2. Mechanics specialising in Toyotas will not travel to Luhansk due to the instability of the region.
3. The closest workshop can be found in Kharkiv.
4. If my brother-in-law brings his car to Kharkiv, everything will be fixed in a flash, and to the highest quality.

Naturally, my brother-in-law was not about to hire a tow truck and travel through the checkpoints to Kharkiv. As such, we saved the repairs until better times.

Time passed.

We still had no petrol.

We could not travel during the bombing.

Travel was also daunting — there was a real risk of being left without a car. The more expensive the car, the bigger the risk. The separatists just take everything, and that's it.

It looked like the car was doing bird in the garage — no coming out.

Yet I phoned a month later and heard, to my surprise:

"I fixed the car."

"What? By yourself?"

"Well no."

"You didn't go to Kharkiv, did you?"

"No. Our guys did it, some locals," my brother-in-law giggled nervously. "It was a bit of a joke…"

My brother lived in a private detached house. Without electricity, TV, and internet, the neighbours often would go out and chat on the street. Old vendettas and grudges were forgotten. Their common misfortune had brought them together.

Three separatists came onto their street in a car, wearing camouflage and with rifles. The neighbours fled the areas from fright, peeking through the holes in their fences. The car stopped by my brother's yard. All the other neighbours breathed a sigh of relief. The militants piled out of the car and started banging on his gate. My brother-in-law, pale, dolefully opened the gate and looked out.

"Are you Vitya?"

"Yes," he said, growing even more pale.

"I talked to you about the Toyota."

"You're a mechanic?" He felt a wave of relief.

"Yes. Where's the car?"

My brother-in-law held the mechanic's rifle while he rummaged around in the car.

After half an hour, everything was done, and the car was once again on the road.

The mechanic got his payment.

The militants went off to fight.

The neighbours once again flooded onto the street to talk.

Episode 11
2nd June 2014, Luhansk

People who side with the separatists always like to rile me up in arguments by saying that the war in Luhansk started with a Ukrainian plane firing on the Luhansk administration. Like, as if that was the point of no return.

I remember that day one of my brothers-in-law — on the separatist's side — phoned me and told me in a booming voice:

"Damn those bloody fascist terrorists! Look how many people have died! Look at the blood! The hospitals are overwhelmed with corpses and the wounded! You go look at the families grieving over there! We can't come back from this! FASCISTS!"

And then he slammed the phone down. At first, I thought he was taking the piss. You wouldn't believe it, but he copied my exact words! MY EXACT WORDS! It was those exact words I used with him after Crimea was annexed. Only I used them for the *separs* (separatists) and what they've done.

It was those exact words I used to describe to him the death of Volodymyr Rybak, the Horlivka city councillor whose mutilated body was found after trying to tear down the DPR flag from the town council building, that I used to describe the seizure of the state administrative buildings, the dispersal of peaceful demonstrations, and the beatings of pro-Ukraine citizens. I used these exact words to comment on all the outrages committed by the separatists and 'Russian tourists':

"Fascists! Damn those bloody Russian fascist terrorists!"

But in Luhansk they thought that the point of no return was that exact hour: 3 pm on the 2nd June 2014. As if before that moment everything was still fine, that we could have turned back somehow. Have you ever heard such shameless and insolent nonsense?!! Even if you don't delve into the ugliness of the Russian spring, just take that second day of summer, the 2nd June. I remember that day well. We awoke at 4 am due to the loud and frequent sounds of shooting. Rounds from machine guns and rifles. The loud crackling noise of mines and grenades. This is how the separatist attack on the border troop detachment in the Mirnyi quarter began. We did not live far away, and the rounds and explosions were heard loud and clear that quiet summer night. The separatists hid behind housing blocks, firing at the border troops from the roofs and windows of high-rise buildings. The fighters filmed all of this themselves and even uploaded the videos on the internet. That is why I felt like I myself was there. The border troops fought off the cowardly attacks from the separatists for 14 hours! 8 of them were seriously wounded! All the soldiers were locals, from Luhansk, our own countrymen.

None of them were Banderovites or some great Horde coming in from the West.

It was then the troops brought in the Sukhoi Su-25 jet for aerial support. But there was little point in it. The border forces were located in a residential area, surrounded on all sides by high-rises. The separatists were hiding in them. The Sukhoi couldn't shoot into buildings where people lived. The troops had become a sitting duck. But they also couldn't shoot into windows where people lived.

Can't that be a point of no return?

The centre of the city can be seen straight from my balcony. My daughter and I went out onto the balcony when the Su-25 plane flew from the border troop detachment into the centre of the city.

The jet circled high above the centre of the city.

"Dad, what's that plane doing?"

"It's just flying."

Dark clouds began to appear and fade halfway between the plane and the ground.

"What's that, Dad?"

"Those are the bad guys shooting at the plane."

"Why?"

"They want to shoot it down."

"But when they shoot it down, what's it going to fall on?"

"On the houses in the town."

"And people are there right now?"

"There's lots of people there."

"But then they'll die?"

"Yes."

"That means you shouldn't shoot down the plane?"

A 12-year-old had enough sense to make the right decision.

The jet flew overhead for a long time. We went inside…

I didn't see the actual plane crash. I only heard the explosions. That's why I can't say any more on that matter. The video that was later uploaded also doesn't give us any solid answers.

In any case, there is a big difference between shooting at residential buildings, and shooting a building occupied by separatists.

SUMMER OF 2014

Yuliia Ablamska

*Linguist and translator,
now working in Kyiv as head of HR
at a firm evacuated from Luhansk*

I often think back to the time it all started. Now I live in a strange city, with my commute taking more than an hour there and back. In the evenings, I often get off a stop early to walk home and think. At home I always walked. Luhansk is a small city; everything I needed was right on my doorstep. The walks are muscle memory, I guess. More often, during these long walks I silently hold the following conversation with myself: I ask myself the question of when this nightmare all started. My answer is always long, full of unnecessary details; never anything concrete. I do not remember the exact date the war entered my life. I often hear or read how others state: 'We already knew back in March that we had to get out of there. We sold our flat off to our neighbours on the cheap, but not as cheap as they're going now. We quickly moved on to Kyiv / Ivano-Frankivsk / Kharkiv / Zhytomyr.'

I find these people hard to believe. At the time, I did not see or understand what was happening. I worked well, and hard, and 2013 was a good year for our company and for me personally. We completed a large order and made plans for both the short and long term. We had installed equipment in the production shop and thought about expanding. We designed new models and prepared for exhibitions in Donetsk, Kyiv, Moscow, and Warsaw. There was no sense of impending disaster.

I found out about the Maidan protests on the train from Luhansk to Moscow in January 2014, when I went on some business or other. At the Russian border, an elderly lieutenant colonel entered the cabin in which I was travelling alone. He saw the navy-blue passport on the table and was ready to throw hands, yelling at me about the threat to the Rostov region from the 'Bendery'. I clearly remember asking him what threat Moldova could pose to Rostov-on-Don, seeing as Bendery is a town in the unrecognised breakaway state of Transnistria.

"The whole of Ukraine sits between Russia and Moldova! And besides, these are two different nations! How could there be a threat?" — was my response.

I nearly got clobbered over the head with my own passport. The lieutenant colonel roared and thundered, shouting, *"Yankee pigs!"*, *"What a great country we were!"*, and *"There is no Ukraine and Moldova, only great Russia!"* and so on, and on and on the train plunged into the Russian winter, and I deduced that the protests in Kyiv were behind his incoherent shouting, which, according to his authoritative opinion, were anti-Russian, of course.

On my return home I plunged myself into work, renovating my flat, working towards the next holiday. Did I realise that something extraordinary was happening? No. I found out about the attacks nearby quite by accident from one of my friends, and I remember the feeling of time collapsing in on me and the ground falling away from beneath my feet. The memories of what happened next have smeared together, like butter on bread: it is difficult to gather them up and discern their exact taste.

My friend and I stood in the yard of an old printworks after our English lesson. Winter was already over, though the puddles were still covered over with ice, when the muddy snow dampens your mood, but we had already stopped wearing our down jackets and were instead freezing in our wool coats. For some reason the streetlamps were not working, only one above the entrance right in front of us. We stood in its white beam, hoping that my friend's husband would pick us up soon in his warm and comfortable car, but for now our teeth were chattering desperately as we looked out into the dark. Our eyes accustomed to the darkness, and we were able to distinguish several outdated buses that looked like the ones which took miners to work. Only just what miners' buses had to do outside an old printworks at ten in the evening, I did not know…

When the first passengers appeared, we had already grown so used to the darkness that we could see that the old rust-buckets were missing number plates. The passengers were also funny looking — young lads in identical black tracksuits, some of them wearing balaclavas and knitted black beanies, and all of them were holding long metal rods. They slowly walked towards the three buses, waving the rods around and looking at us. They could not have missed us, as we were the only bright spot in a pitch-black yard. Did we understand then that something bad was happening, and that we had to run? No… we were stupid and careless; we were scared half to death by a band of thugs carrying piping, but we did not use our heads and connect what was happening in the city to them. It was lucky our friend's husband grabbed us by the arm and took us out of that terrible yard back to our safe homes. That was at the very beginning of March. We were not yet aware of the catastrophe to come.

Articles about the beginning of the war have piled up by the tonne; there are thousands of photographs and videos. For those who know what it's like to find themselves under attack, lie on the floor, scream the words of a prayer thought up on the spot, there is no need to talk about the war. For those who don't — there is no point in talking about it. It is impossible to fully convey that animal state you sink into, when the fear grabs you by the throat, by your stomach, when it traps your head in an iron vice. Words cannot transmit the feeling of inhuman relief when the volleys and the explosions subside, and you get up and check whether you can still hear, whether you can still speak, whether all four walls of your home are still standing. You understand that, for today, you got lucky, that the shell hit the next building, and not yours. Words cannot transmit that euphoria, which immediately gives way to a shame that burns your insides: there are people living in that house too; they could have died. But you have no strength to leave, your knees do not bend, your fingers do not obey you, to the point where tying your shoelaces becomes an unachievable task. Besides, it's curfew, and they'll notice you — and shoot you either on the spot or in some basement. You don't know which is best. And so, day by day, you lose your human side. The fear sucks you dry of your dignity, pride, and self-worth, drop by drop. To add to this are the daily fights for survival: looking for food, water, when you are almost out of money; then you understand how even the most cultured person can turn into a wild animal. For me, there was no victory in survival; it was only a question of how quickly you stop acting like a human being — the quicker the process, the greater likelihood of living till tomorrow.

Electricity kept cutting out for the whole of July in the occupied city: the fridge had long since blown its fuse, and my laptop held on thanks to its long-lasting battery. But on the 2nd of August, it still happened — the end of the world. The water was cut in a city that burned like hell, and pumps were installed. There was no electricity anywhere: not even in the hospitals or in the morgues.

A vaguely recognisable number appeared on the screen on my still-operating phone:

"Can I come over?"

"Of course. Can you no longer manage on your own?"

"I need someone to talk to."

Later:

"Come in! What is that smell! Oh my God, I think I'm going to throw up!"

"I was at the morgue. There's no more space and the freezers are no longer working. *They* — you know what I mean — are just lying on the street. My childhood friend's mother phoned me, I'm the only one who didn't leave. Someone said her son who went missing three weeks ago was there. At the morgue. That is, not in the morgue, but on the street outside. They identified him by his tattoo."

"Why you?"

"We were good friends when we were kids. Then I went to university and he went to technical school. We became different people. He disappeared three weeks ago, and his mother's arthritis means she can barely walk. Someone told her they saw him there, outside the morgue. She could only find my number — my landline, not my mobile. So that's where I went."

"Did you find him."

"No."

"Here's some bottled water. Please throw away my towel after using it."

"Don't you need it?"

"No, it smells like death."

The morning began with a tiresome hygiene regime: a shower, and brushing your hair and teeth. Water is precious: it just does not exist. After dragging yourself over to the pump, you often would find that it was out of water, and you would run over to the next one. Many people stopped washing, and you could smell them from a mile away in the baking heat of a city perched on the steppe. I soon found out that my olfactory receptors got used to it, and stopped picking up on this cacophony of odours. There was no water running through the sewage pipes, either. Food left behind in abandoned houses rotted in people's fridges. People quickly debased themselves, but this already did not bother anyone else. Drunken separatists brought water, drawing kilometre-long queues of worn-out, stinking crowds. The water, however, emitted a distinct scent of sewage water and death.

I would walk up to four kilometres a day to the pump by the private houses on the edge of the city. My neighbour loaned me her flatbed trolley, thanks to which I could bring back four or even five 5-litre demijohns of water. These trolleys were now going for unreal amounts of money at the local markets, alongside candles, batteries, and cheap Chinese receivers, which were now in high demand.

* * *

Once, my neighbour and I, trudging through the block next door, found a *barrel* there! It was a dark-blue plastic barrel, hoisted onto the trailer of an old Zhiguli car. Smoking next to it was a melancholy-looking chap, clearly from the countryside — its owner. He was a real salt-of-the-earth sort, there was no other way about it. He emanated the kind of earthiness, solidity, and a measured serenity that is only gained from country life. He sold us the water for one hryvnia a litre. Though it seemed expensive, considering the cost back then of the petrol to refuel the generator connected to the pump and to fill up the old Zhiguli, which then used up loads of petrol at checkpoints, then this old farmer was basically carrying it for free — for the very right to carry it! My neighbour and I squealed for joy and counted out the hryvnia that were carefully withdrawn from credit cards in happier times. In fact, he charged us the six-litre bottles as five-litre ones, meaning that every sixth litre went for free. We did not have to then walk far. The water was actually clean, with no funny smell, taste, or sediment left after we boiled it. We did not stay so fortunate for long. The man did not come on the sixth day. He never came after that, after a skinny lad in camo with rotten teeth and touting a machine gun came out of the entrance of one of the old blocks of flats and said something like the following:

"What, so you're parasiting off the backs of hard-working people here?"

The man tried to explain himself, talking about the price of petrol and how hard it was to get through the checkpoints. I saw the plumes of dust rise up from the bullets which landed at the base of his water-trailer. He dived into his Zhiguli, followed by the cry of:

"You'll be dead if I ever catch sight of you again!"

And so, we resumed our daily wanderings in search of water.

* * *

A puppy once jumped out at us in the same yard. He was half-grown, about six or seven months old. A type of setter, not ginger like an Irish setter, but black and tan — a Gordon setter, most likely. The friendly beastie was tied to a garage on a long lead, with a bowl of water and leftover food, meaning he clearly lived outside, right next to the garage. He had been abandoned, like many other animals that summer. That was the first time I saw whole hordes of purebred domestic cats on the street: Persians, British Shorthairs, even Sphinxes. The man who has lost his humanity quickly betrays those who once called him master.

Some local men who we had seen next to the water barrel were smoking next to the garages.

"Can I stroke him?"

"Sure, just he's very jumpy. He'll lick you and dirty your trousers."

That is just what happened: I plopped down onto the dust, and the dog immediately jumped onto my knees and was purring like a kitten.

"Archie, stop!" — shouts one of the old blokes there.

I once had a dog called Archie. I understood that this puppy and I would become companions, like the old story of the cat and the parrot, because I just could not leave him there tied to the garage. I hug him, and he licks me on the nose, and tears well up in my eyes — but I should not cry! I asked them if they knew whose dog it was.

This actual human being stroked his chin, then suddenly said, "I think he's mine…"

Then, sighing, he unties this fabulous dog and takes him home. I then met them every day. Both looked completely and utterly happy.

* * *

"Do you even remember that I was at yours yesterday? I stayed over."

"Yes, I remember. You slept on the sofa bed in the guest room. We were drinking away our fears, weren't we?"

"Why do you sleep on the floor in the hall?"

"I've got a window in my room, opposite my bed. If some shrapnel hits the window, I'll be covered in shattered glass. I still have to live; I have stuff to do."

"I was at my friend's mum's place, you know, the one who disappeared. She sleeps in the bath."

"I have a shower, not a bath. It's glass, remember? You washed the smell of corpses off you in it."

"Yes, it's just strange, going to a girl's house and she's got a bed in the hall…"

* * *

There is a shop on the ground floor of our building, an ATB supermarket. I saw the manager, a young guy who had clearly come from somewhere in the west of the country.

"Hello! I live in this house, above you, it turns out! You're the shop manager, if I'm not wrong?"

"Yes; hello!" — he says, replying in Ukrainian to my Russian.

"You see, the city council published a list of bomb shelters and it turns out that ours is in the basement of your shop. And we live above you. Your shop is on the ground floor of our building. If something happens… you know, a bombing or something… we won't make it to another place. Only me, my neighbour with her invalided elderly mother, a disabled family on the first floor and our girl Katya on the fourth floor are left. Would you open the door to the shelter? Would you take us? After all, we live above you!"

"I hope you're joking…" he replies in Ukrainian.

"Why would I be joking?". I then add in Ukrainian, "We're not joking here, it's a war!"

"What war? It'll be over in two days!"

"What, are you not going to let us into the bomb shelter?" — I switched back to Russian.

"Of course not! That's where we store our wares!"

* * *

We had no water for twenty days already. The relentless fear had chased all thoughts out of my head. At night I would read Ilf and Petrov and Bulgakov. My skin would grow cold reading Bulgakov: it was uncanny how the events of a century ago were repeating themselves.

Each day was strictly regimented: I would go and look for water, boil it, look for food, try and cook something, wash my clothes, and once again fetch water, eat dinner with my neighbours, and talk about 'when our boys would finally come here and tear this all apart; we can rebuild it all after, just we need to be freed from this…', followed by a long and complicated dishwashing effort. This happened amongst interruptions for the shelling, since the Grad rocket launchers stood right in my yard, and they tried to put their equipment between the houses in the schoolyard, so that the answering fire would cause even more misery.

One morning my neighbour knocked on my door:

"Look what I found! If we find batteries, we can turn it on, I think…"

She held a huge brown polished box, covered with cloth. It was a radio, probably dating from the sixties. We managed to work it — I cannot remember to which station we tuned it, but we listened to news snippets and reports from the front in Ukrainian. We listened to it twice a day — at 2 pm and 4 pm. When we first heard Ukrainian, we could barely contain ourselves. We wanted to whoop and howl from happiness, listening to our native language, and from the pain of having to listen to it in secret. It was some connection with reality, even if it was unstable. For occupation did not just mean no water or electricity — it meant no information, and this was what we hungered for the most.

* * *

"Put your glasses on."

"Why? I hate sunglasses. I only like them when I'm by water, on holiday in my swimmers on the beach. When I get a frying pan full of mussels straight from the ocean on, and I can dangle my feet in the sea… Why would I need sunglasses in Luhansk?"

"Your eyes could burn them! Hate is oozing from you like poison. You don't need to say anything, they'll definitely feel it. I'm afraid to look at you! Put them on, I'm begging you."

* * *

Our city used to be full of roses. Someone saved them amidst the chaos of the nineties, and they were recently planted on the side of the road. Yellow and pink roses, white ones, and your classic red ones all adorned our rather unsightly town. I dragged my trolley with the empty water bottles alongside the flowerbeds and thought to myself, 'How are they surviving?'. We had had no rain for two months already, the heat was unbearable, yet here they were: blooming, not wilting. Three women, also with trolleys and empty water bottles, were walking around not far from me. They wandered slowly, heads bent, backs bowed; the quintessential signs of despair. Suddenly, a humongous car carrying a tank with the logo 'Blue Key' (a brand name for tap water, popular before the war, later seized by our valiant separatist rebels). It was being chased by a green minibus. The camo-clad separatists hopped off the bus, awkwardly turned on the taps of the hoses and began to water the roses. Water! Some fashionably-dressed people who were visibly freshly bathed and perfumed dismounted from the bus with a sprightly jump, carrying cameras and microphones. I halted my two-wheeled transport and decided to watch the filming. But for the women, having seen the water pouring onto the ground, water they spent every day breaking their backs over to find, pulling muscles, dragging weights — it was too much. One sat on the tarmac and keeled over. The other took the two trolleys and rushed over to the water:

"My dear boys, please pour us some water! We've been a whole month without water! I've children at home... my grandson is disabled, please help!"

The clean TV reporter girls looked at the hysterical woman, the other sitting on the tarmac and at her friend fanning her with a rather dirty handkerchief and wetting her face with her spit.

"Oi, get out of here! Can you not see we're filming? Shoo, I said! Silly old women, where have you come from?"

(I omit here the obscene vocabulary, since I think we can all guess exactly what the men used to address these poor women).

The muzzles of three rifles were pointed at the three sobbing women, who could have been the same age as each gunman's mother. The cameras and microphones were put down.

"My son, please... Water!"

She fell on her knees and crawled towards him; hands held as if in prayer. One of the separatists motioned a kick in the air, showing her what he would do to get rid of her. Her friend dragged her up and pulled her to where she came from. They picked up their bottles and, bending over almost in half, they slowly wandered off, howling. The others carried on watering the roses, the cameras were turned back on, and the squeaky-clean girl with the microphone smiled with her pearly-white teeth, and ran up to the same tanned 'hero' in clean combat gear who was about to kick the old woman. Lights, camera, action.

* * *

Everything ended for me on the 25th of August. It was the day after Ukrainian Independence Day, which we quietly celebrated with our neighbours by singing the national anthem about fifteen times, it felt. Our neighbour from the next building, a quiet primary school teacher, brought a blue and yellow flag, and we all sang and drank together. Again, we drank, and sang songs about 'putting our bodies and hearts on the line for freedom'. Two stripes: blue and yellow; this was the symbol of our choice, though internal, of freedom and loyalty. That morning we embraced and said farewell without tears or complaints, and the next thing I found around me was the unbearably hot bus, with the whistle of shells and gunfire overhead. We were a crew of about fifteen strangers, sitting with chins to our chests, holding our passports above our heads. We passed through three separatist checkpoints, who were easily recognisable with their unsteady gait, plastic sandals, and tattered socks. We already did not notice the stench rising off us. By that time, we had had no water for a month in our hot, southern city — in some districts for even longer than that. Fresh as a daisy we were not. Unexpectedly, at the next checkpoint, we saw different feet that stood firm, clad in combat boots.

The driver's voice rang in my head: "Don't raise your eyes, just don't look at them! Look at the floor, I say! Hold your passport up! Raise it up!"

I could not bear it any longer, and my gaze slowly creeped over to their camouflage. I see it: two stripes on their sleeves. Blue and yellow. I had not cried for two months: not even when

I was spat in the face by some camo-clad scumbag in the ex-regional state administration building, not even when I got hit by a rifle butt on the back of my neck. Not even when a shell hit the next building; not even when someone got killed in the queue for water. And yet here… not for two whole months. I only remember the whole bus pouncing on me after I started sobbing. I was on my knees, hugging the soldier's legs, and he stroked my head, comforting me, in Ukrainian:

"Enough now, everything will be alright. You're alive, and thank God for that."

Holding his hand, I tried to stand up, and kissed his chevron. I do not know how I managed to let go.

Now I am in a strange city, in a strange house, with a little flag of my country sitting on my desk. For me, this flag, in its colour and its form, represents my freedom. This is my choice, and this is my country.

Glory to Ukraine!

HERE WE GO AGAIN...
THE SHAME...

RAISA SALNIKOVA

www.facebook.com/raisatroeglazova

2nd August 2014

Today I received a call from a couple from the city of Horlivka (or Gorlovka) near Donetsk. They cremated their child yesterday, who did not survive his operation at the Amosov cardiac clinic in Kyiv. They asked to meet me to talk about what they should do next. The clinic gave them my number — who, and why, I do not know.

We met at the station.

Thank God they did not raise the matter of accommodation, though before our meeting I got permission to take them in at Teteriv, but as a very last resort, since children live there. However, and once again, thank God, some relatives in Myrhorod were ready to take them in, and they were leaving for there tomorrow.

The grief-stricken parents brought various papers with them: documents including the child's birth and death certificates. They asked whether they could get an allowance in Kyiv for burying the child and how to do this. It was a completely out-of-the-ordinary situation and therefore an unknown for me. I try to return to the 'beginning' — the birth — and ask whether they received child benefit. It turns out they did not manage to, since they immediately left the Horlivka maternity hospital for Kyiv, to Amosov's clinic, for an emergency operation.

Together we turned to the representatives of the Department for Social Protection for advice, to ask whether the parents —

who were now refugees from the 'anti-terrorist operation zone' —
could issue and receive all of the benefits due to them, but outside of their place of permanent residence.

We were advised to turn to social security services with
a query about their place of residence. We repeat ourselves, explain once more the sensitive and extraordinary nature of this
situation — Horlivka was in the occupied area, the child had already died and been cremated in Kyiv, and they were carrying
around the urn with the ashes… Social security categorically declares that here, all situations are 'extraordinary', and without
a crumb of sympathy they insist on us joining the queue to register. I explain that the parents of the child that died *two days
ago* can and want to go to their relatives as soon as possible. The
question is whether they can get benefits, and which ones at that.
With a look that told us we were total idiots, the officials suggested we went to the Ministry of Health. Remembering that today
is a Saturday, they suggest we call the hotline.

That was it. The limits to our patience and courtesy are exhausted. I feel shame for the employees of the Department for
Social Protection. After all, they could have 'looked into things',
consulted with their colleagues at corresponding administrative
branches or departments. But no… I feel ashamed of our government.

I parted with my fellow countrymen on the terms that they
were going to their relatives in a safe place, and that they would
appeal to social and health services there… If they are told to
'eff off' there as well, they would call me. I would pull together all
those politicians who are supposed to have an 'interest' in Kyiv…

The main question that did not let me rest for many days afterwards was the following: 'What was the point?' I would prefer to
use less-delicate words to say this, but this will do: what was the
point in having *eight (!) specialists* in various state social services
sitting in the reception area for internally displaced persons?'

How do I ask that question?

RECOLLECTIONS

* * *

*The author of this testimonial
asked to remain anonymous*

My story is probably a very typical one for those times. When everything kicked off in Luhansk, very few people actually got what was actually happening. This wasn't surprising, because we had a very vague idea about what war was: what we knew came from stories from our grandmothers and grandfathers, or from books or films. And then, instead of being recounted for what it was, war was turned into something heroic, featuring fearless guerrillas or Red Army soldiers fighting the fascist 'baddies'. Of course, by then, the battle in Slovyansk had already happened and there had been clashes in other places, but the newsreels on the telly and the realities of daily life were two very different things. I therefore didn't see the point of hiding from anyone my pro-Ukrainian position or my negative attitude towards collaborators, who I called traitors to their face. In the end, this turned out to be pointless. I realised this later when I heard about a file of denunciations against me from 'well-wishers', written long before I was detained.

On one of those June summer days, I was simply taken from my house, flanked by the barrels of semiautomatic weapons, accompanied by the joyful shouts of some of my neighbours about 'these Banderovites who deserve it'. I was taken to the basement of the Luhansk regional state administration, where no-one saw the point in conducting any interrogations. I was just beaten with rifle butts, some sort of pipe, and then with the fists and feet of a dozen or so 'separatist heroes'. They had this one particular form of entertainment — they'd stick a gas mask on their face and blow 'spice', the synthetic drug, into it. They used to call it *'slonik'*, or 'little elephant'. They would then beat people up till they lost consciousness. There was even talk of them cutting off your ears, or them sending you in a car full of explosives to the town of Shchastya, which the Ukrainian Aidar battalion had just retaken, to either get shot by Ukrainian snipers or blow yourself up and the Ukrainian troops with you. To my good fortune, this didn't happen in real life. Funnily enough, the name 'Shchastya' means 'good fortune', although the place was no longer a very fortunate one.

Another lad, Oleksii, was taken down into the basement with me. He was born in Kamyanka, a village near Luhansk. He was a soldier in the regular army and had served in Crimea. After our troops were withdrawn from Crimea, they were allowed to terminate their contracts early. He didn't want to fight, as far as I understood, so he took advantage of this and went home. But to his misfortune he decided to pass through Luhansk on his way back, to go see his sister. When the separatists checked his documents at the entry checkpoint, they found a military ID on his person — which was, of course, enough for him to be included in the ranks of 'Ukrainian saboteurs' who were swelling in number, according to separatist propaganda.

I learned all this from him later, when he came to after nearly a whole day and night spent lying unconscious after his 'conversation' with the 'valiant defenders of the Donbas'. I regained consciousness a bit before him in our so-called 'cell'. It was actually a normal lift shaft extending out into a basement. One time, two people from the banana republic formerly known as Luhansk Oblast accidentally took the lift from the upper floors of the regional state administration, which cheered us up a fair bit. In fact, we had a lot of laughs down there, strange as that may sound. And over such seemingly *unfunny* things, such as when my cellmate was hit over the head with a rifle butt. Apparently, it was actually made of poor-quality plastic. Such are the paradoxes of the human psyche. We begged each other not to make each other laugh too much, since it hurt our sore ribs. This meant our cell actually commanded a funny sort of respect from the separatists, because even though the majority of its inhabitants had been sorely beaten, we never lowered ourselves in front of them. They hardly bothered us after, and even held cigarettes for us so we could smoke them. I wanted a smoke the whole time. Later I would find out — and this surprised me even then — those who tried to kowtow the separatists were treated worse. The reward for this 'servility' turned out to be quite the opposite. They only received more beatings.

Two of my 'brothers in misfortune' were two local soldiers serving in the Aidar battalion who were mistakenly stopped at a separatist checkpoint. They were saved from certain death by the fact they were dressed in civvies. Their comrade in camo travelling with them was beaten to death in the corridor of our basement. Before the war he was a teacher at the police academy in Shchastya, from what I could gather. I wish I knew what happened to them afterwards, especially since one of the 'commanders' of this sorry band of rebels promised to shoot one of them the day I managed to escape. I really like to hope they survived.

I still remember when we burnt the ballots from the so-called 'elections'. One day, a panic began to spread among the 'heroes of Novorussia' that Ukrainian troops were on the advance, and their 'handlers' ordered all evidence of falsification to be destroyed. That night, all of the prisoners were driven out the back door of the administration and we were lined up in a chain from the window of the room where all the wastepaper was stored to the furnace in the next building. We spent half the night destroying the evidence of treason against the regional government.

I remember one old man who was put in our 'cell' for being

***

caught drunk during their curfew. He said that he had been an active agitator for the 'Russian peace' and worked in their propaganda office near the state security service building. Yet now he was sitting there, crying, saying over and over, 'This isn't what we wanted', and, 'I didn't think they'd turn out to be such scumbags'.

We were taken out to dig trenches in the town of Metalist, where we were being guarded by a band of rebels from Severodonetsk, which was also occupied at the time. We became inadvertent eavesdroppers to their private conversations, which, trying to stay as close as possible to the original, went something like:

"While the Luhansk fighters were sent to old Severo' to go take our women, we got sent out here to die with no reinforcements, and one magazine clip per person."

Everything was led by the Russian armed forces, who based themselves in a large building that used to be the public baths, not far from the regional state administration. Back then they didn't really hide who they were. I saw them in person and talked to them. There were plenty of Russian journalists representing various media channels. I would find it pretty amusing to hear people afterwards spin yarns about a 'civil war', the *'ikhtamniets'* (or 'little green men') and of the people *'tired from war'*, when all they knew about war came off the telly. The local rebels who dug trenches with us as a punishment for drunkenness or looting would talk a lot about the camps in Rostov-on-Don near the border, where they were trained, and about their 'handlers' from Russia.

I only got out of that cellar alive due to a fortunate turn of events: some separatists came over from the fighting then taking place in Metalist to change over with our guards.

"We're out there losing our lives — you guys here are just robbing people, nicking cars, and holding people at ransom in a basement!" — complained the newcomers.

They had a fair point. As such the newcomers decided to check all the 'cells' according to their lists of who was there and why they were being detained. My name wasn't on the list, which meant, I logically concluded, I wasn't supposed to leave there. I saw my chance. Playing the fool, I told their commander that I didn't understand why I was there and that maybe, in the middle of this bedlam, I'd been forgotten about. He asked me for my documents and let me call someone. I dialled the only number I knew by heart — my own — since I left my telephone at home during my arrest. To my good fortune, my family was next to the receiver and within ten minutes my passport had arrived at the building.

Due to this very fortunate turn of events, I was released. I could have written far more about what happened, but this calls for resurfacing painful memories. Plus, I'm no writer. I am not about to spew out as many words as I can for the sake of it.

I shall sum up my piece like this: it's for those who think that war won't affect them, as long as they stay neutral. When war has already creeped up to your front door, it affects everyone: people both on the left and right, nationalists and pacifists, patriots and people who don't care what flag they live under. Shells and bullets don't care whose house they hit, whether it belongs to a 'Russophile', a 'neutral', or a true Ukrainian. One must look after his own, or become a victim. The scariest thought for me when I was sitting there in that cursed basement was the idea of dying without having done anything for my children, my mother, or my homeland, at the end of the day. That's why I got into doing good deeds, after my bones had set and bruises had healed a little. But that's another story. I apologise if my conclusion comes across a bit sentimental. I wrote it from the heart, because this is what I really feel.

***

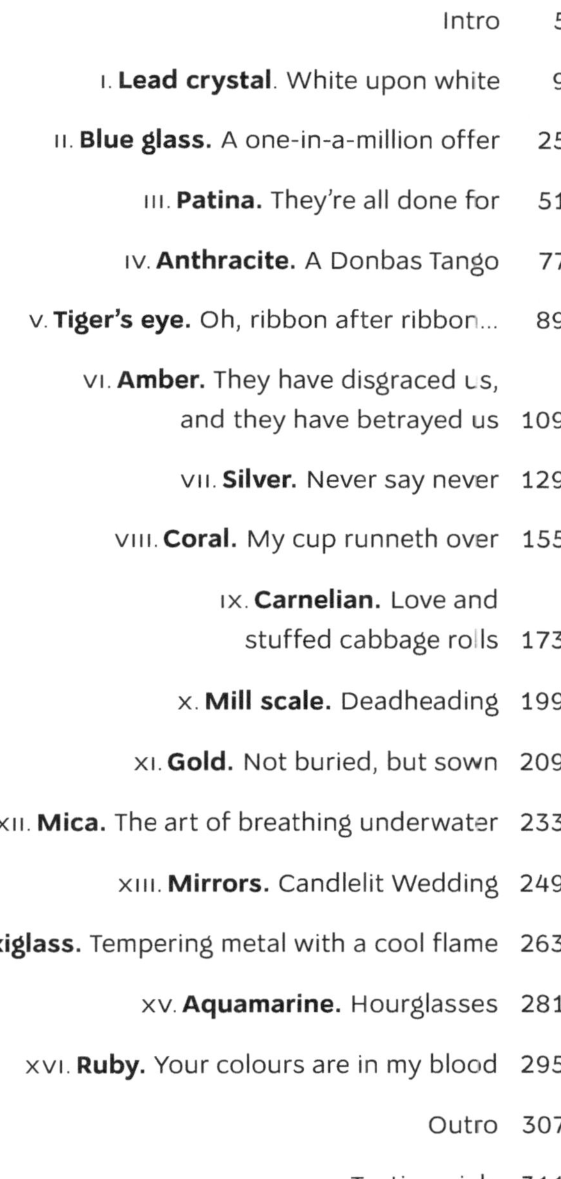

CONTENTS

Tamara Horikha Zernya (Tamara Duda) was born and raised in Kyiv. A poetry and prose author as well as a songwriter, she holds a degree in journalism from Taras Shevchenko National University in Kyiv. *Daughter* is her debut novel and has received favourable reviews from both literary critics and well-established Ukrainian writers.

With the outbreak of war in Eastern Ukraine, Tamara took a leave of absence from her career to serve as a volunteer at the front. In 2014 and 2015, she and her husband raised funds for, purchased, and delivered equipment and aid to Ukrainian soldiers to the front. The author spent a full two years on the road in combat areas, and refers to this period as the most tragic, fascinating, intense, and inspiring years of her life — years that have changed not only the country but also each and every Ukrainian citizen.

Tamara Duda

DAUGHTER

English translation by Daisy Gibbons

mosaicPRESS